JOHN HADFIELD

LOVE ON A BRANCH LINE

D0994554

PENGUIN BOOKS
BBC BOOKS

PENGUIN BOOKS
BBC BOOKS

Published by the Penguin Group and BBC Enterprises Ltd
Penguin Books Ltd, 27 Wrights Lane, London W8 5TZ, England
Penguin Books USA Inc., 375 Hudson Street, New York, New York 10014, USA
Penguin Books Australia Ltd, Ringwood, Victoria, Australia
Penguin Books Canada Ltd, 10 Alcorn Avenue, Toronto, Ontario,
Canada M4V 3B2
Penguin Books (NZ) Ltd, 182–190 Wairau Road, Auckland 10, New Zealand

Penguin Books Ltd, Registered Offices: Harmondsworth, Middlesex, England

First published in Great Britain by Hutchinson & Co. Ltd 1959
Published by Penguin Books and BBC Books,
a division of BBC Enterprises Ltd 1994

3 5 7 9 10 8 6 4 2

Printed in England by Clays Ltd, St Ives plc

Love on a Branch Line is also available as a spoken word cassette
from the BBC Radio Collection. It is available from stockists of BBC Books

For Anna

Readers who happen to know the more inaccessible parts of Suffolk and Norfolk may recognize some features in the landscape through which this Branch Line runs. I want to emphasize that all the characters, if not the scenes, are wholly imaginary.

I must, however, acknowledge the kindness of the late John Copinger Hill, who allowed me to borrow an episode from his family history (there is no other resemblance). I also wish to acknowledge gratefully the guidance on trains and traction engines given to me by the late L. T. C. Rolt, and on the history of jazz music by my son Jeremy.

J.H.

WOODBRIDGE
SUFFOLK

The woods of Arcady are dead,
And over is their antique joy;
Of old the world on dreaming fed;
Grey Truth is now her painted toy;
Yet still she turns her restless head. . .

W. B. YEATS

'Yes, I know; Jasper *is* a bore.' The words nibbled at my mind as I sat there in the early morning despondency of the Piccadilly Tube. The only consolation was that so far I had not had to give up my seat. But now several people were standing, some of them female.

The only rule of life I remember my father giving me was that a gentleman always gives up his seat to a lady. Now the dictum has a positively archaic ring. I wondered how many, if any, of the men sitting opposite me had ever heard it. There they sat, some of them manifestly younger than I, hugging their *Daily Mirrors* and their private comfort, and ignoring the girls, the young women, even the middle-aged women, strap-hanging before them. Clearly they had never been troubled by the thought that a gentleman gives up his seat to a lady.

But then most of them were not gentlemen. I, Jasper Pye, happened to be a gentleman. It was something I would never venture to put into spoken words: indeed I would not consider myself a gentleman if I did. But the knowledge was there; and it was that which now compelled me to look up and down the compartment and consider whether or not I could continue the journey sitting. (Further proof, no doubt, that I, Jasper, was a bore.)

I had made it a rule that I allowed 'teenagers to

stand, provided they didn't look too tired, but that I offered my seat to anyone of marriageable age or over. I was usually called upon to do this at Earls Court or Gloucester Road. Today I had sat uneasily as far as South Kensington. But now, as the doors closed, a girl with a pout and a pony-tail, who had been standing in front of me since Gloucester Road, stepped back on to my toes as a grey-haired woman, carrying a suitcase, was pushed towards her by the throng near the doorway.

I gripped my umbrella, clambered rather awkwardly to my feet, and tried to attract the old lady's attention. 'Would you care to take this seat?' I said when I had worked my way past the girl with the pony-tail. The lady turned an anxious glance towards me.

'Thanks ever so,' said a voice behind me. I looked round to see the girl with the pony-tail flop into the vacant seat, giving me what no doubt she supposed to be a dazzling smile.

'I didn't catch what you said?' the old lady asked.

I felt a blush creeping up the back of my neck. 'Oh, I thought there was a seat here, but there isn't,' I said lamely. What could one say? Ask the girl to mend her manners and get up again? Make a pompous ass of oneself? Be a bore? I mumbled a further apology to the old lady and gazed fixedly at a fatuous advertisement for fruit gums over the girl's head.

'Yes, I know; Jasper is a bore.' The words had been echoing through my mind half the night, to such effect that any self-confidence I had possessed was scattered in small pieces round the relics of my self-respect. Why had I gone to that party anyway? I had known I wasn't going to enjoy it. Perhaps there had once been a certain glamour about studio parties in Chelsea. Now they were merely gatherings of advertisement copywriters or commercial artists trying to be 'bohemian' and spongers from Espresso bars in the King's Road trying to get free drinks.

Of course, I knew perfectly well why I had gone to that particular party. I had gone solely because I knew Deirdre would be there. And she *had* been there. And that – I ground my teeth and gazed with intense concentration at the advertisement for fruit gums – was the last occasion on which I would see Deirdre. No doubt about that!

I had elbowed my way through the crowd towards her, trying with only partial success to avoid spilling the drink I had got for her. As I came up behind her I heard the words. She was talking to a young man whom I had not seen before, and certainly would never wish to see again. He had greasy, unbrushed hair, and a weak chin which didn't appear to have been shaved for several days. He was wearing a yellow polo-necked sweater, and was in every detail a caricature of the then fashionable Angry Young Man. And the words I heard Deirdre addressing to this contemptible listener were these – there was no mistaking them – 'Yes, I know; Jasper *is* a bore.'

'Oh, there you are, darling!' The patent insincerity in her greeting when she saw me had only emphasized the revealing candour of the previous remark. Naturally I pretended I hadn't overheard it. No reference was made to it. I went home early, and I went alone, as I had promised my mother I would tie up the branches of the nectarine tree against the garden wall before it got dark. I didn't even say goodbye to Deirdre: I don't suppose she noticed.

It was, admittedly, a ridiculous episode. And it was ridiculous of me to make so much of it. But truth often reveals itself in trifles; and this trifle, coming from Deirdre as it did, when it did, was going to loom very large indeed in my life.

At breakfast, after a sleepless night, I had told Mama of my decision to resign from the Civil Service and go to Paris. It must have sounded somewhat melodramatic, coming from me. But Mama, not for the first time, had astonished me by her quiet, unquestioning acceptance of something which, on the face of it, was not a little surprising.

'It's not for me to guide you, Jasper dear,' she had said. 'As long as you are happy, that's all that matters to me. But what are you going to do in Paris?'

I told her I was going to take up painting again: I had always felt I had a genuine talent for it, and, although I was conscious of my limitations, I couldn't help noticing how superior were my efforts to those of most of the other exhibitors at the Whitehall Arts Club.

Mama never even mentioned the financial aspect. She was extraordinarily trustful in such matters, and since she herself was reasonably provided for, and I had certainly not lived up to my income during the nine years I had been at the Ministry, I assumed she relied on me to look after myself.

And now, as I stood in the heat and crush of the Piccadilly Tube, studying that nauseating advertisement for fruit gums, I realized that a new chapter in my life was about to open.

A bore indeed! That was not how Mark Fairweather would view me when I handed in my resignation. I could picture the amazement in his face. Suddenly the sting went out of the word. For some reason I began to feel extraordinarily elated. It was all rather fun! I laughed out aloud.

'Did you speak?' the old lady next to me inquired. 'Did you say there was another seat?'

I pulled myself together. 'No, ma'am,' I replied, 'but I think this young lady here is going to offer you hers.'

The pony-tail looked up at me with a puzzled stare.

'Aren't you?' I added, with ponderous emphasis.

The girl blushed and got up. 'I don't mind,' she said, ungraciously.

'Thank you so much, my dear,' said the old lady as she sank into the seat.

'Don't mention it!' said the girl, looking daggers at me.

To her astonishment – and, I must admit, to my own – I gave her a pronounced and vulgar wink. What would have happened if the train had not then drawn into Green Park Station I cannot imagine.

Up in the sunshine I still felt light-headed. As I walked down St James's Street towards the Park I rehearsed the speech I was going to make to Fairweather. After nine years I knew him pretty well – and he, no doubt, thought he knew me pretty well. In his mind I was almost certainly classified as a bore – though he, by virtue of his temperament and his position, probably thought the better of me because I was a bore. What would he think when I told him that I was going to shake the dust of the Ministry off my well-polished, hand made, Dowie and Marshall shoes, and was going off to Paris to become an artist?

The morning walk across St James's Park, which I always enjoyed, even to the extent of adding another five minutes to my journey from Barons Court, was particularly enjoyable this morning. The sun shone; the fresh green of the trees had not yet been sullied by smoke; the ornamental duck were sporting amorously; there was almost a hint of Paris in the air.

Stéphanie – was that the name of the girl I had met in La Coupole? No doubt she had moved on by now: it was four years ago, after all – more than a year before I met Deirdre. But it would be fun to go to La Coupole, and look round. I might meet some fellow artists there.

Mark Fairweather might understand how I felt about

La Coupole; he would probably understand, too, about Stéphanie – if that was her name. What he wouldn't be able to understand was exchanging the sober security of a Grade 3 pensioned post in the Ministry, with every prospect of regular advancement to an Under-Secretaryship, for the undisciplined insecurity of a studio in Paris. He was the kind of man who would feel quite lost without his desk, his in-tray and out-tray, his regulation square of carpet, his briefcase, and his umbrella.

His umbrella. For some reason I particularly associated Mark Fairweather with his umbrella. It had an outrageously large knobbly cane handle. But I, too, was an umbrella man, in my own way. As I walked over the bridge across the lake in St James's Park I held up my own umbrella and considered it. It was a good, restrained umbrella, by no means the cheapest to be bought at Smith's in New Oxford Street. I looked after it well; I had the ferrule and the elastic replaced when worn; and I kept it immaculately rolled.

Now, however, I saw it as a symbol of my Civil Servitude. It would have to go. And the sooner the better. Let this be the first gesture of revolt. À bas le parapluie!

Beside the asphalt walk through the Park was a magnificent bed of delphiniums just coming into bloom, their brilliant blue flower-stems rising densely to head height. I stopped to admire them, then looked to right and left along the pathway. Nobody was in sight. I leaned forward and plunged the point of my umbrella into the soil behind the tallest, most luxuriant delphinium. Then I stepped back and surveyed the bed again. There was no visible sign of the symbol of servitude.

I plucked an outsize floret from one of the delphiniums, put it in my buttonhole, and walked briskly to the Ministry, vaguely aware – but proudly so – that my right hand had nothing to hold on to.

'What's that in your buttonhole?' asked Fairweather, leaning on his desk and peering at me over his heavy horn-rimmed spectacles.

'Delphinium,' I answered.

'Never saw that in a man's buttonhole before.'

I looked out of the window, over the Park, and mumbled vaguely. This was not how I had intended to begin the conversation.

'The flowers that bloom in the spring, tra-la!' said Fairweather, with unconscious relevance to the point at issue. I waited for him to make the next move. He, after all, had sent for me, before I had had time to ask to see him. Let him say his piece first, before I threw my bomb-shell across his tidy desk.

'Lovely time of year!' he continued. 'Would you like a holiday?'

'Holiday? But I'm not due for any more leave this year.'

'I don't mean leave. Just a break in routine.'

I was a little taken aback. Was he, in some curious way, anticipating me? 'I don't quite understand, Mark,' I said, introducing the Christian name in order to give myself some reassurance.

'I mean what I say, Jasper. A break in routine – a change from all this.' And he waved his hand over the in-tray, the out-tray, and the regulation square of carpet.

It was uncanny how he was edging his way – quite unwittingly, no doubt – onto my ground. I decided to take the offensive. 'As a matter of fact, Mark, I would like a break. And although it may surprise you, I've already decided to make it. I was intending to tell you today, in any event.'

Now it was Fairweather who looked puzzled. But only

15

for a moment. He was a pretty accomplished diplomat. 'I can't say I'm surprised, dear fellow,' he said. 'We've been a bit fussed lately, I know. And you've not been given a fair chance. It isn't easy to fit everyone into the post-Budget pattern. But we shall do.'

'Not me, I think. I'm not interested in the post-Budget pattern, Mark. I want to get right away from it.'

'How well I understand your feelings, Jasper!' said Fairweather, unexpectedly. 'And how fortunate that you feel like this just at the moment!'

What did he mean? Was he accepting my resignation before I had even offered it?

'What do you mean, Mark?'

'Just what I say, Jasper. How lucky for us that at this moment you're feeling the spring fever in your blood and wanting to remove yourself from the frustrations of Whitehall.'

A new and unwelcome thought struck me. Was it possible that I had been put in the list of Civil Servants who were being politely told that they were redundant under the new Treasury scheme for economy?

'You aren't by any chance trying to tell me, Mark, that the Ministry doesn't want me any more?'

Fairweather grinned in mock malice.

'Suppose I said yes? Ha! Of course, it isn't easy to make the adjustments which this confounded Treasury direction demands. But I dare say we can still find some use for you, Jasper.'

My reaction to this rather patronizing irony was confused. I felt I was being put in a false position.

'Don't worry, Mark,' I said. 'As it happens, I was going to break the news to you today that I want to resign.'

'You want to resign? Come, come, Jasper!'

'Yes – for purely private reasons. Whatever the staff situation may be, I want to go.'

Fairweather took off his glasses, rose from his desk, and walked over to the window. For a moment he stood there, his well-tailored back to me, as he gazed reflectively over the trees in the Park. This, I knew, was a well-rehearsed gesture of his, designed to suggest the weighing of grave decisions. In actuality its sole purpose was to enable him to gain time.

'Shall I go along to Establishments and make the necessary arrangements now?' I asked.

He made no movement. He continued to gaze impassively out of the window. I couldn't help admiring his self-command, his air of relaxation.

'No, you're not going, Jasper. You are not, as the Americans say, expendable.'

I blinked. So he hadn't been trying to axe me! Or had he suddenly changed his mind? But that was not the way things happened in the Ministry. I felt confused. Perhaps I should let him finish what he intended to say before I made it clear that my decision was irrevocable.

'Are you prepared to spend a week in the country, Jasper?' he asked suddenly.

'Well,' I hesitated. 'Yes and no. Actually I was intending, when everything had been cleared up, to go to Paris.'

'Paris? Oh, indeed! What for?'

'To paint,' I answered, lamely.

'Of course, I see.' He brushed the matter aside. 'I'd forgotten your painting. Extraordinarily good it is, too, if I may say so. But you don't necessarily have to go to Paris to do it, do you?'

'We seem to be at cross-purposes, Mark. I'm talking about what I'm going to do after I've resigned.'

'*Resigned*, my dear fellow!' exclaimed Fairweather, in a tone of horror. 'Whoever said anything about you resigning?'

'I did,' I confessed, like a schoolboy owning up to some peccadillo.

17

'Well, Jasper, I think – if you don't mind – we will pass from that rather hypothetical subject to the one under discussion. Are you prepared to spend a week in the country?'

'Well, yes,' I admitted grudgingly. What else could I say?

'Immediately?'

'I suppose so, if there's something urgent to be done.'

'There is,' said Fairweather. He spoke decisively now. This was the other part of his act – the swift, effective administrator at work. I had to admire the performance. 'Yes, there is. Something a little out of the ordinary. Something that may call for peculiar tact and finesse. And I'm asking you to tackle it, Jasper, *because* it's out of the ordinary. It's not quite the kind of assignment I'd like to give to any of the Under-Secretaries. Excellent as they are, they might lack the flexibility, the imagination, that this problem demands. That is why I asked for you to have a word with me.'

'I'm flattered, Mark.' The implied compliments, insincere though I guessed them to be, were heartening.

'May I therefore have your co-operation, Jasper?' Fairweather asked, with an air of humility that was quite touching.

'Why yes, of course,' I said, 'until we've sorted out the other matter.'

'Forget the other matter,' he said, with a disarming smile. 'Let's just deal with this for the moment.'

'Very well.'

He looked solemn. 'May I assume I have your confidence?'

'My confidence? Of course you have my confidence, Mark – in anything concerning the Ministry,' I added as a sop to the spirit of revolt.

'Perhaps I don't make myself clear. What I intended to suggest was that the matter under discussion must be regarded as confidential between us.'

'Oh, I see! "Secret", or "Very secret"?'

'Not exactly either.' Fairweather laughed uneasily, and I noticed that for the first time some of his self-possession was lacking. 'No, this is in rather a different category. It is nothing of consequence. But it affects the prestige of the Ministry. And with the House and the Press so eager to look for administrative mistakes we want this investigated by one of ourselves, without publicity.'

I couldn't help becoming interested. For a moment or two, the alluring vista of La Coupole receded. Fairweather continued: 'You know, of course, that there are several outlying divisions of the Ministry, some of them only loosely linked with the main establishment. They are scattered about the country – Reading, Chester, Lincoln, and so forth.'

I nodded. The strange habitats of the Ministry's field forces were a constant subject of satirical comment in Whitehall.

'Considering that the Ministry is a recent growth,' Fairweather went on, 'and that we started with only a handful of Permanent Civil Servants such as myself, we haven't done a bad job administratively. But there have been mistakes, inevitably. Here and there, loose ends. Of course, they've mostly been tied up.' It was the bureaucratic build-up again. Fairweather was once more putting on his act – this time, I suspected, the famous face-saving performance.

At last he came to the point. 'I've been looking over the ground for this Treasury inquiry, and I've found one unit which seems to have become a little isolated from headquarters. It is an offshoot of Purvis's division, which was set up rather hurriedly in the Battle of Britain period, and for some unaccountable reason has avoided all subsequent reorganizations.'

'What! Since 1940?' I did not try to hide my astonishment.

Fairweather looked self-conscious. 'Yes, I know it sounds odd. But it's just one of those things. Apparently Purvis's predecessor set up a small unit called "Output Statistics". Its purpose was to collate and analyse the output of foreign publications. Quite frankly, its work seems never to have been of more than academic value. Reports have been regularly submitted, but nobody seems to have paid much attention to them. And, owing to some curious lapse on the part of Administration and Control, the unit has never been screened for redundance.'

'You mean, in plain terms, that the Ministry has forgotten all about it all these years?'

'Not quite that, my dear chap.'

'What is its strength?' I asked.

'Oh, nothing much. It's in the charge of a man named Pollux – he seems to have been an obscure university don. And he has an assistant named Quirk, with, I believe, one secretary.'

'Where are they?' I asked.

'They are in a wing of a big house on the borders of Suffolk and Norfolk – belongs to a backwoodsman peer, the Earl of Flamborough.'

'Do we rent it?' I asked. 'Or does it come under the Ministry of Works?'

'Well, that's the odd thing,' said Fairweather. 'Apparently Lord Flamborough lets us have it for nothing. When it was requisitioned during the war he refused to take any rent or sign a lease. That's one reason, incidentally, why nobody's bothered much about the unit.'

'But what about the salaries?' I asked. 'Surely they have come up for revision from time to time?'

'I suppose so,' said Fairweather. 'But Professor

Pollux only gets a nominal salary – one of those gentleman's agreements that came about in wartime. Quirk, the assistant, is on loan from the Stationery Office, and as there's no job for him there they've been quite content to leave him where he is. The secretary is paid out of a local allowance, and as it's so small, and so unvarying, it seems to have slipped through every year without anyone noticing it. All a result of divided responsibility, you know.' Fairweather attempted to finish strongly on a cardboard generalization.

'Well, I'm astonished, I must admit. Do they still produce any evidence of their existence?'

'Yes, yes, certainly,' said Fairweather, picking up a large folder of typescript. 'Here are their reports for the last three months.'

He passed the folder over to me. I glanced at the first few sheets. They consisted partly of summaries of the different kinds of printed matter produced by the Ministry for circulation overseas, and partly of statistics which I was sure nobody but the compiler had ever read.

'Well, Jasper,' said Fairweather briskly, 'what about it? If it won't interfere with your personal arrangements I'd like you to go down there as soon as possible, stay for a week or so, scrutinize the work and personnel of the whole unit, and submit recommendations without delay.'

'But is this quite my line of country?' I asked. 'Statistics are Greek to me.'

'Nonsense, my dear Jasper! You don't have to give an expert opinion on the statistics. We can take them as read. All I want you to do is to sum up the general purport of the work, and decide whether there is any reason why it should not be discontinued. We hope, of course, you will consider it has had its value up to now. But a recommendation that it is redundant today will, I am

21

sure, be entirely in line with Treasury requirements.'

I continued to turn over the pages of the reports. There was something rather pathetic about this conscientious outpouring of memoranda, analyses, and figures – unappreciated, unwanted, unread. Presumably Professor Pollux conceived it to be of value, if no one else did. If the Ministry had ignored his existence for so long, why should I be instrumental in doing him out of his job?

'I'm sorry,' I said. 'This really isn't my cup of tea. Can't you find someone else to do it? I'd rather go my own way and let the regular people deal with this sort of thing.'

'What is this talk of your going your own way?' Fairweather was irritated. 'I shall begin to think that you *want* to resign.'

'But I do.'

'Piffle!' exclaimed Fairweather. 'What I'm afraid you're trying to say is that you find this little task outside your range. Forgive my being frank, Jasper, but I think you're becoming a little timid in your approach to fresh problems. This, clearly, is a delicate and unusual mission. You appear to be slightly scared of it.'

'Nothing of the kind, Mark!' This was an absurd turning of the tables.

'I'm afraid so. You talk airily of going to Paris and painting, but the fact is that you're becoming just a shade – how shall I put it? – stuffy. You know, my dear fellow, if you don't take such opportunities as this – of tackling fresh or piquant situations – you run a very real risk, as we all do, of becoming a bit of a bore.'

I was stunned. I could think of nothing effective to say.

'You're quite misunderstanding me,' I protested.

'I apologize, Jasper,' he said, in a contrite voice. 'I don't know what made me become so personal. Of course you'll take this on, won't you?'

'Of course.'

'You can get away tomorrow?'

'I'll go tomorrow,' I said.

'Good chap!' Fairweather beamed. 'Take your painting kit. I dare say you'll find some subjects there. Norwich School stuff. Or is it the Constable country?'

'What is the name of the place?' I asked.

Did I imagine that a gleam of irony darted from Fairweather's eyes? 'It's called Arcady,' he said. '*Et in Arcadia ego* . . . You know the tag?'

'I do,' I said. 'Well, now I'll check the facts, arrange about expenses, and pack my bag.'

'I rather like that delphinium in your buttonhole,' said Fairweather, irrelevantly.

As I walked back across St James's Park I couldn't resist the temptation to look into the flower-bed to see if the park gardeners had discovered my umbrella. No, there it was, the dark cane handle just visible behind the delphiniums. Extraordinary that no one had spotted it all day!

I stopped, and looked up and down the path. There was nobody in sight. Quickly I leaned forward and grasped the handle. It was, after all, a good umbrella; and it might rain – even in Arcady.

The woman opposite me in the train put down her needlework and leaned forward with a hesitant gesture of inquiry. 'I see you are looking at the cricket scores,' she said. 'Forgive my intruding, but could you tell me how Leicestershire are getting on?'

I read out the scores. 'You follow county cricket?' I asked.

'I love it!' she exclaimed, with a schoolgirlish titter that came incongruously from someone of uncertain years and unmistakably greying hair. 'My brother used to keep

23

wicket for Clifton, you see, and my sisters and I used to bowl and field for him on the lawn at home. I wasn't much of a bowler myself. But' – she smiled – 'I was rather good at retrieving the ball from the shrubbery.'

I smiled too. 'Leicestershire are not doing very well just now,' I said.

'No, they have no amateurs. It isn't quite the same when they're all professionals, is it? I mean, it used to be such a gentlemanly game. Not that I'm snobbish about it. I always used to think Hobbs and Sutcliffe two of the nicest men you could possibly meet. And some of the other ones – the rough diamonds like Parkin or Macaulay – they all fitted in somehow, didn't they? Just like the village blacksmith or the poacher on the village green. But all that is a thing of the past now, isn't it?'

'I wonder if it really is?' I said, looking out of the window at the vistas of parkland through which the train was passing. 'Suffolk, at any rate, looks much as it must have done thirty years ago. There's an unchanging look about this part of the world, isn't there? I should think that tradition still counts for a good deal here?'

'Oh, I hope you're right,' she said earnestly, taking up her needlework again. 'I can't bear to read about the breaking-up of estates, and all those lovely old houses going to rack and ruin, or being taken over as government offices or lunatic asylums.'

'I'm on my way to one that's been taken over by the Government,' I said. 'I wonder if you've heard of it? Arcady Hall?'

She sat up in surprise.

'Arcady! Of course I have! That's Lord Flamborough's place. How interesting that you are going there! Are you a Civil Servant?'

'Well, I have been one for some years. But I'm resigning in a week or two.'

'Oh, how thrilling!' she exclaimed, though it was not

quite clear which of my two statements thrilled her.

'So you know Arcady Hall?' I asked.

'Well, I only knew it as a girl. My father, Canon Tidy, was Rector of Flaxfield, the little town nearby, and sometimes I used to go to the Hall for fêtes and that sort of thing. I'm afraid I couldn't describe it to you very accurately, but it had a marvellous Tudor gatehouse, and a moat, and walled gardens surrounded by a park. And there was a lake, and a temple, and a ruined chapel in the woods – I remember that clearly.'

'It sounds enchanting. Did you ever meet the present Lord Flamborough?'

'Well, yes.' There was a certain hesitation. 'Oh yes. I quite often met him when I was a girl' – she pronounced it almost as 'gel'. 'But after the war – I mean the first war, of course – parsons' daughters couldn't quite compete . . .'

There was another hesitation.

'Then he married – a really topping person, Lady Flamborough – Mabel. And there are those girls . . .'

'Has he any sons?'

'No, that's the tragedy. Only those girls.'

'How many daughters has he?'

'Three. But I only knew Chloe, and Belinda when she was a baby. Matilda was born after Daddy resigned the living and we'd gone to live at Loughborough.'

'Chloe, Belinda, Matilda – what charming names!' I said.

'Yes, I suppose so. But a little *outré*, don't you think? Dear Bertie Flamborough, he always had rather odd ideas; and then he had that terrible accident in the General Strike, which made him odder still.'

'What happened to him in the General Strike?'

'Oh, didn't you read about it? But' – Miss Tidy glanced at me with momentary embarrassment – 'of course, you're much too young. The General Strike was in the 'twenties, I suppose.' Her thoughts seemed to wander for a moment. Then she continued. 'Bertie Flamborough volunteered to drive an engine. He had always been mad about trains – model trains, you know. When he was a boy he used to be allowed to ride on the engine, on the Branch Line between Arcady and Flaxfield. The General Strike was a wonderful chance for him to play at trains on the grand scale. But, poor dear, he nearly lost his life through it.'

'How was that?'

'Well, he was at Norwich, or somewhere, getting up steam, or whatever one does, before he took his engine out for a trip, when some of the railwaymen who were on strike molested him. He was polishing the brass on the name-plate, I believe, when they got into the cab and took the brake off. The engine started to move, and as Bertie tried to clamber on to the footplate he fell under the wheels.'

'How ghastly!'

'Yes, run over by his own engine!'

'Was he badly hurt?'

'He had to have both legs amputated. Never walked again, except on crutches.'

'What a horrible end to one's hobby!'

'Bad show!' she said.

'I suppose he's more or less a cripple nowadays.'

'I doubt it, knowing Bertie,' Miss Tidy reflected. 'But I haven't seen him for over twenty years. In fact this is the first time I've been to that part of the world since the war – the second war, I mean. I'm going down now to see my old Nanny, who has her eightieth birthday on Sunday.'

Miss Tidy picked up her needlework again. It was a large and apparently elaborate design, in brilliant colours.

'I suppose we both get out at Flaxfield,' I said.

26

'Yes.' She looked out of the window. 'We should soon be there. Why, there's the windmill! And still in full sail! Daddy always started getting the bags down and telling us to put our coats on when we saw the windmill. "Only three minutes from Flaxfield," he used to say. Always a stickler for punctuality, Daddy was.'

She put her wool away in her hand-bag, and began to roll up her needlework on her knee. 'That's the cross-stitch finished, anyhow,' she said.

'May I see it?' I asked.

'Well, I hardly dare to show it to you,' she said with a titter. 'You're an artist, I can see by the painting things you've put on the rack. And you won't think anything of my humble effort.'

'I'm only a very humble amateur myself,' I said, though secretly I was a little flattered. 'Do let me look.'

She unrolled her needlework again and hesitantly held it up for my inspection. I was astonished. I had expected to see some floral composition of an entirely conventional kind. But this was a striking design, in vivid colours, which had the air of an abstract painting by Braque.

'Do you like it?' she asked, holding it up before me.

'I certainly do. It's most unusual.'

'I thought I'd try a classical theme,' she said, with that hesitant, schoolgirlish titter again. 'I'm not sure it isn't a little beyond me. It's supposed to be Pan.'

I looked more closely. Yes, I could see that it was Pan.

Through a brilliant pattern of emerald green and gold leaves danced a fantastic figure, with horns, goat's feet, a torso of Etruscan virility, and features which were almost Mephisthophelean.

She rolled it up and got to her feet as the train drew into Flaxfield Junction.

'This is quite like old times,' she said. 'I wonder if

27

anyone is playing cricket on the rectory lawn.'

'And whether,' I added, 'there's anyone to retrieve the ball from the shrubbery.'

'You was wholly lucky to get here as quick as you did,' said Mr Pott, the landlord of the Virley Arms. 'Those people in London had no business to sell you a ticket to Arcady. The Branch Line was closed down four year ago. Closing 'em all down in this part of the world, they are.'

'It seems a pity,' I said; 'but I suppose Branch Lines don't pay for themselves nowadays.'

'Redundant, dearie; that's what they are,' said the landlord's wife.

The word seemed to have followed me from Whitehall.

'We're all of us redundant, here in Arcady. That's so, isn't it, Percy?' The speaker was a florid, sandy-haired man in tweeds and a yellow waistcoat. His eyes were slightly bloodshot. He spoke with a curious over-emphasis. 'All redundant here – except the Prof.'

Mr Pott made no comment. Mrs Pott, having helped herself to a sweet from a tin behind the bar, turned to me with a twinkle in her eye. 'Pay no attention to Mr Lionel,' she said. 'It's just his little joke. Speaking for myself, I can't say I feel redundant – except for the first hour or two on a Monday morning.'

'Good for you, Dimple!' said the man called Lionel, emptying his glass. 'We can't have the Virley Arms closed down like the Branch Line, can we! Not till the whisky runs out, anyway.'

Percy Pott took the empty glass and refilled it. 'There's been a pub in Arcady as long as there's been Virleys at the Hall,' he said. 'There's their coat of arms' – he pointed to the plaster mouldings over the chimney-piece – 'and there's the date when the pub was built –

28

1562. Very interesting old house this is. You should hear the Professor talk about it.'

'Oh, flip the Prof!' said Mr Lionel. 'Anyone would think that ruddy old mountebank owned the place.'

'Steady, Mr Lionel!' said the landlord. 'Where would the Virleys be without the Professor, I'd like to know. Many's the family in these parts that's had to sell up their places since the war. And I don't doubt his Lordship would have had to do the same if it weren't for the Professor.'

'Flip the Prof again,' exclaimed Mr Lionel. 'Give me another, Percy. And make it a double.' He turned to me. 'Will you join me? Lionel Virley my name is – part of the furniture here, "with all faults", as the auctioneers say.'

'Thank you very much,' I said. 'My name's Pye.'

Percy Pott filled the glasses. His wife, whose generous build seemed to require constant sustenance, helped herself to another sweet.

'Who is this professor you've been talking about?' I asked.

Mr Lionel drew himself up in mock dignity, and, assuming an exaggerated Scots accent, said: 'Duncan McAlistair Pollux, ma dear sair, Professor of Pomposity in the University of Abairdeen and self-appointed Curator, Historian, and Bailiff at Arcady Hall.'

'Pollux!' I exclaimed.

'Aye, ma dear sair,' said Mr Lionel, still in the mock Scots accent. 'And kindly remember to spell it with a P and not a B.'

He made a show of raising his eyebrows pompously; then collapsed into ribald laughter.

'Don't take no notice of him, dearie,' said Mrs Pott to me with a wink. 'It's just his little joke.'

I smiled non-committally, uncertain whether or not to admit any concern with Professor Pollux and his activities. I had not written to announce my visit to Arcady Hall, and had intended to stay inconspicuously at the Virley Arms for a couple of days before I got involved at the Hall.

'Mr Lionel and the Professor don't always see eye to eye,' Percy Pott explained. 'But it's quite right what I was saying. The Professor's done a lot of good for Arcady, him and the Government; and his Lordship would be the first to admit it.'

'Lord Flamborough, you mean?'

'Yes. His Lordship hasn't got what you might call a head for business. Wouldn't expect him to, brought up the way he was. And he needs someone like the Professor to manage the estate for him. Wholly civil to me, the Professor is, I must say. More than I'd say of some of the bailiffs we used to have about here. Good evening, Mr Jones. What can I get for you?'

The last words were addressed to a short man with surprised eyes and a little toothbrush moustache who had just come into the bar.

'Pig's ear, Perce,' said Mr Jones. ' 'Evening, gents!' He nodded to Lionel Virley and myself. 'Lovely time of year for the weather.'

'Mr Jones,' said the landlord, when he had drawn his glass of beer, 'here's something will wholly make you laugh. Those people in London sold this gentleman a railway ticket to Arcady Station. Can you beat it? Ought to know where their own trains go to, didn't they? The Branch Line's been closed for four year.'

Mr Jones turned towards me, his eyes alert with curiosity. 'Haven't still got the ticket, have you, mister?' he asked.

As it happened, I still had it, since nobody had asked me for it when I found there was no connection at Flaxfield. I felt in my pockets for it.

'I'd be much obliged for that ticket, sir,' said Mr Jones, 'if you can spare it. I'd like to add that to me collection.'

30

I found it and handed it over to him. 'You're welcome to it. It's no use to me.'

'Ta, lots,' said Mr Jones. 'This is a collector's item. Liverpool Street to Arcady, and dated four years after they closed the line. Boy, this is something! What can I let you have in return? Interested in cigarette cards? I've a few swops of Wills's Cricketers, 1901, or I might spare you an Ogden's Golden Guinea if you're a real collector.'

I thanked him for the offer, but admitted that I was not a collector of cigarette cards.

'Autographs, then? How about a Little Tich or a Bobby Jones? You're only too welcome.'

'That's very kind of you,' I said, 'but I don't want anything in return for that ticket. I'm happy to give it to someone who values it.'

'Much obliged to you, sir,' said Jones, shaking me warmly by the hand. 'I dare say you don't realize the value of a curiosity like this to a student of serendipity like meself.'

'Serendipity,' said Mr Lionel, enunciating the word with exaggerated care. 'What the blazes is serendipity? Something naughty, I'll be bound?'

'Serendipity,' said Jones, 'is what you might call the collecting bug. Pleasure in pickin' up unconsidered trifles. And,' he added, with an air of innocence, 'I don't mean pickin' up glasses in a bar.'

'Eh?' Mr Lionel glanced at him suspiciously. 'That's meant for me, is it?'

'Steady, Mr Lionel,' interposed Mrs Pott. 'Mr Jones likes his joke same as you do.'

'I can take a joke as well as the next man,' said Mr Lionel, looming unsteadily over the diminutive Jones. 'But if any twopenny-ha'penny cockney pipsqueak who's only here on sufferance is going to make offensive remarks about—'

'Time, gentlemen, please!' called Percy Pott, switching the lights off and on several times in quick succession.

'Have one with me before closing time?' I said to Mr Lionel. 'And you, too, Mr Jones?'

'Ta, lots,' said Jones.

'That's very civil of you, sir,' said Lionel.

Percy Pott, having made his gesture to legality by switching the lights off and on, was quite ready to refill the glasses and accept a drink himself and one for his wife.

'Your good healths!' said Lionel. 'Yours too, Dimple, my dear!'

'All the best, dearie!' said Mrs Pott.

'Cheery-ho!' said Jones. 'Mud in yer eye, Dimple!'

·Lionel swayed towards me. 'Don't want you to think I can't take a joke,' he said. 'This chap Jones is all right really. Bit of a gadfly, though, aren't you, Jones? Thinks we're a lot of has-beens down here, don't you, Jonesy? And I expect you're right.'

He stared fixedly at the Virley coat of arms above the fireplace. Alcoholic rivulets of sweat ran slowly down his forehead. 'See the family motto over there? *Hic manemus* – "Here we stay." Relics, that's what we are. Relics from the past. Collectors' pieces. And that's why Jonesy' – he turned and bowed to the little cockney with a gesture that was half ironical, half apologetic – 'that's why this picker-up of unconsidered trifles finds us of interest. Something to stick in your scrap-book, eh, Jones?'

'Time, gentlemen, please!' said Percy. This time he didn't turn the lights on again. A cool air came from the open door. We picked our way towards it by moonlight.

The sharply contrasted figures of Jones and Mr Lionel moved down the village street in diminishing silhouette.

Before they turned the corner Mr Lionel stumbled, and I saw Jones take his arm. Then they were gone. The echoes of their footfalls died away.

The air was warm and still. The fresh, sharp smell of dew on summer dust rose up and mingled with the odours of thatch and lichen-clad walls. Huge elms loomed unreally in the moonlight; and beyond them, outlined in the turquoise of the afterglow, stood the church tower.

I crossed the road and went into the churchyard. The headstones stood in moonlit groups, like ghosts in mourning. As I walked towards the Norman porch the only sound was the soft crunch of gravel under my feet.

The door was unlocked, and it swung smoothly on its huge hinges. Within, the lime-washed walls caught and reflected the chequered moonbeams with a brightness almost of candlelight. For so small a village as Arcady it was a surprisingly large church. The pews had heavy, ornate bench-ends carved in the shapes of dragons, griffins, basilisks, and wyverns. High above the nave I caught glimpses of angels' wings outspread from the bosses of the roof.

The walls of the nave were bare and austere, but on the north side of the chancel was a massive monument in black and white marble. An Elizabethan lady and gentleman reclined in effigy above a frieze of eleven children, their little hands pressed together in prayer. The carving of the arcaded recess and the supporting columns was rich in swags and strap-work, Tudor roses, fleurs-de-lis, laurel wreaths, masks, allegorical animals, and cherubs on the wing.

As the moonlight poured through the windows of the chancel I could just discern the inscription in the arched recess above the effigies. It commemorated two of the earliest Virleys to live at Arcady Hall. Surrounding the inscription was a profusion of carved emblems of mortality – skulls and crossbones, hour-glasses, moths, worms, picks, and shovels. And beneath it I could just read the Virley motto – *Hic manemus* – 'Here we stay.'

As I stood there, I seemed to hear again Mr Lionel quoting the family motto in the Virley Arms. There was a tragic contrast between his down-at-heels, tipsy irony and the bold assurance of this Elizabethan monument. I wondered whether I had come to Arcady to be a chance witness to the end of the House of Virley.

As though in echo of Mr Lionel's voice there came a desolate shriek from over the high elms in the churchyard. It was extraordinarily vibrant for the hoot of an howl, but an owl I assumed it must be.

Gradually I became conscious of a certain dankness in the atmosphere of the church and of a current of cold air playing round my ankles. I turned, hurried down the moonlit aisle, and let myself out through the massive south door.

Outside, the air had the soft reassurance of early June, and in the breeze I caught the scent of wild roses.

On the far side of the churchyard was a high brick wall. A footpath led to a wrought-iron gate in it, and, supposing that it led back to the road, I opened the gate and went through.

I found myself in an avenue of lime trees. They stood in ranks, on either side of the path, their branches outstretched and meeting overhead like the swords of a guard of honour at a wedding.

As I walked between them, my feet treading silently on the grass, the dog-rose scent rising to my nostrils, and my shadow seeming to dance ahead across stepping-stones of moonlight, I felt I was passing from the mortuary world in which Mr Lionel and the owl exchanged cries of lamentation into the Arcady of the original Virleys, a land in which the self-assurance of the Elizabethans blended with the poetry of Shakespeare and Sir Philip Sidney, and life was eternal summer.

Then, as though transmuting my moonlit fancies into historic fact, there loomed up before my eyes the majesty of Arcady Hall.

I saw it as I stepped out of the tunnel of trees at the end of the lime avenue. At my feet was a flat and shaven lawn, across which a wide path passed between sentinels of yew to a balustraded bridge over a moat. Beyond the bridge, rising sheer from the waters of the moat, were the twin towers of a gatehouse which seemed to ascend, like Jacob's Ladder, to the skies. Each of the two towers appeared, as far as I could see, to be octagonal, and each was decorated with terracotta mouldings, trefoil patterns in brick, and tiny windows, shaped like clover leaves, rising one above the other, storey after storey. The tops of the towers, as I saw when I had overcome my wonder at their height, were crenellated like the turrets of a medieval castle.

Between the towers of the gatehouse was a Tudor archway leading inwards from the bridge over the moat, and, above it, two huge eight-light windows, with stone mullions and arched transoms, which caught and reflected the moonlight in innumerable leaded panes. On either side of the gatehouse, rising directly from the waters of the moat, were the wings of the building. Their brick walls were patterned with mullions and surmounted by castellated cornices and crowstepped gables. From the apex of each gable rose octagonal chimneys which seemed to reach for the sky in mimicry of the cloud-capped towers soaring above them.

I stood rapt in amazement at the sight. The longer I looked at it the more unbelievable it seemed. In the radiance of the moonlight it was as unreal as an architectural fantasy by Desiderio.

I could hardly have been farther removed from Whitehall and Mark Fairweather's problems of redundance. Not even Paris could compete with this. As I stood there, an uninvited guest at this private view

35

of faerie land, the beauty of it all seemed to have a sudden poignancy. Oh, why did Deirdre have to be left out of this?

As though in answer, from the top of a vast cedar which grew beside the moat came the same wild bird cry that I had heard when I was in the church. But this was not the hoot of an owl; it rose in a harsh, desolate, continuing shriek, like the death rattle of some mythical creature – a griffin? a wyvern? a basilisk?

Then I saw it – a peacock, perched high on an arm of the cedar, its long pendant tail outlined in black against the starshine, and its cruel, prophetic head flung back in an ecstasy of lamentation.

Next morning I decided to make myself known at Arcady Hall. Perhaps I had been unwise to arrive without writing to Professor Pollux beforehand, but when I telephoned from the Virley Arms he was not available, so I left a message explaining who I was and saying I would arrive at the Hall about midday.

When I set out from the Virley Arms in the middle of the morning the sky had that luminous clarity which it seems to achieve only in East Anglia. There was very little wind; a few cumulous clouds stood guard round the horizon; the trees surrounding the village green were statuesque in the sunshine. It was an early June day made exactly to the specification of lyric poets and popular song-writers.

I thought it unbefitting my official status to approach the Hall through the lime avenue from the churchyard; so I walked over the village green towards the main entrance. As I went I noticed that despite Lionel Virley's talk of change and decay the village green was mown like a lawn, and in the middle of it was a beautifully prepared cricket pitch.

The grounds of the Hall were surrounded by a high brick wall, which skirted the far side of the village green. Behind this was a belt of oak trees. As one walked over the green there was no hint of the architectural grandeur that lay beyond.

Beside a door in the wall there was a small Ministry notice announcing that this was the entrance to the Department of Output Statistics. Inside, I found myself in another of the enclosed walks which seemed to be a feature of the garden plan. On one side was a high wall, on the other a flower border, edged with lavender and backed by a tall yew hedge.

At the end of it was a garden house, built of brick, and surmounted by a miniature castellated turret. As I walked towards it everything I saw seemed just as it might have been four hundred years before. And the illusion was heightened, indeed perfected, when, through the arched doorway of the garden house, with deliberate and pompous gait, stepped the peacock.

He paused, stood very erect, then put his head on one side and regarded me curiously with a large, reflective brown eye. It was odd that I immediately noticed the Vandyck brown of his eye, for the metallic blue of his neck and breast was of much more startling brilliance, and the glitter of gold and green which ran down his back and along the full five or six feet of his tail was like a cascade of jewels. Such, however, was the bird's dignity and air of command that when he paused, as it were, to interrogate me, I had to meet his eye.

In shape and bearing it was an imperious head he had, with the long, thin, flexing neck, and the aquiline beak. But the foppish elegance of his feathery coronet, and the curious parchment-like mask of white skin round his eyes, gave him a certain air of benevolence, like that of an elderly Edwardian clubman with puckered cheeks and a butterfly collar.

We gazed at each other for a time in mutual assessment. Then he moved on, picking up his spurred feet with unhurried deliberation, and drawing his jewelled train behind him.

'Are you the man from the Ministry?'

It was a woman's voice, but it took me some moments to discover the speaker.

'I'm up here,' she said. Glancing upwards, I saw a dishevelled head of brown hair leaning out of the upstairs window of the garden house.

'Yes, I suppose I am,' I replied, hesitantly.

'They told me you were coming. Wait a minute and I'll come down.'

In the room overhead a door slammed; there was a scurry of footfalls down creaking stairs; and through the doorway came a short, well-built young woman dressed in jeans and a blue shirt. Her hair was cut short, and in tousled disarray. She wore no shoes or stockings and I saw that her toes were sunburnt.

She stopped and examined me with a surprisingly frank and open curiosity. She had large, widely set brown eyes, a wide forehead, thick dark untrimmed eyebrows, and a broad snub nose. She had the tomboyish air and figure of a girl of seventeen – the kind of girl one sees hanging round the stables at a riding school.

'You're not what I expected,' she said, with a candour matching the frankness of her gaze. There was a self-assurance in her voice – a husky contralto – that made me realize she was older than she looked.

'What *did* you expect?' I asked.

'Grey-striped trousers, an umbrella, and a bowler hat,' she answered. 'And probably pince-nez.'

'I'm sorry to have disappointed you.' I didn't mention that I had an umbrella back at the Virley Arms.

'Crikey! I'm not disappointed,' she said, with a grin.

'You'll do excellently. We're distinctly short of able-bodied men in these parts. What's your name, by the way?'

'Jasper Pye. And yours?'

'Belinda.'

I was slightly surprised at the omission of her surname, but, remembering my conversation with Miss Tidy in the train, I put two and two together.

'You must be Lord Flamborough's daughter?'

'Yes, one of them – the wicked one.'

I didn't know what rejoinder to make to that.

'Are you married?' she asked.

'No.'

'Girl friend?'

'Not now,' I answered, reluctantly.

'All clear, then? Whizzo!'

The schoolboy expletive would have sounded absurd on the lips of anyone of her age in London. Here, uttered by this quite unaffected young woman, it seemed spontaneous.

I asked which way I should go to find Professor Pollux.

'No good looking for him now. You'd only find Quirky, who'd bore you with the latest batting averages. The Prof has gone to Flaxfield to arrange about the marquee for the Fête. Won't be back till this afternoon. You'd better come along and see Daddy first. He's always glad of company. I'll take you.'

I thanked her, and followed her through a wrought-iron gate which opened into another long walk, with high yew hedges at either side.

'What a labour it must be, keeping all these hedges trimmed,' I said, to make conversation.

'We leave all that sort of thing to the Prof,' said Lady Belinda, 'though Mummy sees to the flowers: she's a mad-keen gardener.'

'I'm rather fond of gardening myself,' I ventured.

Lady Belinda looked at me with curiosity.

'Then you'll make a hit with Mummy,' she said. 'I can see you settling down here for quite a while. Have you brought plenty of clothes, or only a toothbrush? Anyway, Daddy or Lionel can fix you up with anything you want. You can't go till after the Fête, that's certain.'

'When does this Fête take place?' I asked.

'On Whit Monday – next Monday.'

'Is it in aid of something?'

'Fallen Women.'

'I beg your pardon?'

'The Fund for Fallen Women,' Lady Belinda enunciated clearly and with relish. 'Girlies like me, but who haven't been quite so careful. It's Mummy's pet charity; at least, she inherited from Grannie, and she's never had the heart to chuck it up.'

'Of course, I'll make a contribution,' I said. 'But I doubt if I can stay as long as that. And, to be quite honest, it doesn't sound quite in my line.'

We walked along in silence for a while. The path seemed to go on and on.

'Not interested in fallen women, then?' Lady Belinda asked, with a sidelong glance at me.

I hunted for an appropriate answer. 'No, not as a social problem, I must admit.'

'Not in the mass, you mean?'

'No, not in the mass.'

'But individually, perhaps?'

'Perhaps, yes,' I admitted.

'Thanks be for small mercies, anyway,' she remarked, with a sigh.

I felt I had been absurdly pompous. 'I don't mean I've no feeling for them,' I said. 'I mean it just isn't a problem I've come up against.'

'You will,' said Lady Belinda laconically.

At that moment we arrived at a junction in the walk, where four or five paths debouched in different directions.

'No, not that way. This way!' said Lady Belinda.

I turned first to the left, then to the right, and in the confusion stepped hard on Lady Belinda's bare toes.

'Ow!' she exclaimed.

'I'm terribly sorry!' I put out my hands to steady her as she bent forward and rubbed her foot.

'No harm done,' she said, in a matter-of-fact voice, and nestled cosily under my chin. Involuntarily I put an arm round her.

'That's a lot better,' she said huskily, sliding her arms under my jacket and round my back. 'I think you've got more feeling for fallen women than you think you have.'

We stood for a moment in this unpremeditated and slightly ridiculous pose. Then she kissed me, lightly and tantalizingly, on the lobe of my ear, and we resumed the walk. I felt more unnerved by the incident than she appeared to be.

'This seems a very long way round to the Hall,' I said after a while.

'We're not going to the Hall,' said Lady Belinda. 'Daddy doesn't live in the Hall any longer. He's down at the station – across the park.'

I wondered what she meant. We came at last to the end of the yew-lined walk, went down a flight of steps in a ha-ha, and began to cross the park.

'Do you like being kissed?' she asked suddenly.

'Well, yes – I mean, of course. But I don't know . . .' I really couldn't think how to answer that question, coming just when it did.

'What I mean is some men don't like being kissed. They prefer to do the kissing themselves.'

'Oh, I see. You mean there's a difference between active and passive kissing.'

'Yes, if you like to put it that way. I like both, as a matter of fact. First I like to be active, and then passive – and then both at the same time.'

If anyone else had started to talk like that, without any conversational preliminaries, I should have shied off, or assumed she was a tiresome exhibitionist. But Lady Belinda was so naïvely matter-of-fact that I found myself slipping without qualms into the mood of the conversation.

'I suppose I ought to say that I like kissing more than being kissed,' I said. 'It's a more manly attitude, really. But though I wouldn't have dreamt of kissing you when I trod on your foot just now I admit I did rather like being kissed by you.'

Having said this, I was a little embarrassed. After all, I had only met her ten minutes ago: I hadn't met her family; and I was supposed to be on a delicate mission which might involve them all in disagreeable negotiations.

Lady Belinda, however, seemed quite unconcerned. She walked a little ahead of me, with long strides, swinging her hips, and plucking grass shoots as she went.

'You ought,' she said, 'to see how you like being the kisser, instead of the one who's kissed.'

'Ought I?' I temporized.

'Yes, you should,' said Lady Belinda. 'When we reach that little copse beyond the stile I'm going to offer you my lips, or cheek, or ear – whatever you choose, and you can see how you like it.'

'Supposing,' I said apprehensively, 'I said I'd rather not risk it? I mean' – I stumbled on – 'I don't mean that discourteously. But' – I saw my way out – 'supposing I didn't want to spoil the savour of the first kiss, and preferred to wait a little while before the next.'

'Oh, I suppose I'd understand, if you put it as nicely as that.' We came to the stile, and she lightly vaulted over it. 'But I'd be jolly disappointed.'

I climbed over the stile after her. She stood just inside the copse, sucking a shoot of grass, and solemnly gazing down at the ground like a despondent child. Despite the extraordinary freedom of her conversation there was something naïve about her dejection.

'I wouldn't dream of disappointing you,' I said, startled by my own words.

She looked up at me with innocent wonder in her eyes. 'You really want to?' she asked.

'Yes, really,' I said, wondering what I was letting myself in for.

'Then which would you prefer – lips, cheek, or ear?'

She stepped towards me and offered me her lips. For a moment I was overcome by shyness. Then I felt the chains of my reserve snapping.

When I became rationally aware once more of what I was doing she had buried her face in my chest and I was kissing her hair. 'You seemed to like them all,' she whispered. 'But I think you liked my eyes best.'

She tilted up her chin. With an unaccountable twinge of guilt I found myself thinking of Deirdre. Then Belinda closed her eyes. I kissed her eyebrows, her eyelids, her eyelashes. I was thinking of Deirdre no longer.

'Whizzo!' Belinda murmured. 'You kiss beautifully.'

I have no idea how long we had been standing there when a woman's voice rang through the copse. 'Belinda, will you stop spooning for a moment and give me a hand over this stile?'

I started from Belinda's arms to see a hatless woman, with greying hair, clambering over the stile. She was dressed in shabby green tweeds, and under her arm she carried a box of plants.

Belinda, who seemed much less disconcerted than I, called out, 'Coming, Mummy!', ran towards her, took the box of plants, and helped her over the stile.

'Why your father chooses to exile himself to the far side of the park I cannot imagine,' the newcomer said. 'I wish he'd get a girl friend to look after him, and save my poor feet.'

'Never mind, Mummy, it keeps you fit,' said Belinda. 'And Jasper will carry your plants.'

'Of course!' I said, stepping forward self-consciously.

'How d'you do!' said Lady Flamborough to me, abruptly, but without a hint of surprise.

She had the same huskiness of voice as her daughter. I saw, too, that she had the same widely spaced brown eyes, and the same broad nose and mouth – a peasant's features, one would have said, if one had passed her in a country lane. And her clothes, though tailor-made, were as well-worn and homely as any peasant's.

'Thank you so much,' she said, as I took the box of plants from her. 'Now, 'Linda dear, you'll have to interrupt your studies and go up to the Hall. Quirky wants someone to help him unpack the bunting.'

'I was taking Jasper to see Daddy,' said Belinda.

'Jasper can come with me,' said Lady Flamborough. 'Who is Jasper, by the way?'

'He's the man from the Ministry,' said Belinda.

'Didn't know we were expecting one. Still' – she turned to me – 'you'll lunch with us, of course?'

'Thank you very much, Lady Flamborough,' I said nervously.

'Now get along, 'Linda,' said Lady Flamborough. 'And make sure Quirky gets out the Flags of All Nations as well as the bunting.'

'See you later,' said Belinda. She lightly brushed my cheek with the back of her hand, vaulted the stile, and ran back across the park.

'Didn't realize you were one of the Professor's people,' said Lady Flamborough, as we set off in the other direction. 'I thought you were just one of 'Linda's suitors.'

I cleared my throat apprehensively. This, it seemed, was where I had to account for the situation in which she had surprised me.

'I must apologize, Lady Flamborough—' I began.

'That's quite all right. There's always plenty of lunch. Bertie eats enough for three, and it will do him good to go without his third helpings.'

'It's very good of you to have me,' I said lamely. 'But after our rather embarrassing meeting I thought perhaps—'

'I'm never embarrassed. And, if you take a middle-aged woman's advice, you'll never be embarrassed either.'

'But I really ought to explain—' I said.

'Don't try! The ways of the Ministry are quite inscrutable. You may be an agent from MI5 for all I know. But it doesn't make the slightest difference, so long as you don't mind carrying the bridal wreath.'

'The bridal wreath?'

'Yes, a bridal wreath. One so seldom sees them nowadays. But I think it's such a charming traditional ornament.'

I couldn't imagine what she was talking about. Then a frightening thought came into my mind. She had referred to me as one of her daughter's 'suitors'. Did she – surely she couldn't – suppose that I was contemplating marriage?

'When I was a girl,' Lady Flamborough continued, 'any number of the cottagers used to have bridal wreaths. They were supposed to bring good luck. But they have quite gone out of fashion.'

I felt I must disillusion her immediately.

'I must explain that the situation in which you found us was quite . . . fortuitous.'

45

'Fortuitous!' echoed Lady Flamborough. 'How amusing! I've never heard cuddling described like that before. But tell me, how do you like the bridal wreath?'

The conversation was getting out of my depth.

'I don't really know what a bridal wreath is. But I'm sure it's charming.'

'*Francoa ramosa*,' said Lady Flamborough. 'I'll get one for you, if you like.'

'But I've no intention of getting married,' I said, desperately.

'No?' said Lady Flamborough, with an unexpected lack of interest. 'But I'll let you have a bridal wreath all the same, if you'd like one. You can train it up a stick.'

I was nonplussed. 'Can you please tell me, Lady Flamborough, exactly what a bridal wreath is?'

'You've got one under your arm now,' she said, pointing to the box of plants I was carrying.

'You mean this pot-plant? The one with leaves like a turnip?'

'Yes,' she said. 'Haven't you ever seen them in cottage windows? They're scarce nowadays, I know. But I took some cuttings from a plant in the village, and I'll let you have one if you'd like it.'

'Thank you so much. I'd love one!' I said, with a sigh of relief. Thank heaven the conversation had recovered its sanity! 'I'm rather keen on window plants. I have quite a lot in London.'

'They tell me the aspidistra is all the rage in London now,' said Lady Flamborough. 'You must see the ones I keep in the saloon. I'm growing them out-of-doors, too. It's really too cold for them in East Anglia, but I've planted them in the shelter of the chapel ruins. Come and look.'

We were passing a thicket, dense with fallen tree-trunks, ivy, and ground elder. 'We can get through here,' said Lady Flamborough, plunging into the undergrowth, regardless of waist-high nettles and trailing bramble shoots.

I followed. Inside the thicket it was damp and dark, and there was a rank smell of rotting vegetation. 'Wonderful accumulation of humus here,' said Lady Flamborough. 'See how it suits my primulas!'

We came out into a glade, where the sunlight found its way between the branches overhead and fell upon rivulets of blue and purple blossom running through the grass.

'Grow as freely as bluebells, don't they?' said Lady Flamborough. 'And here are the aspidistras – flourishing like stink-horns.'

She pointed ahead, where I saw a wall of flints rising some twenty or thirty feet out of the undergrowth. At the top it was crumbling into ruins, which were precariously sustained by dark buttresses of ivy and crowned with vivid yellow clusters of stonecrop. Round the foot of the wall, in deep shadow, grew the aspidistras, throwing up their glossy spear-shaped leaves in luxuriant profusion. They were scarcely recognizable as the dusty pot-plants of the Victorian villa.

Lady Flamborough bent down and lifted up some of the leaves. 'Look, they're flowering!'

Low down at the base of the leaves were little cup-shaped flowers, with chestnut-coloured pointed petals.

'I don't believe I've ever seen an aspidistra in flower before,' I said.

'Amusing, aren't they?' Lady Flamborough said delightedly.

'What a romantic sight this is,' I said, looking round me at the ruins of the chapel rising from an almost tropical labyrinth of greenery.

'Slugs,' said Lady Flamborough. 'All done by slugs. They fertilize the blossoms.'

We picked our way round the walls of the chapel. Inside it there was little of the fabric still standing, except one high pointed arch rising out of a thicket of holly and brambles like a characteristic detail in a water-colour by Cotman.

'How long has this been in ruins?' I asked.

'As long as anyone can remember,' replied Lady Flamborough. 'But they used to hold village weddings here when Bertie was a boy – quite irregular, I believe; but the village people still have an idea that if a child is fathered on one of the girls here it ranks as being born in wedlock, whether the parents are married or not.'

'What a convenient legend!' I said.

'A prickly place for a tryst,' said Lady Flamborough. 'But it certainly suits the aspidistras.'

We made our way round to the other side of the chapel, where there were the relics of a fine Decorated window, with flowing tracery. It overlooked a more open expanse of herbage, amongst which primulas were growing as freely as cowslips in a meadow.

'They look just like native wildflowers,' I exclaimed. 'But I suppose they really come from Kashmir or Tibet?'

'I get them from Thompson and Morgan,' said Lady Flamborough. 'A shilling a packet. Grow them from seed. No trouble at all.'

She pointed to a group of flower-spikes, almost waist-high, bearing blossoms of a rich apricot yellow. 'That's *Bulleyana*. And that' – pointing to some rosy purple flowers – 'is *burmanica*. And this is *Florindae*, a Chinese species. And this is *gemmifera zambalensis*.'

I was standing there, marvelling at her botanical knowledge as much as the flowers, when I became aware that we were not alone. Perched on the inner ledge of the chapel window, her knees drawn up to her chest and her head thrown back against the tracery, was a girl, dressed entirely in white, with a chaplet of primula blossoms woven into her long black hair. She seemed unaware of our presence.

'This yellow one is a new introduction from Assam,' Lady Flamborough continued. '*Prolifera*, it's called. And this drooping one is *microdonta*, the Moonlight Primula.'

The girl sat motionless, ignoring our presence. Framed in the stonework of the window, she seemed quite unreal, as though she were a painting by Burne-Jones or Rossetti. I found it difficult to concentrate on Lady Flamborough's botanical discourse.

'What is that violet one over by the window?' I asked, hoping she would see the girl and summon her to life.

'That's one of the *denticulatas*,' she replied. '*Cashmiriana*, I think. Quite hardy.'

She saw the girl.

'And that's my daughter Matilda. In one of her gothick moods, I imagine. Wake up, Tilly! It's nearly time for lunch.'

Lady Matilda made no reply.

'We'd better get along,' said Lady Flamborough. 'Bertie doesn't like being kept waiting for his victuals.'

We began to pick our way through the primulas back towards the path. When we approached the window of the chapel Lady Matilda moved for the first time. Slowly she turned her head towards me as I passed, and gazed at me intensely from dark, deep-set eyes. Not a word was said. A little self-consciously I returned her glance, muttered a greeting, and hurried past.

'That was your youngest daughter?' I asked, as we regained the pathway.

'Yes,' said Lady Flamborough. 'Tilly's only sixteen. Funny girl. Spends all her time reading old-fashioned thrillers like *The Mysteries of Udolpho* and waiting to be seduced by a sinister monk. She'll grow out of it.'

Lady Flamborough's matter-of-fact tone removed some of the romantic improbability from the encounter, but as we walked along I found my mind's eye dwelling on that strange immobility of pose and that searching glance from deep, dark eyes. Somehow it was even more disturbing than her sister Belinda's total lack of reserve.

'We're nearly there,' said Lady Flamborough, as we crossed a meadow and entered another spinney. 'I'm sorry you've had to carry that bridal wreath all this way. But Bertie will give you a stiff drink.'

I followed Lady Flamborough out of the spinney to find myself at the back of a gaunt, narrow building, in the Victorian Tudor style, with white-painted railings at either side. I took it to be a keeper's cottage, now deserted. Lady Flamborough walked ahead of me through an arched doorway into a high bleak hall, devoid of any furniture or decoration, apart from an ancient poster advertising the attractions of Skegness.

'This way,' said Lady Flamborough, opening another door on the far side.

I stepped out after her and found myself, to my astonishment, on the platform of a railway station. The platform was only some fifty yards long, but there was all the usual station equipment – verandah roof with fretted edge, a bench, hanging oil lamps, a door marked 'Waiting Room', and a few tattered timetables. A single rail track ran out of sight. Standing in the station were three coaches, coupled to an ancient locomotive.

There was not a porter, ticket-collector, or guard in sight, but Lady Flamborough strode to the door of the nearest coach – it seemed to be some sort of restaurant car, with doors at the ends – and threw it open.

'Bertie!' she called, as she clambered in. 'I've brought a man from the Ministry to lunch.'

I stepped in after Lady Flamborough, passed a pair

lavatory doors, marked 'Gentlemen' and 'Ladies' respectively, and entered a full-length Pullman compartment, sumptuously panelled with inlaid mahogany and sandalwood, and furnished with enormous armchairs, upholstered in plush and hung with heavy lace antimacassars.

The windows of the coach were edged with decorative borders in frosted glass. From the ceiling, whose elaborate plaster-mouldings were patterned in gilt, hung flamboyant gas chandeliers. On each side of the doorway was an aspidistra on a carved ebony *jardinière*. At the far end of the carriage, seated in an invalid chair, was the Earl of Flamborough.

As we came in he was leaning over an archaic gramophone with the original type of HMV horn, shaped like an arum lily. A record began to revolve; he lowered the needle arm; and a harsh scraping sound filled the saloon.

Lord Flamborough raised a leonine head of grey hair and fixed me with a keen glance.

'Can you dance the Charleston?' he asked.

Before I could reply the gramophone began to emit the wheezy but emphatic notes of some vintage jazz band playing 'Yes, sir, That's my Baby'.

'Bertie,' shouted Lady Flamborough, against the din of the gramophone, 'this is Jasper – don't know his other name. Give him a stiff drink: he's carried my plants across the park.'

'Damn decent of you,' said Lord Flamborough. 'What'll you have? Like to try one of my Manhattans? Or my special Dark Lady? Or Angel's Tears?'

I asked him to give me whatever he was having himself. He decided it should be a Dark Lady, and propelled his wheel chair to a cabinet stacked with bottles.

As he mixed the ingredients I studied his features. His hair was grey, and appeared not to have been brushed for some days, but he was a singularly handsome man, with a large aquiline nose, commanding blue eyes, high bushy eyebrows, and full lips. A certain puffiness of the cheeks and a tendency to a double chin merely accentuated the resemblance to a Regency buck or one of the later Roman emperors.

'Learned to shake a cocktail from Harry Craddock,' he remarked, 'the fellow who used to be at the Savoy. He invented the cocktail. Dead now, I dare say. But I use my own recipes. See how you like this.'

The cocktail he gave me was almost as dark in colour as port, but had a surprisingly light, dry flavour. I asked if one of the ingredients was Dubonnet.

'No,' replied Lord Flamborough. 'I colour it with beetroot. Cheaper.'

'It's delicious,' I said. It had both a fortifying and a relaxing effect. My somewhat bizarre experiences of the morning began to take on a less dream-like aspect.

'I take it you have a private coach on this line, sir?' I asked.

'I own it,' said Lord Flamborough.

'You own the coach?'

'I own the railway,' replied Lord Flamborough. 'I bought the Branch Line, stations and all, when they closed it down four years ago. The railway people made me a present of the locomotive – it's an old Great Eastern "Intermediate" – used to run between Cambridge and Mildenhall.'

'And the coaches?' I asked, attempting to pursue rationally a conversation that verged on the fantastic.

'A fellow called Jones found them for me, in a siding at Palmer's Green. Hadn't been moved for years, they tell me; the line was bust up in the blitz. But Jones—'

'Is he a short man, with a little toothbrush moustache?'
I asked.

'That's it. Know him?'

I told him I had met Jones in the Virley Arms.

'Well, Jones told me about these coaches – he's a bit of a dealer, you know, always travelling around, buying and selling things. And I said I'd like 'em if he could get 'em for me cheap. So he went to the Railway and they told him he could have 'em for a song if he'd take them away.'

'How did he get them here?' I asked.

'Well, that's a story,' said Lord Flamborough. 'Jones read in the papers that the footplate men were threatening to come out on strike. Now I happen to have had my legs chopped off through some idiot railwayman's carelessness in the General Strike. So, a day or two before this footplate strike was due to begin, Jones went along to the local branch of the Union and told 'em that he'd arranged for me to appear on Television, waggle my stumps at the audience, and tell the world how the footplate fellows behaved in 1926. Sheer blackmail! I wouldn't have done it, of course; haven't been to London for twenty years, except for the Coronation. But Jones pitched 'em the yarn. Naturally they didn't like it – thought it might turn public opinion against 'em. So Jones told them that I didn't really bear 'em any ill will, and if they'd run these three coaches down to Flaxfield for me I'd call off the Television act. They ran the coaches down here while the strike was on – there was a bit of confusion on the railways at that time. Very decent about it, they were. Cleaned the coaches and oiled round the engine before they went. And elected me Vice-President of the Flaxfield Branch of the Union.'

Lord Flamborough put his hand to the lapel of his jacket and displayed the Union badge in his buttonhole.

Whilst he was talking Lady Flamborough had left

the saloon. Now she reappeared and announced that luncheon was ready.

'Give me a push, there's a good fellow,' said Lord Flamborough.

I took hold of the handles of his invalid chair, and wheeled him into the next coach, which was a dining car. One of the banquettes had been removed to make room for Lord Flamborough's chair. Lady Flamborough and I sat opposite him.

'Always did enjoy eating on a train,' said Lord Flamborough, 'though the meals weren't always what they might have been. Now I get the best of both worlds – home cooking and a change of scene.'

As he spoke there was a sudden loud hissing sound, and a white cloud drifted past the window.

'Is Chloe in the cab?' Lord Flamborough asked.

'Yes, dear,' his wife replied.

Lord Flamborough picked up a guard's peaked cap that was resting on the window ledge and put it on his head. Then he took a large gold watch from his waistcoat pocket.

'One seventeen,' he said. He put the watch away, took a whistle from another pocket, and blew two sharp blasts on it. There was an answering toot from the locomotive.

'Care to flag her out?' asked Lord Flamborough.

I was not sure what he meant until I realized that Lady Flamborough was handing me a green flag.

'We haven't got a guard's van,' said Lord Flamborough. 'You have to use the door behind me. Wait till you hear the "away" whistle.'

Hesitantly I got up, took the green flag, walked down the car and stepped out on to the platform.

Leaning from the cab of the engine was a fair-haired woman, dressed in brown overalls. From within the dining car came a long shrill whistle. I gave a tentative

54

wave of the flag and the woman's head disappeared. With a burst of smoke from the funnel and a clanking of coupling rods the train began to move.

I jumped back into the coach and shut the door after me. As I returned to my seat and handed the green flag to Lady Flamborough her husband was studying his watch again.

'One nineteen precisely,' he announced.

'Will you have soup?' said a low, soft voice at my shoulder. I turned to see Lady Matilda holding a silver soup tureen on a tray.

'Thank you,' I said.

She gave me a long searching glance, just as she had done in the ruined chapel, then helped me to a portion of steaming mulligatawny.

'Don't slop it, Tilly,' said her mother.

'Go into the saloon, Tilly,' said her father, 'and put "Bughouse Blues" on the phonograph.' The word 'phonograph' seemed to be his term for the vintage gramophone.

I looked out of the window. In imperturbable calm the sober Suffolk landscape was gliding by.

Fifty-eight minutes later, by the Earl of Flamborough's gold watch, the train drew up at the Halt for Arcady Hall. During that time we had eaten an excellent four-course lunch, served by Lady Matilda, and the train had travelled to Flaxfield Junction and back again.

At Flaxfield Junction, as though to mark the distinction between British Railways and the Earl of Flamborough's Folly, the Branch Line terminated abruptly in a high corrugated iron fence which had been thrown across the rails some fifty yards from the station platform. A group of local children had gathered at this unimpressive terminus to watch the train steam in, and

Lord Flamborough leaned out of the dining-car window to make a distribution of some sticky sweets which he called Arcady Rock. The train eventually made its departure from Flaxfield Junction to the accompaniment of shrill cheers from the spectators. Evidently its visit was a daily occurrence which afforded much innocent pleasure.

The line from Flaxfield to Arcady passed along the edge of the park surrounding Arcady Hall, but for most of its course the Hall was hidden by high hedges or woods. There was only one opening through which the whole building could be seen from the train, its gatehouse rising from the placid landscape like some castle of the imagination sketched in the background of a Flemish primitive by Dirk Bouts or Memling.

In this opening was the Halt, which comprised a short wooden platform and a very small but elegant brick-built shelter, with Gothic windows, a Regency verandah, and castellations round the roof.

'Here you are, my dear fellow,' said Lord Flamborough. 'It's only a couple of hundred yards from here up to the Hall.'

'Aren't you coming too, sir?'

'Not me. The Hall is entirely in the Professor's keeping. I live in the train.'

'You sleep here, too?' I asked.

'Of course. The front coach is a sleeper. And very comfortable, too. Now off you go, or I shan't be back at the terminus on time. There's Quirky on the platform, waiting to welcome you.'

As I stepped out and shut the carriage door behind me I heard the blast of Lord Flamborough's whistle, and the green flag appeared through the window. The female engine-driver, whom I took to be the Flamboroughs' eldest daughter, waved to me and set the train in motion.

'I'm Quirk,' said a gruff voice behind me.

'I'm Jasper Pye,' I said, turning and shaking hands with the Archivist to the Department of Output Statistics.

'The Professor sent me along to welcome you,' said Quirk. 'We heard on the grapevine that you'd probably arrive on the Flamborough Flier. Hope you're none the worse for your experiences.'

'Not at all,' I said. 'Lord and Lady Flamborough were most hospitable, and I had an excellent lunch.'

'Huh! I usually get roped in as fireman,' said Quirk.

He would be a serviceable stoker, I thought, glancing at him as we walked towards the Hall. Though he appeared to be in his late fifties he had the weather-beaten air and springing step of a sailor or an athlete. In his club tie and slightly moth-eaten blazer, he looked less like a Civil Servant than the games master at a prep school – an impression that was strengthened when he took a cricket ball from his pocket and began to toss it from hand to hand.

'I gather,' he said, 'that you're on a tour of inspection.'

'Oh, hardly that,' I answered, reassuringly. 'I've just come down to talk over the work with Professor Pollux.'

'He wasn't expecting you – not till he got your message this morning. But you'll find everything ship-shape. Always is. The Prof's a stickler for order and method.'

'Oh yes, I'm sure,' I said. 'And what a lovely place you have to work in!'

We were approaching the Hall at a different angle from that at which I had seen it the night before. The gatehouse was now at the farther end from us, and we were walking over a lawn that flanked the main buildings, though it was separated from them by the moat.

'Fond of fishing?' asked Quirk. 'There are some

decent trout in the moat. It's fed from a spring and runs into the river.'

As we drew closer I looked down into the water. It was crystal clear, with a chalky bottom, and here and there a clump of watercress. The walls of the Hall rose straight from the moat's edge. From any of the tall mullioned windows one could have cast a fly on to the water.

'Clean, isn't it!' said Quirk. 'Every autumn we go round in a punt and mow the weeds with a scythe.'

'It's certainly very well kept up,' I said. 'Unlike some of these ancestral homes.'

'All the Professor's doing,' said Quirk, with a note of reverence in his voice.

We rounded the corner of the moat, and the full glory of the gatehouse and the main façade came into view. In the sober afternoon sunshine it was almost as impressive as it had appeared in moonlight. The sun was just moving off the face of the building, but it still caught the edges of the octagonal towers and the projecting oriel windows, throwing dark, unlikely shadows over the intervening spaces.

We walked over the bridge across the moat towards the high arched doorway at the base of the gate tower. As we drew near there was a rattle of bolts and chains and the door swung slowly open. Framed in the doorway, in silhouette against the sunshine in the courtyard beyond, stood a man of commanding stature, with deep-set, searching eyes, improbably thick eyebrows, and the high tonsure of a priest. He stood quite still, regarding me for a moment or two with an odd, whimsical air of appraisal. Then he said, in a beautifully articulated voice with a Scots timbre, 'Welcome to Arcady, Mr Pye!'

'How do you do, Professor?' I said, shaking hands. 'I hope I haven't arrived at an inconvenient time.'

'In Arcady, Mr Pye, we are fortunate in having mair

58

time at our disposal than you restless people in London. Our place of business was erected some four hundred and seventy years ago – mair than a hundred years before the fragment that remains of your Palace of Whitehall. Wi' so much time behind us, Mr Pye, we should be churlish if we didna' spare a wee bit for so rare a pleasure as a visitor from the Ministry.'

He delivered this formal speech as though it were a lecture to students; but under the measured periods and elaborate courtesies I detected a note of irony – or was it mistrust?

'You are certainly fortunate,' I said, 'to have a building like this as your place of business.'

The Professor, who had led me through into the courtyard of the Hall, turned and subjected me to a disconcerting stare from beneath his outsize eyebrows.

'It is mair than good fortune, Mr Pye,' he said solemnly. 'It is a preevilege. And a preevilege of which we hope all concerned will prove worthy.'

Was it just his magisterial manner which made me feel that I had been reproved? I noticed that Quirk was standing by with a self-conscious grin on his face, like a schoolboy in the presence of the Head.

'I think, sir,' he interjected, 'that I'd better take Mr Pye along to my room for a wash and brush up. Then I'll bring him along to the Great Gallery.'

'Guid!' said the Professor, turning on an expansive and somewhat frightening smile. 'Make yourself comfortable, ma dear chap,' he said to me, 'and then I will show you roun'.'

Quirk took me back into the gatehouse entrance, and up a spiral stairway.

'You'll bear in mind, won't you, Mr Pye, that this place means a lot to the Professor. Being here is more than a job of work, as far as he's concerned.'

'You mean he's become attached to the place for its own sake?' I asked.

59

'More than attached,' said Quirk. 'He's quite potty about it – loves every brick.'

'How about yourself?' I asked, as I was washing my hands.

'Oh, I'm fond of the old place, too. But I haven't got the Professor's sense of history. I'm just a camp follower. I'm happy enough if I get my game of cricket now and then. But I've a great admiration for the Prof. I'd do anything for him.'

As though embarrassed by this declaration of loyalty Quirk took the cricket ball out of his pocket again and began bouncing it lightly against the wall of the room.

'I'll take you up to the Great Gallery,' he continued, 'and then I'll walk over to the Virley Arms and collect your bag. You'll be sleeping here, of course?'

'Yes,' I said, 'if that's convenient. But I'll go and get my bag myself. No need for you to bother.'

'No bother at all,' said Quirk. 'I want to run a roller over the wicket, and that's on my way.'

Having washed, I followed him up the spiral staircase, which was like no other staircase I had seen. It was entirely built of brick, even to the handrail, which was made of moulded bricks inset in the outer wall. At intervals there were little quatrefoil windows with opaque, leaded panes. The whole effect was medieval.

We came to a massive oak door leading off the stairway. Quirk opened it and ushered me into a room whose length and proportions and luxuriance of decoration almost took my breath away.

'This is the office,' said Quirk, 'and this is Miss Mounsey.'

I was so overwhelmed by the magnificence of the Great Gallery that I hardly noticed the girl whom Quirk introduced to me.

'Oh, how d'you do, Miss Mounsey?' I said, shaking hands with her.

'I'm sorry to say,' remarked Quirk, with a boyish grin, 'that Miss Mounsey is commonly known at Arcady Hall as the Mouse. But I don't think she bears us any ill-will because of it.'

Miss Mounsey smiled and lowered her eyes. She was pretty, in an indeterminate way, and had fine eyelashes, but I surmised that the nickname fitted her.

'What a marvellous room!' I exclaimed. 'However can you manage to get any work done in here?'

'Oh, it's most convenient,' said Quirk, taking my question quite seriously. 'You see, it used to be the library, and all these little alcoves between the bookcases are just right for filing cabinets. The Mouse sits here by this window, where there's a good light for typing coming over the left shoulder. I sit opposite the fireplace at that refectory table, which is large enough for all my files. And the Prof sits at the far end, when he's in here – up on the dais.'

At that moment the door swung open and the Professor came in. I had not noticed before that he was wearing a suit of old-fashioned plus-fours, in Harris tweed of a bold sporting pattern. Striding into the Great Gallery, with that commanding presence of his, he created the illusion of a landed gentleman or laird entering his ancestral home.

'Ah, Mr Pye,' he said, 'I see you are impressed by our workroom – and rightly so. These bookcases were carved by Grinling Gibbons for the fourth Earl. The ceiling is Jacobean – a hundred and twenty years later than the house itself. But it is, I believe, the earliest of its kind, and antedates the somewhat similar examples at Blickling Hall and Boston House, Brentford ... Don't let me interrupt you in your duties, Miss Mounsey.'

Miss Mounsey blushed and bent over her typewriter.

'I expect you know Henry Peacham's *Minerva Britannia*,' continued the Professor, 'a book of emblems which was published in 1612. These panels' – he pointed up at the ceiling, which was decorated with a series of panels containing embossed pictorial devices – 'these panels are emblems of the senses and other human characteristics, adapted from Henry Peacham's book. This gentleman playing a lute to his lady represents, as you see, "Hearing" – *Auditus*. That undressed lady astride a wee dragon exemplifies *pulchritudo femina* – the beauty of women. Indeed, Mr Pye, as I tell Quirk when he has any bother with his filing system, one only has to look at the ceiling and one can find clearly described, analysed, indexed, and cross-indexed, the human character in all its foibles and quirks.'

'Foibles and quirks,' echoed Quirk, gleefully, with a glance of schoolboyish delight at the Professor, whose face had broadened into an indulgent smile.

I laughed dutifully, and studied in all seriousness the remarkable work of craftmanship overhead. The room must have been fifty or sixty feet long, and the whole of the ceiling was intricately patterned with ribs, scrolls, and strapwork, framing the panels in which the emblems were set. The brilliant white of the plaster was in striking contrast to the dark oak panelling. In the middle of the room was a fireplace, set in an elaborately worked stone chimney-piece of Jacobean design, embodying three coats of arms, painted in red, blue, and gold.

'Those, I suppose, are the arms of the Virley family?' I said.

'Aye,' the Professor replied. 'They indicate the relationships by marriage upon which the family fortunes were based. Indeed there are few, if any, members of the family today – or connections by marriage – who couldna' trace their descent from one or other of the unions commemorated by those arms. It is quite extraordinary, Mr Pye, how the Virley family has kept itself to itself. Since the seventeenth century there has hardly been a single instance of a Virley marrying anyone who wasna' in some degree related to the family. Perhaps that is why they have played so little part in politics or national affairs. They have lived in a world of their own, and hardly anybody from the outer world has entered it.'

'Was the present Countess of Flamborough related, then?' I asked.

'She is a second cousin of her husband,' said the Professor. 'And their eldest daughter, Lady Chloe, is married to a first cousin of the next generation, Lionel Virley, who is now – for better or worse – the heir to the title and the estate.'

The Professor was now escorting me through a series of smaller rooms which led from one to another, in what I took to be the west wing of the house. They were very sparsely furnished, though the walls of some of them were hung with tapestries.

'I have met Lionel Virley,' I said, 'at the Virley Arms.'

'That,' said the Professor drily, 'is where you would meet him.'

We descended a flight of stairs and entered a long room on the ground floor, which apparently was below the Great Gallery.

'This is the Eating Room,' said the Professor. 'Most people would call it the Dining Room, but in fact it is marked on a seventeenth-century plan as the Eating Room, and that is how it is still described today. Although the company which sits down at that refectory table – it is twenty-nine feet in length – usually consists of one Civil Servant and two Temporary Civil Servants, we have a decent respect for tradition, and we adhere to

63

the auld terminology. I hope, Mr Pye' – the Professor gave me a sardonic glance – 'that you willna' refer to it in your report as the "canteen".'

'I have some regard for tradition myself, Professor,' I said. 'And, in any case, my report will not be concerned with the topography of your office, but with the work done.'

The Professor stopped in his tracks, turned, and looked down at me reflectively.

'So you *are* going to write a report, Mr Pye? I had put ma ain interpretation on your visit, but this is the first direct intimation I have been given of its purpose.'

What an idiot I had been! How could I have been so unguarded as to fall into his trap?

'Perhaps,' continued the Professor, relentlessly, 'you would rather not waste any mair time looking at antiquities. Let us go upstairs to my room and I will conduct you, file by file, through the work of the Department.'

He opened the door of the Eating Room, stood aside, and with a curt inclination of the head indicated the way I should go. I walked upstairs, feeling, for some reason which I could hardly explain to myself, as though I had been guilty of ill manners to my host.

'To your right at the top, Mr Pye,' the Professor called up to me. 'Then straight through to the wee room with the spears and chain mail over the fireplace.'

As I followed his directions I tried to phrase some reassuring statement about the purpose of my visit; but after the penetrating glance the Professor had given me I felt sure he would see through any attempt at prevarication. He obviously realized the implications of my coming. I decided I must be honest with him.

The room in which I now found myself was in complete contrast to the grandeur of the Great Gallery. It was a small, square chamber, apparently, as I deduced when I looked out of the tall brick-mullioned window, an upper room in the gatehouse. The walls were of bare brick, and there was a brick floor. At either side of the fireplace was an alcove, lit by three small arched windows. The fireplace itself was of extreme simplicity, under a simple Tudor arch. Hanging from the wall above it were a helmet, a suit of chain mail, and a pair of mailed gauntlets. At either side hung six crossed spears. The only furniture in the room was a small oak trestle table and two panelled oak chairs.

'Perhaps I need not apologize for the austerity of ma office,' said the Professor, as he followed me into the room. 'It may commend itself to your masters in the Treasury. Here, as you see, we are no' making free wi' the taxpayers' money. We do not even boast the regulation square of carpet. Sit doun, Mr Pye – but not too heavily, as we canna' afford a cushion for the chair, and there is, I fear, woodworm in the seat.'

The Professor's exposition of the nature, purpose, and value of his work was fluent and exhaustive. He may or may not have been an outstanding statistician – I was no judge of that – but he was certainly a skilful advocate. At one point I asked him why he chose to hide himself in obscurity when he might have been making a name for himself at one of the universities or in Whitehall.

'You have only been in Arcady for two days, Mr Pye,' he replied. 'So I canna' expect you to understand ma reasons. But, in the seventeen years since the chances of war brought me here, Arcady has given me much. I want, while I can, to give something in return.'

I did not quite understand what he meant, though there was no doubt about his sentimental attachment to the place. But that was not a matter that concerned the

Ministry. It was essential that I should maintain my detachment. I did, however, make one concession to sentiment: I agreed to stay at Arcady, and defer making my report, until after the Fête. I was a little surprised to find that this loomed as large in the Professor's mind as in the eyes of the Flamborough family.

When the conference was over, and we had had tea, I walked out into the garden. I made my way to a wrought-iron gate in the wall beyond the lawn. This seemed to be approximately where I had emerged the night before. When I opened it, however, I found myself in a small formal garden, enclosed by a brick wall on all sides, and divided by low close-clipped box hedges into an intricate pattern of what I took to be flower-beds. As I looked more closely I saw that there were no flowers in the beds: each was filled with pebbles of a different colour – some a gravelly red, some blue, some white, some almost black. I had never seen anything like it before. I assumed it must be an Elizabethan knot garden.

In the evening sunshine the box hedges exhaled a gentle fragrance. The air was calm, the sky without a cloud. Time and the elements seemed to stand still. It was unbelievable that only a little while ago I had been discussing Departmental statistics.

I sat down on a bench against the wall and began to gather together my impressions of the day. My normal routine did not include visits to moated gatehouses and Elizabethan knot gardens. I knew several 'characters' in the Ministry, but none of them, so far as I was aware, grew aspidistras beside ruined chapels or lived in private trains on their own Branch Lines. Whether or not any of the young women in Whitehall were connoisseurs of the kiss, like Lady Belinda, I just didn't know.

After a few minutes of meditation, however, it occurred to me that I was not nearly as surprised by the events and encounters of the day as I might have expected to be. When I had walked down the lime avenue the night before, had seen the gatehouse in the moonlight, and heard the peacock uttering his wild cry, I seemed to have stepped on to a different plane of existence from that on which I usually lived. Although I was less than a hundred miles from Whitehall the atmosphere and environment were as distinct and other-worldly as if I were in some land of legend.

'Oh, there you are! Thought we'd lost you.' My thoughts were brought rudely down to English earth by the voice of Quirk, who appeared at the entrance to the knot garden, wearing white flannel trousers and carrying a cricket bag.

'I've paid your bill at the Virley Arms,' he said, 'and I've brought your things down here. I wonder if you'd care for a turn at the nets?'

His bland assumption that I played cricket was rather odd; but in fact he had guessed right, though I had not played much in the last year or two.

'I didn't suppose you'd come prepared for cricket,' said Quirk, 'so I've put a spare pair of trousers and a shirt in here. And I've got a pair of boots, size ten, up in the pavilion.'

Everything seemed to have been arranged for me. I followed him through the knot garden into the lavender-bordered walk where I had met Lady Belinda earlier in the day.

'Do you bat or bowl – or both?' inquired Quirk.

I made modest sounds indicating that my batting was not quite as indifferent as my bowling.

'We shall be very glad of you for the Flaxfield match on Saturday,' said Quirk. 'We're always a bit short of players at haysel. And this year is the hundredth annual match between Arcady and Flaxfield – what we regard as the local Derby.'

We stepped out of the doorway in the park wall on to the village green. At one end of the green a practice net had been set up. Just beyond it was a little thatched pavilion with white-painted Gothic windows. Three or four men and boys were standing about in shirt sleeves and braces.

'Now get changed into these whites,' said Quirk, 'while I go and dig Jones and Mr Lionel out of the Virley Arms.'

By the time Quirk had completed his mission I had changed my clothes, and three of the players had taken their turns in the net. I was surprised to see how cultured their stroke-play was. Now and again they let fly at the ball in the conventional rustic style, but they had evidently been well coached – presumably by Quirk – and their standard of play was much higher than I had expected. So – fortunately – was mine, when my turn came to bat.

'Very pretty, sir!' cried Quirk, as I executed a surprisingly effective square cut.

'That's a stroke I used to play at Oxford and Cambridge and Battersea Technical College,' said Jones in mock BBC accents with a strong flavour of cockney. 'Now try this on yer piano!'

He bowled – he was left-handed – a slow, high-flighted ball which pitched outside my legs and knocked back my off-stump, to the delight of all present. 'Knocked 'em in the Old Kent Road,' said Jones, bowing to his audience.

Mr Lionel, having removed a bottle of beer from each pocket of his shooting jacket, and set them carefully down behind the net, bowled an extremely fast full toss which whistled past my shoulder.

'Steady, the Buffs!' cried Jones.

'Not enough ballast,' said Mr Lionel, and walked with unsteady steps to the back of the net, where he opened one of the bottles of beer.

After I had had my turn Quirk batted, with extreme correctness but apparently some difficulty in sighting the ball. Jones, who followed, turned out to be a stone-waller, who hardly lifted his bat from the crease but defied every bowler's efforts to get past it.

By the time it was Lionel Virley's turn to bat he had drunk both his bottles of beer and was in ebullient humour. His style of play was evidently familiar not only to the other players, but to the assembled children, who scattered over as wide an arc as the area of the green allowed.

'Half a pint on the stumps,' he announced as he took guard at the wicket. 'And a large Scotch for anyone who catches me.'

The reason for the distinction between the two awards became apparent when he had played half a dozen balls. He was by no means an incorrect player, but his intention was to hit every ball out of the ground. He missed a good many, and was bowled three times; but he made a surprisingly large number of contacts, and whenever this happened the ball travelled for a prodigious distance, at great height. Much of the bowlers' time was spent helping the children to search for balls in the long grass against the park wall.

Having bowled him once, thereby earning half a pint of beer, I delivered another ball of the same length and pace, only to see it rise steeply towards long on, pass high over an oak tree at the edge of the green, and fall into the shrubbery beyond the gate in the park wall. As the village children were occupied elsewhere I set off myself to find it.

Behind the wall was an overgrown, uncultivated part of the garden. On either side of the path there was a tanglewood of box and yew trees, Portugal laurel, and rhododendrons. Here and there the undergrowth thinned out into a narrow glade, but the chances of the

69

cricket ball having fallen into an open space were remote. I decided not to search very seriously, but to take the opportunity of cooling down.

As I picked my way between the bushes I could hear the shouts of the cricketers on the green and the leathery crack of bat on ball. It was refreshing to be in the scent-laden stillness of the shrubbery and enjoy the sounds of activity vicariously. I sat down for a moment on a fallen tree-trunk and lit a cigarette.

'You won't find anything unless you look.'

Was I imagining things, or was that a voice? I peered through the bushes but could see nobody. And yet, from the way the words were spoken – almost in a whisper – the speaker must be quite near.

'You won't hear anything unless you listen.' There could be no mistake this time: it *was* a voice – speaking in a curiously low and confidential tone, with just a hint – so it seemed to me – of mockery. Still there was nobody to be seen.

'Who's that? Where are you?' I asked, rising to my feet.

There was silence, except for the cries of the cricketers in the distance. I began to feel slightly uneasy, and a little ridiculous. It was almost as though I were suffering from an hallucination. To cover my confusion I started to look methodically for the cricket ball, walking backwards and forwards where I assumed it had fallen, and kicking up the dead leaves with my feet.

'You won't find what you want by looking on the ground.'

Of course! The voice came from above: the speaker must be up a tree. I looked upwards. But I could see nobody. It seemed hardly possible for anyone to perch up in the yews and hollies amongst which I was standing. But some yards away, close to the wall of the park, there was an oak of huge girth with a crown of massive

70

branches some ten feet from the ground.

'You're in the oak tree, aren't you?' I said.

No reply.

I pushed my way through the bushes and came to the foot of the tree. 'Who are you?' I asked.

'I'm the ghost of Bonny Prince Charlie, in the Boscobel oak,' said a voice above me – a boy's voice or a girl's voice, I could not be quite sure.

'It wasn't Bonny Prince Charlie who sheltered in the Boscobel oak,' I said. 'It was Charles the Second.'

'Well, I'm the ghost of Charles the Second, then,' said the voice. 'Who are you?'

'I'm Oliver Cromwell,' I replied, fatuously.

'I must take good care,' said the voice, 'or I may become one of the ruins that Cromwell knocked about a bit.'

'You'd certainly better take care,' I said, trying to enter into the spirit of the charade. 'We Roundheads can be pretty drastic.'

'I should rather like some drastic treatment,' said the voice reflectively. Yes, it was obviously a girl.

'You seem to be the wrong sex for Charles the Second,' I said.

'I'm a hermaphrodite, actually,' said the voice. 'I'm a Lost Soul. I can take on human form, male or female, at will.'

'How about materializing now?' I suggested.

'Oh no, I couldn't,' said the voice. 'I'm feeling very ghostly at the moment.'

'Then perhaps you could make my cricket ball materialize instead?'

There was silence, except for the hum of midges in the undergrowth and the remote shouts of the cricketers on the green. A brimstone butterfly fluttered down the glade ahead of me.

'Can you catch?' said the voice.

71

'Of course I can catch,' I answered. 'I'm a newly elected member of the Arcady Cricket Club.'

'Can you catch with your eyes closed?'

'I could try.'

'Well, walk forward until you stand underneath the lowest bough of the tree,' said the voice.

I did as I was told.

'Now hold out your arms and close your eyes.'

I did so. There was a sound of scrambling in the branches above me.

'Remember, you must keep your eyes tight shut,' said the voice. 'If you open them I shall put a spell on you, and you'll become a Lost Soul, too.'

'My eyes are tight shut,' I said.

'Catch!' the voice commanded.

There was another rustle in the leaves above me, and with an alarming jolt an unquestionably human form dropped into my outstretched arms. Before I realized what had happened I was rolling in the grass with a pair of slim but determined arms wrapped round my neck and a pair of equally purposeful legs twined round my waist.

'Remember, you promised to keep your eyes closed,' a voice murmured in my ear – quite superfluously, as my head was enveloped in what seemed to be the hem of a cotton frock.

'You are rather a butter-fingers, aren't you?' said the voice, as we lay locked together on the ground.

'I'm sorry I dropped you,' I said. 'But I wasn't prepared for such a handful. Would you mind loosening your stranglehold and letting me get up?'

'Only if you swear faithfully to keep your eyes shut.'

'I swear,' I said.

The arms and legs were uncoiled and the cotton frock fell away from my face. I sat up in the grass.

'Are your eyes tight shut?'

'Tight,' I answered truthfully.

I felt the light, glancing touch of lips on my cheek. 'Count ten, and then you can open your eyes.'

'One, two, three, four' – I heard the swish of grass and a scampering of feet – 'five, six, seven, eight, nine, ten.'

I opened my eyes just in time to see the back of a slim, girlish figure in a white frock vanishing down the glade.

At that moment there was a rustle of dead leaves and a sound of footsteps approaching from the opposite direction. As I turned and scrambled to my feet another figure emerged from the undergrowth. It was the parson's daughter with whom I had travelled down in the train.

'Miss Tidy!' I exclaimed, adjusting my clothes. 'Whatever brings you here?'

'I've found the ball,' she said, holding it out to me.

After dinner, which I took in the Eating Room at the Hall, the Professor invited me to go with him to a conference in Lord Flamborough's train to decide on the programme for the Fête.

'To a Londoner like yoursel',' said the Professor, 'this may seem much ado about nothing. But there has been an annual Fête here as long as anyone living can remember.'

'Why,' I asked, 'is it in aid of the Fund for Fallen Women? I've never heard of such a fund.'

'It exists,' said the Professor. 'It was founded in the eighteen-fifties by the widow of the twelfth Earl, whose sentiments were stirred by a problem picture exhibited at the Royal Academy by Augustus Egg. It is a matter of family honour that the Fund should be maintained. One wouldna' pretend that the present organizers and participants in the Fête are greatly concerned with the welfare of Fallen Women, but all are on their mettle to make a success of the Fête. I hope, ma dear Pye, that you will be able to contribute some fresh ideas to our discussion.'

'I can't promise to be much help, Professor,' I said. 'But I take it as a compliment that I'm invited to join in.'

The Professor paused in his stride as we began to mount the steps of the little railway station in the park. 'Aye, ma dear Pye,' he said, gazing intently into my eyes, 'you *are* going to join in, are you not? You, too, are in Arcady now.'

He continued to regard me solemnly for a moment or two. Then, with a quizzical lift of his dark, bushy eyebrows, he turned away and led me to the door of the Pullman coach.

'Come in, Prof!' cried Lord Flamborough, who was sitting in his invalid chair beside the gramophone. 'I'm glad to see you've brought this young fellow from the Ministry. He'll have some ideas for us. He tells me he can dance the Charleston.'

'He's a useful opening bat, too, sir,' remarked Quirk, who was sitting with Miss Mounsey on an elaborately carved mahogany sofa which looked like a relic of the 1851 Exhibition.

'You didn't know whether you was doing the Charleston or the Black Bottom when I bowled you that Chinaman this evening, did you, Mr Pye?' said Jones, whose sparrow features emerged from the foliage of one of the aspidistras. Beyond him, sitting quietly in the far corner of the saloon, was a golden-haired woman in her late twenties, whom I recognized as the driver of the railway engine. I assumed her to be Lady Chloe, who was married to Lionel Virley.

'Shall we begin?' said the Professor, calling the

74

meeting to order. 'I should like to propose that his Lordship takes the chair.'

'Seconded!' said Jones.

'Declined!' said Lord Flamborough decisively. 'I never could be trusted with Fallen Women. Let's take our orders from the Prof, as usual.'

The Professor made unconvincing sounds of protest.

'The Lord has spoken,' said Jones. 'I have much pleasure in seconding the Professor for the Chair of Female Deliquency.'

Everyone present murmured 'Agreed!'

'I appreciate your confidence in me, my Lord, ladies and gentlemen,' said the Professor, pulling a bundle of papers out of his pocket, 'though I canna' regard Mr Jones's witticism as being either apt or humorous.'

'Sorry, Guv,' said Jones, with a grin at me. 'I'll sack me gag-writer.'

'Let us proceed to business,' said the Professor. 'I have to report that I have concluded arrangements with Messrs Sneezum and Corder for the hire of the marquee, and with Mr Percy Pott to undertake the catering. With the co-operation of the tenantry I have arranged for the provision of a pig and a set of bowls with which to bowl for it. I have also secured a Suffolk ham which will be suspended from a tree and awarded to the competitor who succeeds in pinking it with a foil or épée blind-folded.'

'Why not use a sabre?' interjected Lord Flamborough. 'The lads might express themselves more whole-heartedly in slashes than in thrusts.'

' 'Ear, 'ear!' said Jones. 'The fencing caper is a bit la-di-dah. You want something more 'omely. "Cut yerself a slice of ham! Sixpence a slash." That's the way to sell it.'

'I hope you've arranged for the St John Ambulance people to be present,' said Lady Flamborough.

'Aye, in fact I have, your Ladyship,' said the Professor, 'though I had assumed – wrongly, it may appear – that their presence was merely a formality.'

'Jones has got the right idea,' said Lord Flamborough. 'You can use that *scabiola* that's hanging in the Great Gallery; it's devilish sharp, and has a double edge.'

'Cuts both ways!' said Jones. 'Just the ticket.'

The Professor raised his bushy eyebrows in a gesture of resignation. 'Verra well. If it is your wish, we borrow the *scabiola* and announce this wee attraction as "Slicing the Ham".'

'Agreed!' said everyone.

'We must have fireworks!' With this vigorous statement of policy Lady Belinda, her hair dishevelled and her shirt buttons coming adrift, burst into the saloon.

The Professor turned his magisterial glance upon her. 'We hav'na' yet reached that item in the agenda, Lady Belinda, though the meeting has been in progress for some while.'

'Sorry I'm late, Prof,' said Lady Belinda, 'but I've been helping Lionel with his new toy.'

'Where is Lionel?' inquired Lord Flamborough.

'Need we ask?' said the Professor, looking at his watch. 'It isna' closing time yet.'

'Lionel's on the way,' announced Lady Belinda with a reassuring glance at her sister.

'To resume,' said the Professor, tapping irritably on the arm of his chair, 'I have also had the assistance of her Ladyship in organizing a flower show, and the Lady Chloe is arranging a sweet stall. I propose to call upon Mr Jones to put his talents as a salesman at our disposal and run the jumble sale.'

'Jumble!' exclaimed Jones. 'Jumble! Not on yer life, cock! Glad to oblige and all that, but you'll kill the business stone dead if you call it "jumble". "Relics and Curios", if you like, or "Treasure Trove" – but cut out the jumble, Prof. We got to move with the times, be dynamic.'

'As you wish, Mr Jones,' said the Professor. 'It's your responsibility. But I trust you will bear in mind that this is Arcady and not Yarmouth Pier. I hope your dynamism willna' gang so far as fluorescent lighting and what I believe are called juke boxes. And now I think we have assigned some task to all present except Mr Quirk and Miss Mounsey, who will assist me in administration, and our newcomer, Mr Pye.' He turned to me. 'Have you any suggestions, Mr Pye?'

I hadn't a thought. Fortunately, before my lack of resource became painfully obvious, Lady Belinda spoke. 'What about me, Prof? Shall I provide the fireworks?'

'No doubt you'll do that, 'Linda,' said Lady Flamborough, 'whatever task is allotted to you.'

'But I'm serious, Mummy. We must have fireworks – super fireworks – rockets, Catherine wheels, golden rain . . .'

'And a set piece, I suggest,' said Lord Flamborough 'illustrating a Woman in the Act of Falling.'

'*Flagrante delicto*,' said Quirk, unexpectedly, and then cleared his throat in sudden embarrassment. The Professor glared at him, but before he could administer a reproof there was a heavy tread out in the corridor, the door swung open, and Mr Lionel lurched into the saloon. His countenance glistened in the gaslight as he stepped with excessive deliberation across the floor.

'I'm all lit up,' he announced, 'all lit up like a Christmas tree. If you're talking of a firework display I sugges' that all you need do is set a match to my breath.' He collapsed on the sofa between Miss Mounsey and Quirk, and appeared to fall asleep.

Lionel's incursion appeared to occasion no surprise, though Miss Mounsey extricated herself from the over-laden sofa and moved to a chair beside me.

'We will proceed,' said the Professor, 'leaving the pyrotechnics in the care of Lady Belinda, with – or without – the assistance of Mr Lionel.'

'What about Mr Pye?' asked Lady Flamborough.

'Ah yes, what about Mr Pye?' echoed the Professor, turning an appraising and – I thought – ironical glance on me.

'Perhaps' – I racked my brains – 'perhaps I could arrange something in the nature of a treasure hunt?'

There was a pause.

'Sounds a bit South Ken to me,' said Jones.

'I didn't intend anything elaborate,' I protested. 'Just burying a prize in the ground and inviting people to stick tallies as near to it as possible.'

'That,' said the Professor, 'is something that has already been arranged. It will be organized by the kiddies – from the Primary School.'

'Think again, chum,' said Jones, throwing a line to me in my discomfiture.

'Can't he put on a demonstration of the Charleston?' suggested Lord Flamborough. 'I'd provide the music. I dare say the village girls would gladly pay sixpence a time for a hop with him.'

If the proposal had been made by anyone but Lord Flamborough I should have been indignant. But his innocent outrageousness was disarming. I endeavoured to laugh the suggestion aside.

'Perhaps Mr Pye has a gift for fortune-telling,' said Quirk. 'We did very well with "Madame Fatima" last year, you remember. But the chiropodist from Flaxfield who obliged on that occasion has moved to Brightlingsea.'

'What d'you say to that, Mr Pye?' said the Professor.

Lionel stirred. 'Used to know a little girl in Brightlingsea once. Name of Ada; platinum blonde. But she threw me over for a pork butcher. Pity. Still, never mind; I've got Susie now.' And he went to sleep again.

'Ignoring that interruption, Mr Pye, what d'you say to impersonating Madame Fatima?' asked the Professor.

'Well, really,' I temporized. 'I've never done anything like that, and I don't think I'd be very convincing.'

'Susie's a smasher!' announced Lionel irrelevantly.

'I know what Mr Pye could do convincingly,' said Lady Belinda, gazing innocently at me. 'He could offer to kiss the girls at a shilling a time.'

'Really, Lady Belinda!' I exclaimed.

'Well, half a crown, then,' suggested Lord Flamborough.

'You got something there, Lady B.,' said Jones. 'A money-spinner. Put Mr Pye in a dark tent labelled "Errol Flynn" and let the girls inside for half a dollar a minute.'

'Isna' this slightly improper, Mr Jones?' said the Professor. 'Or am I being auld-fashioned? I have an idea Mr Pye is no' amused.'

'Perhaps it's a role more suited to Lionel,' said Lord Flamborough.

'I'm not going to kiss any of the girls,' said Lionel, opening his eyes and sitting up. 'I've got Susie to think of.'

'Mr Lionel, this is no' the time nor the place ...' The Professor's voice was heavy with disapproval.

'I'm bringing Susie, no matter what that old wind-bag says,' announced Lionel, glaring red-eyed at the assembly. 'Susie's a smasher!'

'Who is Susie?' asked Lady Flamborough, with a side-long glance at Lady Chloe.

'Is she that chorus girl from Lowestoft?' asked Lord Flamborough blandly.

'Shall we proceed wi' the business?' said the Professor hurriedly. 'We still hav'na' found a function for Mr Pye.'

'How about an ankle competition?' said Lady Flamborough. 'I'm sure Mr Pye is a good judge of ankles.'

79

I was beginning to get irritated by the assumption that I was interested in kisses and ankles and generally acting the part of an Errol Flynn. But Lady Flamborough's suggestion seemed less offensive than the other, so I accepted it with as good a grace as I could muster.

'That's that,' said the Professor. 'Is there anything else we want?'

'I want Susie,' proclaimed Lionel, from the sofa. 'And we're going to have a Traction Engine Rally.'

'A what?' said the Professor.

'Traction Engine Rally,' repeated Lionel, thickly.

'Never heard of such a thing,' said Lord Flamborough. 'Has Lionel got DTs again?'

'No, but I've got Susie,' said Lionel, grinning vacuously at his father-in-law.

'Mr Lionel, please control yourself,' said the Professor testily.

'Chloe, lock him up in the dungeon for the night!' said Lord Flamborough. 'And turn the fire hose on him.'

'You may think I'm drunk,' said Lionel, struggling to an upright position. 'And in fact I am. But I'm doing my best for the Fallen Women, and I've actually – I mean actually – arranged a Traction Engine Rally.'

'You've arranged it!' said Lady Chloe.

'Yes, ducky,' said Lionel, blowing his wife a kiss. 'I've been round the pubs in Thetford and Diss and Beccles and Bungay, and I've rallied the black caps.'

'But what *have* you arranged, exactly?' the Professor asked.

'Traction Engine Rally.' Lionel repeated the words with elaborate care. 'Eleven engines will assemble on the green at noon on Whit Monday. And Susie, darling Susie, will be there.'

With this final defiant statement he collapsed again on the sofa.

Lady Flamborough turned to Belinda. 'Who is this Susie?' she asked. 'Do you know? It was a girl called Gladys last time.'

'He's got Susie outside,' said Belinda, grinning.

'Outside!' exclaimed Lady Chloe. 'Really, Lionel!'

'Yes, out in the station yard,' said Belinda.

'Mr Lionel!' said the Professor sternly. 'This is too much. You really might keep your – er – lady friends at a decent distance.'

Lionel sat up, fixed the Professor with a drunken stare, then gave a lewd wink.

'Steady, the Buffs!' said Jones, coming from behind the aspidistra, and putting a restraining hand on Lionel's shoulder.

'Go and play with your cigarette cards!' said Lionel, pushing him aside and staggering to his feet. 'I'm going to introduce Professor Duncan McAlistair Pollux to my friend Susie.' He grabbed the Professor by the arm. 'Come along, Prof, and broaden your education.'

'This is preposterous!' the Professor fumed. But Lionel, as I had observed when he was playing cricket, was a man of uncommon strength. He bundled the Professor unceremoniously out of the train, followed by Belinda, Jones, and Quirk, who were presumably attempting to preserve law and order.

Lord Flamborough, who had been rummaging among his records and winding up his gramophone, turned to me. 'Go and have a look at her, my dear fellow,' he said. 'And come back and tell me what she's really like. One never can be sure with Lionel's girls.'

With an apologetic glance at Lady Flamborough and Lady Chloe I followed the party out of the train, across the platform, and through the station exit. In the twilight I saw the five of them – Lionel, the Professor, Belinda, Jones and Quirk – grouped round an object in the station yard.

81

'Meet the girl friend!' said Lionel, stumbling forward and giving something a resounding slap.

I stepped forward, adjusting my eyes to the half-light. Belinda burst into peals of laughter. Lionel was leaning against the boiler barrel of an aged traction engine. A wisp of smoke trailed from its chimney. On an elaborately embossed brass plate just above Lionel's shoulder I read the name 'Susie'.

'Weel, weel!' murmured the Professor. 'We appear to have fallen into an error of deduction.'

Across the station yard, from the half-open windows of the Flamborough Flier, I heard the wheezing strains of his Lordship's gramophone playing 'If you knew Susie like I know Susie, Oh, oh, oh, what a gal!'

Lock him in the dungeon, Chloe,' repeated Lord Flamborough, 'and put some of Tilly's white mice in there to keep him company.'

We had all returned to the railway coach, and Lionel had now subsided on the floor behind one of the aspidistras.

'That, I think, terminates the meeting,' said the Professor. 'We are now agreed that there shall be a Traction Engine Rally as well as the other attractions arranged for. We only hope that Mr Lionel will have recovered sufficiently by then to organize the mechanics of it. Thank you for your hospitality, Lord Flamborough. My staff and I will withdraw. Are you coming, Mr Pye?'

' 'Arf a mo, Mr Pye!' said Jones. 'If you and me each took hold of one of Mr Lionel's arms I dare say we could show 'im the way to go home.'

'Certainly!' I said, answering a silent appeal in Lady Chloe's eyes.

We caught hold of Lionel under the armpits, dragged

him out from behind the aspidistra, and hauled him to his feet.

'Susie's the girl!' he muttered, as Jones and I assisted him towards the door of the saloon.

'You'll have to leave her all alone in the moonlight, Lionel boy,' said Jones. 'It's beddy-byes and a nice cup of Ovaltine for you!'

'Ovaltine, Jones!' Lionel stopped in his tracks as we made our way across the station platform. 'D'you realize what you're saying? Many a man's been asked to choose his weapons and meet at dawn for less than that.'

'Pye and me may be up at dawn, Lionel boy,' said Jones. 'But something tells me you'll be sleeping the sleep of the unjust.'

'Damn sleepy, I mus' admit,' Lionel murmured, putting his arms round our shoulders and resuming his unsteady progress towards the Hall. 'What I need 's a stiff brandy-and-soda. Nothing like a b-and-s when one's had a hard day.'

'A stiff Alka Seltzer is what you're going to get,' said Jones. 'Lift yer feet, cock! We aren't 'ospital orderlies.'

'Steady, the Buffs, eh?' grunted Lionel. 'Left, ri'; left, ri'; left, ri'! *Hic manemus!*'

At last we got him up to the Hall, over the drawbridge, and into the gatehouse.

'Where's his room?' I asked.

'Across the courtyard,' answered Jones. 'He and Lady Chloe 'ave a flat in the far wing.'

'Where's my wife?' asked Lionel. 'Chloe, what've you got f' supper?' he shouted.

'A brace of roast pheno-barbs, I dare say,' said Jones, renewing his grip on Lionel's elbow, and directing him firmly across the courtyard.

'I've often thought,' Jones said to me, ' of letting 'im walk into the moat and seeing whether 'e'd float. But

83

somehow I've never 'ad the nerve to chance it. I can't swim meself, you see, and I wouldn't like to watch 'im drown. Might get me into trouble with the RSPCA.'

A door in the far wall opened, and Lady Chloe came out.

'Thank you so much, Mr Jones,' she said. 'And you too, Mr Pye. Lionel must be over-tired after driving that traction engine all the way from Flaxfield. He's so silly to overdo it like this. Now I'll put him to bed.'

'Brandy-and-soda, ducky! Tha's all I need,' said Lionel, lurching through the doorway. 'Bring me a b-and-s and we'll go on to a night club.'

'Come along, Lionel dear!' said Lady Chloe, taking his arm. 'I've got it waiting for you upstairs.'

'All present and correct, Lady C.?' said Jones. 'Shall we help you to get him up the apple-and-pears?'

'Pears, Jonesy,' said Lionel, turning at the foot of the stairs, 'make a very palatable mild drink, called perry. You sh' try it some time. With a dash o' Curaçao.'

'A dash of soda bicarb, more likely!' said Jones. 'Well, cheerio, cock! Happy dreams!'

Jones turned to go. 'Coming my way?' he asked me.

'I'm sleeping at the Hall tonight,' I said.

'Do come in and have a night-cap,' called Lady Chloe from the top of the stairs. 'You can't want to go to bed yet.'

Supposing that she might want some help with her husband I said good night to Jones and followed her upstairs. There I found her trying to cajole Lionel into his bedroom.

'Can I do anything?' I asked.

Lionel looked round. 'You're the man from the Ministry, aren't you?' he asked, with an owlish stare. 'Why don' you join us at a night club? Only takes an hour or two to run up t' the West End. Bubbly, that's what we all want now. Magnums. Jeroboams.'

'You're going to lie down for a little while first, Lionel,' said Lady Chloe, gently. 'Come on, darling, take your coat off and get on to this bed.'

'Jus' like a wife,' said Lionel. 'Always fussing like an old hen. Bring me the brandy, ducky.'

'Wait there, darling,' said Lady Chloe, 'and I'll see if I can find it.' She pulled a blanket over him, turned out the light, and came on to the landing, shutting the door behind her.

'He's just over-tired,' she said to me, with a strained smile. 'He'll fall off to sleep now. He usually does.'

She seemed unaware that her last three words tore the shreds of pretence from her pathetic efforts to excuse Lionel.

'Let's go down to the Buttery and have a drink ourselves,' she said in a weary voice. 'I could do with one.'

The Buttery, into which she took me, was a narrow, high, panelled room, containing a carved oak refectory table and a couple of broken-down wicker armchairs. Along one wall, above the panelling, was a line of old-fashioned bells, on coiled hangers, with the name of a room below each one.

'Do you mind sitting in one of these awful old chairs?' Lady Chloe said to me. 'I'll see what there is to drink.' She went to a panelled door in the wall, and unlocked it with an iron key which she appeared to keep tucked in the top of her stocking.

'I keep this door locked when Lionel's in one of his moods,' she said. 'I don't like to risk him going down the dungeon steps and breaking his neck.'

'Is that really a dungeon?' I asked.

'Well, we use it as a wine cellar now, but it used to be a dungeon, so the Professor says. Just a minute, while I get the drinks.' She lit a candle and went below. I listened to the diminuendo of her descending footsteps.

I was grateful for the momentary silence and solitude

which followed. I had been a little bewildered by the inconsequence of the discussion in the railway coach; and although nobody seemed to be much perturbed by Lionel's drunkenness, I, as a stranger, was rather embarrassed by it.

Lady Chloe seemed to be taking some time to collect the drinks, and I began to read the names below the bells on the wall. The bells were, presumably, early Victorian – but some of the names seemed to go far back into history. There were the conventional 'Blue Room', 'Parlour', and 'Morning Room', but there was also a 'Moonlight Room', a 'Damask Room', a 'Gilded Turret', a 'Gothick Chamber', and 'Sir Almeric's Room'. I wondered whether the bells still worked, and whether any of them ever vibrated with a ghostly tinkle from the past.

Was the Hall haunted? In a building with so much history there was bound to be some legend of haunting. I must ask the Professor about it.

As my thoughts took this turn I became aware of an undercurrent of sound in the silence – an odd impression of moaning or whimpering. It was not the wind: it was a singularly still night. And it didn't sound like Lady Chloe's movements in the wine cellar. I could not place it.

I stood up and walked to the window. No, it was not outside. I paused by the refectory table and listened again. Was it below me? Diffidently I stepped across to the dungeon door. There was silence below. What was Lady Chloe doing? I wondered.

Then I heard the sound again. Undoubtedly it came from the foot of the dungeon steps, and it sounded very much like someone sobbing.

'Can I give you a hand?' I called nervously.

There was no reply.

I waited for a moment. Then I heard the sobbing again. Despite a certain bristling of the hair on the nape of my neck, I had no alternative but to pull open the dungeon door and feel my way down the steps into the darkness.

'Are you all right?' I called.

There was no reply; but as I rounded a bend in the stone steps I saw Lady Chloe in the candlelight, kneeling against a stone slab which was covered with bottles. Her flaxen head was bent forward.

'What's the matter?' I asked.

In answer she buried her face in her outstretched arms and her shoulders quivered.

'Have you hurt yourself?' I said, coming to her side.

Her shoulders shook.

'Please, please forgive me!' she sobbed. 'Perhaps you'd better go away.'

'But what's the matter?' I said, dropping down on my knees, a little self-consciously, beside her.

'Oh, everything,' she said, raising her head and gazing hopelessly into the darkness. Seen in profile, her clear-cut Roman features outlined in the candlelight, she was, I realized, strikingly beautiful.

'Can I help?' I said.

'Oh no, I'm afraid not,' she said, in a tone of dull despair. 'I wouldn't like to ask you, anyhow.'

'Is it to do with Lionel?' I asked, diffidently.

She nodded.

I put my hand on her shoulder.

'You're very sweet,' she said, laying her forehead down again on her folded arms. 'But it's no concern of yours, is it?'

'I'd like to help, if I can,' I said.

'Nobody can help.' She began to sob again.

I put my arm round her shoulders.

'Nothing's really as bad as it seems.' It was the only comforting phrase that came to my mind.

'I know it isn't,' she said. 'That's why I feel so ashamed of myself for behaving like this.'

'Perhaps you're tired,' I said. 'You may feel better tomorrow.'

She lifted her head and turned her eyes towards me.

'I just can't bear to think of tomorrow,' she said quietly.

Her fair hair, silhouetted round her shadowed face, was intensely moving; I was reminded of one of those lovely candlelight paintings by Georges de la Tour.

'Relax for a moment,' I said.

Hesitantly, she leaned forward and pressed her face against my chest. I put my arms protectively round her. She began to weep again.

'Chloe, poor Chloe!' I murmured.

She sobbed for a while, and then was silent. The candle spluttered once or twice as the charred wick curled over. Then the flame rose steadily and clearly again. There was an almost tangible stillness and quietness. We seemed singularly isolated and alone. And, despite the bottles ranged along the stone slab, there was no mistaking that it *was* a dungeon.

I shuddered. Chloe seemed to awake from her reverie. She raised her head and looked up into my eyes.

'You are so sweet,' she said, and kissed me, gently, with very tender lips, full on the mouth.

'Now we must get those drinks,' she said. She rose to her feet, picked up the candlestick, and began to rummage amongst the bottles.

'Here's some sloe gin,' she said; 'will that do?'

I said yes, and she handed me the bottle.

'I'd better go first,' she said.

As I made my way up the steep stone steps behind her I was vividly, poignantly, aware of her hand in mine.

For my bedroom I had been given the Moonlight Room. When I closed the door and peered about me by the light of the candle which Chloe had given me, I realized why that was its name. The walls were so closely hung with pictures that the frames almost touched; and every picture was of a landscape in moonlight. Some were river scenes and were evidently Dutch; two of them bore on their frames the name of Aert van der Neer. There was a vivid little painting of a moonlit church by Alexander Cozzens, and there was a set of four dramatic landscapes, with moons shining over precipitous crags and ravines, which were by Joseph Wright of Derby.

I deduced that some member of the Virley family, about the end of the eighteenth century, had been caught up in the Romantic Movement and had made a collection of the then fashionable 'moonlights'. I looked forward to studying them next morning. In the dead of night, however, with only a single candle as illumination, I found the repetition of white orbs and crescents, shining palely from dim cloudscapes over shadowy mountains and dark rivers, a little eerie.

I was reassured by the familiar sight of my leather briefcase, my umbrella, and my travelling bag, neatly grouped at the foot of the bed. Presumably Quirk or Miss Mounsey had brought them up from the Great Gallery.

As I unpacked my pyjamas and dressing-gown, and arranged my shaving tackle and toothbrush on the old-fashioned washstand, I tried to sort out the day's experiences.

I had made a good start in my investigation of the work done by Output Statistics, but at the moment the official purpose of my visit seemed to have faded into insignificance beside the communal activities of Arcady. I found it difficult to apply to the problems of administration a mind which at the moment was blurred by a confusion of somewhat bizarre impressions. Images of the peace and beauty of Arcady Hall and its gardens alternated fantastically with recollections of the walk round the ruined chapel with Lady Flamborough, the conference in the railway carriage, or the drunken Lionel slapping the boiler of 'Susie' in the twilight.

I couldn't put out of my mind the picture of Matilda framed in the arched tracery of the chapel window, gazing at me so earnestly from those dark, deep-set eyes. Could it have been Matilda with whom I had had that strange encounter underneath the oak tree? I couldn't be certain, for I had, indeed, kept my eyes closed as I had been bidden – even when she had kissed me. But there undoubtedly had been an air of Matilda about the white frock dancing into the distance down the glade.

How different – how abundantly real – was Belinda! There was a naturalness, a spontaneity, about her which was extraordinarily refreshing after the guarded or calculated sex-appeal of the girls I was accustomed to meeting in London. Was Belinda consciously aware of sex, I wondered? Was she, perhaps, at heart an innocent – a sort of *belle sauvage* of the Suffolk backwoods? As I pulled on my pyjamas and got into bed I couldn't deny to myself that I was still tingling with the physical contact of that kiss in the coppice. And yet – and yet – only half an hour ago I had been kissing Chloe in the dungeon!

I had an intensely vivid impression of that almost theatrical scene – the cool, damp air, the deep silence, the spluttering candle, Chloe's features in profile, and then the extreme softness of her lips. Despite the melodramatic trappings, that kiss had seemed to mean something, to be an expression of true emotion.

As we had sat and sipped the somewhat sickly sloe gin Chloe had asked me about my job, my home, my interests. We had talked about my mother, the house I lived in, my painting. In the short time we had sat together in the Buttery she had even elicited a few facts about myself and Deirdre. Oddly enough, I found I could talk to her about Deirdre without any feeling of disloyalty or distress. Chloe had the natural gift of sympathy, of inspiring confidence – and confidences.

I blew out the candle and lay back in bed watching the chequered patterns made by the moonlight shining through the diamond-panes of the window. There was something odd and improbable – yet rather piquant – about the real moonlight falling on the imitation moonlight in the paintings.

Odd and improbable – yet rather piquant: a fair summing-up of my first twenty-four hours in Arcady. Moonshine – yes, perhaps it was all moonshine – the girl in the tree just as much as the peer in the Pullman car. Maybe it was all a midsummer night's dream from which I should awake to sober reality in the morning. I closed my eyes and tried to go to sleep. It must be nearly midnight, and I wanted to be fresh next morning for my rather delicate negotiations with the Professor.

Gradually I became drowsy and my thoughts began to drift on a tide of their own. Moonshine – yes, it was all moonshine; and yet I could still feel, almost tangibly on my lips, the imprint of a kiss. Was it the unselfconscious, sensual kiss of the *belle sauvage*? Was it the tender, self-revealing kiss of a woman seeking consolation? Or was it, perhaps, the insubstantial salutation of the unseen girl from the tree?

I must have been slipping over the borders of sleep when there was a sudden whirr and thud across the room. I sat up in alarm. Had a bat flown in at the window?

I reached for the candle, fumbled with the matches, and struck a light. At first I could see nothing unusual. Then, in the far corner of the room, opposite the window, I saw something that had not been there before – a stick or shaft of some sort projecting from the wall. I got up and crossed the room. Embedded in the wall – between the frames of two of the moonlight pictures – was an arrow, a real and actual arrow, some two feet long, with a wooden shaft and a feathered tail.

I glanced across the room towards the window. Yes, it seemed wildly unlikely, but it must have been shot into the room through the open window as I lay in bed. Who on earth could be practising archery at this time of night?

I was about to grasp the weapon and pull it from the wall when I saw that just in front of its feathered tail a piece of paper was wrapped round the shaft and secured with white cotton. I got my penknife – which I always laid out beside my money on the dressing-table before going to bed – cut the cotton, and unwound the sheet of paper. Holding it in the candlelight I saw that it had a message pencilled on it, in bold capital letters: COME TO ME AT MIDNIGHT IN SIR ALMERIC'S ROOM.

As I read it the silence was rent by the harsh, unearthly shriek of the peacock calling across the park.

I stood for some time, in amazement, reading and re-reading this extraordinary missive. Then, in a mirror across the room, I caught a glimpse of myself – a man with tousled hair, wearing Austin Reed pyjamas, holding a letter in one hand and a candle in the other, and standing beside an arrow embedded in the wall. I almost laughed aloud at the wild incongruity of it.

What should I do now? Presumably the flight of the arrow into my bedroom was not accidental, but the result of skilful marksmanship. Or was the arrow intended for someone else? No, that was hardly likely: as far as I knew I was the only person sleeping on this west side of the house. The Professor, Quirk, and Miss Mounsey all had quarters on the east side of the quadrangle, while Lionel and Chloe occupied the south end. The other members of the Virley family, presumably, slept in the railway coach.

No, the message must be intended for me. But who was the sender? The whole performance was so absurdly theatrical that I found it impossible to associate it with the Professor or Quirk, who were, after all, the people most likely to want a meeting with me. The Professor was a queer fish, certainly, but far too dignified to shoot arrows into the air at midnight – though one could never be quite certain about Scotsmen. Quirk, it seemed to me, was altogether too pedestrian for such behaviour. It might well be one of the Virleys, of course: they were peculiar enough, in all conscience. But it obviously was not Lord Flamborough; he could hardly practise archery in his invalid chair. Could it be Lionel? It might well have been; but when I had last seen Lionel he was much too drunk to handle bow and arrow – to say nothing of aiming so accurately. Jones – could it be Jones? I wasn't too sure. There was more to Jones, I felt, than might appear. And he seemed to have a somewhat equivocal position in the household – or among the hangers-on.

Anyhow, why should I pay attention to such an absurd jape? I couldn't take it seriously: it must be someone's idea of a practical joke.

Then a fresh thought came to me. Why should the archer be necessarily a man? Archery was just as much a woman's sport nowadays. It would not be Chloe, of course: she wouldn't act like that, and I'd been talking with her only about half an hour ago. Belinda – ah yes, it might be Belinda! I could well imagine *la belle sauvage* disporting herself with bow and arrow.

I glanced at my watch. It was ten minutes to twelve. Quickly I took off my pyjamas and began to get into my day clothes. There was no time to lose.

As I dressed, my doubts and hesitations seemed to slip

93

away and be replaced by a curious feeling of exhilaration. Moonshine, it was all moonshine! The candle flickered, and one of Joseph Wright's crescent moons gave me a decidedly knowing look. If other people were crazy, why shouldn't I be crazy too? I was no longer the bore of Barons Court. I was the man who had shaken the dust of Whitehall off his feet. I was the new Arcadian.

I gave a finishing twist to my tie, put a clean handkerchief into my breast pocket, picked up the candlestick, and turned towards the door. To Sir Almeric's Room!

Outside, in the tapestry-hung corridor, I stopped dead. Where *was* Sir Almeric's Room? I realized that I had not the faintest idea. I looked at my watch: it was now five minutes to twelve. How could I possibly find the uncharted Sir Almeric's Room in five minutes? I had only a rough idea of the layout of the Hall, and certainly none of the rooms I had been shown during the afternoon had been referred to as Sir Almeric's.

Why, then, was the name familiar? Of course! I had seen it underneath one of the bells in the Buttery. But that was no help. There was no indication in the Buttery as to the whereabouts of the rooms. I would just have to explore the house as rapidly as I could. For the moment I would eliminate the Buttery wing, as Chloe and Lionel were there, and also the East wing, where the Ministry people slept. Something told me that Sir Almeric's Room would not be on the ground floor: I had seen most of the ground-floor rooms anyway. It must either be one of the rooms leading off the corridor where I now stood, or it must be one of the upper rooms in the gatehouse.

Cupping my free hand round the flame of the candle I hurried down the corridor. None of the doors were locked, and I hastily glanced into one room after another. They were mostly unfurnished, and rather small. None of them seemed very appropriate for a tryst.

Having investigated the first-floor rooms in the West wing, I hurried back towards the central block. My only way to reach the unknown part of the building was through the Great Gallery. Although it was the hub of the Ministry's work at Arcady Hall I assumed that nobody would be there at this time of night, and I pushed open the great nail-studded door without ceremony.

To my dismay I saw, on the Professor's raised desk at the far end of the Gallery, a lighted lamp. I drew back hurriedly, and listened for sounds of movement.

All was silence. I slowly opened the door again and looked about me. I could see no sign of anyone in the room, though there might be someone hidden in one of the recesses formed by the Grinling Gibbons bookcases.

I decided I should only seem ridiculous if I were found tiptoeing surreptitiously through the Gallery, so I walked briskly forward, my candle in my hand, trying hard to think of some reason to account for my presence if I were accosted. To my surprise, however, all the library bays were empty: there was nobody at all in the whole length of the room.

Perhaps the lamp had been left burning through inadvertence when the Professor went to bed. I stepped up on to the dais and glanced at the desk. No, there were no papers there; everything seemed to have been cleared away except for a visiting card which was propped against the base of the lamp. I bent forward and read the conventional copperplate script. In the middle of the card was engraved the name *Miss Muriel Tidy*, and in the lower left-hand corner the address, *St Biddulph's, Loughborough*.

I felt a little deflated. I had no idea what had brought Miss Tidy here to see the Professor. But it was not Miss Tidy I was looking for. She seemed to have a knack of intruding, in person or by proxy, at inconvenient moments. However, she was obviously not here now. I turned down the wick of the lamp on the desk, and blew out the flame. Then I made my way to the door into the gatehouse at the far end of the gallery.

Out on the spiral brick staircase the air was surprisingly cool. I waited until the flame of my candle had adjusted itself to the draught, and then began to climb the stairs. As I passed one of the curious trefoil window-openings I looked out and saw the landscape bathed in moonlight.

'Moonshine!' I said to myself, wryly. There was altogether too great a chasm of improbability between the prosaic matter-of-factness of Miss Tidy's visiting card and the ridiculous will-o'-the-wisp I was chasing up the spiral staircase!

I arrived at the turn of the stairs opposite the doorway to the Professor's room. That, I felt sure, was not Sir Almeric's Room. With his guide-book mentality the Professor would surely have mentioned the name to me when I had my session with him earlier in the day. I went on up the stairs.

At the head of the next flight there was an oak-panelled screen, but there was no door in it. The stairs continued upwards, and so did I.

Round the next turn in the spiral the stairs ended before a low, narrow door, heavily encumbered with great iron hinges, latches, and locks. Was this Sir Almeric's Room? Was I going to find it barred and bolted after all?

I caught hold of the heavy iron ring of the latch and turned it. To my surprise the door swung smoothly outwards. I stooped and stepped through.

When I raised my head I realized that I was not in Sir Almeric's Room; I was on the leaded roof of one of the turrets. Ahead of me and on my right were the castellations of the wall. On my left was a flagstaff; and at the foot of it, his tonsured head bowed over folded hands, sat Professor Pollux.

He gave no immediate sign of being aware of my presence. Then he said, slowly and distinctly, the Latin tinged by his Scots burr, '*Et in Arcadia ego.*' Whether he was talking to himself or to me I could not tell. I stepped back towards the stairs. Then I realized I could hardly make my escape without his noticing me and wondering what I was doing, so I hesitantly cleared my throat.

The Professor sat quite still. Then, without raising his head, he asked quietly: 'Is that you, Quirk?'

'No,' I answered. 'It's Pye, Jasper Pye.'

'Pye?' he repeated, with a note of interrogation, but still not raising his head. 'Pye? Is there some deep significance in that name? Surely wee Jack Horner had some transactions with a Pye? Did he pull out a plum? Or was it Pye in the sky?'

I was at a loss for a rejoinder. Was he being whimsical, or profound – or slightly insulting? Or – this thought rushed into my mind – was he talking in his sleep? I had a sudden suspicion that he might be a somnambulist.

'I apologize for intruding on you, Professor,' I said in a clear voice.

At last he did raise his head; but he still looked away from me. He seemed to be surveying reflectively the vistas of moonlit landscape that could be glimpsed between the castellations of the turret.

'Intrusion,' he said, after a while, 'is a term capable of several interrpretations. I maself am an intruder here, just as you are, Pye.' I realized now that he was awake.

'My name is no' Virley,' he continued, 'and because of that I too am an intruder in Arcady. But in seventeen years I have almost established squatters' rights. When I perceive a newcomer approaching, whose aim may no' be intrusion so much as extrusion, I fancy that I too hear ancestral voices prophesying war.'

97

'All I meant, Professor,' I said, 'was that I apologized for intruding on your privacy. I was just wandering round the house – as I didn't feel sleepy. I hardly expected to find you up here.'

'You are interrested in the house, Pye?' he asked, turning and looking at me for the first time.

'Of course!' I replied. 'I find it intensely interesting. I should like to know much more about it.'

'If you really were interrested, and were no' merely being diplomatically polite, I might tell you mair.'

I thought I saw my chance. 'When I was in the Buttery with Lady Chloe,' I said, 'I was looking at the names below the house bells. Most interesting they are. Sir Almeric's Room, for instance; which one is that?'

He paused – tantalizingly – before replying.

'Sir Almeric,' he said at last, 'was one of the few Virleys who have made their mark in the larger world. In the reign of Henry the Eighth he became Lord Mayor of London. He became rich, and added considerably to the estate and the fabric of the Hall.'

'Which is his particular room?' I interjected.

'I will show you in due course,' said the Professor. 'There are other points of particular interest about Sir Almeric Virley. He was a noted archer, and was appointed Archer-in-Ordinary to the King.'

'How very interesting!' This piece of information was indeed relevant. For an absurd moment my imagination conjured up a ghostly Sir Almeric practising archery in the dead of night. But no: the arrow that had embedded itself in the wall of my room was unquestionably solid and material. Still, the conversation was on the right lines. A little more encouragement and the Professor might tell me where Sir Almeric's Room was. I glanced at my watch in the moonlight. It was nearly midnight.

'Sir Almeric,' continued the Professor, 'also suffered from ringworm.'

Ringworm! Whatever irrelevancies were we going to discuss next?

'An odd bit of historical information, Professor,' I said, abruptly. 'But I'm more interested in architecture. What would interest me most would be to see Sir Almeric's Room.'

'That, ma dear Pye, is where you are making a mistake. Sir Almeric's ringworm is perhaps the most cherished phenomenon in the family history of the Virleys.'

'But why?' I asked. 'They don't all suffer from ringworm, do they?'

'Of course not,' said the Professor testily. 'An ironist might consider that all the Virleys are a wee bit touched i' the head – but not by ringworm.'

From beyond the avenue of limes came the clang of the church clock chiming the hour. The Professor was silent as the chimes ended and the clock struck twelve. I checked the time by my watch, and became as obviously restless as I dared.

'Another day!' said the Professor, standing up and surveying the landscape.

'About Sir Almeric . . .?' I prompted him.

'Aye,' he said, sitting down once more. 'You fail – understandably – to see the significance of Sir Almeric's ringworm.'

'Never mind his ringworm, Professor. Which is Sir Almeric's *Room*?'

'But you ought to know about his ringworm, ma dear Pye. That disagreeable ailment gave rise to the most romantic tradition in the Virley family history. King Henry the Eighth, distressed by the disfigurement and discomfort of his Archer-in-Ordinary, gave him royal leave to wear his hat when in the King's company. Since then the head of the Virley family has always claimed and been granted the right to remain covered when in the presence of the King or Queen. There is, I believe, only one other person in the United Kingdom who enjoys that right.'

Despite my impatience I couldn't help being interested.

'I noticed,' I said, 'that when I had lunch with Lord Flamborough he wore a cap. Was that anything to do with this tradition?'

'Certainly,' said the Professor. 'The Virleys have a way of carrying things to extremes, and the present Earl invariably wears a hat at meals. The fact that it happens to be a railway guard's cap rather than a coronet is, in his Lordship's view, a matter of no moment.'

'All this originated with Sir Almeric?' I said.

'Aye,' said the Professor, rising to his feet again. 'I promised I would show you Sir Almeric's Room. Should we go now, or would you rather wait till daylight?'

I hesitated, and again consulted my watch. It was five minutes past midnight. Should I be too late? And how could I shake off the Professor?

'Let us glance at the room on our way down to bed,' said the Professor, making up my mind for me.

I lit my candle, which had gone out whilst we were talking. We turned and went down the spiral stairway. As we came to the landing where the wall was panelled in oak the professor called to me to stop.

'You wouldna' be likely to find Sir Almeric's Room without a guide,' he said, as he passed his fingers round the edge of one of the wooden panels. 'Only privileged visitors have the opportunity of discovering this room.'

Quietly and smoothly a section of the panelled wall swung inwards.

'Yon is the largest of the secret rooms in Arcady Hall,' said the Professor.

Holding my candle ahead of me I stepped through the secret door in the panelling and found myself at the head of another, much steeper and narrower, flight of stairs. I went down. At the foot of the stairs was another panelled door.

'Press the bevelled top edge of the right-hand panel,' said the Professor.

I did so, and the door swung open, to reveal a long but narrow room, its walls entirely hung with tapestries depicting scenes of the chase. At the far end of the room was a heavily carved oak four-poster bed hung with embroidered silks.

'This is Sir Almeric's Room,' said the Professor. 'And that is the bed he slept in.'

There was nobody in the room, but as I stepped forward to look at it more closely I had an odd impression that the huntsmen and horses in the tapestries along the wall were moving. Was the surface of the tapestry rippling in the draught caused by our entrance into the room? Qr was it an illusion caused by the flickering light from my candle?

'There are no less than four secret entrances to this room,' said the Professor. 'All except that through which we entered are hidden by the tapestries. Qne leads doon to a tunnel which runs under the moat and up into an arbour in the garden.'

I was looking at the bed-hangings, which were richly embroidered with foliage and figures of birds and beasts, woven in colours of surprising brilliance. 'This must be Tudor embroidery,' I said.

'It is indeed,' he answered. 'There is a tradition that much of it was embroidered by Ann Boleyn ... But wha'ever is this doing here ...?'

He leaned forward over the bed, and picked up a long object which I had scarcely noticed against the pattern of the embroidered bedspread.

'Sir Almeric's long-bow!' he exclaimed. 'One of the great treasures of Arcady. What, in heaven's name, is it doing here?'

Again I had that queer illusion of a movement in the tapestry. Or was there something moving behind it?

'Shouldn't it be here?' I asked.

'Certainly it shouldna',' said the Professor, in tones of the utmost gravity. 'It is supposed to be on loan to the Victoria and Albert Museum in London.'

There was a sudden draught of cold air. The flame of my candle fluttered and expired. Somewhere, nearby, but yet not within the room, I heard, unmistakably, the sound of low, mocking, feminine laughter.

Unquestionably it was going to be another fine day. The sunshine streamed through the leaded window panes as I brushed my teeth, shaved, and folded my pyjamas. In the brightness of the morning the Moonlight Room seemed much less sinister than it had at dead of night. There was something very placid, too, about the distant sound of doves cooing in the lime trees.

Nonetheless, although I had slept soundly and dreamlessly from the time I had finally gone to bed until I was awoken by my travelling alarm clock, I still felt curiously exalted.

Had it really happened?

Having put my keys, my money, my fountain pen, and my Eversharp pencil in their appropriate pockets, I went over to the chest of drawers and opened the bottom drawer. Yes, the arrow was where I had put it, underneath my shirts. It was infuriating that I had dropped somewhere in one of the passages the piece of paper bearing the cryptic message; but even in the sober light of day I was positive I had not imagined it.

Should I say anything about it? I decided that it was a matter which concerned only myself and the writer of the message. I might, at an appropriate moment, mention it to *her*. Meanwhile, what was to be done with the arrow? I decided to leave it where it was, underneath my shirts.

I breakfasted alone in the Eating Room, where I found toast and coffee and boiled eggs awaiting me. I was relieved that I did not have the Professor's company: he might have wanted to discuss the events of the night and the unaccountable reappearance of Sir Almeric's longbow. That was one mystery with which I was not going to concern myself.

After breakfast I went up to the Great Gallery. It seemed as deserted as it had been at midnight until I saw Miss Mounsey bending down behind a filing cabinet in one of the library bays.

'Good morning, Mr Pye,' she said. 'The Professor and Mr Quirk have gone to see the Rector – about the arrangements for the Fête. Can I do any letters for you?'

Her words and her secretarial demeanour were reassuringly matter-of-fact.

'How long have you been working here, Miss Mounsey?' I asked.

'Let me see: I suppose it must be nearly five years. I came here after six months in the Ministry of Works at Lambeth. Mr Quirk got in touch with me through a cricketing friend of his in the MOW, and I thought Suffolk would make a pleasant change from Dulwich Village, where I lived.'

'And has it?' I asked.

'Well, yes,' she answered, with some hesitation. 'I've nothing to complain about, and everyone is very nice to me. But it's rather difficult for a girl to fit in here in quite the way the Professor and Mr Quirk do, for instance.'

'They do fit in here, then?' I asked, feeling slightly uncomfortable at seeking information from a typist in this way.

'Oh yes, they're really part of the place. You'd think they'd always been here. Of course, it's the Professor

103

who is really mad about Arcady. Mr Quirk is mostly interested in the cricket and the village life. But the Professor knows every detail of the history and architecture of the Hall, and I'm sure he knows much more about the Virley family than Lord Flamborough himself.'

'Lord Flamborough doesn't mind the Professor and the rest of you being here?'

'On the contrary,' said Miss Mounsey, 'I'm sure he's very grateful for it. I don't suppose he could afford to keep the place going himself.'

'But I dare say you know that the Ministry pays no rent for the house?'

'Oh yes, I know that: I do all the accounts, as it happens. But it's not the money Lord Flamborough wants, so much as the care and attention and management that he gets from the Professor. He'd never find a land agent or bailiff who'd look after the estate the way the Professor does.'

'He leaves all that sort of thing quite happily to the Professor, does he?'

'Oh yes,' she said, 'he never interferes. Quite honestly, I don't think he'd dare to. Everyone is just a bit frightened of the Professor, you know.'

'You mean, he has a forceful personality?'

'Yes. And he's so terribly single-minded. He's devoted himself heart and soul to Arcady since he came here; and he's a bit like a headmaster; he regards any opposition or criticism as disloyalty to the school.'

'One has to watch one's step with the Professor, then?'

'One certainly has,' said Miss Mounsey, with a twinkle in her eye. It occurred to me that she was probably shrewder than one might suppose; perhaps the nickname of 'Mouse' was not entirely appropriate.

'Are you interested in statistics?' I asked, changing the conversation.

'Honestly, I can't say I am,' she replied. 'But I don't have much to do with the statistics, apart from typing them. Mr Quirk is the statistical expert. He loves figures. You should see the marvellous graphs and permutations and combinations he works out in connection with the County Cricket Championship.'

'And you have no other staff?' I asked. 'How do the Professor and Mr Quirk manage when you go on leave?'

'Well, they used to get a temporary typist from Norwich or Yarmouth or Saxmundham. But since Lady Belinda has been living at home they have got her to lend a hand when I'm away.'

'Lady Belinda can type, can she?'

'Lady Belinda is a very capable person,' said Miss Mounsey.

'So I gather,' I said. 'Someone was saying, I think, that she went in for archery.'

'Archery?' exclaimed Miss Mounsey, with a flutter of her long eyelashes. 'Not Lady Belinda – not to my knowledge, anyway. But—'

There was a sound of voices on the stairs, the great oak door swung open, and I heard Quirk saying: 'If Northamptonshire won eight out of their remaining twelve matches and Surrey won ten, Northamptonshire would still lead by two points. This is the Great Gallery, Miss Tidy.'

'Ah, another of my cricketer friends!' exclaimed Miss Tidy, advancing towards me, a parasol in her hand. 'I hope you haven't lost any more balls lately.'

I felt myself blushing as I shook hands with her.

'Isn't it perfectly splendid to have two such keen cricketers in Arcady?' she said to Miss Mounsey. 'And Mr Quirk tells me that you are an excellent scorer. How very clever of you. I was always so helpless at figures as a girl. And not much better now, I fear.' She tittered.

'Still, Miss Tidy,' said Quirk gallantly, 'you know a lot

more than most ladies about the finer points of the game. I hope very much you'll be with us on Saturday to watch the centenary match between Arcady and Flaxfield.'

'Of course,' she said. 'But we mustn't interrupt Mr Pye in his labours. Could you spare the time to show me round the rest of the house, Mr Quirk? It's so many years since I was here that I've quite forgotten my way about.'

Together they walked through the Great Gallery towards the farther door.

'I see,' said Miss Tidy, pointing up at the moulded plaster ceiling with her parasol, 'that the naked lady riding on the dragon still hasn't got herself a skirt or blouse. I'm afraid dear Bertie's father used deliberately to shock my father by discussing her anatomy when he came to call. But we aren't so shockable nowadays, are we, Mr Pye?'

'Er – I suppose not,' I answered.

'Well, tootle-oo!' she said cheerily as she reached the door. 'I hope we shall see you on the cricket field on Saturday – if you can spare the time from your other duties.'

Blushing again, I turned back to Miss Mounsey and began to dictate a letter to Fairweather reporting my arrival in Arcady.

After I had dictated my letter and had a further discussion with Miss Mounsey, I wandered out into the garden. I paused to marvel at the coloured pebbles of the knot garden, sparkling in the sunshine, and then walked into the walled garden beyond.

All was stillness and seclusion. Great bearded irises stood motionless in flaring grandeur, their veined and velvet petals almost lasciviously reflexed to the touch of the sun. Behind them, in high relief against the green-and-gold of the yew hedge, rose stately groups of tall, sophisticated delphiniums. The air was soft with the fragrance of damask roses and the musky scent of sun-baked lichen on the walls.

I walked slowly to the end of the path, where there was a brick-built garden house with a castellated turret – a twin, it seemed, to the garden house where I had first met Belinda. As I stood and looked at it, time seemed to repeat itself. From the arched doorway, with deliberate and pompous gait, stepped the peacock.

He paused, stood very erect, then put his head on one side and regarded me with a large, reflective, Vandyck-brown eye. This time he seemed to decide that I was worthy of more attention than I had been given on our first meeting. He cocked his head first to one side, then to another. Then he bent his glistening metallic blue neck and pecked reflectively at the grass path, glancing up at me between pecks.

'He wants his mid-morning biscuit,' said a voice behind me. I turned and saw Lady Flamborough coming down the path towards me, a gardening trowel in one hand and a wooden trug filled with weeds in the other. Her tweed skirt seemed even more homely and tattered than yesterday. On her head she wore a very ancient, sun-browned straw hat with a brilliant peacock's feather stuck into it.

'Would you like to give him his victuals?' she asked, taking a biscuit from her pocket and handing it to me. 'Break off a small piece and hold it out to him. He'll take it quite politely.'

I broke off a piece of biscuit and offered it to the bird. He examined it for a moment or two with a curious but courteous eye, then took it very gently from between my fingers and swallowed it. I broke off another piece, and he took that. Quietly and without any haste he ate the whole biscuit, piece by piece.

'Does he have Digestive biscuits for elevenses every morning?' I asked.

107

'Yes,' said Lady Flamborough. 'And they must be McVitie and Price's.'

'Is that all he eats?'

'Oh no,' said Lady Flamborough. 'He eats insects and grass, and wallflowers and phlox, and night-scented stocks and snapdragons. And he has maize for his supper. But at this time of year the maize is apt to put thoughts into his head.'

She put her hand in her pocket again, took out a few grains of maize, and threw them down on the path.

'Look!' she said.

The peacock bent down, picked up a grain, swallowed it, picked up another, dropped it, and shook his head several times, causing his brilliant blue-and-green coronet to quiver and glisten in the sunlight.

Then he gave a little hop into the air and seemed to shake free the long, folded feathers of his tail. Arching his neck, and pawing at the ground with his toes, he backed away from us. As he did so his tail fanned out and slowly rose, with a whirr and rustle as of wind amongst dry leaves.

The tail, some six feet in length, had seemed brilliant enough when lying folded behind the bird, on the ground. When it rose and fell open on either side of his body, forming an eye-studded arc some ten or twelve feet in diameter, the effect was electric.

'It's incredibly beautiful!' I exclaimed.

'It's all caused by sex,' said Lady Flamborough, in matter-of-fact tones.

'It's much more impressive than any expression of the human sex impulse,' I said.

'Look at the dopey expression on his face,' said Lady Flamborough. 'Haven't you seen stockbrokers looking just like that at chorus girls in night clubs?'

There was certainly a bemused expression about the bird's open beak and fixed, staring gaze. But, as though to disprove Lady Flamborough's insulting analogy, he began to claw at the ground, set up again a whirring, sibilant vibration of his tail feathers, and, raising his beak in the air, emitted a series of wild, dervish shrieks.

'That's not very beautiful,' said Lady Flamborough, in the same matter-of-fact tone.

'But the display is exquisite,' I said, fascinated by the kaleidoscope of changing colours as the great gold-and-green eyes of his tail feathers caught and reflected the sunlight at different angles. 'May I get my paints and try to put it down on canvas?'

'Of course,' said Lady Flamborough, 'but you'd better hurry; he won't keep it up for long. His wife has been sitting on eggs for three weeks already, so this performance is only in the nature of an encore.'

I went back to the Hall, assembled the paints, brushes, and portable easel which I had brought with me from London, and hurried out to the garden again. Lady Flamborough had gone, but the peacock was still displaying his tail to spectacular effect, and he greeted my return with a further volley of cacophonous shrieks.

Quickly I set up the easel, fixed a canvas in position, and unpacked my palette and brushes. But I had no sooner picked up a piece of charcoal to make a sketch of his tail than the whole superb panoply slowly subsided, the tail was lowered to the ground, and the peacock began to scratch the back of his head unglamorously with a large ungainly claw.

'Bad luck!' said a voice above me. 'I'm afraid you've had it!'

I looked up and saw Lady Belinda smiling out of the little upstairs window in the garden house.

'Won't he display it again?' I asked.

'Shouldn't think so. Not for some time.'

'Bother! Do you think I'd get him again tomorrow?'

'Might do,' she said. 'But I wouldn't be sure. He's had his sex life for this year. He'll soon be moulting now.'

I began to pack up my paints and brushes again, in some disappointment.

'Wait a minute!' called Belinda. 'I've got an idea.' She withdrew her head from the window and came running down the stairs.

'You really do paint, do you?' she asked, as she came out through the doorway, wearing her usual blue jeans.

'Well, yes,' I said, diffidently, 'but I'm only an amateur, of course. I'm not much good.'

'What sort of thing do you paint?' she asked, examining my chromium-plated easel with curiosity.

'Mostly still life,' I said, 'because it's the easiest subject to arrange. But I've had a shot at landscapes and portraits – even a few abstracts.'

'Have you ever painted nudes?' she asked.

'There was a Life Class at the School of Art I went to,' I said. 'But I haven't really kept it up. Models are expensive.'

'I'm not,' she said. 'I'm free.'

'I mean professional models.'

'I'm not a professional model, I know,' she said. 'But I can keep still for an eternity. And I shan't charge you anything.'

'But really,' I expostulated. 'I don't . . . I don't know that I want to—'

'I'm pretty good, you know,' she said, raising her arms above her head and slowly revolving her torso before me. 'Thirty-five, twenty-three, thirty-six, to be exact. A typical Renoir bust.'

'I dare say,' I said, picking up my easel and dropping my brushes in my embarrassment. 'But I don't think it's quite . . . quite suitable, is it?'

'Oh, not here!' she said. 'I wasn't proposing to strip down in the garden. But there are plenty of suitable places. I know – Sir Almeric's Room – ideal! Whizzo!'

My paint box fell to the ground with a clatter. The peacock, who had been standing beside us quietly preening and grooming his feathers, bent his head and examined the scattered paint tubes with interest.

'I'll pick them up,' said Belinda, dropping on her knees. 'Then we'll go straight up to Sir Almeric's Room. Hardly anyone goes there. There's a north light. There's a handy little alcove for undressing behind the tapestries. And there's a bed – a huge, old, beautifully comfortable bed.'

She finished collecting the paints and brushes and rose to her feet.

'Got everything now?' she asked. 'Let's go.'

The peacock cocked his head to one side and glanced at me benignly. Then, with a curious solemnity, he lowered his eyelid and appeared to give me a slow, deliberate wink.

'You'll probably get the best light if you put your easel to the left of that window,' said Belinda. 'Assuming that you're right-handed.'

'Yes, I'm right-handed,' I said.

'Goody!' said Belinda. 'For some reason I'm faintly mistrustful of men who are left-handed. No idea why. Must be something Freudian.'

Without being really sure whether I was going to paint or not, I set up the easel where she had suggested, and fixed a canvas in position.

'I shouldn't have thought there was anything very Freudian about you,' I said, trying to adjust myself to the situation. 'You surely aren't troubled with complexes, are you?'

'Not normally, I admit,' said Belinda. 'But I suppose

111

that deep down I'm a dreadfully conventional person. It's more conventional to be right-handed, isn't it?'

'It's more usual, of course,' I said, setting out my paints on a table by the window, and arranging my brushes beside them. 'But what's usual isn't quite the same as what's conventional, is it?'

Belinda, who had been sitting on the edge of the bed, combing her hair, got up and began to unbutton her shirt.

'That's a terribly profound remark, isn't it?' she said.

She undid her shirt and slipped her arms out of it. She was wearing no vest or brassière. I suddenly panicked; this seemed no way for a Civil Servant to conduct himself in the course of his duties. 'Look here,' I said hastily. 'Do you think this is quite all right? I didn't come here to paint life studies, you know. I'm supposed to be on duty.'

Belinda glanced up in surprise. 'What's the matter? You aren't still supposed to be mulling over those dreary statistics, are you?'

'Oh no, it's not that.'

'You were just about to paint the peacock, weren't you? Why shouldn't you paint me instead?'

'Well, I suppose it's all right,' I said, hesitantly. 'But oughtn't I to ask your mother first?'

'Ask Mama! What an extraordinary idea! But you can if you like. I expect she's still in the garden.'

Stripped to the waist, she darted to the window, pushed open one of the creaking casements, and leaned far out, her breasts rippling in the sunlight.

'Mama!' she yelled. 'Mama!'

I heard an answering call in the distance.

'Mama! Jasper's going to paint me in the nude,' she shouted at the top of her voice, 'and he wants your permission. That's okay, isn't it?'

There was an indistinguishable reply from far below, and Belinda hauled herself back into the room.

'That's okay,' she said. 'How do you like me?'

She flung out her arms, twisting her hands from side to side, and thrusting forward for my inspection her generously furnished, sun-tanned torso.

'Splendid!' The proportions of the neck, the slight heaviness of the shoulders, and the rounded fulness of the breasts – all had a splendid natural poise.

She put her hands to her waist and started to wriggle her hips out of the jeans.

'No, don't take off anything else!' I said hastily. 'You're marvellous as you are. I'll have a shot at the torso only.'

'Not a full-length? I think I'm better full-length.'

'No,' I said firmly. 'I'm going to sketch you half-length, turned slightly to your right.'

She pulled up her jeans and fastened the belt round her waist. Then she turned half-right as I had suggested.

'Is this how you want me?'

'You'd better sit down,' I said, pushing a chair towards her. 'And lean very slightly forward.'

She did as I told her; but the spontaneity of movement had gone.

'No, that's not quite right,' I said. 'You're hunched up. Throw your right arm forward a little. Be natural.'

The result was even worse.

'Come and arrange me how you want me,' she said. 'Then I might be more natural.'

I went over to her and tried to indicate the pose I wanted.

'Push me about,' she said. 'I don't mind being handled. I like it.'

The simplicity and directness with which she said this seemed quite devoid of flirtatiousness. I took hold of her arms and arranged them in the pose I had visualized. I put my hand under her chin and raised it a little.

'Breasts okay?' she asked.

'Quite okay,' I said, returning to the easel. 'Now relax, and I'll try to compete with Renoir.' I started to sketch the outline.

'I'm all right, am I?' she asked.

'You're perfect,' I said. 'As a model you can certainly compete with Gabrielle.'

'Who's Gabrielle? Girl friend of yours?'

'Gabrielle was Renoir's model,' I said, with a touch of severity. 'He painted her scores of times, and when you say you're the Renoir type you probably mean that you're rather like Gabrielle . . . which you are.'

'But surely those Renoir women had no waists, and enormous bottoms. I'm not like that, you know.'

I found that I was getting a far better sketch than I could have imagined possible. I went ahead without a pause, handling the brush with more freedom than I had ever done before.

'My comparison with Gabrielle goes only down to your waist,' I said.

'I'll show you the rest as soon as you've finished,' she said, 'and you can judge for yourself.'

'It's only your torso I'm interested in,' I said sharply. The sketch was beginning to work out marvellously, and I wanted to concentrate every thought and effort on it.

'Oh, what a pity!' said Belinda, gazing at the floor ahead of her with a look of dejection that was oddly appealing.

'Hold it! Hold it just like that!' I cried. 'The eyes and mouth are just perfect. Don't move: I must just catch that rather sulky look. *Please* don't move,' I said, as I saw she was about to speak. 'Keep quite still and don't say a word.'

For several minutes I worked as fast and intently as I could. Belinda, to do her justice, remained quite still, and retained, with surprising self-control, that wide-eyed, dejected expression which I wanted to capture.

At last I felt I had done all I could with her facial expression.

'You can ease up now,' I said. 'I've finished with the eyes and mouth.'

'I wasn't actually sulking, you know,' said Belinda. 'I never sulk. It's boring. I was merely disappointed – because you said you were only interested in the top half of me.'

'Oh, don't be absurd,' I protested. 'I never said anything of the kind.'

'Yes, you did,' she said. 'And I honestly think the bottom half is just as good. Wait till I get my trousers and pants off.'

'Maybe,' I said. I was ceasing to be embarrassed by her outrageous frankness, and was beginning to take it for granted. 'But we've got quite enough to do with the top half today. To tell you the truth, I'm getting really rather excited about the result.'

'I'm glad you're getting excited about *something*,' she said. 'I was beginning to think you were rather a cold fish.'

'Look here, Lady Belinda,' I said severely, setting down my palette. 'The question whether I'm a cold fish or not doesn't enter into the conversation at the moment. I'm engaged on painting a picture, for which you have very kindly consented to sit, and the all-important thing is to get that picture painted – or at any rate the first rough sketch done – without allusions to people's characters.'

'Oh dear, I am sorry,' she said abjectly. 'I always say just what comes into my mind. And I know I shouldn't!' Gazing sadly and wide-eyed at the floor, her lower lip almost imperceptibly trembling, she looked like a contrite child about to burst into tears.

'That's what I like about you,' I said in a conciliatory tone; 'your spontaneity.'

'I'm glad you like something about me,' she said. 'Now I'm prepared to sit here, quite still, for as many hours as you want. You won't have any more trouble with me. I'm frozen into immobility.'

I painted, in complete silence, for about half an hour. Belinda remained miraculously still. She might well have been a professional model. The rhythm of the brush strokes, and the intense concentration required, had an almost hypnotic effect on me. As the painting took shape, however, I had to admit to myself that the exhilaration I was now feeling, as I endeavoured to recreate her on the canvas, was not wholly aesthetic.

At last she spoke. 'This Gabrielle you mentioned. Was she Renoir's mistress?'

'I haven't the least idea,' I replied. 'She was his servant. She looked after his children.'

'I'd like to be your servant,' said Belinda. 'I'd look after your children quite competently, I think.'

'But I haven't got any children,' I expostulated. 'I'm not married.'

'I know you're not married. But you might have children just the same.'

'Really, Lady Belinda,' I said, in some exasperation, 'I'm not that sort of person.'

'Oh dear!' she said. Then, after a pause: 'But that's no reason why you should address me as "Lady Belinda". Couldn't you drop that convention, at any rate?'

'Of course . . . Belinda,' I said. 'I'm afraid I was being a bit pompous. People sometimes say I'm pompous. I suppose I am.'

'You're not pompous,' she said, breaking the pose and looking straight into my eyes. 'You're sweet.'

Trite though the remark was, I felt myself glowing with pleasure.

'You're sweet, too,' I said, keeping my eyes fixed firmly on the canvas.

'Do you really mean that? Or are you only being civil?'

'Of course I mean it,' I said emphatically.

'Then you think we might be friends?'

'I'm quite sure we shall be friends.'

Now the portrait was really coming to life. I began putting in the highlights. Belinda was still holding her pose perfectly, but the slightly sulky expression had been replaced by one of thoughtfulness.

'Do you think we shall be lovers?' she asked suddenly.

I drew back just in time to prevent a smudge of terre verte ruining her left eyelid.

'I wish you wouldn't throw leading remarks at me without any warning,' I said irritably. 'I'm trying to concentrate on the underlying form, and it presents rather a lot of problems.'

There was another long silence, during which I recovered my equilibrium and made some further progress with the painting.

'I imagine a lot of things present problems to you, don't they?' she said at last.

I pondered the question while I tried to flick a few glints of light into the hair. 'You may be right. I suppose I tend to look for difficulties.'

'I don't,' she said. 'I always do what's easiest. It's much pleasanter.'

All of a sudden, to my astonishment, I found myself dropping into her irresponsible way of thought. 'And you think it would be easy for us to become lovers, do you?' I asked, putting down my palette and brushes and starting to wipe my hands.

'I'm not quite sure about that,' said Belinda, breaking the pose and looking at me with a disturbingly direct gaze. 'It might present difficulties. But I'm sure they could be overcome.'

'Well, I've finished now,' I said. 'At least, I've finished all I can do at one sitting.'

'May I see?' she said, standing up. 'Or would you rather I didn't see it till it's quite finished?'

'Have a look if you'd care to. But bear in mind it's only a rough sketch.'

117

She came over to the easel and stood beside me. For several minutes she examined the painting with great care. Then she turned and looked up at me with awe. 'Gosh, Jasper! You're absolutely super! However do you manage it?'

Her unsophisticated, unreserved pleasure was so heartening – so utterly different from the usual banalities uttered by people who looked at my pictures – that I put my hands on her bare shoulders and kissed her forehead.

'Thank you very much, Belinda, for modelling for me. Now I'd better pack up these things and put them away somewhere. I don't want everybody coming and staring at this sketch – at any rate until it's finished.'

'You could put everything behind the tapestry,' she said. 'There's an alcove in the wall over there. Nobody ever looks there except when the tapestries are spring-cleaned.' She drew one of the tapestries aside. 'Here you are. There's plenty of room for the easel.'

I picked up my things and carried them behind the hangings into a little niche lit by a tiny slit window.

'You'll find a shelf there for your brushes and paints,' Belinda called from the room behind me. I set everything out neatly, washing the brushes in turpentine and drying them on a clean cloth. Having wiped down the palette and propped it against the wall, I felt for the gap in the tapestries, drew them apart, and came back into the room.

For a moment it seemed that Belinda had disappeared. Then I saw her jeans and knickers lying in a heap in the middle of the floor.

'Now you can see me full-length.' My eyes followed the voice to the bed, where Belinda was lying on her belly, quite naked, across the rich gold and blue and green embroidery of the Tudor bedspread.

'D'you like me?' she asked, rolling over on to her back

118

and stretching out her arms and legs like a cat.

How I should have answered that question I don't know, for at that moment there was a creaking of hinges at the head of the stairs leading down into the room, followed by the voice of the Professor, saying in ponderous tones: 'Allow me to go first, Miss Tidy.'

'Crumbs!' said Belinda, jumping up from the bed. 'I suppose this may be liable to misinterpretation.'

'Quickly!' I whispered. 'Behind the tapestry!'

'Keep smiling!' she whispered back, with a grin; then blew me a kiss and darted across the room.

Despite my extreme embarrassment I could not help admiring the unconscious animal grace of her naked body as she parted the hangings and disappeared into the alcove where I had put my easel and paints.

'This,' boomed the Professor's voice behind me, 'is Sir Almeric's Room, so called after Sir Almeric Virley, who was Archer-in-Ordinary to King Henry the Eighth. Hello! What's this? I didna' know you were up here, Mr Pye!'

I just had time to kick Belinda's clothes under the bed before turning to confront him.

'Er – yes, Professor,' I said. 'I thought I'd have a shot at painting this room.'

'Painting the room?' The Professor stared at the walls. 'Ah, you mean painting a picture of the room. I remember they told me you were a painter. May I see what you've done?' He looked round. 'I don't see your paints and brushes.'

'I . . . I've left them downstairs,' I stammered.

'Well, it will be interesting to see wha' you can do,' said the Professor. 'May I introduce Miss Tidy. Miss Tidy, Mr Pye.'

'Mr Pye and I are already acquainted, Professor,'

said Miss Tidy. 'We've met before, haven't we, Mr Pye, in other circumstances.'

The Professor regarded us quizzically in turn, and then proceeded with his guide lecture. 'I have already told Mr Pye about Sir Almeric Virley's curious disability, so I willna' bore you with that story, Miss Tidy. But I am sure you will appreciate the hangings in this room, which are some of the most precious things we still retain here at Arcady Hall.'

'These tapestries are exquisite,' said Miss Tidy. 'How old are they?'

'They are no' by any means the auldest examples of needlework at Arcady,' said the Professor. 'They date back only to the early seventeenth century. They were made at Mortlake. As you see, they are mostly based on classical themes. You could find the subjects of most of them in Ovid's *Metamorphoses*, which was one of the favourite books of the educated gentlemen of that day.'

'I always understood it was rather a naughty book,' said Miss Tidy. 'Isn't that so, Mr Pye?'

'I don't think I've ever read it,' I said.

'I'm sure you have,' said Miss Tidy with a titter. 'I'm sure it must have formed part of your education.'

The Professor gave her a searching glance, under his dark eyebrows, and continued his discourse.

'I assume that this tapestry,' he said, advancing to the one hanging in front of my easel and Belinda, 'depicts Actaeon, the celebrated huntsman, son of Aristaeus, who was changed by Artemis into a stag.'

'He doesn't seem to have become a stag yet,' said Miss Tidy, approaching to examine the needlework. 'Who is the lady without any clothes on?'

I drew a quick breath; then realized she was pointing to a figure in the design of the tapestry.

'That is Artemis, or, as the Romans called her, Diana,

the huntress. She is, as ye ken, the maiden-divinity, who is never conquered by love. A dangerous lady, eh, Pye?' He turned to me with a ponderous smile. 'Mr Pye, being nearer to his education than I am, would be able to tell you how Artemis, when her chastity was threatened by Orion, slew him with an arrow.'

I shuddered; and I could have sworn I heard a giggle behind the tapestry. But the Professor boomed on. 'In this design you see Artemis being spied on by Actaeon, whilst she is bathing.'

'And she changed him into a stag?' said Miss Tidy.

'Exactly,' said the Professor. 'The consequence of Actaeon's intrusion upon the naked Artemis was that, transformed into a stag, he was torn to pieces by fifty dogs.'

'Oh dear, what a lesson for Peeping Toms!' said Miss Tidy. 'What I admire so much about these tapestries is the closeness of the weave. May I feel it?' She reached for the edge of the hanging.

I stepped forward hurriedly and took her by the arm. 'This is what you'll admire even more, Miss Tidy,' I said, leading her away from the Mortlake tapestry towards the bed. 'These bed-hangings are of infinitely finer workmanship.'

The Professor looked at me with respect.

'Mr Pye is even quicker-witted than I thought,' he said – whether with irony or not I couldn't be sure. 'These bed-hangings are indeed of superb quality and verra great historical interest.'

'How exquisite!' exclaimed Miss Tidy. 'These enchanting animals and birds and insects – and all with their names embroidered underneath.'

'You will observe the quaint archaic spelling, Miss Tidy,' said the Professor. 'A rabbit spelt RABET, and a hawk spelt HAUKE.'

'What a hawk, too!' said Miss Tidy. 'Look at the

121

keenness of his eye! He'd miss nothing, would he? Rather like yourself, Professor!' she tittered.

She turned to me. 'I'm sure you wouldn't like being a rabbit if that hawk were after you, would you, Mr Pye?'

I murmured something incoherently.

'Who's been disturbing this bed?' said the Professor, bending down and straightening the embroidered bed-spread. 'It almost looks as though someone has been lying here. You haven't been taking a siesta, have you, Pye?'

'Perhaps it was Artemis or one of her nymphs,' said Miss Tidy. 'But we don't want you turned into a stag, do we, Mr Pye! Not before Saturday's cricket match, anyway.'

'Well, if you've seen all you want, Miss Tidy,' said the Professor, 'perhaps we should move on.'

I began to breathe again.

'I should mention,' he continued, 'that this room has no less than four exits. The only apparent way in is up the stairs by which we approached. But in fact there are three other ways out. One leads to a subterranean tunnel which goes under the moat and up into that wee arbour in the garden.'

The Professor, who had moved over to the window, pointed to a little brick-built arbour facing the knot garden. As our eyes followed his arm a naked figure emerged cautiously from the arbour and ran swiftly to the gate in the walled garden.

'Great Scott!' muttered the Professor.

'Artemis?' asked Miss Tidy. 'Or one of her nymphs?'

The Professor closed the window hurriedly and turned back into the room. 'There are, as I was saying, four secret doors and sliding panels in this room. They are hidden behind these tapestries. Here, for instance.' He walked over to the edge of the Mortlake tapestry, behind which I had set up my easel and canvas, drew it to one side, and looked behind it.

I closed my eyes and started to count ten.

There was an audible silence. The Professor reappeared, wide-eyed and faintly flushed.

'I was mistaken,' he said, gazing at me with what seemed to be amazement rather than indignation. 'The sliding panel must be in the other wall. But perhaps we should move on, Miss Tidy.'

'I must have just one more look at those bed-hangings,' said Miss Tidy, returning to the bed. 'Do you know who did them?'

'Ann Boleyn,' said the Professor curtly.

'Really! Ann Boleyn herself?'

'Aye,' said the Professor. 'I will tell you the whole story when we get back to my room. Shall we go back the way we came?'

'Exquisite! Exquisite!' exclaimed Miss Tidy, bending over the bed and lifting up the edge of the bedspread. 'It's a combination of *gros point* and *petit point*. And – yes, you're right, Professor! I didn't really believe you, but here is the monogram of Ann Boleyn – A.B. What a discovery! How romantic!'

'I think we should go,' said the Professor impatiently, turning to ascend the staircase. 'Will you follow me up the stairs, Miss Tidy? I shall see you later, Mr Pye.'

Miss Tidy, who had been on her knees examining the embroidery of the bedspread, rose to her feet.

'Well, I never!' she exclaimed. 'The things one finds!'

'I beg your pardon?' I said.

'That marvellous needlework!' she said, in an awed voice. 'And that monogram of Ann Boleyn!'

'Yes,' I said, waiting for her to go. 'I'm sure the Professor can tell you a lot about it.'

She drifted towards the door. 'That very, very keen-eyed hawk, I'm sure he'd miss nothing,' she said reflectively. Then she turned to me. 'I shall look forward to seeing you at the cricket match, Mr Pye. I hope you'll be in good form. And – oh dear! I was nearly going off with it – I think this must be your handkerchief: I picked it up by the bed.' She handed me a crumpled slip of white silk. Then she followed the Professor up the stairs.

I looked down at what she had given me. It was the one garment Belinda had been wearing underneath her jeans.

After the events of the morning I felt unequal to sitting down to lunch with the Professor. I left word with Miss Mounsey that I had to absent myself for the afternoon, and I walked into the village, had some sandwiches at the Virley Arms, and caught a bus to Flaxfield.

I spent the afternoon in Flaxfield, a picturesque little town – really no more than a large village – with a medley of white and pink stud-and-plaster buildings jostling each other at unaccountable angles along both sides of a broad, tree-lined thoroughfare. At one time, presumably, it had been a busy market centre: now, in the afternoon sun, it seemed half-asleep.

I went into the strangely large and lofty church, which had a fifteenth-century porch, built of brick, and a tower which showed traces of both Saxon and Norman work. There was a fine hammer-beam roof to the nave, and there were lovely traceried windows in the aisles.

After I had had tea at a little rose-clad tea shop where, as the sole customer, I was treated as a very important person, I set out to walk the three miles back to Arcady.

Although there was an occasional transient roar from aircraft passing high overhead, and in the distance I could sometimes hear the hum of a tractor, I became increasingly conscious of the remoteness and isolation of Arcady from the outer world.

Flaxfield, itself a relic of the past, was the nearest centre of population. There was apparently no main road within four or five miles in any direction. The lanes were narrow, twisting, and deep-set in banks of grass and sheep's parsley. I passed no garage, and only one tumble-down pub. Now and again I would see across the fields the tiled roof of a pink-washed farmhouse, half-hidden amid a protective cluster of tall elms, with, as often as not, a massive Tudor chimney-stack to testify to its age. I passed nobody on the road except an occasional farm worker on a bicycle or a roadman sharpening his scythe. As I approached Arcady I noticed that the landscape became less open and more wooded: there were an increasing number of copses and spinneys and tall elms and oaks in the hedgerows.

The lane passed a hundred yards or so from the Arcady station on the Branch Line, and I stopped to see whether Lord Flamborough's train was standing in the platform. As I saw no sign of it I decided that I might as well cross the line at the station and take the short cut back to Arcady Hall through the park.

There was something curiously poignant about the desolate air of the deserted platform – the paint peeling off the wooden railings, the timetables yellowing with age. Docks and thistles sprouted between the sleepers; cobwebs festooned the hanging lamps.

I sat down on the sun-blistered bench which stood against the platform railings, below the bleak sans-serif letters which still proclaimed the name ARCADY. As the sun beat down on me, and I watched, far up in the sky, the convolutions of some almost indistinguishable but incredibly fast-moving aircraft, the contrast between the vapour trail of the jet plane and this decaying relic of the 'permanent way' was so emphatic as to seem unreal. At any moment I expected some decrepit ticket-collector with an Emett moustache and the sad voice of Horace Kenney to appear out of the dusty desolation of the booking office.

I sat there for some time, dozing in the evening sunshine after the exertions of my walk. I realized that I was going to be late for dinner at the Hall, but I was not hungry, and I felt reluctant to return and face the Professor. What deductions he had drawn from our unfortunate encounter in Sir Almeric's Room I didn't know, but I couldn't help feeling that any moral authority with which I may have been invested through my status in the Ministry had now been hopelessly undermined.

At last the sun dropped below a bank of cloud on the horizon. I got up and made my way to the exit through the booking office. It seemed incredible that the ancient poster of the Jolly Tar advertising the bracing air of Skegness should still be stuck up here. I remembered it from my childhood; but I hadn't seen it for years. I now studied it with curiosity. It had a sort of period gaiety about it: one visualized the Jolly Tar beckoning to crowds of Bank Holiday-makers in straw hats and silk blouses, attended by vast families of children in sailor suits, clutching buckets and spades. And here he was, jolly as ever, beckoning across the dusty booking office of a deserted station on a disused Branch Line.

I was about to go on my way when, out of the corner of my eye, I saw a railway ticket lying on the ledge outside the closed window of the booking office. I stepped across and picked it up. It was a used ticket, clipped in two places and brown with age, entitling the bearer to make a single journey between Flaxfield and Arcady. I turned it over to see if I could read the date.

The date stamp had been smudged, and the date was indecipherable. Round the edge of the ticket, however, was written, in capital letters, MEET ME IN THE CHAPEL RUINS AT TWILIGHT.

It was ridiculous; it was absurd; but still I couldn't resist the conviction that the message was intended for me.

There was no supporting evidence, of course. How long the ticket had been lying there I had no idea. Days or weeks, possibly. The message may have been written by some village lad for his girl, months or even years ago. Anyway, nobody knew that I was coming through the booking hall at that particular time on that particular day.

Still, the conviction remained. Life in Arcady had already provided so many improbabilities that I was quite prepared for another. And, of course, there *was* a certain similarity to a message I had received on a previous occasion.

I looked at my watch. I was surprised to see that it was after eight o'clock. I left the station yard and began to saunter slowly down the path through the park. This was the path along which I had walked with Lady Flamborough the previous day. It passed, as I now recalled, only a few yards away from the ruined chapel.

When I came to the edge of the thicket which surrounded the chapel and hid it from view I looked again at my watch, and then at the sky. The sun had not set, but it had gone down behind a bank of cloud, and there was an evening glow in the west. Not quite twilight yet, however. I sat down beside the path and leaned back against the trunk of an oak tree. I decided that I would definitely miss dinner at the Hall. If they wondered where I had got to – let them wonder. I saw no reason why I should not for an hour or two play up to the spirit of fantasy that seemed to be in the air.

I hadn't long to wait before fantasy made its next move. I was so well prepared, so inured to the improbable, that I hardly jumped at all when I heard the whirr and the thud above my head as the arrow embedded itself in the bark of the oak.

I scrambled to my feet and detached the message from

the arrow. I experienced something of the cool detachment of an actor playing a well-rehearsed part as I
unfolded the paper. The message was written in
verse:

> Come to the raven's bleak abode;
> Come to th' apartment of the toad;
> Come where the vixen safely feeds;
> Come where the pois'nous adder breeds.
> Come where the spider sits and spins
> Her cobwebs over untold sins.

I read the missive twice. Whether it was a quotation
or an original composition by the sender I had no idea.
But its purport seemed clear enough. I had been right
about the message on the railway ticket. I began to push
my way through the nettles and brambles towards the
ruined chapel.

Within the thicket there was a hushed and humid stillness and a pervasive odour of decay. As I made my way
towards the clearing my hands and ankles were stung
by nettles and my jacket torn by trailing bramble shoots.
How anyone had shot an arrow through such a tanglewood I could not conceive. In the distance a wood-
pecker uttered his mocking cry.

Then the incandescent blue and purple of the
primulas came into view, and, rising out of it, like the
shell of some long-lost temple of the Aztecs or Mayas,
the ivy-encrusted walls of the chapel.

I picked my way through the sparkling sea of primulas
and walked slowly round the ruins. There was nobody to
be seen. I took off my jacket and began to remove the
burrs and bramble shoots that had attached themselves
to it. As I did so I became aware of a voice singing, in a
high-pitched but curiously delicate tone, somewhere
above me. I stood still and listened.

> 'Her face was like an April morn,
> Clad in a wintry cloud;
> And clay-cold was her lily hand
> That held her sable shroud.'

There was a pause. I looked about me. I could see no sign of the singer, but the voice seemed to come from somewhere up above the high-pointed arch of the chapel.

> 'But love had, like the canker-worm,
> Consumed her early prime:
> The rose grew pale, and left her cheek;
> She died before her time.'

Yes, the sound certainly came from above the arch. I pushed past a holly bush that was growing in the middle of the ruined chancel and approached the foot of the wall. 'Whoever you are,' I called out, 'you seem to be alive at the moment. May I see the rose in your cheeks?'

There was a further pause. Then the song continued:

> 'This is the mirk and fearful hour
> When injured ghosts complain;
> Now dreary graves give up their dead
> To haunt the faithless swain.'

There was now little doubt in my mind that the singer was hidden among the yellow stonecrop growing on the top of the wall. 'You're no ghost,' I called. 'I believe I've met you before. You dropped out of an oak tree then. Are you coming down? I'll close my eyes if you want me to.'

The song was resumed:

> 'How could you say my face was fair,
> And yet that face forsake?

How could you win my virgin heart,
   Yet leave that heart to break?

'How could you say my lips were sweet,
   And make the scarlet pale?
And why did I, young witless maid,
   Believe the flattering tale?'

'You're not by any means witless, maid,' I said. 'And I don't remember saying any of those things to you. But I might say something pleasant if you'd only show yourself.'

I was answered in song:

'That face, alas! no more is fair,
   Those lips no longer red;
Dark are mine eyes, now closed in death;
   And every charm is fled.

'And take a lesson from that, Sir Jasper,' continued the voice, falling to a conversational level at last.

'I'm not Sir Jasper,' I said. 'I'm a plain Mister. And perhaps you'd tell me: are you a plain Miss? Or are you her Ladyship?'

'That is something you will have to find out for yourself,' said the voice.

'How do I do that?'

'For a gentleman of your reputation, Sir Jasper, you don't seem very resourceful.'

'Never mind about my reputation,' I said. 'Tell me where you are.'

'Isn't it obvious, Sir Jasper, that I live on a higher plane than you?'

'You mean that you're hiding on the top of that wall? But how do I raise myself to your level?'

'By prayer and fasting, I suppose,' said the voice. 'But

130

I don't suppose that would appeal to Sir Jasper at all. Sir Jasper will no doubt act as a deep-dyed villain should, if he's to gain his dastardly ends.'

'How should a deep-dyed villain act, in present circumstances?' I asked.

'Really, Sir Jasper, it isn't for me to further your devilish ends. You must use your eyes – and perhaps your hands and feet as well.'

I was now quite certain where the voice was coming from; and, if the speaker had climbed up there, presumably I could, too. The top of the wall was some thirty feet above the ground, but there was a gnarled and ancient ivy growing all the way up the wall, and it might afford a foothold. I put down my jacket and investigated. Yes, the trunk of the ivy seemed substantial and there were signs that it had been used already as a ladder.

'Is this ivy safe?' I called.

'It's poison ivy,' replied the voice.

'I know, but is it safe to climb up it?'

'I shouldn't have thought Sir Jasper would hesitate to take a risk like that,' said the voice. 'Is he perhaps a rather faint-hearted villain, after all?'

'He's nothing of the kind. He's merely cold and calculating.'

'That's better!' said the voice, laughing. 'Then perhaps he will rise in the world.'

'He's on the way up already,' I announced, gripping the main stem of the ivy and setting my feet in the tangle of branches.

It was, in fact, by no means difficult to climb the tree. Bruised leaves and worn places on the branches were evidence that someone was in the habit of making the ascent. I made good progress until I was within about a yard of the top of the wall.

'Oh, Sir Jasper!' – the mocking voice was only just

above my head now – 'are you going to pursue me into my very sanctuary?'

'I'll be with you in half a minute,' I said, removing one hand from the ivy stem to brush the hair out of my eyes. 'Are you sure this ivy is quite safe?'

'I'm not at all sure that *I* am safe,' the voice murmured.

I gave a final haul and pulled myself level with the top of the wall. The final stage of the climb was more difficult than I had expected, as the ivy had been broken off just short of the edge of the stonework, and there was nothing for my hands to get a grip on.

'What do I do now?' I asked.

'Really, Sir Jasper, it isn't for me to say,' said Lady Matilda, with a hint of surprisingly adult irony in the dark, deep-set eyes which were gazing into mine from a distance of only a few inches. She was lying at full length on the top of the wall. 'A defenceless maid is hardly expected to assist her pursuer.'

'Very well, then,' I said, 'I shall have to heave myself up unaided. I only hope this stonework doesn't come adrift.'

The stonework did not come adrift, but, as I jerked myself upwards, the pressure of my feet proved too much for the ivy, which suddenly detached itself from the face of the wall and swung backwards into space.

'Help, help!' I cried. 'Catch hold of me!'

With astonishing quickness and presence of mind Lady Matilda flung her arms round my shoulders and tightly gripped me by the shirt.

'Hang on!' she said. 'I'm afraid the ivy's letting you down.'

Indeed it was. My feet shot out into the void, carrying the whole superstructure of the tree with them. Only the grip of my hands on a stone cornice, and Matilda's surprisingly tenacious hold on my shoulders and shirt,

132

saved me from following the ivy in its backward dive into the brambles and nettles below.

'Put your toe into that ledge below you,' said Matilda. 'I've got hold of your shoulders.'

'But I'll pull you down,' I gasped, as my legs scrabbled wildly along the face of the wall trying to find a foothold.

'I'm all right,' said Matilda quietly. 'I've crooked my legs round a thorn tree.'

To my intense relief one of my feet slipped into a cavity in the wall and found a foothold. Slowly and cautiously I prised myself upwards. I was hauled by Matilda over the edge of the wall into safety.

'Phew! I thought I was going!' I said, as I pulled my legs up and stretched myself out flat on the top of the wall. 'Thank you so much for showing such presence of mind.'

'Thank you for the honour of your company, Sir Jasper,' said Matilda, releasing her grip on my shirt and uncoiling her legs from around the stunted thorn tree which was growing so conveniently out of the top of the wall.

I was relieved to see that the wall was about three feet wide and seemed fairly substantial. It was carpeted with yellow stonecrop upon which lay, alongside Matilda, a bow and a quiver full of arrows.

'Is this Sir Almeric's long-bow?' I asked, when I had got my breath back.

'No,' said Matilda. 'The Professor collared that. After all the trouble, too, that I'd had in getting it back from London.'

'So it was you who stole it from the Victoria and Albert Museum?' I said.

'Stole it! I never stole it!' she protested, her dark eyes flashing. 'It belongs to us. It should never have gone to London at all.'

'But did you bring it back?' I asked. 'The Professor seemed quite put out about it.'

'Of course I brought it back!'

'D'you mean you went and asked for it?'

'No. I don't suppose they'd have let me have it – without a letter from the Prof. I took it.'

'But you can't just *take* things from the V and A,' I said. 'I know; I live near there. They're frightfully strict about people going in or out with bags or parcels – to say nothing of long-bows!'

'I know,' said Matilda thoughtfully. 'I had to climb in and get it. But then I like climbing, as you know.'

'I suppose I'd better not ask any more questions,' I said, 'or I shall become an accessory after the fact.'

'But it wasn't stealing,' insisted Matilda, with great earnestness. 'It's our long-bow, you see. It belongs here.'

'Good for you, anyway!'

'That's better,' said Matilda, sitting up and tidying her long black hair. 'I was afraid you were going to disapprove of me, like everyone else.'

'Good heavens, no!' I said. 'I admire you. But I rather wish you wouldn't shoot arrows at me on the least provocation. I'm beginning to get nervous.'

'You don't need to be,' she said. 'My aim isn't likely to falter. One day I shall win the Six Gold Badge: I've shot four several times.'

'I don't understand archery,' I said. 'But that's good, is it?'

'Only two women have shot six arrows running into the Gold – that's the middle of the target. I shall be the third one to do it.' There was a note of quiet confidence in her voice.

'I can see that you're a very determined person,' I said.

'Yes, I'm determined,' said Matilda in a matter-of-fact voice. 'You see, everything's easier for me; I lead a life of the spirit.'

I didn't quite know what to say to that. Feeling slightly uncomfortable – physically as well as mentally – I changed my position and rose up on to my knees. But the sight of the sheer drop on either side of the wall was too much for me. I shuddered and lay down on my stomach again.

'You're afraid of heights, aren't you?' said Matilda. 'I expect it's because you're so sexy. The two things go together, I'm told.'

'You aren't afraid of heights, then?' I asked, declining to discuss the other topic.

'No. I'm not sexy, you see – not in the way you are, or my sister Belinda is. I'm intensely romantic, and I might well become a *femme fatale*. But I'm not interested in sex. Perhaps some man will kill me one day. But it will be because I'm really unattainable.'

'You don't seem perturbed at the idea of being killed,' I said, 'so you're hardly likely to be afraid of heights. Are you afraid of anything?'

Matilda plucked a blade of grass and sucked it for a moment whilst her dark eyes pondered the question. 'No, I'm not afraid of anything – except bats.'

'Bats! Are you afraid of bats?'

'Yes,' she said solemnly.

'But they don't hurt you, you know – not the bats you get in this country. It's an old wives' tale about them getting into your hair. They're just as anxious to avoid you as you are to avoid them.'

'Actually,' she said, 'my hair is rather long, and they might get into it. But it isn't that. You see, bats are more than they seem. They are evil spirits.'

'You haven't been reading *Dracula*, have you?' I asked.

'No,' she replied. 'What's *Dracula*? A book? Would I like it?'

I was silent. It hardly seemed to me the moment for a literary discussion.

'I expect you think I'm dotty,' said Matilda, biting the

blade of grass. 'Everyone does. Or else they say I'll grow out of it. But I won't.'

'I don't think you're dotty at all,' I said, with a half-guilty sense of not quite telling the truth. 'I think you're unusual; and obviously you think a lot more about things than most girls of your age.'

'I'm not all that young,' she said, defensively. 'I'm over sixteen. You could ravish me with impunity if you wanted to.'

'I wouldn't dream of such a thing!' I was really rather shocked. 'You have the most extraordinary ideas about me.'

'I wouldn't mind, actually,' she said, looking with disconcerting candour straight into my eyes. 'One must accept life as it comes. But I dare say I don't appeal to you. I expect you prefer my sister Belinda. I suppose you've ravished her, haven't you?'

'Look here, Matilda!' I said indignantly, rising up on to my knees again. 'This isn't the sort of conversation I'm accustomed to having with – er – 'teenagers.'

Again I became sickeningly aware of the drop on either side. I flopped down on my stomach once more.

'What is a 'teenager?' asked Matilda.

'What is a 'teenager?' I echoed. 'Do you mean to say you don't know what a 'teenager is? Don't you read the papers?'

'No, I don't, as it happens. I prefer *The Monk* and *The Mysteries of Udolpho*. What is a 'teenager?'

'A 'teenager is just someone of your age,' I said.

'How dull! I thought it meant something interesting, like a werewolf or a zombie.'

'Most people nowadays consider 'teenagers extremely interesting,' I said.

'Not me,' said Matilda. 'I like people who are old, and experienced, and disillusioned. Like you, Sir Jasper.'

'I'm not old,' I protested irritably. 'And I'm not Sir

Jasper. I've not been knighted.'

'Then you're a baronet,' she said eagerly. 'That's much better. Perhaps your line goes back nearly as far as ours. I expect you're terribly degenerate and effete.'

'I'm just a plain Mister, I keep on saying. And I'm not effete.'

Matilda nodded reflectively. 'You protest too much, Sir Jasper. I don't believe a word you say. I mistrust you intensely.'

'Oh dear!' I said. 'We don't seem to be getting on very well, do we!'

'I think we're getting on very well indeed,' said Matilda. 'I'm enjoying you quite a lot.'

'Thank you,' I said stiffly. 'I'd be enjoying myself a good deal more if we weren't perched up here.'

As I said that an alarming thought entered my mind. I wriggled to the edge of the wall and looked down. Then I moved over to the other edge and looked down there. The ivy lay spread out on top of the holly and brambles in the chancel below. 'I say. There doesn't seem any way of climbing down now that the ivy's collapsed. What do we do?'

'We shall have to spend the night up here,' said Matilda.

'But we can't do that!'

'I don't suppose it's the first time you've spent the night with – with a 'teenager, is it?' she said blandly.

I let the suggestion pass. 'But it's infernally uncomfortable,' I said. 'And we might roll off.'

'Oh, it's your fear of heights that's worrying you; I see. Well, I'd better send a message for help.'

She jumped up, causing me a spasm of apprehension lest she lost her foothold, and ran along to the end of the wall, where the corner stones rose above the level of the rest. She lifted up one of the stones and from behind it

137

took out a pencil and book and some sheets of writing paper. She sat down and scribbled a message.

'I'll make it sound desperately urgent,' she said. 'I'll say I'm about to be betrayed by a deep-dyed villain. But it's just a matter of luck whether anyone passes by and finds it.'

'Half a minute!' I protested. But she picked up an arrow, rolled the paper round the shaft, and fixed it in position with a rubber band which she took off her wrist. Then she stood up again, with the bow in her hand, took up the archer's stance, drew the bow, and shot the arrow through the trees towards the pathway.

'That should strike the ground just under that oak tree where you were sitting,' she said. 'Someone may pass by on the way to the station.'

'What do we do till then?' I asked.

'I could read to you.'

'Yes, do!' I said gratefully.

'What would you like? I've got several books here.' She made me wince with apprehension again as she tripped along the wall to her hiding place, her white frock outlined against the darkening sky. 'I've got *The Moonstone* and *In a Glass Darkly* and *The Monk* and *The Midnight Bell*, or *The Abbey of St Francis*.'

'Let's have *The Monk*,' I said. 'I've heard of it but I've never read it.'

She picked out the book, sat down on the wall with her feet dangling over the edge, and began to read. She had a soft and low but expressive voice, and she obviously enjoyed reading aloud. Although she appeared to take the absurdly melodramatic story quite seriously, she gave the high-flown phrasing just enough emphasis to bring out the period flavour. After a time I forgot the discomfort of my posture and my doubts about our prospects of being rescued, and became absorbed in the story. Certainly the story didn't lack incident.

'. . . As she uttered these last words, she lifted her arm and made a motion as if to stab herself. The friar's eyes followed with dread the course of the dagger. She had torn open her habit, and her bosom was half exposed. The weapon's point rested upon her left breast: and oh! that was such a breast. The moon-beams darting full upon it enabled the monk to observe its dazzling whiteness: his eye dwelt with insatiable avidity upon the beauteous orb: a sensation, till then unknown, filled his heart with a mixture of anxiety and delight; a raging fire shot through every limb; the blood boiled in his veins—'

'Stop!' I said. 'I believe I can hear someone walking along the path.'

'Oh, bother!' exclaimed Matilda. 'You've interrupted one of my favourite bits.'

'I'm sorry, but I'm sure I can hear voices.'

We listened and we looked. It was beginning to get dark, and there was little chance of seeing anyone in the shadows between the trees. But undoubtedly there were voices.

'They may not see the arrow,' I said. 'We'd better call out.'

'Help, help!' shouted Matilda.

There was a silence: then the voices seemed to come closer.

'Help, help!' shouted Matilda again.

There was a crackle of branches as someone began to push through the undergrowth towards us.

'It came from the chapel, I think,' a voice called out. It sounded like Quirk's.

'Go ahead, I'll follow ye.' There was no mistaking the voice of the Professor.

Matilda stood up and waved her book in the air.

'For heaven's sake don't fall off now someone's coming at last,' I said sharply.

'I'm as safe as houses,' she answered gaily, executing a *pas seul* with terrifying abandon.

Then suddenly she ducked and threw her arms up in front of her face. 'Oh no, I'm not!' she cried, in panic.

'Who's there?' The Professor's voice called out from below. 'Who is that, Quirk? Can you see?'

'Help, help!' screamed Matilda, and to my dismay there was hysteria in the cry. Even more to my dismay, she threw herself down on top of me and flung her arms round me.

'Help, help, help!' she screamed.

'Stop it, Matilda!' I said sharply. 'Don't be silly! We're all right now.'

'Help, help, help!' she screamed. 'The bats!'

Clutching desperately at her to stop her rolling off and carrying me with her, I lifted my head and looked along the wall. Sure enough, flickering innocuously past us in the twilight were a pair of bats.

'Help, help! Save me!' the shrieks continued.

'Leave the lassie alone, sir!' the Professor bellowed. 'You'd better be careful. We have two witnesses here.'

'It's all right, Professor,' I gasped, holding Matilda firmly down on top of the wall. 'It's only me.'

'Pye, by God!' the Professor exclaimed. 'It's Pye again, Quirk!'

'Don't get alarmed, Professor,' I called. 'Everything's quite all right. But Lady Matilda is a little nervous. Can you get a ladder or something?'

'Quirk,' the Professor barked, 'run over to the station and look under the signal box. There should be a ladder there. Bring it as quickly as you can ... Stay quite still where you are, Mr Pye. We'll soon reach you. Have no fear, Lady Matilda. I've got ma eye on him.'

* * *

140

Breakfast on Saturday was an uncomfortable meal. The Professor made a show of being absorbed in his morning's mail. Quirk seemed to be deeply concerned with the county cricket reports in his newspaper. No reference was made to the events of the previous evening. Whether they had accepted my explanation – my entirely truthful explanation – I could not tell. Probably not: I had to admit that all the evidence suggested quite a different interpretation.

I was about to make some jocular comment on the episode, in order to relieve the tension, when Miss Mounsey appeared. 'A message has just come up from the station,' she announced, 'to say that his Lordship would be much obliged if Mr Pye would call on him this morning.'

The Professor looked up from his correspondence and subjected me to a frigid smile. 'Perhaps you'd better be going along, Pye,' he said portentously.

'Dear me!' said Quirk in a fluster. 'This is rather upsetting. I wanted to give Mr Pye a few balls in the net this morning, to get his eye in for the match this afternoon.'

'Cricket isna' the be-all and end-all of life, Quirk,' said the Professor. 'I think his Lordship has something rather important to say to Mr Pye.'

I gulped down the last of my coffee and rose to my feet. 'I'll go now,' I said, in as casual a tone of voice as I could muster. There was a pregnant silence as I left the room.

Walking through the park to the railway station I felt like a schoolboy on his way to a painful interview with the headmaster. Admittedly I had nothing on my conscience; but I knew only too well from my schooldays that an appearance of guilt was just as damning as guilt itself. It was perhaps doubtful whether Lord Flamborough would prove as intimidating in the role of headmaster as, say, the Professor would. Still, Belinda and Matilda were his daughters, and my relationship with the two of them must appear compromising, to say the least.

The train was standing in the station, a curl of smoke rising from the funnel of the engine into the bright, still summer air. I walked down the platform and put my hand on the door of the Pullman coach.

Should I knock before entering? It seemed unnecessary to knock at the door of a railway coach, but it also seemed a little presumptuous for a virtual stranger to burst into a private drawing-room unheralded. After a moment's consideration I opened the outer door, entered the vestibule of the coach, and knocked on the inner door of the saloon. At that very moment Lord Flamborough's gramophone wheezed into motion, with a strident rendering of ' "Maggie?" "Yes, Ma!" "Come right upstairs!" '

I waited outside the door for a while, wondering whether my knock had been heard; then hesitantly I turned the handle and went inside.

The saloon presented a scene which was almost surrealist. The sun was shining in through the enormous plate-glass windows on to the plush armchairs, the antimacassars, the inlaid mahogany panelling, and the gilt chandeliers. At the far end of the saloon, framed by a pair of aspidistras on their carved ebony jardinières, the Earl of Flamborough was sitting in his invalid chair. With a rapt expression on his face, and a drumstick in either hand, he was beating an energetic percussive accompaniment to ' "Maggie?" "Yes, Ma!" ' on a battery of drums and cymbals.

He was so absorbed in his performance that I stood unnoticed until ' "Maggie?" "Yes, Ma!" ' wound itself to a climax and the gramophone groaned to a halt. Then, having wiped the perspiration from his brow, Lord Flamborough saw me.

'Are you hep?' he asked.

'I beg your pardon?'

'Are you hep?' he repeated. 'I think that's how they put it nowadays, isn't it? We didn't bother with words like that in the 'twenties, of course: we just enjoyed ourselves, without any palaver.'

'I don't really know what "hep" means,' I admitted. 'It's a 'teenagers' term. I don't use it myself.'

'A 'teenager is what we used to call a flapper, isn't it?' said Lord Flamborough.

'I suppose so,' I said. His Lordship was evidently more up-to-date than his youngest daughter.

'Do these 'teenagers really enjoy themselves nowadays?' he asked. 'I read about them sometimes in the *Sunday Pictorial* – Dimple brings it over to me from the pub each week: we only have *The Times* here. I'd like to see them doing this Rock-'n'-Roll. Looks rather like the Charleston to me.'

'It isn't quite the same,' I said.

'You can do the Charleston, can't you?' said Lord Flamborough. 'How about doing a solo now? Can't provide you with a partner: the girls are up in the village. But you'd probably get on better solo.'

'I'd rather not,' I said. 'I believe there was something you wanted to see me about.'

Lord Flamborough frowned. 'Yes, I believe there was something. But it'll wait. Let's have a quick Charleston first.Which would you prefer – "Fascinatin' Rhythm" or "I Wonder Where My Baby is Tonight"?'

'I'd really rather not,' I said uncomfortably. 'You see, I think there's been some misunderstanding, and I'd like to clear it up.'

'What's that?' said Lord Flamborough, looking puzzled. 'Don't know what you're driving at. But if there's any bother you must clear it up with the Prof. He's in charge: he deals with everything. Now, we might try

143

"Sweet Hortense". It's a bit early for the Charleston, but the rhythm's right.'

'Yes, it is a bit early,' I said, clutching at the straw. 'I really don't feel I could dance the Charleston at this hour of the morning.'

'I wasn't talking about the time of day,' said Lord Flamborough, impatiently. 'I mean that "Sweet Hortense" belongs to an earlier period than the Charleston. But it's got the right beat. Try it.'

He pulled a record out of the cabinet and began to wind up the gramophone. 'You can say what you like about modern gramophones, but you don't get that same, harsh, tinny tone out of them that you get out of this. You need that for jazz. Gives the flavour to it. The only trouble is getting the right needles. Jones gets them for me now – don't know where, but Jones can find anything. Now we're ready. Let it rip!'

He released the catch on the instrument and was about to lower the needle on to the disc when Lady Flamborough walked in. 'I've been swindled, Bertie,' she announced. 'That isn't a *damascena versicolor* at all; it's a *gallica*.'

Lord Flamborough stopped the record.

'What are you talking about, Mabel?'

'That rose I got from Piggott and Heginbotham in the autumn. It's just come into bloom and it isn't a York and Lancaster after all; it's a Rosa Mundi.'

'Sickening!' said Lord Flamborough, perfunctorily. 'Now don't interrupt us, Mabel. This fellow from the Ministry is going to do a solo Charleston.'

'Really, Lord Flamborough,' I protested. 'I'd rather not.'

'It's the word *versicolor* that confuses,' said Lady Flamborough. 'They are both called *versicolor*, but the York and Lancaster is a damask rose and the Rosa Mundi is a *gallica*.'

144

'Perhaps you'd rather have a genuine Charleston tune?' said Lord Flamborough. 'Let's change over to "I Wonder Where My Baby is Tonight".'

'Couldn't we leave it for another time?' I said miserably. 'I feel we must clear up that other matter first.'

'What they won't grasp,' said Lady Flamborough, 'is that the York and Lancaster doesn't have red and white stripes on the same bloom: it has quite distinct blooms – some red and some white.'

The gramophone blared into the conversation.

'Hotcha, hotcha!' shouted the Earl. 'Give it all you've got.' And he launched another assault upon the drums. Lady Flamborough retired to the domestic quarters.

Reluctantly, and in extreme embarrassment, I began to swing my arms, dip my knees, and agitate my ankles into a Charleston.

'Okay, buddy!' Lord Flamborough yelled. 'That's the rhythm.' And he began to sing, in a curiously high, refined tenor voice:

'I wonder if my Baby does the Charleston, *Charleston*!
I wonder who is teaching her the Charleston, *Charleston*!
I wonder where she's gone,
And how she's getting on.
I wonder where my Baby is tonight.'

Imperceptibly my embarrassment slipped away and I began to throw myself into the idiotic frenzy of the dance. It was, after all, an extraordinary catchy rhythm, if only one could capture it; and, as it happened, I had the knack. I let myself go, and worked through all the variations and convolutions of the dance that I could think of. I even improvised a few cross-over steps and side-kicks.

Lord Flamborough, meanwhile, was giving a

145

demonstration of every gesture and flourish of the old-time dance-hall drummer. He sang; he bobbed up and down in his invalid chair; he threw his drumsticks in the air and caught them as they fell. He ended the performance with a clattering attack upon the cymbals.

'Oh boy, oh boy!' he exclaimed in ecstasy, as the record ended and we both relaxed, breathless. 'I haven't had such a work-out for months.'

I mopped my forehead and wiped the inside of my collar with my handkerchief. I felt very hot, and, now it was all over, very self-conscious.

'Reminds me of the old days at the Forty-Three,' said Lord Flamborough. 'Before your time, of course. Towards dawn Mrs Merrick used to let me play the drums. We used to burn the place up. Pity the bobbies had such a down on the old girl. She was a sweetie. Dead now, I believe.'

'That, I suppose, was before you lost your—' With horror I realized I was touching on a subject about which the Earl might be highly sensitive.

'Before I had my legs chopped off, you mean?' he said cheerfully. 'Yes, just before. I went back once or twice afterwards. But it wasn't quite the same. The girls seemed sorry for me, you know. Used to get morbid when they'd had a glass or two of bubbly. No good being morbid at the Forty-Three. So I packed it up, and came down here for good. Haven't been up to Town at all since then, except for a couple of Coronations.'

Listening to this matter-of-fact recital I found myself feeling very sorry for him.

'What bad luck, sir,' I said, haltingly.

'Bad luck? Wasn't bad luck at all! My own silly fault. Don't you start getting morbid too. Nothing to get morbid over. I've no complaints. Happy as a sand-boy. If one can't be cheerful sitting down one isn't likely to be cheerful standing up. What about another number?

Shall we try "Sweet Hortense" this time?'

'Don't you think, sir,' I said, 'that we ought to deal with this other matter first?'

'Oh yes,' said Lord Flamborough, looking puzzled. 'There *was* something I had to say to you, wasn't there? Can't for the life of me remember what.'

He twisted his chair round and wheeled it towards the door. 'Mabel!' he yelled. 'What was it I had to say to this young fellow?'

There was no reply. Whether Lady Flamborough had gone back to her rose garden, or was tactfully absenting herself from an embarrassing conversation, I could only guess.

'Never mind,' said Lord Flamborough, wheeling himself back to the gramophone. 'It'll come back. Let's put on another record. If you're too puffed to do another Charleston we might have something different. What would you say to "Riverboat Shuffle" or "Blackbottom Stomp"?'

'I'd love to hear either of them,' I said. 'But I'm supposed to be going up to the nets to get some practice for the cricket match. If you can't remember what it was you wanted to see me about, perhaps I'd better be going.'

'Cricket match? Oh, I remember what it was!' said Lord Flamborough. 'Of course! How stupid of me! It's about the Fête. We want you to present the prizes at the Fête – on Monday. Will you?'

'Present the prizes at the Fête!' I echoed, amazed. 'You want *me* to present the prizes?'

'Of course, my dear fellow! We'd be delighted if you would. My wife usually does it. But she's longing for a break.'

'But *me*. Why me?'

'Why not you?' said Lord Flamborough. 'You're the man from the Ministry; you're the big shot. And you've

147

made a hit personally down here. Everyone's pretty impressed by you – especially the women. You've got what it takes, you lucky devil!'

'B – but,' I stammered, 'what will the Professor think of this?'

'The Professor? Actually it was the Professor who suggested it – came to see me last night about it. You seem to have impressed him as much as anyone.'

I was completely at sea. 'Was . . . was that all you wanted to see me about?' I asked.

'Yes, my dear chap. That was it. Silly of me to have forgotten. But you'll say Yes, of course?'

There seemed to be nothing else I could say.

'That's fine!' said Lord Flamborough. 'Now let's have another Charleston. I'd like you to try "Sweet Hortense". It's got a peculiarly quick but unobtrusive beat. Tricky. You'll like it.'

About noon I managed to stem the flood of vintage jazz and tumble out, dazed, but also surprisingly exhilarated, on to the station platform.

'Don't forget about the Fête,' Lord Flamborough called after me.

Forget about it! I was still so astounded at having been asked to present the prizes that I could think of nothing else. Here was I, a stranger – indeed, an interloper – and I was being accorded the position of honour at what was evidently a time-honoured local ceremony. What was even more extraordinary was that my encounters with Belinda and Matilda, which, on superficial evidence, might well have revealed me in a very unfavourable light, seemed to have gained for me an undeserved prestige. I was baffled by it all.

On the other hand I couldn't help feeling flattered – and indeed a little elated – at the success I seemed to be having. Lord Flamborough had become more and more genial as we had worked our way through his record collection, from New Orleans to Swing, and from King Oliver to Duke Ellington. There wasn't a hint that I had overstepped the bounds of propriety with his daughters: indeed he had made one or two jovial and appreciative references to what he called my 'way with the women'.

Equally surprising was the fact that the Professor, of all people, had suggested me for the prize-giving at the Fête. I must have misjudged him completely; I had certainly got the impression that he viewed me with suspicion and disapproval.

I found myself whistling snatches from Lord Flamborough's records as I walked through the park to the Hall. Overhead the sky was a pellucid blue, such as one never saw in London. On the horizon rested a few puff-balls of pure white cloud which threw the blue into even more vivid contrast. The sun blazed down. The hedges were bright with wild roses and honeysuckle in bloom. Bees buzzed, birds sang, and summer was all it ought to be.

I walked briskly across the lawns towards the Hall, crossed the bridge over the moat, and walked through the open doorway of the gatehouse into the courtyard.

'Mr Pye! Mr Pye! We couldn't think what had happened to you.' Miss Mounsey came out of the stairway door and ran towards me. 'Mr Quirk was waiting to give you some cricket practice,' she said in a fluster. 'But he couldn't wait any longer, and he's had to go up to the green. They're all having lunch at the Virley Arms before the match. You're to join them there. I've put your cricket clothes out on the bed in your room – the ones Mr Quirk lent you, I mean – and I've cleaned the boots with whitening, and I think you'll find everything ready.' She ran out of breath.

'That's terribly kind of you, Mouse,' I said. 'I'll go up and change at once.'

Miss Mounsey appeared to be a little taken aback. 'I must get along to the green,' she said, blushing; turned, and hurried away. It was not until she had disappeared over the bridge that I realized I had unwittingly slipped into the prevailing convention of addressing her as 'Mouse'. Why it had embarrassed her I couldn't imagine.

However, it was very sweet of her to have got my cricket things ready. I went up to my room to change. White shirt, flannels, white socks, a white silk scarf, and an old dark red blazer were laid out neatly on the bed; a brilliantly blanco'd pair of cricket boots stood by the dressing-table. It merely remained for me to justify myself on the field. I changed as quickly as possible and ran downstairs again, carrying the cricket boots under my arm.

For some reason which I could not quite explain to myself – it was not solely due to Lord Flamborough's invitation to present the prizes at the Fête – I felt as though I now belonged to Arcady. I felt almost a school-boyish anxiety to do well in the cricket match – to take a few wickets or bring off a spectacular catch; perhaps even to score twenty runs or so. Unfortunately I realized how out of practice I was. And I recognized only too clearly that sinking feeling in the pit of the stomach which was the form my nervousness had always taken when I went on to the cricket field.

Out in the courtyard I ran into Lionel Virley. He was wearing a sun-tanned panama, an almost tangerine pair of flannels, and a faded I Zingari blazer. He was carrying a large and impressive leather cricket bag, from the opening of which protruded the necks of several bottles.

'All ginned-up for the joust or tourney?' he said

genially, running an appraising, watery eye over my cricket clothes.

'I wish I were,' I said with a laugh. 'I feel rather nervous.'

'Nervous, dear boy?' Lionel tapped the side of his nose. 'I've got the sovereign remedy. Never been known to fail. Come into the Buttery.'

'I don't really want to get ginned-up,' I protested hastily. 'I thought you only meant it as a figure of speech.'

'Of course I did, dear boy. Gin is useless on such occasions. Impairs the vision. Engenders false confidence. No, I've got something better than gin. Follow me.'

A little apprehensively I followed him across the courtyard and into the Buttery. He put his cricket bag down and went over to a cupboard. 'Hold these,' he said, handing me a couple of champagne glasses, 'while I pick the lock.'

He approached the door at the head of the steps to the dungeon, and took from the pocket of his blazer a curious metal contraption which seemed to consist mostly of bent wire.

'My dear wife keeps this door locked, y'know,' he said, 'in case I fall down the steps when I'm drunk. But I met a burglar one day in a pub in Ipswich and he let me have this gadget for picking locks. Surprising how effective it is.'

He inserted the bent end of the device into the keyhole, wriggled it about for a moment or two, and then twisted it. The lock turned. He opened the door.

'Down you go!' he said. 'Oh, just a minute; you'll want a light.'

He reached for a candlestick, lit the candle, and gave it to me. 'You go first. I'll follow.'

I climbed down the steps.

'Don't drop those glasses,' he called, as he pulled the door to after him.

I reached the foot of the stairs and held up the candle so that he could see his way down.

'I apologize for this cloak-and-dagger stuff,' he said. 'But it becomes necessary as one grows older to evolve a *modus vivendi*. My wife's ideas don't always coincide exactly with my own, and I find it more convenient to make independent arrangements for access. Now we mustn't be too long. It would never do for us to be late.'

He picked his way through the shadows to a wine bin against the far wall. 'Shine the light here, dear boy.'

I followed him and held the candle in front of the bin, which appeared to be stacked high with bottles, of different colours and shapes, all bearing white paper labels lettered in ink.

'What a cellar you have!' I said.

'Not bad, is it?' he said, leaning forward and searching along the shelves. 'All home-made. All my own vintage. Ah, here's the bottle I want!' He gently extracted a champagne bottle. The cork was held in position by wire. There was a written label on the side.

'You don't make your own champagne?' I asked, in surprise.

'Not from grapes, dear boy. But I think this is even better.' He held the bottle up for my examination. On the label was written, in an old-world copy-book hand, *Elderflower Champagne*.

'It's a bit of a gamble,' said Lionel, 'because it doesn't keep. You have to take it on the flood – drink it at the moment of truth.'

He undid the wire round the neck of the bottle and gently loosened the cork. 'Have the glasses ready,' he said.

The cork flew out with a resounding pop. Lionel filled both glasses with a sparkling amber fluid which fizzed and danced with bubbles.

'Here's to your century!' he said, raising his glass to his lips.

'Here's to yours!' I responded.

My instinctive apprehensions were soon dispelled. The wine was light and dry and singularly refreshing.

'Like it?' said Lionel.

'Yes, I do. It's certainly got a champagne quality. And it's beautifully dry.'

'I think we've got this at the right moment,' said Lionel. 'It was bottled three weeks ago. Won't keep more than four.'

'Is it really made from flowers?' I asked. 'Not from the berries?'

'Not from the berries,' said Lionel. 'Elderberry Wine is quite different – don't care for it myself. Elderberry Port isn't too bad, though. Got a few bottles over there. Won't be ready for a couple of years. But this stuff is made from the flowers. Nothing else in it but sugar, a sliced lemon and a spoonful or two of white vinegar. Have another glass?'

'Thank you,' I said. 'I hope it isn't very intoxicating. I'm not used to home-made wines.'

'Wouldn't harm a child,' said Lionel.

'It's certainly very light, and delightfully fizzy,' I said.

'Everything depends on the day when you pick the elder flowers,' said Lionel, re-filling my glass. 'You have to keep watch for the Bees' Day.'

'The *what*?'

'The Bees' Day. That's the day when the flowers are in full bloom, and it's sunny and still, and the bees cling to the blossoms all day as though they were too tiddly to fly. The very next day you must pick the blossoms – pick them when they're warm with the sun. Then, when you drink the wine, the scent of flowers should rise with the bubbles from the glass.'

In the candlelight, with his champagne glass raised

before his eyes, I seemed to see quite a different Lionel Virley from the rather boring toper I had encountered before. He was talking almost like a poet, and there was the gleam of the artist in his red-rimmed eyes.

'Mustn't be too long,' he said. 'But before we go I want you to compare a glass of Gooseberry Champagne. Shine the candle down here, will you, dear boy?'

He stooped down again and came up with another bottle.

'Are you sure this won't put us off our game?' I said.

'The very opposite,' said Lionel firmly, untying the wire and pulling the cork. 'Here, hold your glass out. It's empty, isn't it?'

I drank the last of the Elderflower, and Lionel filled my glass with Gooseberry.

'Here's to your hat-trick!' he said.

'Here's to yours,' I responded.

The Gooseberry Champagne was pink and had more body than the other, but it was not unduly sweet. As I drank it I felt the muscles of my stomach relaxing in a warm glow, and the nervous tension slackening.

'I never thought gooseberries could taste like this,' I said.

'This is a mature wine,' said Lionel. 'It's made from red gooseberries, of course. I make it in June; then it has to lie in the cask till the following April. I draw it off and bottle it when the gooseberry bushes are in flower again. Have another glass?'

'Thank you, I will.'

Lionel refilled my glass and his own.

'Has it put new heart into you?' he asked.

'It certainly has.'

'That's the brandy in it, of course.'

'Oh dear! Is it very potent?'

'As gentle as a mother's kiss,' said Lionel. 'It's mellow, you see. Mature.'

154

'How old is it?'

'Four years. And that reminds me; we'll be too late to make our centuries and do our hat-tricks if we don't get along. Drink up, dear boy. We must finish the bottle.'

I drank up. We finished the bottle.

'I think there's still a drop of the Elderflower left,' said Lionel. 'We'd better finish that.'

We finished the Elderflower.

'Speaking for myself,' said Lionel, 'I feel a new man. How are your nerves?'

'Gone,' I answered. 'I feel in fine fettle.'

'What impresses me,' said Lionel, 'is my clarity of vision. Goodness knows it's dark enough down here, but I can see you with singular luminosity. That promises well for my performance at the wicket.'

'We really ought to go now,' I said. 'It wouldn't do to turn up late.'

'You're right, dear boy. The thought had passed through my mind that we might feel even fitter if we topped off with a drop of Applejack. But perhaps we should go.'

'We certainly must go,' I said decisively, draining my glass. 'Will you go up the stairs first, and I'll follow with the candle.'

'A small glass of Applejack would have been agreeable,' said Lionel, wistfully. 'But we can't let the side down. To the wicket! *Marchons!*'

He handed me his empty wineglass, felt in his pocket for the lock-picking device, and made his way to the foot of the stairs.

'You must watch your steps as you follow me,' he said. 'These stairs are a bit tricky if you don't know them.'

He walked briskly up the steps. I followed closely behind him, carrying the empty wineglasses and the candle.

'I could find my way up here blindfold,' said Lionel.

155

'Damn and blast!' He appeared to trip over the turn in the staircase, lurched forward, and measured his length on the steps. As he fell his arm swung round, brushed against the candle, and extinguished the flame. Fortunately I was able to retain my grip on the candlestick and keep my balance.

'Damn and blast!' repeated Lionel, scrambling about in the darkness ahead of me. 'I've never done that before. I do apologize, dear boy.'

'Never mind,' I said. 'It was my fault for following too closely behind you. Stay where you are whilst I light the candle again.'

I set the two champagne glasses down on the steps and felt in my pockets for my matches. I had none. Evidently I had left them in the pocket of my suit when I changed into my cricket clothes.

'Can you let me have a match?' I asked. 'I don't seem to have any.'

I heard Lionel fumbling in his pockets. 'I'll see if I have any,' he said. 'But I've just given up smoking. And I've given up carrying matches, too. No, I haven't got any. Are you sure you haven't any?'

I felt in all my pockets again.

'Quite sure,' I said. 'We'll have to manage without a light. Lucky that you can find your way up these stairs blindfold.'

'No need to be sarcastic, dear boy,' said Lionel. 'It was pure mischance that I tripped at that corner. Now watch how I find my way up.'

'I can't watch you, you ass! It's pitch dark,' I said. 'But carry on. I'll stay here till you've opened the door.'

I heard Lionel's footfalls as he climbed the stairs. There was no hesitation: he certainly knew his way. 'What did I tell you?' he called gaily, as he reached the top.

There was a pause.

'I say,' he said in a less confident tone, 'I haven't got the lock-picking gadget. I must have dropped it when I fell. Feel around, dear boy, and see if you can find it.'

'Do you mean to say you locked the door behind you when we came down here?' I asked querulously.

'Of course, dear boy. I didn't want Chloe to come back unexpectedly and find it unlocked. She might have smelt a rat.'

'Then we're locked in?'

'We're locked in, dear boy . . . until you find that lock-picking affair and pass it up to me.'

I put down the now useless candle, knelt on the steps, and began to feel around for the burglar's tool.

'Search for it methodically,' said Lionel. 'Start two or three steps above where I fell, and work your way down.'

'That's precisely what I'm doing,' I said irritably.

'No need to get shirty, dear boy,' said Lionel. 'We could be locked in a worse place.'

I worked my way backwards down the stairs, running my hands methodically over each step. Eventually I touched something, but before I realized what it was there was a crash of splintering glass on the stone floor below.

'For heaven's sake, man! What have you done?' cried Lionel. 'Don't say you've broken the wineglasses?'

'I'm afraid I've broken one of them,' I said. 'But I've got the other safely, here.'

'The Lord be praised! Hold on, now. I'm coming down.'

'What are you going to do?'

'I'm going to take that wineglass from you,' said Lionel, 'and put it in a safe place.'

He stepped down to me with surprising assurance, felt for my hand, and took the wineglass from me.

'Now follow me,' he said, 'and be careful where you put your feet.'

157

Cautiously we felt our way down to the foot of the stairs.

'Now go on searching for that lock-picking gadget,' said Lionel, 'while I deal with this wineglass.'

I went down on my knees again, and methodically searched every step from the bottom up to the turning where Lionel had slipped.

'I don't suppose it's on the stairs,' called Lionel from below. 'I expect it fell right down to the bottom. Come down and search the floor.'

I descended cautiously to the foot of the stairs again, and began to run my hands over the stone floor of the dungeon.

'I don't see any hope of finding it,' I said, after searching for some time. 'It's probably fallen somewhere among those wine bins.'

At that moment I put my hand down hard on a sharp and jagged object.

'Damnation!' I exclaimed. 'I've cut myself on the broken glass.'

'Sorry about that, dear boy,' said Lionel. 'Is it bleeding much?'

'How can I tell?' I said sharply, getting to my feet and wrapping a handkerchief round the injured hand. 'I'm not a cat. I can't see in the dark.'

'Suck it and see,' said Lionel with a jolly laugh.

'That doesn't seem to me to be in the least funny,' I said curtly. 'And what about the cricket match? Whatever will people think of us – failing to turn up like this?'

'Keep calm, dear boy,' said Lionel, feeling his way through the darkness towards me. 'Take a sip of this. It's just what you need when you're suffering from shock.'

'I'm not suffering from shock,' I said angrily. 'I've merely cut my hand.'

'Well, take a sip of this in any case,' said Lionel soothingly, and he put the remaining wineglass into my hand.

'I hope you won't mind if we share the same glass. But I felt I had to have a nip to pull myself together after that nasty tumble I took.'

Everything seemed so hopeless that I did as he suggested, and gulped down the contents of the glass.

'Better?' said Lionel.

'Phew!' I gasped, catching my breath. 'Whatever's that? Fire-water?'

'Don't be offensive, dear boy,' said Lionel. 'That is my very finest, seven-year-old Applejack. I don't believe you'd find a liqueur to equal it in the best restaurant in London.'

I felt a curious tingling in my cheeks, and a warm, expansive glow in my midriff.

'It's not bad at all,' I admitted, 'once one gets over the initial shock.'

'Have some more,' said Lionel, replacing the glass in my hand.

I had some more. It was certainly an unusual and tasty – if somewhat fiery – beverage. And its tonic effect was instantaneous.

'I don't see any point in continuing the search for that burglar's gadget,' said Lionel. 'We can't have you cutting yourself on bits of broken glass. Sit down here on this packing-case, and we'll wait till someone rescues us.'

'Do you think they will?' I asked, sitting down as he had suggested. As I did so there came the pop of another cork being pulled.

'No doubt about it,' said Lionel. 'They can't start the match without their two best players; so they'll have to send out a search party. Meanwhile I'd like you to tell me what you think of this.' He reached out to make sure where I was, and put the wineglass into my hand again.

'D'you think I ought to go on drinking like this?' I asked.

'I do,' said Lionel. 'No doubt about it.'

I drank. This was something different. It had a slightly

earthy flavour, but was agreeably dry, and had a noticeable kick.

'Carrot Whisky,' said Lionel. 'May I have the glass back so that I can taste it myself?'

I passed it back to him. We had now got a certain sense of each other's whereabouts in the darkness.

'How do you know it's Carrot Whisky?' I asked. 'You can't see the labels on the bottles.'

'I know that one by the shape of the bottle,' Lionel replied. There was a pause while he poured out another glass for himself and drank it.

'That last question of yours,' he said, 'has put an idea into my head. Why don't we open half a dozen bottles, from different bins, and see if we can identify them in the dark? Excellent practice, you know. Everything will depend on the palate.'

It seemed to me an absurd idea, but I felt too weary to demur. Lionel rose to his feet and I heard him stumbling round the cellar, collecting bottles from different places and feeling his way back with them to the two upturned packing-cases which had become our headquarters.

'Never thought of doing this before,' he said, as he began to pull the corks. 'But it's an extremely interesting exercise. We shall miss the pleasure and piquancy of the colour, of course, but it'll be a hundred-per-cent test of flavour and bouquet. Pity we can't rinse out the glass between tastings, but I'll swill it out each time with some of the wine we're going to taste next, so that one won't contaminate another.'

I heard the gurgle of another drink being poured. 'Try this,' he said. 'Bouquet first; then a sip or two.'

I took the glass and held it to my nose. There was a lovely aroma of flowers in bloom; but what flowers I couldn't say. I took a sip; two sips. Delicious. But I hadn't the faintest idea what it was.

I handed the glass back to Lionel. A few moments later

he gave his opinion. 'It might be Marigold. Or it might be Cowslip. I can detect the brandy in it, anyway. On balance I think it's Marigold. Now for the next.'

There was an interval, during which I heard sounds of movement, of splashes, and of liquor being poured. 'I'm pouring the lees into an empty cask,' said Lionel. 'They won't be wasted. Now let's have your verdict on this.'

I took the glass from him again, sniffed it, and drank the contents. 'Elixir of the gods,' I said.

'Nice of you to say so,' said Lionel. 'But we must try to be more exact. Let me have the glass, dear boy, and I'll see if I can identify it.'

Some time later – I think I must have dozed as a result of having been so long in the dark – I heard Lionel delivering his judgment. 'It's either Birch or Sycamore. Almost certain it's one I made from the sap of a tree. You have to tap the trunk, you know. Tricky operation. But the result's well worth while. A bit too effervescent if you aren't careful. But the flavour's distinctive. I'm almost certain this is Birch. Now we'll try another.'

'I think,' I said, 'I'm going to sit on the floor. Then I can lean back against this packing-case and relax.'

'Good idea,' said Lionel. 'Essential to relax. Concentrate all your energies in the taste-buds. No distractions.'

At intervals during the next hour or so I felt Lionel shake my shoulder, rouse me, and pass me a fresh glass of wine. They were all delicious, but I left the identification to him.

'This,' I heard him say, 'is undoubtedly Citron Water. I can taste the balm in it.' Or: 'I believe we've got Oak Leaf here. But there's just a chance it may be Walnut – made from the leaves, of course; you get something altogether different if you use the nuts.'

We must have sampled about a dozen bottles when I

began to get cramp in my thigh from the coldness of the stone floor. I heaved myself up on to the packing-case again.

'I believe we're drinking Hawthorn now,' Lionel was saying. 'They say it's a very good tonic for the heart. Just the thing to drink before one goes in to bat.'

I scrambled to my feet in sudden alarm, kicking over the cask of lees as I did so.

'Steady on, dear boy,' said Lionel. 'What's bitten you? Relax, relax!'

'Lionel,' I said, in a sudden access of dismay. 'We ought to've been out on the cricket field hours ago. It's the big match. We're letting the side down.'

'By Jove, you're right!' said Lionel. 'I was so absorbed in the wine-tasting that I'd quite forgotten the time.'

'What is the time, Lionel?'

'No idea, Jasper. I used to have a timepiece with a luminous dial, but I popped it last week in Saxmundham. Had to realize all my assets, y'know, to buy that traction engine. Good old Susie! Susie's the girl!'

'Never mind about Susie,' I said with decision. 'We've got to get out of here. We're letting the side down if we don't.'

'Entirely agree with you, dear boy. But how d'you set about it?'

'Can't think,' I said, sitting down suddenly; the darkness made me feel rather dizzy.

'No use hunting for that lock-picking gadget,' said Lionel. 'You'd only cut yourself again on the broken glass. How is your hand, by the way? Are you bleeding to death?'

'I've no idea. But I don't feel at all well.'

'Have another glass of Applejack,' said Lionel. 'That'll pull you together.'

'No,' I said firmly. 'I'm going to get out of here. I'm going to rattle the door until someone hears me.'

162

'Carry on, dear boy!' said Lionel. 'Excuse me if I don't come with you, but I've got just one more bottle here which I haven't opened yet.'

I stood up. 'Can you direct me to the stairs?' I asked. I had the curious illusion that the darkness was revolving around me. It was distinctly disturbing to my sense of balance and direction.

'If you walk directly away from me,' said Lionel, 'I think you will walk into the wall. You ought to find the stairs then, a little to your left.'

I turned round and followed his instructions. Now that I was moving I felt rather better. After five or six steps I barked my shin on a solid stone object. I bent down and found I had walked into the foot of the stairs.

'You all right?' inquired Lionel.

'I'm in acute pain,' I replied in Spartan tones. 'But I've found the stairs, and I am now going to ascend.'

'Take care, dear boy. You don't want to fall and fracture your skull. I think this last bottle, incidentally, is Hip.'

'Hep?' I said. 'I've never heard of a wine being hep. What are you digging?'

'I said Hip – H-I-P,' said Lionel. 'And I'm not digging; I'm drinking.'

'Hip, hip, hooray!' I said wittily.

'It's made from crushed hips,' continued Lionel, 'and—'

'That's neither right nor proper,' I interjected, 'like the chorus girl's left hip.' I couldn't help laughing for a long time at the aptness of my joke.

'I'm not referring to chorus girls' hips,' said Lionel stuffily. 'I'm talking about hips and haws. Haws with an "h", of course, not a "w".'

'I'm on my way up,' I announced.

The sharp pain of barking my shin against the stone edge of the steps had somehow cleared my head and given me fresh energy. I stepped quite briskly up the stairs, guiding myself with one hand on the wall.

The door at the stairhead was just discernible in the darkness by the tiny cracks of light down either side. I ran my hands over it until I found and grasped a heavy iron latch.

'I've got hold of the door,' I called to Lionel, 'and I'm going to rattle it like mad until somebody comes.'

'Don't let me stop you, dear boy!' said Lionel. 'But I don't suppose there's anyone there to hear you. They'll all be up on the village green. It's the big cricket match today, you know: Arcady versus Flaxfield.'

I lifted the latch with both hands and gave it a violent shake. To my utter astonishment the door immediately flew open. I pitched headlong across the floor of the Buttery.

Blinking in the glare of the daylight I staggered to my feet and stumbled back to the head of the dungeon steps. 'Lionel, you damn fool,' I cried, leaning through the doorway, 'the door wasn't locked all the time.'

Lionel came lurching up the steps. 'What'n extraordinary thing!' he exclaimed as he emerged into the light, holding the wineglass in one hand and a bottle in the other. 'Must be something wrong with the lock-picking device. I certainly twiddled it in the key-hole when I came down.'

'You idiot!' I shouted at him. 'I don't suppose it's intended to lock a door – only to unlock it.'

We looked at each other, and then both of us burst out laughing.

'Well, I never thought of that,' said Lionel, pouring out the last drop from the wine bottle and sipping it reflectively. 'Still, never mind! We've had a most int'resting experience, and a first-class party. Now we must get along and score our centuries.'

'Do our hat-tricks, too,' I added.

Lionel leaned forward and picked up his cricket bag. I was sorry to see that he seemed to be a little unsteady on his feet. I took his arm. As we walked into the sunshine I heard the church clock strike five.

We walked together through the garden towards the village green. It became apparent to me that Lionel was distinctly the worse for his experiences. His speech was halting and indistinct; he swayed from side to side of the path. Twice he caused me to stumble and fall into the lavender hedge.

I, on the other hand, was in remarkably good shape. The dizziness and lassitude which I had experienced when we were down in the dungeon had given way to an unwonted sense of energy and power. I had some slight difficulty in focusing my eyes on objects a little distance away, but that, no doubt, was due to the contrast between the brilliant sunshine and the darkness from which we had emerged. As for my nerves, they had been completely quelled by the glass or two of wine which I had taken, and I now felt relaxed, self-confident, ready to face anything.

As we stepped through the door in the wall that opened on to the village green there was an outburst of clapping and groans, and one of the batsmen started to walk towards the pavilion. The fieldsmen gathered round his wrecked wicket.

'That's Percy Pott just been bowled,' said Lionel. 'We're batting. Help is on the way!' he shouted.

The spectators round the edge of the field, sitting on benches or deck-chairs, leaning against trees, or lying in the long grass, turned and regarded us with curiosity. Then there came a shrill cheer from a group of children by the scoreboard. 'It's Mister Lionel! Good old Lion!' Quirk, wearing pads and carrying a bat, broke away

165

from the group of players outside the pavilion and came running towards us.

'Where have you been? Whatever have you been up to?' he cried. 'Come quickly! We've only three more wickets in hand.'

'Steady, dear boy!' said Lionel, reassuringly. 'I'm sorry we're late, but we were unavoidably detained. Now we're here, and *hic manemus*. How's the game going?'

Quirk grabbed hold of Lionel's bag and hustled us towards the pavilion. 'We're in a tight spot,' he said, breathlessly. 'We put them in to bat and got them out by tea-time for 104 . . .'

'Not bad,' said Lionel. 'That's nothing to worry about.'

'Not bad at all,' said Quirk irritably, 'considering we were without two of our best players and had to field a couple of substitutes. But when we went in to bat, after tea, nothing seemed to go right.'

I glanced at the scoreboard. 'We appear to have lost six wickets for 48 runs,' I said. 'That doesn't look promising.'

'It doesn't,' said Quirk, propelling Lionel through the door of the pavilion. 'Now it all depends on you – and the umpires,' he added bitterly.

'The usual umpire trouble?' said Lionel, with a meaning glance.

'Worse than usual,' said Quirk. 'The umpire the Flaxfield people have brought is Charley Aspall, the publican from The Fox and Goose. He's not only outrageously partisan; he's also drunk.'

'Disgusting!' said Lionel.

'He disallowed every appeal we made when Flaxfield were batting, and he no-balled Jones eight times,' said Quirk. 'Now he has given four of our men out lbw and one caught out off a bump ball.'

'Disgraceful!' said Lionel. 'But what's our umpire been doing all this time?'

'Our umpire is the Professor,' said Quirk miserably. 'And, as you know, he's as upright as a judge. He wouldn't dream of giving a decision that wasn't in accordance with the facts.'

'Absurd! Quite absurd!' said Lionel.

'Well, you know the Prof,' said Quirk. 'He's got this idea that cricket's only a game, and should be played according to the rules.'

'Ridiculous!' said Lionel.'Now, when do I go in?'

'As you weren't here,' said Quirk, 'I put you down as number ten. I'm number nine, and Mr Pye is number eight. You're next man in, Mr Pye. You'd better get your pads on.'

I was leaning against the rustic woodwork of the pavilion, enjoying the gracious and typically English scene unfolded before me, when the significance of Quirk's words sank in. For a moment I felt a return of my earlier apprehensions.

'Oh dear! Couldn't I go in last?'

'No,' said Quirk. 'We're keeping Jones till last, in case we need some stone-walling. You're a stylist, Mr Pye. We're looking to you to impress these Flaxfield chaps. Go inside and put your pads on now. A wicket may fall at any minute.' He handed me pads and batting gloves, and pushed me into the pavilion.

I sat down on a bench, changed into my cricket boots, and began to strap on the pads. As I leaned forward I felt a recurrence of the dizziness I had experienced in the dungeon. I laid my head on my arms.

'Are you all right, dear boy?' asked Lionel, who was fumbling in his cricket bag.

'I feel a bit dizzy,' I admitted. 'It must be the effect of sitting in the darkness for so long.'

'We'll soon put that right,' said Lionel, and pulled a flask out of his hip pocket. 'Take a swig at that,' he said, passing it over to me.

I took a swig, and a glow of reassurance ran through me. Almost at once the dizziness disappeared.

'Better?' said Lionel.

'Much better,' I said.

Lionel took the flask from me and had a drink himself. 'It's the ever-faithful Applejack,' he said. 'Absolutely infallible as a pick-me-up. Strong, mind you. Doesn't do to take too much.'

'I think I've had just the right amount,' I said. 'I feel on top of the world now.'

'That's the spirit!' said Lionel. He bent over his cricket bag and pulled out a bottle. 'Better refill the flask, in case of emergencies.'

I finished strapping up my pads, chose a bat from several which Quirk had set out for me, and went outside.

'Come and sit here, Jasper darling,' said a familiar voice. Lady Belinda was sprawling on the grass beside an empty deck-chair, regarding me with a provocative smile. She was wearing her usual blue jeans, and was eating an ice-cream. I sat down in the deck-chair beside her.

'Are you in good form?' she asked.

'I feel on top of the world,' I said with conviction.

'You look smashing,' said Belinda. 'You'll get a rousing reception from the village maidens when you go in to bat.'

'I shall need it,' I said, 'judging by the state of the scoreboard.'

'Are you very drunk?' asked Belinda. 'Mummy's got some smelling salts in her bag over there. I'll get them for you if you'd like a sniff. Oh, crumbs! They've given Albert out.'

I looked out to the wicket, to see the umpire pointing inexorably to the skies, and a youthful Arcady batsman wending his way in dejection towards the pavilion.

'You're next, Mr Pye,' said Quirk. 'It all depends on you.'

I rose with deliberation, and drew on my batting gloves. I became aware that all faces were turned towards me.

'Jolly good luck to you!' called Miss Tidy, who was sitting beyond the pavilion with Lord and Lady Flamborough.

'Try some of those fancy Charleston steps,' said his Lordship.

'Steady, the Buffs!' said Jones, patting me on the shoulder.

'*Hic manemus!*' cried Lionel hoarsely, from within the pavilion.

I observed that even the peacock had turned out to watch my performance, though at the moment he seemed more interested in studying his own reflection in the bumper of one of the spectators' cars.

I bent down to pick up my bat. 'I am not drunk,' I said to Belinda firmly but quietly. 'And I do not require smelling salts.'

'Darling, you're divine!' she answered, rolling over in the grass and blowing me a kiss. 'I simply adore you.'

'I shall be watching you every moment,' said a low voice at my elbow. 'And I shall be *willing* you to cover yourself with glory.'

I turned and found myself gazing down into Matilda's dark and mesmeric eyes.

'I shall see what I can do about it,' I said. I walked out to the wicket amidst gratifying manifestations of goodwill.

Having taken guard, I prepared to receive what I was told would be the last ball of the over. I noticed that all sensations of nervousness had departed from me. Indeed, I felt so self-confident that I hardly saw the bowler's approach to the wicket. Before I could shape for a stroke the ball approached me from an entirely unexpected direction and struck me sharply on the back of the hand. Thence it rose into the air in a graceful curve, mid-way between myself and the bowler.

As the bowler ran eagerly forward to catch it some sixth sense told me that the situation called for decisive action.

'Come on! There's a run there!' I yelled to my partner at the other end, and I set off briskly down the pitch. With equal speed, though with a look of incredulity on his face, my partner responded to my call.

Neither of us, as we sped down the pitch, had taken into account the fact that the bowler was doing likewise. Despite last-minute attempts at evasive action my partner and I arrived in mid-wicket simultaneously with the bowler. The three of us collided, with no little degree of violence, just as the bowler was holding out his hands to receive the ball.

'I do apologize,' I said earnestly to the bowler as we all three picked ourselves off the ground and my partner and I scuttled back to our starting-points.

'Apologize!' growled the bowler, a wizened, ferret-like creature, as he stooped to pick up the ball. 'Obstruction! That's what that was. Umpire, I appeal for obstruction – obstruction of the field.'

'H'out!' said the square-leg umpire, who was, so I understood, the landlord of The Fox and Goose in Flaxfield. 'Definitely h'out for obstruction.'

He had not, however, reckoned with his learned colleague at the other end. 'I am sorry to have to differ from you, Mr Aspall,' said the Professor in his most pontifical tones. 'But if you study the Laws of the Game as printed in *Wisden's Cricketers' Almanac* you will find that the umpire officiating at the bowler's end, as I am the noo, has jurisdiction in a case of this kind. It was evident to me that Mr Pye, though obviously suffering pain from the blow on his hand, made every effort to avoid the bowler.

The collision which unfortunately occurred was sheer mischance.'

'What's the old bleeder talking about?' said the bowler, glancing round the field.

'I pronounce the batsman No' Out,' said the Professor decisively. 'And that is the end of the over.'

'The old bleeder!' muttered the bowler, tossing the ball to his captain as the fielders crossed over.

Feeling, as I did, a little ruffled by this unfortunate incident, I was rather glad that we had not been able to complete our run, and in consequence I did not have to take the first ball of the next over. I had already noted that the bowler who was about to perform at the other end delivered the ball with extreme speed. In contrast to the ferret-faced bowler (who was still muttering imprecations on the Professor) he was heavily built, with long, pendulous arms and ape-like shoulders. He had a lock of long red hair which flashed across his forehead when he delivered the ball.

My fellow batsman, having adjusted his pads and brushed the dust off his trousers, prepared to take the first ball of the over. I stood to the side as the ape-man started his run, accelerated, and lashed the air with his arms.

The ball was very wide on the leg-side. The batsman swung round at it, misjudged it, and snicked it hard on to his pads.

'Howzatt!' screamed the ape-man.

'H'out!' said Mr Aspall of The Fox and Goose, without an instant's hesitation.

'But I hit it,' murmured the batsman.

'H'out!' repeated the umpire, holding up his hand and shaking his index finger. 'Leg before wicket.'

The batsman turned reluctantly, and walked slowly to the pavilion.

'Disputing the h'umpire's decision, was he!' said Mr

Aspall, breathing fumes of whisky over me. 'I don't know what these young fellers are coming to. H'out? Of course he was h'out. Leg before bleeding wicket. H'out.'

Quirk was the next man in. His trim bearing and his sun-tanned, weatherbeaten countenance inspired confidence. I noticed the fieldsmen glancing with respect at his faded Free Foresters cap. He took guard carefully, studied the placing of the field, and then settled himself at the crease.

The ape-man pounded up, whirled himself into the act of propulsion, and delivered an extremely short ball, on the off-side. Quirk flashed his bat at it in an elegant square cut, but missed it by about a foot. The ball landed with a thud in the wicket-keeper's gloves.

'Howzatt!' the ape-man yelled again, throwing his flaming forelock out of his eyes and glaring at the landlord of The Fox and Goose.

'H'out!' said Mr Aspall, holding up his hand. 'Well caught, Harry!' he added.

Quirk lingered at the wicket for a moment in an agony of disbelief; then gradually the public school spirit mastered his resentment, and he turned without a word of protest or complaint, and retraced his steps to the pavilion.

I felt extremely sorry for him. I was also deeply shocked. It was a disgraceful decision – a travesty of sportsmanship. But what could I do? I glanced at Mr Aspall, who was openly receiving the congratulations of the Flaxfield players. 'Plumb h'out!' he repeated, drunkenly. 'Not a shadow of doubt. Caught at the wicket. Plumb h'out. Could 'ave 'eard the snick a mile off.'

I turned away in disgust and perceived Lionel Virley, still wearing his ancient panama, and with an I Zingari scarf knotted round his neck, rolling jovially towards the wicket, to the accompaniment of delighted yells from the juvenile element in the audience. He arrived at the crease and took guard.

'Middle-and-leg, please, Charley!' he called. 'And how's yourself? Drunk, as usual?'

The landlord of The Fox and Goose leered at him with some semblance of geniality.

'Speak for yerself, Mr Lionel,' he said. 'For me own part, I could do with a pint. A little more towards you. That's right. Covers the two.'

'Thanks, Charley boy,' said Lionel cheerfully. 'Did you ever hear the one about the cauliflower and the Scotsman's kilt?'

'Eh, what's that?' inquired Mr Aspall.

'It'll keep,' said Lionel, preparing to take the bowling.

The ape-man pounded past me and delivered a fast good-length ball on the direct line of Lionel's middle stump. Lionel swung his bat vigorously and hit the ball over the long-on boundary. His supporters in the crowd, both young and old, screamed with delight.

The ape-man glared. His next ball was a bumper, very short. With majestic ease Lionel hooked it into the long grass beyond square-leg. There ensued a cacophony of screeches, clapping, and cat-calls. 'Bravo, Lion!' the children yelled.

In a fury of frustration the ape-man returned to the attack. 'Bowl one at 'is head!' muttered Charley Aspall. 'He's always so pickled he's bound to miss it.'

The next ball was indeed aimed with remarkable accuracy at Lionel's head. As he shaped to hook it I went cold with apprehension. To my intense relief, however, Lionel checked his stroke at the last moment, ducked, dropped his bat, and fell flat on the ground. The ball flew harmlessly over his head and went for four byes.

'Missed him! Blast it!' exclaimed the ape-man.

Lionel lifted himself to his feet, picked up his bat, and gave me a broad wink.

'There's one more ball to come, isn't there, Charley?' he called to the umpire.

'Yus,' said Charley Aspall dourly.

'I'll try and get up to your end,' said Lionel gaily, 'so I can tell you that one about the cauliflower and the Scotsman's kilt.'

The next ball was a good-length one, on the leg-stump. Lionel played a cow-shot, of the most agricultural type, and skied the ball deep into the outfield towards the scoreboard. I saw a fielder running round the boundary to take the catch.

'Come on, dear boy!' shouted Lionel. 'We can get a run there. He'll probably drop it.'

We ran a quick single, then turned to see what was happening in the outfield. Lionel was right. As the Flaxfield fielder ran to take the catch a dog tore out from the group of children standing round the scoreboard, and threw himself, yapping enthusiastically, between the fielder's ankles. The fielder tripped, pitched forward, and turned a double somersault, to the gratification of the dog and its juvenile coadjutors.

The dog was the first to extract himself from the mêlée. He picked up the ball in his mouth, and began to run at top speed towards the pavilion.

'Come on, dear boy,' yelled Lionel. 'There are two or three more runs for the asking.'

We ran – two, three, four more runs.

Then I heard warning cries, and I saw one of the Flaxfield fielders throw himself upon the dog, remove the ball from its teeth, and throw it hard back to the bowler's wicket.

'That's all we can manage,' I shouted.

'And quite enough, too,' gasped Lionel, staggering to the bowler's end as the ball flew in from the outfield and broke the wicket.

'Howzatt?' screamed the ape-man, jumping in the air and pointing triumphantly at the shattered stumps.

174

'H'out!' said Charley Aspall.

'Charley, Charley! What's this I hear?' said Lionel, when he had regained his breath.

'You're h'out, Mr Lionel,' said Charley. 'Run yourself h'out.'

'Well, who'd have guessed it?' said Lionel ruefully, gazing down at the stumps. 'Ah well, *c'est la vie*. Now, Charley boy, I'll tell you about the cauliflower and the Scotsman's kilt.'

He took Charley Aspall by the arm.

'Thirsty?' he asked.

'Not 'arf,' said Charley.

'Have a nip of this,' said Lionel, pulling his flask out of his hip pocket.

'I don't mind if I do,' said Mr Aspall.

'Well,' said Lionel, handing him the flask, 'this Scotsman went into a greengrocer's shop and . . .' he lowered his voice. After a few moments a series of convulsions in Mr Aspall's belly indicated that the anecdote had been well received.

'I must be going, I suppose, Charley,' said Lionel, 'since you've given me out.'

'Sorry, Mr Lionel!' said Charley sheepishly. 'I couldn't 'elp but do it.'

'Well,' said Lionel, 'you'd better hang on to my flask and assuage your conscience with drink.'

'That's very decent of you, Mr Lionel,' said Charley, as Lionel ambled off towards the pavilion, where he was received with considerable warmth. In the present state of the game his rapid contribution of sixteen runs had been invaluable.

'Over!' called Charley Aspall, and took himself off to the square-leg position, where I saw him celebrating, with the aid of Lionel's flask, the removal of three members of the Arcady eleven, by barefaced miscarriages of justice, in the course of six balls.

The last man in was Jones. As he stepped jauntily

175

towards the wicket I saw that the total on the score-board was 72. Jones and I had to score thirty-three runs for the last wicket if we were to win. Whether we did so or not seemed to depend less upon Jones and myself than upon the activities of Charley Aspall.

The last run had brought me to the batting end. I pre-pared to face the ferret-like slow bowler, secure in the knowledge that for the next six balls, at any rate, the administration of the laws would rest primarily in the Professor's hands.

The first ball from the ferret was tossed gently into the air a little way outside the off-stump. I saw it with singular clarity, advanced my left leg down the wicket, and executed a copy-book cover drive. To my chagrin, however, the ball evaded the bat, disappeared from view, and ended up in the wicket-keeper's gloves, well to the leg-side of the wicket.

'Extraordinary!' I ejaculated.

'Watch out for the chinaman, Mr Pye,' called Jones. Evidently I had been deceived by the spin.

The next ball was a full toss, a little to the leg. It was a gift to any batsman. I decided to make that easy sweep to leg which used to be a favourite stroke of Denis Compton's. I crouched down, fixed my eyes on the approaching object, and swept with all my force.

'How's that?' yelled eleven players as the ball landed on my left toe.

The Professor gulped, reflected for a moment, and then shook his head. There were rebellious murmurings round the field.

The next ball pitched on the leg-stump. I played it defensively with that assured dead-bat stroke so char-acteristic of Trevor Bailey. For some unaccountable reason, however, the ball changed direction. It passed three inches outside the bat, and about half an inch outside the off-stump.

I was baffled. For the first time in my innings I felt a certain ebbing of confidence. I also began to feel a recurrence of that dizziness which had afflicted me down in the dungeon. I must stop poking about, I decided, and have a go. The next ball was short, and I had plenty of time to watch it as it rose, quite slowly, to a convenient height from which I could hook it for six over the mid-wicket boundary. As I played my stroke, however, I was momentarily unbalanced, and the ground ahead of me seemed to rise up and obscure my view. The next thing I knew was that the ball had hit me in the pit of the stomach.

'How's that?' eleven voices cried.

'No' out!' said the Professor irritably. Then he lowered his voice. 'For heaven's sake, Pye, do hit the ball next time.'

Bending forward and attempting to regain my wind. I felt somewhat resentful of this unwarranted exhortation by one whose sole function was to administer the rules. I decided to show the Professor what I thought of it.

The next ball was rather short and some way outside the off-stump. A less experienced player than I might have seen fit to slash it through the covers for four. I, however, stepped smartly in front of the wicket, raised my bat high above my head, and permitted the ball to pass by innocuously without making a stroke.

It was at this point that I became aware of critical judgment being passed by some of the spectators. A few isolated comments, of a ribald or sarcastic nature, had greeted my efforts up to date; but now an unmannerly section of the crowd began to engage in what I could only assume to be a slow hand-clap.

My dizziness had returned, as a consequence of my energetic motions, and the heat of the sun was now creating the illusion that the ground was rising and falling, like waves at sea. I determined that the next ball was going to be hit for six.

'Try an' pick out the middle one, cock!' exhorted Jones, as the ferret began his run. Before the ball had left the ferret's hand I was several yards down the pitch, waiting for it. As it travelled towards me I flourished my bat and gave it all I knew.

I had a moment of black-out; then I heard Jones crying 'Come on!' I ran rapidly to the far end of the wicket, where, on arrival, I found that I no longer had the bat in my hands. One of the opposing players retrieved it from square-leg and handed it back to me.

'Thank you so much,' I said. 'Did I hit that one?'

'No, Guv,' he replied. 'But the ball hit you on the hip and you've scored a leg-bye.'

It was the end of the over. I heard the Professor muttering as he stalked away to the square-leg position. He appeared to be expressing the view that I should not last long against the combined onslaught of the ape-man and Charley Aspall. The latter, I noticed, was swaying in his stride as he walked to take up his position at the bowler's end. Then I noticed that several of the Flaxfield players also seemed to be lurching from side to side. I wondered whether perhaps they were not all a little the worse for drink.

However, icy-cold, and still completely self-possessed, I took guard. As the ape-man came thudding towards me, his features contorted with venom, I experienced a god-like sense of superiority and calm.

The ball flew towards me, at full pitch, in the direction of my forehead. I stepped adroitly back towards my wicket and shaped to play a model short-arm hook. A rank bad delivery such as this deserved to be smacked without ado over the square-leg boundary. As I began the stroke I saw, out of the corner of my eye, the Professor at square-leg, ducking to avoid the consequences. . .

Some minutes later I opened my eyes and saw, with interest, that the Professor was leaning over me. Deep concern was written in his face.

'Pye, Pye!' he murmured in anguished tones. 'Are you all right, ma boy? Lie still na', lie still!'

I sat up. I was surrounded by a ring of players who were expressing, with varying degrees of insincerity, concern for my welfare.

'What happened?' I asked.

'You took it slap on the cranium, puir chap,' said the Professor. 'It must have knocked you right out. How d'you feel the noo? Have you recovered sufficiently for us to carry you off the field?'

'Carry me off?' I said, puzzled. 'Why? I'm going on with my innings.'

'But you canna do that,' said the Professor. 'You may have concussion. You must go and lie down.'

'I feel perfectly all right,' I said, running my fingers over my forehead.

'You may think you do,' said the Professor. 'But I expect that's merely the effect of the liquor. You won't feel so guid when ye're sober.'

'Are you suggesting I am not sober?' I said, scrambling to my feet. 'I will show you whether I'm sober or not.' I grasped my bat and took up my stance at the wicket.

'I've warned you, Pye,' the Professor pleaded. 'I'm sure ye're no' in a fit state to resume.'

'Go back to your position, please, Professor Pollux,' I said firmly. 'I'm ready to take the next ball.'

In the distance, above the buzzing in my ears, I heard a murmur of sympathetic cheers. The agreeable thought entered my mind that I was now being regarded in a more favourable light.

'Sorry, ole boy!' said the ape-man, with an apologetic leer. 'The ball slipped.'

'Never mind,' I said manfully, as he made his way back to the bowling crease. 'It was my own fault for missing it.'

The ape-man reached his mark, turned, and began his run. It was clear from the outset that I was not going to be treated as an invalid. He threw himself into the fray with his usual ferocity, threshed the surrounding air with his arms, and launched his missile with maximum velocity and perfect length directly down the line of my middle stump.

This, as it happened, was precisely the kind of delivery for which I had subconsciously prepared myself. I swung my bat in an easy, graceful parabola, made contact with the ball as it rose sharply from a length, and drove it high and decisively over the far sightscreen.

The applause could only be described in the cliché: it was deafening. Shrill treble shrieks and whistles rose above a deep ground swell of bass and tenor jubilation. The ape-man subjected me to an amazed and resentful stare; then walked back slowly to his mark.

The next ball was delivered with an even greater show of fury. It pitched somewhat short, well outside the off-stump. I square cut it, with the very middle of the bat, within inches of the left ear of silly point, who flung his arms in the air and the rest of his person on the ground as the ball sped past him to the boundary.

Ten runs in two strokes. That was an improvement. The pent-up emotions of the spectators burst out in a roar of cheers, yells, and whistles. Apart from a faint humming in my ears I felt calm, self-possessed, and in complete control.

The next two balls were certainly fizzers. Both were of perfect length, one on the line of the leg-stump, the other on the line of the off. I leaned forward and drove the first, every inch along the carpet, to the long-on boundary. To the second I played the kind of cover-drive I had seen executed in my youth by Sir Donald Bradman. My execution was perhaps not quite so polished, but the result was the same: the ball travelled like a shot from a gun between cover-point and extra-cover to the wall of the park.

Amid a pandemonium of cheering, whistling, and shouting – more reminiscent of a soccer cup-tie than a village cricket match – the ape-man started on his run for the final ball of the over. Whether or not 'the ball slipped', or he deliberately tried to repeat his assault upon my person, I do not know, but the ball flew, as before, straight at my face.

This time I achieved precisely what I had intended previously. I picked the ball out of the air some three feet in front of my eyes, gave it the full force of the cross bat, and hit it over and far beyond the scoreboard. The people of Arcady went mad with joy.

In the ensuing bedlam of applause I observed with quiet satisfaction that the over which had just ended had raised the Arcady score from 73 for nine to 97 for nine. We now required only eight runs for victory.

It was Jones's turn to face the ferret-faced bowler. The Professor hurried across to the bowling crease. I had never seen him so manifestly moved. He could hardly control his emotions. 'My dear boy,' he said. 'What a perforrmance! What dash! What boldness! What courage!'

I smiled modestly. 'I just needed that bump on the head to rouse me,' I said.

Jones took guard and faced the ferret. The first ball was a yorker and pitched at Jones's feet. He hardly moved his bat. The ball hit it and fell dead. The next two balls were on the off-side and Jones left them severely alone. The fourth ball broke in from leg and hit Jones, who was trying to avoid it, on his bottom.

181

Immediately the ferret appealed for lbw. The Professor said, 'No' out.'

Jones played at the fifth ball, outside the off-stump, but missed it. The ferret promptly appealed for a catch at the wicket. The Professor shook his head.

Off the last ball of the over Jones got a snick towards mid-wicket. We ran a quick single.

As the field changed over for the next over Jones walked anxiously down the wicket towards me. 'I wish to gawd you'd got the bowlin',' he said in a low voice. 'I shall never be able to stop this fast stuff, and if I miss it Charley Aspall is bound to give me out. What can we do?'

I fully sympathized with him. We were within seven runs of victory; it would be tragic indeed if Jones were now 'umpired out'. But there was nothing we could do about it. Jones returned anxiously to the batting crease, and the fieldsmen took up their positions. I saw the ape-man rubbing the ball on his handkerchief and hitching up his trousers in evident anticipation of getting an easy victim.

Just as he was about to start his run, however, there was a surprising diversion. The landlord of The Fox and Goose, who had just taken up his umpire's stance behind the wicket, subsided quietly, like a sack of potatoes, on to the ground.

'Get up, Charley!' said the ape-man roughly. 'It's not bedtime.'

Charley rolled over on to his back and began to snore.

'What's the matter with him?' asked the Flaxfield captain, coming over from mid-off and shaking Charley Aspall by the shoulder. 'Sunstroke?'

'Gin-stroke, more like,' said the ape-man.

The players gathered round and attempted to rouse the recumbent umpire by shaking him, shouting at him, even slapping him. But Charley Aspall had irretrievably passed out.

'I'm much afraid,' said the Professor, who now arrived at the bowler's end, 'we shall have to carry him off. He appears to be both drunk and incapable.'

With none too much gentleness the inert figure was lifted up and unceremoniously carried to the pavilion. As we stood watching the catafalque Jones drew near to me.

'Mr Lionel ain't such a mug as they make 'im out to be,' he said, and he pulled out of his pocket Lionel's flask. 'I picked this up where Charley Aspall fell down. Quite empty. Want a sniff?'

He held the flask to my nose.

'Applejack,' I said. 'The ever-faithful Applejack.'

'Well done, Lion!' said Jones, and put the flask away in his pocket again.

I now observed that some sort of altercation was taking place midway between the pavilion and the wicket. Quirk had appeared, wearing an umpire's coat, and was proposing to take the place of the incapable Charley Aspall. This proposal was being strenuously contested by the Flaxfield captain. He was advocating the claims of a weedy youth who appeared to be the driver of the Flaxfield coach.

It soon appeared that a state of deadlock had been reached. Quirk expressed himself willing to stand down, but he maintained that the Flaxfield coach-driver, so far from being a competent umpire, had been openly maintaining throughout the afternoon his ignorance of the game.

Suddenly we became aware of a fresh party to the debate. 'Would it be a good idea if I umpired, Mr Quirk?' said Miss Tidy, joining the group of disputants. 'I know all the rules, and I'd be quite impartial, because, after all, my dear father was Rector of Flaxfield.'

There was total silence.

'A lady? Can't have a lady umpire!' said the ferret-like bowler.

'And why not, Sticky Palmer?' said Miss Tidy, turning on him with asperity. 'My father taught you all the cricket you know; and I'd like to ask why his daughter isn't good enough to umpire for you.'

'Beg pardon, miss,' said Sticky Palmer humbly. 'No offence meant.'

'I'm sure we'd all be very pleased if Miss Tidy would kindly consent to umpire,' said the Flaxfield captain gallantly. 'Thank you very much, miss.'

'Of course, we'd be delighted too,' said Quirk, helping her into the umpire's coat.

Headed by the new umpire, the players trooped back to the wicket. Miss Tidy took up her position, gave Jones his guard, and called in a resonant, schoolroom voice, 'Play!'

The ape-man, with an apprehensive sidelong glance at Miss Tidy, began his run. The ball whistled past Jones's ear.

'We don't want any intimidation, Dod Hoxen,' said Miss Tidy. 'You've knocked down one man already. Kindly bowl at the wicket, not at Mr Jones's head.'

'Yes, miss,' said the ape-man meekly.

His next ball was on the off. Jones reached out to it; there was a click; and the ball flew on into the wicket-keeper's gloves.

'How's that?' The whole field appealed.

'Not out,' said Miss Tidy decisively. 'You obstructed my view, Dod,' she said sternly to the bowler. 'How can I see whether he's out or not if you run across in front of me?'

'Sorry, miss,' said Dod Hoxen, walking dejectedly back to his mark.

The next ball was on the line of the leg-stump. Jones held out his bat defensively. The ball hit him hard on the thigh.

'How's that, miss?' said Dod Hoxen with diffidence.

'I told you not to bowl at his body,' said Miss Tidy severely. 'Please pay attention to what I say.'

'Sorry, miss,' said Dod Hoxen abjectly.

The fourth ball was an extremely fast straight yorker, which defeated Jones entirely. His middle stump was uprooted from the ground. The Flaxfield players flung up their arms in triumph. Groans of lamentation rose from the men, women, and children of Arcady.

'No ball!' Miss Tidy's clear, emphatic voice cut through the babble. 'You ran at least six inches over the line,' she said severely to Dod Hoxen. 'Go back and try again.' With crest-fallen faces the Flaxfield players returned to their places in the field.

Jones snicked the next ball to third man. We ran a quick single. The score rose to 99.

It thus fell to me to face the sixth delivery of Dod Hoxen's over. The precarious endeavours of Jones to survive the previous five deliveries had raised the temperature of the game to fever heat. There was a tense pause whilst the Flaxfield captain rearranged his field, placing a ring of men round the edge of the field of play to safeguard the boundaries. He stationed himself far behind the bowler's arm, immediately in front of the pavilion. The Arcady supporters, I observed, had mostly risen to their feet, and were delivering themselves of shouts of encouragement and advice to me, and derisory comments on the Flaxfieldians.

I got ready to take the bowling. Dod Hoxen started his ape-like run, glaring and scowling as though bent on homicide. As he reached his climax his whirling arms almost decapitated Miss Tidy and his flying feet executed something between a Spanish cachucha and a Maori war-dance. His lock of red hair cracked like a whip as he flung the ball towards me, straight, very fast, and at perfect length.

I timed it to a nicety, hit it plumb in the middle of the

bat, and drove it, a shade too high perhaps, over the bowler's head.

'Come on!' I called to Jones.

We took a fast single, but as I reached the farther crease I saw, with a pang of dismay, that the ball was falling from the sky straight into the hands of the Flaxfield captain. He stood quite still on the edge of the boundary, just in front of the pavilion, waiting to take the catch.

I turned to take a second run, in desperate hopes that he might possibly err in his judgment. At that moment, into the dead hush with which everyone present, players and spectators, awaited the descent of the ball, there broke a weird, unearthly cackling sound – something between the staccato rattle of a bren-gun and a chorus of witches on a blasted heath.

From amongst the cars parked beside the pavilion there rose into the air a huge winged shape, trailing a long, iridescent tail. Uttering a cacademoniac cry of desperate sadness and ear-splitting timbre it zoomed over the Flaxfield captain's head.

The fielder made every effort to disregard this wholly unforeseen intrusion; but the peacock passed, with ponderous wing-beats, just above his outstretched hands as the ball dropped into them, bounced out, and fell gently amongst the spectators beyond the boundary line.

Hats, sticks, eye-shades, handkerchiefs, ginger-beer bottles, and ice-cream cornets were flung into the air as the inhabitants of Arcady hailed a boundary hit for six, a grand total of 105 runs, and victory over their ancient opponents in the centenary match.

With a sense of something accomplished, something done, I solemnly shook hands with Jones. Then I stood watching the spectators pour on to the field of play from all sides, with the manifest intention of carrying the two of us, shoulder-high, in triumph to the pavilion.

Above the babel I could just hear the *diminuendo* of the eldritch flight-cry as the peacock winged his way over the oak trees by the edge of the park towards the battlemented turrets of the Hall.

By focusing my eyes very deliberately on the face of the big black-and-gold clock which hung above the bar of the Virley Arms I was able to see that the time was ten-fifteen. If Percy Pott closed the pub at the regulation hour of ten-thirty there was a good chance of my still being relatively sober. If there were any laxness in observing the licensing laws I feared that I should be drunk. It seemed that the entire population of Arcady had, at one time or another during the evening, invited me to celebrate my performance on the cricket field. Yet there were still some whose desire to toast me had not been satisfied.

'Darling,' said Belinda, elbowing her way towards me through the crowd, 'aren't you going to have one with me? You were so marvellous. Gin or whisky?'

'I wouldn't dream of letting you buy me a drink,' I said. 'You're going to have one with me. It was entirely owing to your encouragement that I made any runs at all.'

I ordered drinks for the two of us.

'I thought it was the crack on the head that started you off,' said Belinda.

'So it was, dearie,' said Dimple Pott, squeezing out from behind the bar and sitting down at a piano which stood against the wall. 'Made him fighting mad, that did. Oh, what a man! I wouldn't like to run up against him on a dark night.' She gazed at me ardently, her eyelids moist with hero-worship and mascara.

'Yes, you would, Dimple,' said Belinda. 'You'd adore to run up against him on a dark night. So would we all.'

'Oh, Lady Belinda,' Dimple twittered. 'The things you say!'

She turned to me. 'I wouldn't expect to find you in the dark, dearie. You'd be among the bright lights, I guess. The Café de Paris, an' all that.'

'Well, I *have* been to the Café de Paris, I admit,' I said.

'Coo!' said Dimple. 'Lucky you!'

'Dimple!' roared Lord Flamborough, from his invalid chair at the far end of the bar. 'Stop spooning with Sir Jasper, and give us another tune. Something snappy.'

Dimple launched into a vigorous rendering of 'Yes, We Have No Bananas'. Jones led the chorus in a light tenor voice with coster intonation. The crowd gathered round the piano. Belinda pressed herself against me. I felt her arm going round my waist. 'Are you going to run up against *me* some dark night, darling?' she said softly. 'Or do you prefer the heat of the day?'

'I prefer the sunshine,' I said. 'Sun and games.'

'Crumbs!' exclaimed Belinda. 'You *must* have had a bang on the head.'

'It's better now, actually,' I said, feeling the lump on my forehead.

'I'm not so sure,' she said.

'Oh yes, I'm quite myself again.'

'I wonder what you'll be like tomorrow?'

'Fighting fit! Top of the class!' I said, wondering vaguely what I was talking about.

'We'd better make a date, then,' said Belinda, 'so that I can judge for myself.'

'Name the time and place,' I said briskly.

'Crumbs!' said Belinda again, gazing at me with respect. 'How about meeting in the temple by the lake – about three o'clock?'

'In the temple by the lake, about three o'clock,' I repeated.

'In the heat of the day,' said Belinda, with a quizzical glance at me.

'In the heat of the day,' I repeated firmly.

'You're sure you'll be there?'

'I shall be there – if I'm not otherwise engaged.'

'Cad!' she hissed.

'Jasper, dear boy,' said Lionel, looming over us. 'To what do you attribute – I repeat the word "attribute" to show how shober I am – to what do you attribute your sensational success on the field of play? Do you put it down to Elderflower Champagne, or Carrot Whisky, or the occasional thimbleful of Applejack?'

'Applejack,' I said, 'the ever-faithful Applejack.'

'Gentlemen!' bellowed Lionel, silencing the singers at the piano. 'Gentlemen – and ladies, of course – let us drink to Applejack, the ever-faithful Applejack.'

'Does he mean Appleyard?' said Quirk, who was leaning against the bar. 'The Yorkshire slow bowler?'

'The toast is Applejack,' said Lionel. 'And in honour of our brilliant new batsman, Sir Jasper Pye, I have asked Percy to charge all your glasses with a drop of my own shpeshial brew.'

There was a confused roar of voices calling 'Applejack!' 'Sir Jasper!' 'Good old Lion!' and 'Here's my glass, Percy; fill it up!' A very old man with white whiskers, who had been sitting in a corner observing the festivities with a benign but toothless smile, rose shakily to his feet, waved his tankard to and fro, and began to chant, in a quavering voice:

> 'Do be sure your lamb ain't mutton,
> Ere you lose a trouser button.'

The company took up the refrain, to the accompaniment of a curious old-world air played on the piano by Dimple Pott.

'Tomorrow,' whispered Belinda. 'In the temple by the

lake. In the heat of the day.' She drained her glass, set it down on the counter, and was gone.

'What a charming old folk-song this is,' said Miss Tidy, whom I saw, to my surprise, standing primly by the bar, with Quirk. 'I don't believe one would hear it sung anywhere except at Arcady.' Quirk, in obvious embarrassment, began to talk very fast and heartily about the cricket averages.

'Talking of trousers,' said Lionel, raising his glass in salutation to Miss Tidy, 'I wonder if you've heard that one about the cauliflower and the Scotsman's kilt?'

'Lionel!' A reproachful Chloe struggled towards him through the throng. 'Shut up! It's time we went home.'

'Time, gentlemen, please!' called Percy Pott, switching the lights off and on to emphasize the point.

'Time to go home, ducky?' said Lionel. 'But I'm jush off to Flaxfield to see my old friend Charley Aspall. He had a nasty turn this afternoon, you know. I've got to go and see that he'sh making a recovery!'

'Oh, Lionel!' said Chloe, in despair. 'This isn't the time to pay calls at Flaxfield. Do come home!'

'Oh no,' said Lionel. 'Can't let an old friend down. It was partly my fault, you see. Got to do the decent, sporting thing.'

'Got to sample that bottle of Scotch in Charley's back room, you mean!' said Jones.

'Haven't we time for one more tune, Percy?' said Lord Flamborough.

'Well, just one, your Lordship,' said Percy, with an anxious glance at the clock.

Dimple gave a spirited performance of 'Show Me the Way to go Home'. As the applause died down Percy flickered the lights again, and the patrons began reluctantly to stream out into the dusk.

'Wait for me, Dod!' shouted Lionel, draining his glass and stumbling towards the door. 'Run me over to The

Fox and Goose, there'sh a dear fellow.'

'Very good, Mr Lionel,' said the Flaxfield fast bowler with the red hair. 'But I can't bring you back again.'

'Never mind, dear fellow,' said Lionel. 'I'll shleep in Charley Aspall's coalshed. Good night, all! See you in the morning, ducky.' And he blew a kiss to Chloe.

'Sleep in Charley's coalshed!' exclaimed Jones, pulling a face.

Chloe shrugged her shoulders helplessly, and turned towards me with a mute appeal in her eyes. I took her arm.

Outside, between the Virley Arms and the green, the village people stood about in groups as though reluctant to make an end of the day's festivities. There was a grinding of gears and a round of jocularities as Dod Hoxen's car lurched into movement and bore its owner and Lionel away towards Flaxfield.

'Congratulations, once more, Mr Pye,' said Quirk, weaving his way towards me and shaking my hand a number of times. 'You won the match for us: no doubt about it. It was a most magnificent recovery. I hope we shall often have you in the side.'

'But Mr Pye's a Londoner, you know,' said Miss Tidy, who was still with him. 'I expect he usually plays for the Butterflies or the Old Carthusians or someone.'

Quirk took hold of my hand and began to shake it again. 'But now you're an Old Arcadian, aren't you, sir!' he said proudly.

'*Et ego pro Arcadia* . . . ' I replied.

'Arcadia!' exclaimed Miss Tidy solemnly. 'So we're all in the land of Arcadia! Well, I never thought of it like that!'

As though to signalize what seemed, for some reason, to be a peculiarly solemn moment, the old man with the white whiskers stepped out of the shadows into a gleam of moonlight, executed a little shuffle of the feet, and, beating time with a shepherd's crook, began to sing, in his thin, creaking voice:

'In Arcady, bor, in Arcady, bor,
They spin the lasses across the floor!
In Arcady, bor, in Arcady, bor,
They twist the spigot and ask for more!'

In a moment the onlookers had gathered round him and were joining in the ditty. As they sang they bobbed and weaved in a kind of jig. Jones and Dimple Pott appeared to be performing something like 'Knees Up, Mother Brown!' Chloe gripped my arm, and we joined in the dance, which was, I found, a good deal more complicated than I thought. Chloe, however, seemed to know the steps, and she soon had me following her movements.

After four or five repetitions of the song the old man paused for breath, leaning on his shepherd's crook. 'Come on, Chitty!' the dancers cried. 'Give us another one!'

'That'll have to do for tonight, bors,' the old man croaked. 'We must keep something up the spout for Whit Monday.'

The group began to break up. Quirk and Miss Tidy had already gone. Jones called 'Nightie noo, folks!' and went back into the Virley Arms with Dimple. I saw Lord Flamborough bowling across the village green at high speed in his wheel chair.

Chloe and I walked slowly after him, arm in arm. I was beginning to feel tired, and just a little unsteady on my feet, but my senses were amazingly alert and receptive. The air was calm and warm and soft. The smell of dewfall on trodden turf mingled with the scents of dog-rose and honeysuckle against the wall of the park. Chloe's golden hair seemed to turn to silver in the moonlight.

Chloe said nothing. I said nothing. We walked slowly

and in silence across the green, through the door by the shrubbery, and down the path between the high wall and the lavender. As we left the walled garden and the crunch of our feet on the gravel rang out into the stillness, the monumental mass of the gatehouse rose before us like some Dark Tower of legend.

We crossed the bridge over the moat, passed through the gate, and walked across the courtyard towards Chloe's quarters. As she put her hand on the great iron latch to open her door the desolate wail of the peacock rang through the night.

Chloe shuddered. 'Come inside for a moment,' she said. 'I feel so desperately lonely.'

I followed her into the Buttery.

'Before we do anything else,' Chloe said, 'I must look at that wound on your forehead.' She took me by the arm, drew me towards her, and began to feel the bump on my head. The touch of her fingers was exquisitely gentle.

'I think it's only bruised,' she said. 'I shall put some Pond's on it.' She found a medicine bottle, and tenderly dabbed the bruise.

'Now let's go upstairs,' she said. We went up to a tiny panelled chamber that she used as a living-room. She lit a candle, then took off the jacket she was wearing and threw it into a corner.

'If you want a glass of water,' she said, 'you'll find one in the bathroom. Lionel always drinks about two pints of water before he goes to bed.'

'But I'm not Lionel,' I said.

She looked at me for a moment with a kind of desperation in her eyes.

'No. Thank God you're *not* Lionel!' And she flung herself down on the couch and buried her face in the cushions.

I dropped on my knees beside her, and stroked her

golden hair. I had an extraordinary sense of power and tenderness. As I stroked her hair I seemed to feel something of my strength and calmness passing into her.

After a while I put my arm round her shoulders and kissed her neck. In the soft light of the single candle flame the room seemed to enclose us in a private world of our own.

'Will Lionel really not be home until tomorrow?' I said at last.

'No,' said Chloe, biting back a sob. 'He'll be spending the night with a ghastly trollop of his in Flaxfield. Oh dear!' she moaned. 'I shouldn't have said that, I suppose.'

'Poor Chloe!' I said. 'Dear Chloe!'

She lifted her head, and looked for a long time full into my eyes. Then, with a sigh, she sank back on to the cushions.

'Don't be sad,' I said.

'I'm not sad,' she said. 'I'm simply cross.' She suddenly sat up again. 'I'm cross – raging mad, furious, and cross.'

'That's better!' I said admiringly, as her eyes flashed, her nostrils trembled, and the blood ran into her cheeks. 'That's much better.'

'Dear, dear Jasper!' she said, blowing out the candle flame. 'You're such a comfort.'

I was woken by a tentative but persistent knocking at the door. After lying for a little while trying to adjust my eyes to the sunlight I sat up in alarm. Where was I? What had happened? To my relief I realized that I was back in the Moonlight Room. 'Come in!' I called.

The door opened and Miss Mounsey entered, carrying a tray laden with breakfast.

'My dear Mouse,' I said. 'You shouldn't have bothered.'

'Well, Mr Pye,' she said, setting the tray down on the bed. 'It was after ten, and I knew you'd be tired after your triumph yesterday, so I thought I'd bring you breakfast in bed.'

'How very thoughtful of you,' I said.

I looked down at the array of food she had prepared for me. Fruit juice, strawberries, coffee, toast, honey, and marmalade, and, covered with a plate to keep it hot, a large dish of bacon, eggs, and grilled tomatoes.

'What!' I said. 'No kedgeree or devilled kidneys?'

The Mouse's face fell. 'Oh dear!'

'It's all right,' I said. 'It's only my little joke.'

With an expression of relief she put *The Sunday Times*, *The Observer*, and the *Sunday Express* down on the bed beside the breakfast tray.

'We're rather out of the world here,' she said; 'but at least we get the Sunday papers. Now you can relax and have a good read. Oh, just a minute!' She took a cushion out of the easy chair, put it under my pillows, and arranged them comfortably behind my shoulders.

'What a dear creature you are, Mouse!' I said, and kissed her cheek as she bent over me.

'Mr Pye!' she exclaimed. 'Shall I close the window, or would you prefer it left open.'

'Open, please, my dear,' I said. 'It's a fine morning, isn't it?'

'Heavenly,' she said, and, blushing furiously, scuttled out of the room.

I picked up the newspapers and scanned the headlines.

The door opened again and the Mouse put her head round it.

'I forgot to ask,' she said. 'How is your head this morning?'

'My head?'

'Yes, the bump on your head.'

'Oh, it's perfectly all right. I've got just the faintest headache, but that's all.'

'I thought you might have a headache,' she said. 'You'll see a bottle of aspirin on the tray: I should take a couple. Now get on with your breakfast before it gets cold.' And she went out.

I took three aspirins. As I ate my breakfast I tried to think back over the events of yesterday. But yesterday seemed as incoherent as a dream. Moments flashed vividly into my mind – dancing the Charleston in Lord Flamborough's Pullman car, sipping the Applejack with Lionel in the dungeon, square-cutting the Flaxfield fast bowler so sweetly and effortlessly for four, dancing the jig outside the pub. But everything seemed inconsequent and insubstantial.

The only thing that seemed real – vividly and intensely and gloriously real – was the touch of Chloe's lips on mine.

The Sunday papers seemed to be concerned with utterly remote and boring topics, except for the gardening articles. I amused myself with the pleasant daydream that I was the owner of Arcady Hall and could plant the garden with all the uncommon and expensive shrubs and roses and lilies that were so vividly described by the Gardening Correspondents.

By the time I had finished my breakfast my head was quite clear, and I felt fresh and vigorous. I jumped out of bed, and went to the window.

It was the most perfect morning yet. There was not a cloud to be seen; there was not a breath of wind. Already the stone mullions were hot to the touch.

I shaved and dressed in a strange mood of mingled exaltation and contentment. I couldn't remember when I had last experienced such an overwhelming sense of physical well-being and mental energy. As I rubbed myself down after bathing I began to sing old Chitty's ridiculous, lilting ditty:

'In Arcady, bor, in Arcady, bor,
They spin the lasses across the floor!
In Arcady, bor, in Arcady, bor,
They twist the spigot and ask for more!'

What on earth did it mean? What was a 'bor'? Surely it wasn't the kind of 'bore' people talked about nowadays. 'Jasper's a bore.' Oh-ho! Is he? You've got it wrong, Deirdre! Jasper's an 'Arcady bor'; and that's something quite different!

Laughing aloud at the inconsequence of my thoughts I finished dressing and ran downstairs into the courtyard. Faintly disappointed, I saw nobody about. I crossed the bridge over the moat. Still there was nobody to be seen; but Lionel's traction engine was standing in the main drive, and as smoke was curling from its chimney I assumed that Lionel must have returned from his night-out in Charley Aspall's coalshed, so-called.

I decided to walk up to the green and survey the scene of yesterday's triumph. Yes, even the Mouse had referred to it as a triumph.

As I walked through the doorway into the walled garden my face brushed against something soft and silky. I looked up and saw the peacock sitting on top of the wall, the sunlight glancing off his long, pendent tail feathers in a flame of iridescence. He arched his aristocratic neck and studied me solemnly with a keen brown eye.

'Oh, there you are!' called Lady Flamborough, from the middle of the herbaceous border. 'You're just the man we want to resolve our problems for us.'

'What problems, Lady Flamborough?' I asked. As I walked towards her I saw the Professor in the background, holding a rake.

'We're thinking of reorganizing, Pye,' said the Professor. 'And we want yuir advice.'

'Reorganizing what?' I asked, with a sinking of the

heart. I couldn't bear to think of office reorganization on a morning like this.

'Reorganizing the herbaceous border,' said Lady Flamborough. 'We want to get rid of some of these delphiniums and lupins and phloxes, and replace them with something more interesting.'

My spirits rose again. 'What have you in mind?' I asked.

'Some rose species, perhaps,' said Lady Flamborough.

'Good idea,' I said. 'Clumps of the rugosas, for instance, and *Moyesii* and its hybrids, and perhaps *xanthina canarybird*.'

Lady Flamborough and the Professor looked at me with respect.

'Excellent suggestions!' said Lady Flamborough. 'Will you make a note of the names, Professor? This young man seems to know what he's talking about.'

'How d'ye spell them, Pye?' the Professor asked, bringing out a notebook and pencil. I spelt the names for him.

'What would you suggest for the front of the border?' asked Lady Flamborough.

'I should clear out everything that's here,' I said boldly. 'Plant mostly shrubs. A few barberries. *Hookeri*, for instance, which flowers in May, and *atrocarpa*, which is a bit earlier and has those pale yellow flowers. Then you want some unusual evergreens. You might put in one or two *Garrya elliptica* against the wall: they don't mind facing north, and they have lovely glossy leaves, with those curious grey catkins.'

'Are you taking this down?' said Lady Flamborough, turning to the Professor.

'I'm trying to,' said the Professor.

'I don't know whether the soil here is calcigerous or not,' I continued.

198

'Is it calcigerous?' said the Professor to Lady Flamborough.

'No, hardly any lime,' she replied.

'That's fine,' I went on. 'Then you can build up a great bank of azaleas, with some of the more unusual dwarf rhododendrons. And some hydrangeas for later in the summer. *Hydrangea quercifolia*, for instance, with those huge arching panicles of white flowers that turn to a purplish pink.'

'Turn to purplish pink ...' the Professor repeated, writing busily in his notebook.

'And why not Camellias?' I asked.

'I'd love to grow Camellias,' said Lady Flamborough, her eyes glistening. 'But would they thrive?'

'Try *Adolphe Audusson*,' I said.

'*Adolphe Audusson*,' the Professor repeated.

'It is a semi-double, carmine in colour,' I continued, 'and it does quite well out of doors. You're pretty sheltered here, anyway. You ought to be able to grow *Donklaarii*, which has large crimson flowers, semi-double, with white markings. And *Kelvingtoniana*, and *latifolia*.'

'Are you getting all these names down, Professor?' said Lady Flamborough.

'I'm doing ma best,' said the Professor, turning over another page in his notebook.

'Then you might interplant with lilies. They'll like the shade given by the shrubs, and if you plant carefully according to height you'll get some lovely effects. I'm particularly fond of *Lilium auratum* myself – it comes rather late, of course. But there's no end to them. Don't plant too many regales, I suggest. Try *Maximowiczii* – I'll spell that for you, Professor – and the Sunset Lily, *pardalinum giganteum* – it grows up to eight feet. And, of course, lots of Tiger lilies – *splendens* as well as *Fortunei giganteum*. Mix them in with some

199

really handsome hollyhocks – Chaters Yellow, for instance:

> 'Heavily hangs the hollyhock,
> Heavily hangs the tiger-lily.'

'Tennyson!' said the Professor, gazing at me in awe.

'Never mind whether it's Tennyson or Thompson and Morgan,' said Lady Flamborough. 'This young man knows what he's talking about. I'd no idea we had such an expert among us.'

'If you'll excuse me now,' I said, 'I must continue my walk up to the green.'

'Of course,' said Lady Flamborough. 'But we must have a lot more talks about shrubs and rose species – and lilies, too. I'm really delighted to have you here. What fun we're having!'

'Ye'll be back for luncheon, I hope, Pye,' said the Professor, addressing me with an unwonted deference. 'I thought we'd open a decent bottle of claret, to celebrate yuir masterly perrformance yesterday.'

'Of course! A nice thought!' I said. 'Now I must be off.'

I left them poring over the Professor's notebook, and walked briskly down the long walk towards the green. It was surprising how all those plant names had come to me so readily. I had read them all, of course, in the gardening features of the Sunday papers at breakfast. But I should never have believed it possible that I could pour them out so fluently and – I hoped – so convincingly. As Lady Flamborough had said, what fun we were having!

On the green I found Jones, assisted by some village boys, sticking up on an oak tree a poster advertising the Fête. It was a home-made affair, crudely lettered in coloured chalks. To my astonishment I read that the prizes at the Fête were to be presented by "The well-known TV Personality, Sir Jasper Pye, Bart'.

'But I'm *not* a baronet, Jones,' I protested.

'Sorry, cock!' said Jones. 'I'll alter it to "Kt". Or should it be "KCVO"? That would look classier.'

'I'm not a knight of any kind,' I said. 'I'm just a plain Mister.'

Jones stepped back from the poster and looked at me quizzically. 'Come orf it, chum!' he said. 'You can tell that to the Marines, if you like. But you mustn't expect *me* to believe it.'

'But it's quite true, Jones,' I said. 'And in any case, that line about my being a TV Personality is nonsense. I've never even appeared on television.'

'Never mind,' said Jones, 'you will. They can't keep a good man down.'

'But I don't want to appear on television. It's not my line at all.'

'Don't worry,' said Jones, 'you'll find it comes quite easy to you. You'll *send* them, cock: no doubt about it.'

'But it's false pretences to announce me on that poster as a TV Personality,' I persisted.

'Just leave the publicity arrangements to me, Sir Jasper,' said Jones patiently, taking me by the arm and leading me across the green towards the Virley Arms. 'It may be that we're anticipating the BBC or the ITV by a few weeks. But we've got to draw the customers; and, believe you me, they won't cross the street for a Fête unless there's a TV Personality billed. After all, they had Sabrina at Beccles last week. They won't ever bother to come up for the prizes unless they are handed out by someone on a Brains Trust Panel.'

'But I've never been on a Brains Trust Panel in my life, Jones,' I said. 'Nobody's ever heard of me.'

'Never mind,' said Jones reassuringly. 'If we tell them

201

they have, they'll think they have. And, anyway, you're a popular figure already, after that little effort in the cricket match.'

As he spoke, one of the small boys who had been following us across the green ran up beside me, proffered a small and grubby notebook and a pencil, and said, 'Could you be so kind as to give me your autograph, sir?'

'What did I tell you!' said Jones, triumphantly. 'Give me the book, sonny, and I'll show Sir Jasper where to sign.'

Rather than disappoint the small boy, I signed my name in his book. In a moment two other youths had appeared with the same request.

'That'll do for now, laddies!' said Jones firmly. 'Sir Jasper's a very kind gentleman, but we mustn't take advantage of him. You can get all the autographs you want at the Fête tomorrow – at a bob a time.' He waved the boys away and ushered me into the Virley Arms.

'Make way for Sir Jasper!' he cried as we entered. 'Percy, where's that bottle of champagne?'

'Sorry, Mr Jones,' said Percy Pott, 'I'm out of champagne. But what else would do for Sir Jasper? It's on the house, of course.'

'Thank you very much,' I said. 'I'd be quite happy with a glass of beer.'

'There you are, Percy!' said Jones. 'Just wants a glass of beer. No la-di-dah about Sir Jasper. Just one o' the boys, 'e is.'

There was a chorus of 'Hear! Hear!' and 'Jolly good luck!' and 'Your good health, sir!' from the men in the bar. I couldn't help being cheered by their obvious friendliness. As I drank my beer there was a run-by-run discussion of the cricket match. Every stage in the downfall of the Flaxfield Eleven was recounted, discussed, analysed, and applauded.

After a while I ordered a round of drinks for everyone. This was received with the utmost cordiality. Percy Pott was just drawing the last pint when the door opened and, to a burst of jocular greetings, Lionel came in.

' 'Morning, everyone!' he said. 'Am I late for the party?'

'What'll you have, Mr Lionel?' said Percy. 'This one's on Sir Jasper.'

'Jasper, you here before me? How nice to see you, dear boy!' said Lionel. 'B-and-s for me, Percy, if Sir Jasper can rise to it. Got a simply ghastly head this morning! Charley Aspall must have topped me up with methylated spirits last night. Blind as a coot, I was. Ah, that's better!' He took a long draught of his brandy-and-soda.

'How are you, dear boy?' he asked, carrying his glass over to me. 'None the worse for your experiences?'

'No, none the worse, thank you,' I replied, a little self-consciously.

'I hope my old woman saw you safely home,' said Lionel. 'I don't doubt you were nearly as pie-eyed as I was.'

'Yes, she did, thank you.'

'She's a dear, sweet soul, is Chloe,' said Lionel, gazing sentimentally into the bottom of his glass. 'I'm not worthy of her.'

I murmured something non-committal.

'Bet you slept well,' he continued, 'after all the larks you got up to yesterday.'

'Yes, I slept very well, thank you.'

'Can't remember where I slept,' said Lionel. 'When I woke up I was lying alongside Susie.'

'Mr Lionel!' exclaimed Dimple, behind the bar. 'Please remember the company you're in.'

' 's all right, Dimple ducky,' said Lionel, leaning over the bar and putting his arm round her. 'Don't be jealous, sweetie. Susie hasn't displaced you in my affections.'

'Mr Lionel, take your hands off me!'

'Not so huffy, now! It takes all sorts to make a world,

and Susie is "different"; that's right, isn't it, Jones?'

'Susie is only 'is traction engine,' said Jones. 'Blows off steam like any woman, though.'

'Oh, go on!' said Dimple, pouting and tossing her head. 'I know Mr Lionel well enough by now, and if he's gone on anything you can be sure it wears a skirt.'

'That's jus' where you're wrong,' said Lionel solemnly. 'Give me another b-and-s, Percy, there's a dear chap. One for you, too, Jasper?'

I declined.

'I'm a reformed character,' said Lionel. 'I've finished with women. It's boilers, not bosoms, for me in future. Susie! Here's to Susie!' he said, raising his glass.

'Oh well,' said Dimple. 'I suppose there's no accounting for tastes. But what are us girls going to do if you're a reformed character, I'd like to know.'

'You girls?' said Lionel, supporting himself against the corner of a settle. 'I'm passing all you girls over to Sir Jasper. He's the ladies' man. That's right, isn't it, Jasper? You raise your little finger, and they all come running.'

Dimple gazed at me reverently. 'I believe Mr Lionel's right, dearie,' she said to me. 'They all say the same about you.'

'Nonsense!' I said. 'Never heard such tosh!'

I looked up at the clock. It was half past twelve. I really mustn't miss another meal with the Professor: and he was opening a bottle of claret specially for me. 'Good day, everyone,' I said. 'I've got to get on my way.' There was a friendly murmur of farewells. 'All the best, sir!' 'See you again tonight, sir?' 'Best respects, sir.'

'Who's the lucky lady this time?' asked Dimple coyly.

'Yes, which one's next in the queue?' said Lionel.

'As it happens,' I stated coldly, 'I'm lunching with the Professor.'

Lionel made a rude gesture.

'Tell that to the Marines!' said Jones.

To a roar of good-humoured laughter I left the pub. As I walked briskly back to the Hall I couldn't help smiling at the wholly erroneous impression which I seemed to have made on local opinion. And yet – was it really so erroneous? After the events of yesterday afternoon and last night I was beginning to revise my own estimate of myself. Perhaps I was not quite the person I'd always thought I was.

I walked over the bridge into the gatehouse and ran upstairs to wash for lunch. When I came down I saw that it was only ten minutes to one. Perhaps there was just time for me to nip across the courtyard and see how Chloe was.

I found her in the Buttery, an apron round her waist, cooking lunch. She seemed to take a sudden grip on herself, and a blush crept into her cheeks when she realized that I, not Lionel, had come into the room.

'Jasper!'

'Dear Chloe!' I said, and took her in my arms.

We stood quite still for a moment of profound tranquillity. Then Chloe gently pushed me away.

'I think I can smell the Yorkshire pudding burning,' she said, and opened the oven door.

I stood gazing down at her golden hair, with a deep and calm sense of happiness, as she pulled out the baking-tin.

'It was all right?' I asked. 'Wasn't it?'

'Yes, it hasn't actually burnt,' she said.

'I meant – last night,' I said. 'It was all right about last night?'

'Of course it was all right, darling,' she said, pushing the baking-tin back into the oven. 'It was heavenly. You were so very, very sweet. How are you this morning? Have you got a ghastly headache?'

I didn't quite follow her sequence of thought, but I told her I had no headache at all: I said I felt on top of the world.

'Stay there, Jasper darling,' she said, coming close to me again and toying with the lapel of my jacket. 'Stay right on top of the world. That's the place for you. And now you must forget all about people on the lower slopes, like me.'

'But, Chloe,' I protested, 'how can I forget? I love—'

She quickly put her forefinger across my lips.

'You mustn't say that, Jasper,' she said. 'I couldn't say that to you, you know.'

'Well,' I temporized, 'I suppose even love is relative.'

'There's only one Love,' said Chloe simply. 'And whether you or I have found it is something we shall never know. There's sex and there's fun and there's consolation and release – and lots of other things. And we may have stumbled on some of them last night. But that, Jasper darling, was last night. And last night only. We'd be foolish to try and repeat it. It was heavenly – and perhaps it will seem even more heavenly as time goes on. But I have to live on earth, my dear, not in heaven.'

'Chloe!' I murmured. 'We can't . . . You can't—'

She put her arms round me and gave me her lips. We kissed – a long, hopeless, exquisite kiss of farewell.

'Now I can really smell the Yorkshire pudding burning,' she said, releasing herself. 'And if you don't hurry along the Professor won't offer you a glass of his extra special Manzanilla.'

As I walked slowly back across the courtyard I did indeed – and most surprisingly – feel I was on top of the world. I experienced an extraordinary sense of exaltation, of the nobility and fineness and poignancy of hopeless love.

I was in time to be offered two glasses of the Professor's extra special Manzanilla; and very good it was. When we sat down to lunch the Professor placed a decanter of claret on the table before me.

'Tell me what you think of this, Pye,' he said, pouring out a glass. 'You may think it's past its prime. If so, I have a younger one in reserve.'

The claret had a most unusual and elusive bouquet. I took a few sips. It was beautifully smooth, with an uncommon delicacy of flavour.

'It is delicious,' I said. 'I don't ever remember tasting a claret like it.'

The Professor's broad and bushy eyebrows relaxed into a beam of satisfaction. 'I doubt if you ever have, Pye,' he said. 'This is pre-phylloxera wine, made from grapes grown before the *Phylloxera vastatrix*, that pestilential wee greenfly, invaded the vines of Bordeaux in the last century.'

'But how fantastic!' I said. 'I thought claret didn't keep for more than twenty years or so, at the most. Yet this is a lovely wine.'

'I'm delighted that you think so,' said the Professor. 'We are extremely fortunate to be drinking it. I doubt whether mair than a few isolated bottles remain in existence.'

'What is it?' I asked.

'It is Château Latour, 1878.'

'How did you come by it?'

'I found it,' said the Professor solemnly, 'in the dungeon, where I understand you spent most of yesterday afternoon.'

'Not amongst Lionel's home-made brews?' I exclaimed in horror.

'No, ma dear chap. I took the precaution of removing the contents of the dungeon soon after my arrival here, and before Lionel Virley appeared on the scene. There were quite a number of wines that had presumably lain there since the middle of last century. There was a Château Latour, 1858. There was a Léoville, 1868, and several of the eighteen-seventies. There was a Lafite of

1875. There was even a Napoleon Sherry of 1812. I bought them from Lord Flamborough at a proper valuation, of course. It would ha' been sheer wickedness to expose such wines to the ravages of Lionel Virley.'

'I wonder,' I said.

'Lionel may have a certain rough-and-ready guid nature,' said the Professor, 'but he isna' a mon who seeks the highest.'

'I'm not entirely sure,' I said.

'I fear I am right,' said the Professor. 'And sometimes I wonder whether my seventeen years here may not prove to have been wasted after all. Lionel, ye ken, is the heir.'

'Is he?' I said.

'I came here,' continued the Professor, refilling my wine-glass, 'at a time when any sort of fate might have befallen Arcady. It might have been requisitioned by the Army and kicked to pieces by corporals. It might have become a hospital, and had the panelling ripped out, the plasterwork covered with institutional paint, and the Grinling Gibbons bookcases chopped up for firewood. It might, on the other hand, have just been left to decay, for Lord Flamborough couldna' possibly have afforded to keep it up, and he has, dear mon, no head for business at a'.'

'I can well understand that.'

'When I came here, therefore,' the Professor went on, 'I saw maself not merely as a government official engaged in a minor job of war-work, but also as a trustee for the Virleys of yesterday, a *deus ex machina*, dropped by the engines of war to guard and protect this defenceless, decaying relic of the past.'

'And a very capable and conscientious trustee you have proved.'

'You think so? You really think that?' said the Professor, dropping his magisterial mask, and seeming almost to plead for reassurance. 'You consider ma tenancy here has been justified, has yielded fruit?'

'Certainly it has,' I said.

'Perhaps you will somehow contrive to put that point to the people in Whitehall?'

'I can try,' I said.

The Professor leaned forward over the table.

'Forgive me, Pye, if I become perrsonal. But I feel this is a matter which can only be seen in perrsonal terrms. The value of our statistical researches isna', I fear, sufficient to impress our lords and masters of the Treasury. But there is something of greater account than statistics; and that is history. There is something of greater consequence to the nation than the Treasury; and that is tradition. I believe – and I assure you I am not being presumptuous when I say it – that history and tradition would be better served if I were allowed to continue my trusteeship here than if Arcady were left to chance and hazard and Lionel.'

The Professor rose from the table, leaving his food unfinished, and began to pace up and down the Eating Room.

'Dinna' imagine, Pye,' he said, 'that I am afflicted with *folie de grandeur* – that I wish to usurp the rights and inheritance of the Virleys. I see maself, quite clearly and unsentimentally, as their servant. But the present Earl, and Lionel his heir, are no' equipped for the stresses and strains of modern life. They need a guid bailiff. I am that bailiff – a bailiff who serves not only them but their forebears back through fourteen generations, a bailiff who considers himself responsible for every brick, for every joist and timber, for every meadow and tree in Arcady.'

Abruptly the Professor sat down again, and rested his head in his hands. There was a long silence. I continued eating my lunch.

'That is my side of the perrsonal equation,' he said at last, in a low voice. 'What is yours? I wonder.'

I sipped my claret and considered what my answer should be.

'Have some mair claret,' said the Professór, re-filling my glass. 'Let me say how I view your side of the equation. The first fact to note is that you are not the Man from the Ministry whom we all expected. You are, no doubt, experienced, conscientious, and mindful of your responsibilities to Whitehall. But we have all seen, Pye, in these last few days, how history and tradition – the *lares et penates* – have taken you under their wing.' He paused. 'You may have sensed, when you first arrived here, Pye, a feeling of distrust and resentment towards yourself.'

'I did,' I said.

'Perhaps you can now sense that the distrust has passed away. You have shown your sensibility to the sperrit of Arcady: you understand us; you appreciate our values; you respond to the wayward and romantic temperament of the Virleys. I am right, am I not?'

'Yes,' I said, 'I had not consciously recognized the fact myself. But you are right – undoubtedly right.'

'I thought so, ma dear boy,' said the Professor, leaning across the table and clasping my hand. 'There is something here greater than ourselves. There are ghosts – ancient, kindly, tolerant ghosts – behind these panels of oak. There is a *genius loci* of Arcady. There is a living sperrit of the past enshrined in this monumental gatehouse. There are rare and long-forgotten scents in the garden, and ancient gods and goddesses in the woods. And there are voices.'

I sat quite still as this intense and eloquent discourse was delivered across the luncheon table in the Professor's precise and studiously articulated Scottish accent.

210

'You must pay your respects to these gods and goddesses, Pye. You must listen to the voices. You must do what they say – whether they are the voices of history or the voices of myth – whether they are Tudor madrigals or the pipes of Pan.'

I rose to my feet. The meal seemed to have come to an end. The Professor seemed to shiver. Then he too rose to his full height, and smiled at me with a singularly sweet and open smile.

'We are going to stay here, Pye, are we not? Perhaps we both will stay here. *Et tu in Arcadia* . . . But it is up to you, my dear boy, to arrange it.' He leaned over the table and raised the decanter. 'We mustna' leave any of this precious claret,' he said. 'Drink up! A distinguished wine, do ye not consider?'

'Most distinguished,' I said.

'How fortunate,' said the Professor, 'that I had this one bottle left with which to welcome a~verra distinguished guest.'

I looked at my watch. It was ten minutes to three. I quickened my step as I walked through the park towards the lake.

I had caught occasional glimpses of the lake from the turret of the gatehouse and from the window of Lord Flamborough's railway coach; but apart from the fact that it lay somewhere beyond the railway line I had only a vague idea of its whereabouts.

The sun blazed down from a blue sky as intense and vivid in hue as the feathers of the peacock. There was not a wisp of a cloud in sight. As I walked I soon became so warm that I had to take off my jacket and carry it.

I crossed the railway line at the Halt and followed a footpath that led through meadows and copses towards the river. The hedges were bright with dog-roses, hawthorn blossom, and the great white heads of sheep's parsley. There was a green scent in the air.

I paused by a stile, undid my tie, and took it off, and loosened my collar. Already beads of sweat were glistening on the backs of my hands.

Soon I heard the clack-clack of a moorhen's cry: I must be somewhere near water. I walked on. Although the landscape was by no means enclosed there were enough trees and high hedges and copses to preclude any long views or vistas. I experienced yet again that sense of seclusion and remoteness with which Arcady was invested. Out of curiosity I scrutinized the pathway as I went along: I could see no signs at all of human footsteps having recently passed that way. There were only the hoof-marks of the cows which were now standing in immobile groups under the deepest shade they could find, whisking their tails lazily to drive off the flies.

Apart from the cries of the moorhen, which became louder as I walked along, there was a strange silence. After a moment's reflection I realized why it was so noticeable: there was no bird-song. Presumably the song-birds, the thrushes and blackbirds and skylarks, were, like the cows, taking their siesta. As I became increasingly hot and sticky I wondered ruefully why I was not doing the same.

Then to the intermittent squawks of the moorhen was joined the raucous quack of a duck. The lake or the river must be somewhere near. Ahead of me the pathway ran into a belt of trees. As I entered it I picked up the boggy smell of lake-side vegetation. I pressed on. Through the trees I saw the sparkle of water in the sunlight. I looked at my watch: it was five minutes to three.

The belt of trees ran close to the edge of the lake,

which appeared to be the shape of an ellipse some six or seven acres in extent, with a small wooded island towards the far end. The river entered the lake about fifty yards to my right, where there was a decrepit wooden bridge over it, with a high arch, built in an ornamental Chinese style at some time in the eighteenth century, I guessed. Presumably the river ran out of the lake again at the far end, somewhere behind the island. There was a tangle of reeds and bulrushes round the edges of the lake, but beyond it the water appeared fresh and translucent.

I stood by the water's edge and looked round the borders of the lake. There was nobody in sight. Nor could I see any sign of a temple. For the most part the lake was fringed with trees, and it might be that the temple stood somewhere amongst them, a little way back from the water. I set off to investigate.

The barely perceptible track of a path led along the edge of the lake towards the Chinese bridge. I followed it, clambered gingerly over the bridge, and continued along the far side. A fish rose; at intervals there came the clack-clack of the moorhens; but otherwise there was almost uncanny stillness and silence.

As I worked my way round the far side of the lake I saw through a break in the boscage the dome of a little rotunda, supported by slim Ionic columns, set on a mound in the middle of the island. It was, presumably, some sort of ornamental pavilion, now much overgrown by bushes and trees.

I continued my search for the temple, until I had made a complete circuit of the lake and was back at the Chinese bridge again. There was no temple to be found. Nor was there anybody to be seen.

I looked at my watch: it was a quarter past three. I mopped my forehead: this certainly could be described as the heat of the day. For the first time since I had set out I consciously and deliberately asked myself why I had come. Obviously to meet Belinda. But why should I have supposed that the assignation was more than the whim of a moment, arising out of the banter in the pub? Why should I have acted upon it, anyway? I was not especially interested in Belinda. I liked her, and she amused me; but my feelings towards her were quite superficial.

And yet – I couldn't help feeling disappointed that she was not there. And irritated, too. Why make the assignation at all, if she didn't intend to keep it? As I looked over the placid waters, lying in the sunlight like a little lost lagoon, it seemed to me a singularly appropriate and pleasant place in which to pass a hot Sunday afternoon.

I crossed the bridge again and walked slowly along the far side of the lake once more. Where was the temple? Surely it couldn't be the little rotunda of which I now got another glimpse through the undergrowth on the island? That looked more like a gazebo or belvedere: I had imagined the temple as being something more substantial. Yet perhaps it *was* the temple: there was certainly nothing else.

If so, I wondered how Belinda had expected me to get there. The island was fifty yards or so from the nearest point on the bank. And although I had now walked one and a half times round the lake I had seen no sign of a boat or even a boathouse.

Why wasn't Belinda here, anyway?

'Belinda!' I called.

There was no reply.

'Belinda! Where are you? Belinda!'

I stood by the water's edge listening to the echoes of my call. There was no response. I scanned the island and the banks of the lake, but I could see no movement, no indication of any human being. The only sign of life

214

was a solitary black moorhen, with scarlet bill, swimming purposefully towards the reeds.

Damn Belinda! I felt I had been let down. I hadn't thought much about the meeting, but I had expected her to be here; and, in the strangely exalted state of mind to which I had been lifted by the events of the last two days, I felt I needed someone to talk to.

However, Belinda wasn't here. Presumably she had forgotten all about me. I sat down on the bank of the lake. Besides feeling disappointed and irritable I felt extremely hot. I threw my jacket down on the grass. Then I took off my shoes and socks and dangled my feet in the water. It was marvellously refreshing.

Looking towards the island I began to wonder how the stones and mortar and the lead for the domed roof of the little rotunda had been carried over there. Presumably by boat. There was no sign of the island ever having been joined to the bank of the lake by a causeway or bridge. How odd that there was now no boat on the lake! The island looked charmingly romantic, and if some of the trees were cut down and the undergrowth cleared the rotunda would make a perfect setting for a picnic. The Virleys were extraordinary in their neglect of the amenities they should be enjoying. And yet, of course, it was the air of neglect and desolation which invested Arcady with so much of its charm.

My feet were now cool and refreshed, but a cloud of flies had gathered round my head. I longed to take off my clothes and plunge into the lake.

Why not? The water was very clear and clean, and, as far as I could judge, it was quite deep. There was obviously nobody about, and even if anyone did appear I was at the farthest point from the park, and I could easily get out of the water under cover of the rushes, and dress again in the privacy of the undergrowth.

I quickly undressed, stowed my clothes out of sight under a hawthorn bush, and slipped into the water.

Once I had overcome the first shock of the cold on my sweating limbs the sensation was delicious. In three or four paces I was out of my depth. I swam out vigorously for some way whilst I adjusted myself to the temperature of the water; then I turned over on my back and floated. On the surface the water was surprisingly warm; and it was so calm that one could lie quite motionless, with all one's head except one's nose and eyes submerged in the water, and gaze up into the incredible blue of the cloudless sky.

I lay thus for some time, keeping afloat with an occasional twist of the hands, and enjoying the sensation of being one with the elements which can only be experienced in very calm water and in utter solitude.

After a while I rolled over and surveyed the banks of the lake. Not a soul was to be seen or heard. I swam quietly over to the island and climbed up the bank.

The undergrowth was dense and rampant, but I was able to pick my way through it towards the grassy mound on which the rotunda stood, its Ionic columns rising gracefully from an octagonal stone podium. There was a simple carved stone cornice about the capitals of the columns, and upon this rested the leaden dome, green with age, and cracked and battered through neglect.

As I stood looking at this charming, time-worn architectural conceit, its slim columns standing in classical contrast to the unruliness of the surrounding tanglewood, and the green-grey curve of its dome outlined against the empyrean blue, I felt I might indeed be in the Arcadia of myth and legend.

I climbed up the steps of the rotunda. The sun beat down on my back and limbs, and the stone columns were hot to the hand. I walked beneath the dome and looked down over the far side.

Belinda was lying outstretched in a sunlit, daisy-carpeted glade, enclosed on three sides by a thicket of greenery. She was naked. Her tangled hair hung in disorder over her forehead. She held a daisy between her lips.

'Aren't you rather late?' she asked, removing the daisy and throwing it aside.

'Is this the temple?' I asked.

She nodded.

'You never told me it was on an island,' I said, sitting down hastily on the grass as I realized that I was naked too.

'I thought you'd find that out for yourself,' she said, with a hint of a smile. 'As indeed you did.'

'Why didn't you answer when I called?'

She stretched her arms out among the daisies and yawned. 'I was too lazy. And I thought you'd find me if you really wanted to . . . as indeed you did.'

I sat on the bank wondering what was to happen next. The sun was gloriously hot, the scene was idyllic, and Belinda's lithe and sunburnt limbs were extremely agreeable to the eye.

'Where are your clothes?' I asked.

'Not far from yours.'

'So you swam out here too?'

'There's no other way of getting here,' she said, rolling over on her back and flexing her legs, one after the other, in the air.

'So we shall have to swim back,' I said.

'Sometime,' she said, yawning again. 'But you aren't in a hurry, are you? I'm going to stay here all the afternoon. I often do.'

'That's why you're so sunburnt, I suppose?'

'Yes, I suppose so. D'you like it?' she asked, sitting up and surveying herself.

'You're beautiful,' I said.

217

'Rot!' she said. 'That, darling Jasper, was a meaningless remark. I'm not beautiful, and I know it. Chloe's beautiful. Tilly may be beautiful, one day. But I'm just a healthy, reasonably well-developed animal.'

'You're an excellent artist's model,' I said.

'You think so? But that doesn't mean I'm beautiful. It merely means I've got the right curves and proportions. The artist takes the curves and proportions and makes them seem beautiful because of the way he looks at them. Isn't that right?'

'Perhaps so. Perhaps that's why I said just now that you were beautiful. You looked beautiful to me.'

'Darling, you're incorrigible,' said Belinda, getting up and climbing the bank towards me. 'I don't believe a word you say.'

'But I mean what I say,' I protested, as she dropped down on the grass beside me.

'I expect,' she said, looking up into my eyes, 'you've said exactly the same to Chloe. And,' she said with a glint of irony in her eye, 'you meant it then, too!'

'Let's not talk about Chloe,' I said stiffly. 'We were talking – quite objectively – about you.'

'Poor Chloe!' said Belinda, ignoring my remark. 'She *is* beautiful, you know. She's beautiful all through. I'm just a dumb blonde – or would be if I weren't a brunette. I just live on my senses. But Chloe lives on her emotions. It's the rottenest sort of injustice that she should be married to Lionel. She should take a lover. I'm always telling her to. But she never will.'

I was silent. Belinda, who had been picking daisies and weaving them into a chain, hung it over the arch of my foot.

'You don't seem to want to talk about Chloe. Well, what shall we talk about – you, or me, or the scenery?'

'I don't consider myself a very interesting subject,' I said.

218

'You interest a lot of people in Arcady,' said Belinda. 'Me not least.'

'Now I don't believe a word you're saying!' I said.

'But I invariably tell the truth,' said Belinda. 'I find it utterly boring to lie, or flatter, or beat about the bush. I always know exactly what I think, and say so, bang!'

'What, then, as a matter of academic interest, do you think about me?' I asked.

She lay back on her elbows, her breasts rippling in the sunlight, and studied me solemnly.

'I think you have a nice body,' she said. 'Your shoulders are rather too narrow, and they droop a bit. But you've got straight legs, and a flat tummy, and just about the right amount of hair on your chest. You've also got very elegant toes.'

I looked down at my feet with interest and surprise. It had never occurred to me to study anyone's toes aesthetically – least of all my own.

'You're very complimentary,' I said. 'But I hardly expected a summing-up of my figure. I wondered what you thought of my personality.'

'Bodies interest me more than personalities,' said Belinda seriously. 'I envy you your toes. I've got broad, ugly, peasant's toes.'

She held out a foot for my inspection.

'They're broad, certainly,' I said. 'But they're not ugly at all. And what's wrong with being a peasant? One expects to find peasants in Arcady.'

'I'm a peasant all right,' said Belinda. 'I suppose that's one reason why I stay here. I don't feel at home anywhere else.'

'You certainly look at home here. Do you always have this island to yourself?'

'I have company sometimes. And I think I hear them coming now.'

I jumped up apprehensively.

219

'Don't get worried!' said Belinda, her eyes sparkling with amusement. 'There's no need for you to come over bashful. They won't mind in the least whether you're dressed or starkers.'

Down by the bank a duck began to quack. There was a sound of movement in the reeds.

'Look here . . .!' I said.

'I'm looking,' said Belinda mischievously. 'I quite like what I see.'

I began to feel, for the first time, really embarrassed by my nakedness. 'What I mean is, you may be accustomed to lying about in company with no clothes on; but I'm not. I'm not a nudist. I think I'd better beat a retreat.'

'Too late,' laughed Belinda. 'You've got to stay and face the music now. Here they come!' She pointed to a narrow opening at the foot of the glade. Through this appeared a speckled brown duck, waddling vigorously up the slope, followed by a large brood of fluffy gold-and-black ducklings.

Belinda rolled over on to her back and giggled delightedly. 'Poor darling Jasper! How I tease you! Come on, duckies. Duckies, duckies, duckies!'

As she called they came running eagerly towards her, the little ducklings darting ahead of their mother and tumbling over themselves to reach Belinda first.

'How are you, duckies?' she said, holding her hand out to them. The ducklings darted to her, nuzzling and nudging her fingers with their bills. Behind them came the mother duck, waddling from side to side, and emitting deep quacks.

'Jasper darling,' said Belinda, 'run up to the temple, and in the very middle of the floor you'll find a loose paving stone. Lift it up and bring me a handful of the corn you'll find there.'

I did as she asked me. The loose paving stone concealed a small lead cistern, in which there was a bag of wheat. I brought two handfuls back to Belinda.

'Here you are, duckies!' she said, lying down and sprinkling the corn all over and around herself. The ducklings clambered over her, utterly fearless in their greed, squatting on her chest and her tummy as they gobbled up the grain in their eager black bills.

'Will you feed Mama?' said Belinda. I held out a handful of corn to the mother duck, who approached me with sidelong glances of suspicion, and then settled down to a hearty meal off the palm of my hand.

'What breed of duck is this?' I asked.

'Mallard,' said Belinda, who was picking up the little balls of gold-and-black fluff and cuddling them against her breasts. 'Commonly known as wild duck.'

'They don't seem very wild,' I said.

'They know me,' said Belinda.

'Perhaps they regard you as a wild creature, too,' I said.

'Perhaps they do,' said Belinda, rolling over in the grass and letting the ducklings clamber and tumble over her head and shoulders. 'I'm really just an animal, you know. I've nothing inside me. I'm an entirely sensual person. If you look at me you see the whole of me.'

I looked at her, lying among the daisies, her hair tousled, her limbs sprawling in complete unselfconsciousness, and the ducklings perching on her thighs or nestling against her breasts. She was not of the world I knew and lived in.

'Come on, duckies!' she said suddenly, jumping to her feet. 'Let's all go for a swim.' She ran down the bank towards the reeds, followed by the mother duck and a tumbling horde of gold-and-black followers. 'Follow me, Jasper! Come and swim!'

I followed the procession down the slope, and into the water's edge. As I pushed my way through the

221

reeds I saw Belinda's head and shoulders rising from the waters of the lake, encircled by a flotilla of little feathered craft.

I swam out towards her. At the same time another duck appeared from the reeds, with a noisy flapping of her wings, pursued by a handsome green-and-black-headed drake.

'Now, Jasper,' called Belinda. 'Don't be outdone by that lusty young drake. Catch me! Try and catch me!' She plunged under the water, kicked up her heels in the air, and disappeared.

I dived after her, and swam around in the depths, following the gleam of her body in the green under-water shadows. Once I caught hold of her ankle, but she slipped away from me, twisting and turning like a fish.

We both rose to the surface at the same moment, laughing and gasping for breath. 'I see the drake has put you to shame,' said Belinda, pointing into the reeds, where, in a flurry of quacks and splashes, the drake was maintaining a precarious grip on the back of his loved one's neck.

'If you want to be gripped by the hair, submerged, and treated to a general rough-and-tumble, I've no doubt I could do it,' I said, reaching out and grasping Belinda's shoulders.

With a sudden twist she evaded my grip, plunged under the water, then rose unexpectedly close beside me. Twining her legs round my waist she clung to me for a moment, darted her tongue between my lips, then swam off at speed.

I followed, with the swiftest stroke I could muster. But she was a skilful swimmer, and each time I thought I was catching up with her she changed course, or dived, or otherwise escaped me. We made two full circuits of the island; then at last she turned over on to her back, raised both hands in the air, and said breathlessly, 'Now I've got my fingers crossed.'

I swam up beside her, put my hand gently under the back of her neck, and kissed her forehead. Then we swam quietly and slowly, side by side, to the island.

'Who built this temple?' I asked, as we clambered up through the reeds.

'I believe it was built for my great-great-great-great grandfather by a man called William Kent,' said Belinda. 'It was part of a grandiose scheme for transforming Arcady into a vast landscape garden. But my great-great-great-great grandfather gambled his fortune away in a night, and there was no more money for William Kent – or anyone since.'

'How very reprehensible of great-great-great-great grandfather,' I said. 'But I think I like it all just as it is.'

'So do I,' said Belinda.

We lay down on the bank. After the fun and flurry of our chase through the water the touch of the sunshine was exquisitely relaxing and benign.

'What gods or goddesses does one worship here?' I asked.

'Aphrodite,' said Belinda, plucking a daisy and putting it between her lips. 'The goddess of love. Her statue used to be here, but it was taken away and sold.'

'A pity,' I said, lying back and gazing up into the unbelievably blue sky.

'Jasper,' said Belinda, a few minutes later. 'Would you like to worship Aphrodite?'

'Yes,' I said, turning my head and studying the classical beauty of the temple outlined against the sky.

'You still could worship her, you know,' said Belinda, a little while later, 'even though her statue's gone.'

'Could I?' I said, rolling over and looking down at her brown, animal limbs, akimbo in the sun. 'Then perhaps I will.'

223

'When?'

'Just as soon as you take that daisy out of your mouth.'

She lay for some time with her eyes shut and the daisy between her lips. Then she took it out, leaned over me, and twined it into my hair.

The sun was sinking below the tops of the trees across the lake when we swam slowly and placidly from the island to the shore. We dried each other with handfuls of dead leaves from under the trees.

'That was fun, wasn't it?' said Belinda, as we got into our clothes.

'Fun?'

'You don't feel emotional, darling, do you?' said Belinda, coming close to me and putting her hands on my shoulders.

'It's hard to say,' I answered. 'Yes, I suppose I do.'

'I don't,' said Belinda firmly. 'I feel snug, and refreshed, and satisfied – and happy. But I don't feel the least bit emotional. I'm just not made that way.'

'Perhaps I am,' I said.

'Oh dear,' said Belinda, laying her head against my chest. 'I don't think it can ever happen again, if you're going to be emotional. And I so much want it to!'

'So do I,' I admitted.

'To me it's just sheer pleasure,' she said. 'It doesn't involve anything at all except our two bodies and our five senses – there are five, aren't there?'

'I think so,' I said, as we began to walk slowly back towards the park.

'I wouldn't want you to feel involved, though,' she continued. 'It wouldn't be fun any more.'

We walked on in silence for a while. Belinda took my hand. The evening shadows fell across our path; a blackbird was singing. I found my thoughts running back to what the Professor had said to me so earnestly, earlier in the day.

'What do you make of the Professor?' I asked suddenly.

Belinda glanced at me with curiosity. 'The Prof's all right. He's a bit dreary at times, of course. I suppose he would be, being a professor. But he's got the right ideas. Why do you ask?'

'Because at lunch today he talked to me so eloquently and earnestly – almost poetically – about Arcady. I wondered if he genuinely felt like that.'

'The Prof's certainly emotional, if that's what you mean,' said Belinda. 'You've only to see him sitting up on the turret of the gatehouse at night, brooding.'

'I have,' I said.

'For all that schoolmasterish air, the Prof is an involved type – deeply involved.'

'Involved with whom?' I asked in surprise.

'Involved with Arcady. I'm sure he thinks far more about us all than we do ourselves. And it's a funny thing: I'm sure he disapproves of me and my goings-on – he'd hardly be likely to approve, would he? – but yet in an odd sort of way I feel he understands me and wouldn't want me to be any different. I believe he sees me almost as part of the landscape – like the peafowl and the wild duck and the dog-roses in the hedges.'

I reflected on what she had said as we walked through the meadows towards the railway line. 'At lunch today,' I said, 'the Professor told me I should pay my respects to the spirit of the place – the *genius loci*, he called it.'

'He didn't by any chance refer to her as Aphrodite?' said Belinda, looking at me out of the corners of her eyes.

'Not actually.'

'Well, you've paid your respects to her, anyway,' said Belinda. 'And very nicely you did it, my darling.'

I pulled her to me and kissed her unruly hair.

'The Professor also said I should listen to the voices in the woods.'

'There's one!' said Belinda, stopping in her stride. 'The blackbird.' We paused and listened to the measured, deep-throated, reflective notes – the purest and, to me, the most moving of all bird songs. 'And there's another, chiff-chaff.' We listened to its monotonous call. Then we walked on.

'He also mentioned the pipes of Pan,' I said. 'I thought that a bit whimsical.'

Ahead of us the Victorian Gothic shelter at the Halt came into view. Beside it stood Lord Flamborough's train, a haze of steam rising slowly from the dome of the engine.

'The pipes of Pan?' repeated Belinda, with a puzzled frown. 'Oh, I see what he meant! Listen! Can't you hear them?'

I raised my head and listened. The blackbird and the chiff-chaff were now silent; but from the open windows of the Flamborough Flier came the wheeze of his Lordship's 'phonograph'. It was playing 'I Want to be Happy'.

'Come in, dear fellow!' roared Lord Flamborough.

'Join the party! 'Linda, where've you been? Leading Sir Jasper down the primrose path, I don't doubt. Well, fix him up at once with a stiff cocktail. What's it to be, Jasper – a Dark Lady? Or Angel's Tears?'

I chose Angel's Tears. Belinda handed me a glass and then disappeared into the domestic quarters of the train.

'This'll do you more good than those devilish potions

226

of Lionel's you swallowed yesterday,' said Lord Flamborough. 'Not that they seem to have harmed you, judging by your form on the cricket field. You must have a head like granite. Wish I had your constitution. I suppose it's all that dancing you go in for. Nothing like the Charleston for cooling the heels and clearing the head, eh, Jones?'

It was not apparent why this rhetorical question was addressed to Jones, who was sitting in front of Lord Flamborough's record cabinet, surrounded by discs and catalogues and notebooks.

'I can't trace,' said Jones, 'that yer Lordship's collection ever included Albert Ammons's "Boogie Woogie Stomp". It ain't in the catalogue.'

'I'm sure I had it,' said Lord Flamborough. 'It was a Decca record, about 1935 – a very beefy blues-stomp, with a long piano solo, followed by solos on the clarinet and the trumpet.'

'Talking of lilies,' said Lady Flamborough, coming through from the kitchen and addressing me, 'I did have quite a few *Lilium auratum*, but they died off. The leaves went brown, and then rotten.'

'Devilish potions, indeed!' Lionel Virley, who had apparently been lying asleep on the 1851 sofa at the far end of the saloon, sat up and blinked. 'Did I hear you describe my wines, Bertie, as devilish potions? That was a little uncalled-for. Jasper will bear me out that they are singularly bland and mature. And unusual. I don't know where else you'd find some of the vintages I've got.'

'I might find one down the Charing Cross Road,' said Jones. 'But it would cost me money. It must be Ammons's "Boogie Woogie Stomp", I suppose? You wouldn't want the original "Stomp", by Pine-Top Smith?'

'Devilish potions, indeed!' grumbled Lionel.

'I think I've got the Pine-Top Smith "Stomp",' said

Lord Flamborough. 'You'll find it on the second shelf, beyond that Vocalion record of Louis Armstrong's "Tight Like This".'

'Tight like what?' said Lionel. 'I only wish I were.'

'Then the flowers go rotten,' said Lady Flamborough, 'and the whole thing becomes a rather putrid mess, and if you dig the bulbs up they're covered with red spots. It's a nuisance. I had a lovely lot of *Lilium auratum* until that happened.'

'This is a nice little lot o' Louis Armstrongs you've got 'ere,' said Jones, pulling out a bunch of records and studying them. 'There's a pretty keen demand for these original waxes nowadays. Like me to get you an offer for them?'

'Wouldn't dream of selling them,' said Lord Flamborough. 'Best stuff I've got – "Knockin' a Jug", with that shouting trombone solo by Teagarden; "West End Blues" – that's got Zutty Singleton on the drums; and then there's a very early King Oliver recording in which he and Armstrong doubled the trumpet solos – "Dipper Mouth Blues", wasn't it?'

'Botrytis Disease, I should say it was,' said Lady Flamborough. 'It's a fungus. Let's have supper.'

We all got up and went into the dining car, preceded by Lord Flamborough in his invalid chair.

'Lionel, are you sober enough to do the firing?' said Lord Flamborough. 'Chloe's on the footplate, and I promised to pick up the Prof at Flaxfield. A little run in the cool of the evening would be pleasant.'

'I haven't been sober for six months, Bertie dear,' said Lionel. 'But I am not drunk, nor am I high, or stinking, or pissed, or any of those rather disgusting epithets which are flung around so freely in polite society.'

'Well, what are you, dearie?' said Dimple Pott, who appeared at the kitchen door reading the *Sunday Pictorial*.

'I'm exquisitely balanced in a state of equilibrium between the thrust of reality and the counterpoise of delirium,' said Lionel.

' 'Ere, 'ere!' cried Jones, clapping vigorously. 'Nobody who can deliver a curtain line like that can be accused o' bein' – what was that nasty word 'e mentioned? But in the circumstances I propose to offer me own services to Lady C. as fireman.'

'That's extr'ordinarily generous and decent of you, Jonesy boy,' said Lionel. 'I much appreciate it. I shall now go and rub up Susie's brass-work.' He stumbled from the dining car. Jones went to join Chloe on the footplate.

'Tight as a tick,' remarked Lord Flamborough, pulling his chair up to the table. 'No matter. Jones never lets us down. Would you like to flag the train out this evening, Sir Jasper?'

'It would be an honour,' I said, taking the green flag which Lady Flamborough offered me.

Lord Flamborough adjusted his peaked guard's cap on his head and felt for his watch and his whistle. I took the green flag out on to the platform. Chloe, in brown overalls, with Jones behind her, waved to me from the hood of the engine. From inside the dining car came a blast on the guard's whistle. I waved the green flag and remounted the train.

'Good fellow, Jones,' said Lord Flamborough, as I joined him at the table, where, still wearing the guard's cap, he was drinking his soup. 'Don't know why he bothers with us – except that Dimple gives him free board and lodging at the pub. He knows no end about those old gramophone records – some I've had since the 'twenties.'

'Jones is a genius in his way,' said Lady Flamborough. 'But unfortunately he's completely ignorant about plants. Unlike you, Sir Jasper.'

'Please, Lady Flamborough – and you, sir, too,' I said, 'would you mind dropping the "Sir Jasper" and just calling me "Jasper"?'

'Of course, dear fellow,' said Lord Flamborough. 'Don't want to stand on ceremony, eh? Quite right. Anyway, you're one of the family now.'

I wondered vaguely what he meant by that, but the conversation passed on.

'He's our horticultural adviser, too,' said Lady Flamborough. 'He has a quite exceptional knowledge of lilies and rose species.'

I made modest sounds of dissent.

'What would you advise me to plant on the other side of the path?' asked Lady Flamborough. 'I'd like to confine that entirely to roses – the really uncommon ones.'

I put down my knife and fork and considered the question. To my dismay I found that my mind was now a blank: the name of every rose I knew seemed to have passed out of my head.

'Think carefully before you answer,' said Lady Flamborough. 'I want something really distinctive.'

Lord Flamborough was gazing at me with interest. For once he appeared to have got down off his own hobby-horse.

'I should suggest,' I said (what should I suggest?), 'one of the *fruticosas*.'

'*Fruticosa*? That's a new one to me,' said Lady Flamborough. It was also entirely new to me.

'It's a hybrid of *Mancuniensis*,' I said, slipping still deeper into invention.

'Never heard of that one either,' said Lady Flamborough. 'What did I tell you, Bertie! We've got an authority here. I must remember those two names – *fruticosa* and *Mancuniensis*.'

'And he can dance the Charleston, too!' said Lord Flamborough.

'And he goes to the Café de Paris,' said Dimple, who came into the dining car carrying the next course.

'You go to the Café de Paris?' said Lord Flamborough. 'Why, I was there the first night the Prince of Wales went. He made the place, you know. He and a pair of coloured singers, Layton and Johnstone – first-class, they were; used to hunt with the Quorn, too. But that first night the Prince of Wales went – what a party! I didn't go to bed until nine o'clock next morning.'

'I usually go to bed earlier than that,' I said, with a laugh.

'Who with, though?' murmured Dimple, who was clearing away the plates. 'That's the sixty-four-dollar question.'

'You're a demon with the girls, I gather,' said Lord Flamborough. 'So was I at your time of life. We only live once.'

I felt the train slowing up.

'You wouldn't care to marry my daughter 'Linda, I suppose?' said Lord Flamborough. 'It's time she got a husband. She's a dab at the Charleston, but she can never find a partner for it.'

Before I could think of any answer to make, the train came to a stop, Jones's voice called out 'Flaxfield – Junction for London, Glasgow, and King's Lynn,' and Lord Flamborough, after consulting his watch, announced that the journey had taken twenty-seven minutes precisely.

'Good evening, ma Lord and ma Lady,' said the Professor, entering the dining car, followed by Miss Mounsey, Quirk, and the old shepherd with white whiskers who had led the singing the night before. 'I told Chitty Buckthorn that I was sure ye'd gie him a lift as far as Arcady. Ah, guid evening, Pye! Did ye have a pleasant afternoon in the woods?'

'Very pleasant, thank you,' I said.

'Let's all go into the saloon,' said Lord Flamborough. 'Are there any brats outside asking for sweets?'

'I fear so,' said the Professor.

'Open the window, dear fellow, will you?' said Lord Flamborough. Quirk and the Professor pulled the window down.

'Why aren't you loathsome brats tucked up in bed?' roared Lord Flamborough, leaning out of the window. 'I'd cane the lot of you if I were your Dad.'

This threat was received by the groundlings with delighted giggles.

'Johnny,' continued Lord Flamborough, 'what were you doing under Grannie Tuddenham's strawberry net this afternoon? Marilyn, go home at once and take that lipstick off your face. At your age! Scandalous! Gary, give me that catapult I can see sticking out of your pocket. And do your fly-buttons up.'

There was a screech of appreciation from the assembled children.

'Take this, you little horrors!' said Lord Flamborough, throwing a bag of sweets amongst them. 'And never let me catch sight of you again.' He turned to Quirk. 'Would you mind taking over from Jones on the footplate?'

'Certainly, sir,' said Quirk, bustling out on to the line.

'Come and sit down, Chitty.' Lord Flamborough beckoned to the shepherd, who settled down on the sofa, his crook still grasped in his hand.

'I dew loike a-ridin' in a train, your Lordship,' he said. 'Often enough I've a-promised meself a trip on the train to Lunnon, but I ain't never found no toime for it.'

'Well, Chitty,' said Lord Flamborough, 'perhaps you'd like to flag us out.' He handed the green flag to the old man. 'Wave it out of the window when I blow the whistle.'

Chitty Buckthorn rose with great solemnity and performed the task, holding tight to his shepherd's crook as he did so. The train moved off.

'So you've never been to London, Chitty?' said the Professor.

'No, bor,' said Chitty.

'But you can dance the Charleston, eh, Chitty?' said Lord Flamborough.

Chitty grinned. 'I kin dance!' he chuckled.

Lord Flamborough began winding up his gramophone. 'Look in the top shelf of the cabinet, Jasper, and see if you can find "Jazz Me Blues".'

I found the record and handed it to him.

'Girls!' shouted Lord Flamborough. 'Leave the washing-up and come and dance the Charleston.'

Jones pushed the chairs and the sofa back against the walls. The Professor picked up the aspidistras and carried them out into the lavatories. Dimple, Belinda, and Miss Mounsey came in from the kitchen. The gramophone began to grind out 'Jazz Me Blues'.

As her father had said, Belinda was indeed a dab at the Charleston. She flung herself into the rhythm of the dance with a total absence of inhibitions, but her neatness of figure and agility of limb achieved exactly the right precision and bounce. In a moment I had lost all traces of self-consciousness and was kicking up my heels with enthusiasm.

So, too, was Chitty Buckthorn. His version of the Charleston was not quite that of *The Boy Friend*; it was a curiously formal kind of jig, which may have had its origin in the seventeenth century. But it was astonishingly lively for a man of his age, and he hopped round and round delightedly, with one arm round Miss Mounsey's waist and the other firmly tethered to his shepherd's crook.

'Swing it, Chitty!' roared Lord Flamborough, belabouring his drums. 'Hotcha, hotcha!'

Out in the vestibule I saw Jones, enfolded in the ample embrace of Dimple, performing a series of highly individual steps which seemed to derive partly from the Catalan *sardanas* and partly from the Palais Glide.

Belinda concluded a free jiving sequence and we came together again, dancing cheek to cheek. 'Isn't this super, darling!' she murmured. 'You dance beautifully. I adore you.'

'Ditto, ditto, ditto,' I said, feeling ridiculously gay and silly and light-hearted.

'Jazz Me Blues' blew itself out at last in a brassy cadenza and we all fell back, laughing, gasping, and mopping our brows, on to the plush and antimacassars.

'Oh boy! Oh boy!' exclaimed Lord Flamborough with profound satisfaction, as he took off the record and re-wound the gramophone. 'Now let's try a Louis Armstrong – "I Can't Give You Anything but Love". This has got some wizard scat-singing in it, and it's Eddie Condon playing the banjo. You'll enjoy this, Chitty.'

The old shepherd sat on the sofa between Miss Mounsey and Dimple, his vellum features wrinkled with smiles.

'Hey, bor!' he said. 'Would this Eddie Condon be any relation of Rusty Condon, what yewsed to rear turkeys ower beyond Beccles?'

'I doubt it, Chitty,' said Lord Flamborough solemnly. 'Eddie Condon's an American.'

'Ah,' said Chitty. 'One of they Yanks.' He turned to me. 'This here Rusty Condon were a Beccles man; an' a proper caution he were. Swallow six pints in a row, he would, at The Fox and Goose. Then he'd git into his motor-car, start it oop, fall asleep, and drive houme.'

'Fall asleep and drive home?' I repeated.

'Ah, bor! Don' seem possible, do it? But Rusty were a crafty divil – up-to-date, too. Allus yewsed to tune his motor in to a radar beam, like these airyplanes. He jus' went to sleep, and his motor druv itself, on the beam.'

'Extraordinary!' I said.

' 'Twas all right,' continued Chitty, 'until one evening Rusty woke up and saw t'road wobbling from side to side. Motor-car was runnin' dead straight along radar beam, but road was rockin' like a fishin' smack. Police didn't loike that, bor.'

'I should think not.'

'Blarst no, bor!' said Chitty. He leaned forward. 'I reckon trains is better 'n motor-cars or airyplanes. I'd allus feel safer on a pair o' railway lines than on a radar beam, wouldn't yew, bor?'

I agreed with him.

The phonograph started to play 'I Can't Give You Anything but Love'. Chitty Buckthorn hopped to his feet, bowed to Belinda with old-world courtesy, and invited her to dance. I saw Dimple bearing down upon me.

'Will you have this one with me?' I said hastily to Miss Mounsey.

'I'd love to,' she said, jumping up.

We took it as a quick step. The Mouse was a neat but unspectacular dancer, a good deal more reserved in her movements than Belinda.

'I like this record,' she said. 'Don't you?'

'Yes,' I said.

'The floor's quite good, isn't it?' she said.

'Remarkably good, considering it's only a railway coach.'

We danced in silence for a time.

'Have you been to any good shows lately?' said the Mouse at last.

'None to equal this,' I replied.

'Listen to this trombone solo, Jasper!' shouted Lord Flamborough. 'It's played by J. C. Higginbotham.'

'I've never heard of him,' confessed the Mouse.

'Nor have I,' I said.

Dimple and Jones, who now seemed to be attempting a Valeta, collided with us. We danced out of the saloon into the little vestibule. Through the open door of one of the lavatories I caught a glimpse of Lady Flamborough sponging the leaves of the aspidistras in the basin. We danced back into the saloon again.

'There'd be more room in the dining car,' said the Mouse.

The dining car was not only empty but pleasantly cool. Through the open windows I watched the trees and hedges passing like dim ghosts in the dusk. From the saloon came the guttural voice of Louis Armstrong:

'I can't give yuh anything but love, bebbie,
I can't give yuh anything but love.'

Through the windows came the soft summer scents of sheep's parsley and elder blossom. I drew the Mouse closer to me as we danced. She looked up at me.

'Hasn't it been a beautiful day!' she said.

'It's a beautiful evening, too,' I said.

I felt a sudden tenderness towards her – a desire to share my light-heartedness and light-headedness with her. I bent down and kissed her. For a moment her lips welcomed mine. Then I felt her shoulders stiffen, and she turned her head away. We danced back down the gangway to the saloon.

In the saloon we now found the Professor, wearing Lord Flamborough's guard's cap peak to back, and executing a vigorous sword dance. Louis Armstrong was providing the music; on the floor the red and green signalling flags provided the crossed swords. Chitty Buckthorn, Belinda, Jones, and Dimple stood round in a circle, beating time and shouting encouragement.

The Mouse and I joined the circle. For so tall and dignified a figure the Professor displayed surprising dash and agility. His face was flushed; his eyes sparkled; his socks had fallen round his ankles. At intervals he emitted a blood-curdling yell.

An alto saxophone break led into Louis Armstrong's final jungle-cry chorus:

'I can't give yuh anything but love, bebbie,
I can't give yuh anything but love.'

The record ended, and the train drew up at the Halt for Arcady Hall.

'Hotcha, hotcha, hotcha!' gasped Lord Flamborough. 'Oh boy, what a party!'

The Professor was mopping his face and neck. 'I fear, ma dear Pye, that ma performance was a wee bit rude and unpolished. *Ars est celare artem*, but it is difficult to achieve finesse of the foot movements when one's sock-suspenders have fallen doun.'

There were footsteps in the corridor and Lionel appeared, in his panama hat.

'I'd like you all to come and look at Susie's brass-work,' he said. 'While you've been gallivanting across the countryside I've been bulling like a rookie. Have you got a glass of beer, Bertie? I'm devilish thirsty.'

While Lionel poured out a glass of beer for himself we all trooped out of the train, stepped down from the little wooden platform of the Halt, and walked over to Susie, who was standing at the end of the broad footpath leading to the Hall. Even in the twilight one could see the gleam and glitter of her name-plate, her boiler bands, and the other brass accoutrements.

'Jolly good, Lionel darling!' said Chloe, coming along with Quirk from the engine of the train. 'That's going to make a stir in the *concours d'élégance* tomorrow.'

'Tomorrow!' said Lionel, draining his glass of beer and putting an arm round Chloe's shoulders. 'That'll be the day. I think you'll be quite a credit to me, won't you, Susie old girl?' He patted her boiler affectionately.

'How would it be,' he said, 'if I gave her a trial run up the path and round the Hall? I've already got up steam, as you see.'

He clambered on to the driving platform. 'Come up here, Quirky, and give me a hand!'

Lionel eased the regulator momentarily, the flywheel twirled, and the engine delivered itself of several throbbing exhaust beats. Quirk jumped up on to the footplate.

'All away!' cried Lionel. With a resounding clang he engaged the heavy gears. Then he opened the regulator again, and with a brisk coughing sound Susie moved off.

We all followed her, headed by Chitty, who was flourishing his crook and delivering cries of exhortation to Susie, as though she were a sheepdog.

Belinda slipped an arm through mine. A moment later Chloe took my other arm. I felt rather mad and singularly happy.

'I propose to make two complete circuits of the Hall,' called Lionel, above the beat of the exhaust and the loud crunching of iron wheels on gravel.

'Doan run'ee into the duzzy moat, bor!' cried Chitty.

Through the twilight and the clouds of steam and smoke that poured from Susie's funnel the vast mass of the gatehouse loomed into view. As we passed the bridge over the moat Lionel removed his panama hat and bowed ceremoniously towards the Hall. Chitty raised his shepherd's crook like a bandmaster and began to sing:

> 'In Arcady, bor, in Arcady, bor,
> We spin the lasses across the floor!
> In Arcady, bor, in Arcady, bor,
> We twist the spigot and ask for more!'

Chloe and Belinda broke into the bouncy, trotting motion which seemed to be the dance accompaniment to the song. I dropped easily into step and rhythm with them.

Ahead of us Susie was shooting sparks into the night sky. I turned my head and saw that the Professor and Jones and Dimple and the Mouse had also linked arms and were following us in the processional dance. Behind them came Lord Flamborough, propelling his invalid chair and singing lustily.

As we turned the corner of the moat the moon rose, clear and almost full, above the castellations of the Hall.

I blew out the candle flame and sank back among the pillows. I was tired, and I guessed it would only be a few minutes before I fell asleep.

The moonlight shone through the leaded casements, repeating the same patterns on the carpet and the huge oak chimney-piece as it had made two nights ago. The moons in the paintings on the wall frowned or winked or stared coldly back at their original, just as they had done then. Yet, in these past two days, what an amazing change had been wrought in me.

In these two days I seemed to have been living somewhere between Sir Philip Sidney's Arcadia and Alice's Wonderland. I had been experiencing emotions which were in a totally different key from any I had experienced before. I had, as it were, taken leave of my senses. Or was it, rather, that I had discovered them?

The moonlight was so bright that I turned over in bed and shifted my gaze into the shadows of the great open fireplace. I felt my eyelids closing.

> How sweet it were, hearing the downward
>   stream,
> With half-shut eyes ever to seem
> Falling asleep in a half-dream . . .

The lines of 'The Lotos Eaters' crept into my mind like
phrases of some half-forgotten song. Yes, I, too, seemed
to have been eating the lotos. I was heavily under its
influence.

I drifted sleepily into a haze of lotos-dust, through
which I saw, at one moment, the golden hair of Chloe's
head as she bent over the stone shelf in the dungeon; at
another, Lionel ceremoniously doffing his panama as
his traction engine chugged past the gatehouse of the
Hall. The lotos-mist eddied and swirled, and there was
Belinda naked in the grass, the dome of the temple of
Aphrodite silhouetted against the blue sky above her.
Through the mist came half-heard strains of music:

> There is soft music here that softer falls
> Than petals from blown roses on the grass,
> Or night-dews or still waters between walls
> Of shadowy granite, in a gleaming pass;
> Music that gentlier on the spirit lies,
> Than tired eyelids upon tired eyes . . .

Was it the tranquil soliloquy of the blackbird? The
clack-clack of the moorhen in the reeds? Or the distant,
husky wheeze of the mad Earl's 'phonograph' grinding
out jazz?

Yes, it was the gramophone. I could hear the
scratching of the needle on the disc – on, on, it went,
scratching, scratching . . . Why didn't the band start
up? What was wrong? Why this scratching, scratching
of the needle on the disc . . . ?

I was suddenly awake again. Had I been dreaming? The moonlight still streamed into the room: the pattern on the carpet and the chimney-piece was unchanged. But what was that scratching sound, that half-heard scuffling noise? I looked over to the great open hearth. Yes, that was where the noise came from. I listened intently. Jackdaws in the chimney? Or rats?

There was a patter of soot falling in the hearth. I turned over and closed my eyes again. If it were a jackdaw I supposed I should have to get up and let it out of the window. But perhaps it would fly up the chimney again and get out the way it got in.

I must have fallen asleep again almost at once, but I awoke a second time, with a disagreeable start, as another and heavier fall of soot descended into the hearth. I reached for my matches and lit the candle.

The hearth was scattered with soot and little bits of plaster. The scrabbling sound got louder and nearer. Then, with a thud, an animate object, a great deal larger than I expected, dropped into the hearth.

'What on earth...?' I sat up in bed and gazed in astonishment at the creature which scrambled out of the fireplace, wearing gym shoes and pyjamas – bespattered with soot and plaster dust – and with a sooty handkerchief wound tightly round her head.

'What on earth are you doing?' I gasped.

'You don't sound very thrilled to see me,' said Matilda.

'I was hardly expecting you. I thought it was a rat or a jackdaw in the chimney.'

'I'm sorry you were disappointed,' said Matilda sadly. 'Am I much less welcome than a rat or a jackdaw?'

'Don't be silly,' I said irritably. 'I didn't mean that at all. I merely meant that I was astonished to see you.

One doesn't often have young girls coming down the chimney into one's bedroom.'

'Doesn't one?' she said innocently. 'I wouldn't know.'

She pulled the handkerchief off her head and shook it out in the hearth. 'I'm a bit messier than I thought I'd be,' she said. 'Perhaps that's why I've created such a bad impression.'

'You haven't created a bad impression,' I said. 'As a matter of fact you look rather quaint and pathetic, like the chimney-sweep in *The Water Babies*.'

'I suppose it's better to be quaint or pathetic than merely repulsive,' she said. 'But I thought perhaps you'd actually be pleased to see me.'

'I am, my dear,' I said. 'Why don't you sit down?'

She walked dejectedly to the foot of the bed. 'Can I sit here?' she said. 'Or would that be too close?'

'Sit where you like, as long as you don't shed too much soot about the place.'

'I suppose I am a bit sooty,' she said, looking down at herself. 'I didn't think there'd be so much soot: there hasn't been a fire in that hearth for years.'

'How long had you been hiding up there?' I asked.

'I wasn't hiding up there,' she said. 'I've come straight down.'

'Surely you haven't come all the way down the chimney?'

'Yes,' she said.

'I assumed you'd slipped into the room before I came to bed, and just climbed up far enough to hide.'

'No, I came over the roof.'

'Over the roof? But you're crazy! It's a terrible height.'

'I'm not afraid of heights, you know.'

'But I've seen those chimneys from the turret of the gatehouse. They rise high up above the roof. How on earth did you get up there?'

'It wasn't very difficult,' she said. 'It was a bit of a swizz, really. The top of this particular chimney blew off in a storm last winter, and it wasn't any bother to climb into it.'

'Rather you than me,' I said with feeling. 'But what are you going to do now?'

'I suppose I ought to clean up a bit,' she said.

'Pour some water into the basin and have a wash,' I suggested. 'The water's not hot, but it will get the thick of the soot off.'

'Thank you,' she said, going over to the washstand. 'Will you excuse me if I strip down to the waist?'

'Well, yes,' I said hesitantly.

'Actually, I'm not used to undressing with a man in the room,' she said. She took off her pyjama jacket, and poured some water into the basin. Her shoulders were slim and pale in the candlelight. She washed her face and neck and arms.

'Would it be in order for me to borrow one of your towels?' she asked.

'Of course.'

She dried herself. Standing in the far corner of the room, with the candlelight indistinctly illuminating her slim shoulders, her dark hair, and her deep-set eyes, she had an elfin, waif-like air.

'I'm not so messy now,' she said. 'Could I sit on the end of the bed?'

'Your pyjama trousers look a bit sooty,' I said. 'I don't know what Miss Mounsey would think if she found soot all over the blankets.'

'Should I take off my pyjama trousers?'

'Oh no!' I said hastily. 'Put my shirt on the bed, and sit on that. It's got to go to the laundry anyway.'

She did as I suggested, and sat on the edge of the bed. In profile, the long, intellectual, yet romantic line of her nose, contrasting with the delicate, virginal curve of her breasts, was rather lovely.

243

'What happens next?' she said, after a while.

'How do you mean, what happens next?'

'I was asking the question,' she said. 'Not you. I thought perhaps you'd give the answer.'

'I took it as a rhetorical question which didn't call for an answer.'

'I don't know what "rhetorical" means,' she said in a halting voice. 'I only meant that I didn't know what to do next.'

'You could put on your pyjama top,' I said, 'and I'd give you a good-night kiss and hold the door open for you.'

There was a pause. She sat quite still, looking thoughtfully at the moonlight pictures on the wall.

'I suppose,' she said, 'you're playing with me like a cat with a mouse. I suppose it amuses you.'

I sat up in bed and clasped my knees. The situation was gathering intensity. 'Why did you come here tonight?' I asked.

'You must know – quite well.'

'I could think of several reasons,' I said. 'But I honestly don't know which would be the right one.'

'What are they?' She sat quite still, in profile, strangely passive, yet disturbingly attractive.

'You might have come,' I said, 'just for fun, for a lark, for the thrill and amusingness of climbing over the roof and making a dramatic entry, to the consternation of the man in the bedroom.'

'Did I constern you very much?' she asked, turning her head towards me for the first time, and looking at me from those brooding eyes with almost a hint of irony.

'I wasn't actually consterned, as you put it. But I was about to fall asleep, and I was really rather tired. Also I was – how shall I put it? – a little taken aback.'

'I'm glad I didn't actually constern you,' she said,

turning away in profile again. 'But I'm surprised you were taken aback. You aren't usually taken aback, are you? I'd got the impression that you were usually one step ahead of everyone else. Perhaps it was just because you were tired and sleepy: I could understand that.'

'Dear Matilda,' I said, 'I *was* rather tired and sleepy. And, in fact, I still am.'

'Oh dear! I suppose I've made an awful bish.'

'A bish?' I said. 'What is a bish?'

'It's a word they used at a school I went to once. It means a mess-up, a flop, a ghastly miscalculation.'

'But, my dear, you haven't done any of those things. What's the worry?'

'I think I *have* made a bish, Sir Jasper,' she said. 'You see, I was sure you'd want me here tonight. It never entered my head that you'd be tired and sleepy. That wasn't one of the things I took into my calculations.'

'What did you take into your calculations?'

'Nothing, I suppose, on your side. I just thought you'd do as I thought you would. It never occurred to me that you might be tired and sleepy.'

'And what did you think I'd do?'

'You know quite well what I thought you'd do.'

I put out my hand and took hold of hers. 'If I were to do what you thought I'd do, how would you feel about it?' I asked.

'I'm not quite sure,' she said. 'I'm a bit dubious, in fact. But you remember I told you I was not sexy – not like Belinda?'

'Yes, I remember.'

'Well, I've been thinking, and I've come to the conclusion that I was wrong. I think I am a bit sexy, after all.'

'That's not very surprising,' I said.

'So I thought I'd better find out what it all entails,' she said, in a curiously formal voice.

There was a silence.

'Also,' she said, 'it's such a marvellous moonlit night, and I thought how super it would be to lie in this bed with you, surrounded by all these little moons on the walls, while the big moon shone in through the windows on to us. I've always loved this room, you see. I often come here in the middle of the night and lie on the bed alone.'

There was another, longer, silence.

'What happens now?' she asked.

I looked straight into her dark, deep, terribly solemn and romantic eyes. 'That,' I said, 'is quite a weighty problem.'

'Would it help you to solve it,' she said, 'if I got into bed with you?'

'It would help in one way,' I said. 'But it wouldn't be an answer to the main problem that's bothering me.'

'I hope you don't think I'm being forward,' she said, with sudden anxiety. 'I'm not, you know. I'm terribly shy, really. And this sort of thing has never happened to me before.'

She turned her head away and looked intently into the shadows in the hearth. I had the impression that she was nearly in tears.

'I suppose,' I said, 'you'd be surprised if I said it had never happened to me either – not like this.'

She looked puzzled. 'But I don't understand.'

'Nor do I,' I said, shaking my head.

'Aren't you going to ravish me?'

'No.'

Was it an illusion, or did I really see a tremor of relief run through her slim, pale, desperately appealing shoulders?

'I suppose that's because you're tired and sleepy?' she ventured.

'Just because I'm tired and sleepy,' I said.

'So I did make a bish, after all?'

246

'Only a very small and unpredictable bish.'

I threw back the bedclothes and swung my legs out of bed. 'Come here,' I said, 'and let me kiss you. I'm not too tired and sleepy for that.'

She moved hesitantly towards me. I put my arms round her. Her shoulders were unexpectedly cold. She shivered as I touched her, but she did not resist.

I pulled her gently towards me. Through my pyjama jacket I felt her young breasts pressing against me. I kissed her lips. She was passive, pliant, in my arms. For an instant my resolution faltered. Then the thin, cool light of the candle shone into my eyes. I gripped Matilda's shoulders; I kissed her again, on the eyelids and temples, tenderly, softly. Then I lifted her arms, one by one, and put them back into the sleeves of her pyjama jacket.

'I'm tired,' I said, yawning, 'and I'm sleepy. Tomorrow is also a day.'

She got up from the bed, tense and pale, her dark eyes intent upon mine.

'It wasn't a total bish, was it?' she said.

'No bish at all.'

With my hand on her shoulder I walked with her to the door.

'Till tomorrow,' I said, bending and kissing her hand.

'Till tomorrow,' she whispered.

The door swung to; the iron latch fell with a click. As I stood, my head bowed, waiting for the pounding of my heart to subside, I heard through the open window, a long way off, a nightingale singing.

There was an air of bustle and anticipation at the breakfast table. 'Hurry up with the bacon and eggs, Mouse,' said the Professor, 'I must get up to the green to supervise the men with the marquee. Have you remembered those bowls, Quirk, and the pig?'

'Yes, Prof,' said Quirk. 'The pig is laid on; but what's worrying me is rigging up the ropes to keep the traction engines off the wicket.'

'Traction engines! What a thought!' exclaimed the Professor. 'You must keep your eyes firmly fixed on Lionel, Quirk, and keep the liquor out o' his reach until he's got the engines lined up in the enclosure. It's his idea; he's got to organize it.'

The Mouse hurried in and set down bacon and eggs in front of us. 'Did you sleep well, Mr Pye?' she asked.

'Yes, thank you,' I said. 'Another heavenly day, I see.'

'Aye, thanks be,' muttered the Professor. 'How we'd have managed to marshal those traction engines if it had been wet I canna conceive.'

'But it isn't going to be wet,' I said firmly. 'I looked at the barometer in the Great Gallery and it was at Set Fair.'

'Aye, we're lucky, I suppose,' said the Professor. 'But I shall feel happier when the marquee's up, and the ground is pegged out, and the helpers can begin rigging up their stalls. The Virley family, ma dear Jasper, have absolutely no gift for orrganization. At times like this one just has to think of everything oneself. Don't we, Quirk?'

'Don't fuss, sir,' said Quirk, with a surprising show of authority. 'Everything's laid on: the plans are made. Just let things take their course.'

'Of course, Quirky,' said the Professor, with an affectionate glance across the breakfast table. 'I know I'm fussing. But it's the only day in the year when I do fuss, as you know. And I've no' the least doubt that everything will go according to plan.' He turned to me. 'You've thought out a few worrds to say at the prizegiving, Jasper? Not a long speech, of course, but a mention of Lady Flamborough and her interest in the Fallen Women, and thanks to the helpers, *et cetera*.'

'Yes,' I said, 'I'm not used to this sort of thing, but I think I know what's expected.'

'Guid mon!' said the Professor, rising from the table. 'Now I must get up to the green and see how things are moving. Quirk, you'd better check up on Lady Belinda's fireworks: don't leave it all to her: you may need some flower-pots for the rockets. And be sure you take down the *scabiola* from the wall in the Great Gallery for slicing the ham, but put it at the back of the tent where the children canna touch it.'

'Yes, Prof,' said Quirk reassuringly. 'I've got everything under control.'

The Professor departed. A few minutes later, having drunk a second leisurely cup of coffee and briefly discussed with me the prospects of the day's county cricket matches, Quirk followed him.

The Mouse came in, holding a letter. 'That's a very nice suit you're wearing,' she said. 'I like the tie, too.' I was rather pleased: I had chosen my light worsted double-breasted suit, with a chalk line in it, as being most suitable for the prize-giving. And I was wearing a white silk shirt from Harvie & Hudson, with a plain grey tie.

'The post's just come,' said the Mouse. 'There's one for you.'

I took it. The envelope was addressed in Mark Fairweather's hand: the postmark, surprisingly, was Chorley Wood. I opened it and read:

My dear Jasper (he wrote),

I am sending you this personal note because I want to put you in the picture without delay. Late on Friday afternoon – too late for me to write to you from Whitehall – Pilbeam of the Treasury came round to see me, in some agitation. It seems that the Inspec-

249

torate for the Committee on Public Accounts have got wind of the little establishment at A— which you are investigating. Some sarcastic memoranda have passed. Irrespective of your findings as to the value of the work being done at A—, we have had to make a snap decision to discontinue it forthwith, and close down the establishment with the minimum of delay.

If the unit is wound up at once, without any complications, we can, I think, put the relatively small expenditure involved back into last year's accounts, and it will not be subject to the scrutiny upon which the Treasury is insisting in the current year. In these circumstances will you at once give notice to the E— of F— of the termination of our tenancy. (We will make arrangements later for dilapidation, repairs, etc.) It would also be only fair for you to break the news to Professor P— and his staff.

I know I can rely on you to do this with tact and discretion. They will, of course, be receiving appropriate letters of thanks from the Under-Secretary; and Establishments will be looking after the termination of their contracts, superannuation (if any), back pay, etc. I am writing this from home, over the weekend, so that you can speak to all concerned and tie up any personal problems involved before you come back to Whitehall, as I understand you will be doing, on Tuesday.

I hope the weather is being as kind to you as it is to us in Chorley Wood this week-end – also that you've been active with brush and canvas.

Regards.
Yours ever,
Mark.

P.S. It would be just as well, perhaps, to destroy this letter after you have read it.

I threw the letter down on the breakfast table. Although I hadn't realized it, the Mouse was still in the room. 'What's the matter?' she said. 'You look as if you'd seen a ghost. You haven't had bad news, I hope?'

I stared out of the window. Yes, the weather was being kind. Presumably it was also continuing to be kind to the residents of Chorley Wood. No doubt they'd be enjoying a very jolly Whit Monday.

'I've had some news,' I said. 'But I don't really know whether to describe it as good or bad.'

'It . . . it isn't about us, here at Arcady, is it?'

I nodded. After a few moments' reflection I handed Fairweather's letter to her. 'Read it! I can't see that there's anything in it you shouldn't know.'

When she had finished reading it she began to tear it up into small pieces.

'What are you doing?' I said.

'What Mr Fairweather asked you to do,' she answered. 'I'll put it in the kitchen boiler.'

'All right,' I said. 'I suppose that would be just as well.'

'I doubt,' said the Mouse, 'if the way Mr Fairweather expresses himself would appeal strongly to the Professor or Mr Quirk – or, for that matter, to his Lordship.'

'When am I going to tell them?' I asked miserably.

'You'll have to tell them today, if you're going to be back in Whitehall tomorrow.'

'I don't want to spoil everyone's fun, today of all days.'

The Mouse stood and pondered the problem. 'I don't somehow think the Prof or Quirky will be altogether surprised,' she said – it was the first time I had heard her refer to them so informally. 'I believe it would be kinder to tell them this morning, so that the Fête can be a sort of farewell appearance. They'll be utterly miserable, of course, but I believe they'd rather go out with a bang than a whimper.'

'You read Eliot?'

'I do, actually.'

'Very well. I'll go and look for them.' I paused at the door. 'You'll be able to go back to live in Dulwich Village now.'

'Yes, I suppose so,' she said thoughtfully.

'The Ministry will almost certainly keep you on,' I said. 'I'm sure you needn't have any worries about that. You must get in touch with me as soon as things are wound up here. You will, won't you?'

'If you want me to,' she said, beginning to clear the breakfast table.

I found Quirk marking out a square of turf for the Treasure Hunt, assisted by a swarm of Giles-like children from the Primary School.

'Can you spare me a minute, Quirk?' I said.

'Of course, Mr Pye. D'you want me to think up a few okes for your speech? Jones is really the chap you should consult for that.'

'No, I don't want any jokes,' I said. We walked out towards the middle of the cricket field. 'I'm afraid I've some bad news for you and the Professor. It's no good my beating about the bush: the Ministry have decided – over my head and without waiting for my report – to close you down. I'm extremely sorry, and I assure you it's no doing of mine.'

Quirk stood quite still for a moment or two, then he pulled a cricket ball out of his blazer pocket and began to toss it lightly from hand to hand.

'When does this happen?' he asked.

' "Forthwith" is the word I've been given.'

He looked down at the cricket pitch. 'It's a decent wicket we've made this year, isn't it?' he said. 'Good for a lot of runs, I should say.'

'I'm sure you'll be given plenty of time to clear up and make arrangements for the future.'

'For the future,' he repeated slowly, spinning the

cricket ball between finger and thumb. 'The future—'

'I understand,' I said, 'that you are actually on the permanent staff of the Stationery Office: you are only on loan to our Ministry.'

He nodded. 'On loan for seventeen years, so far.'

'You will automatically go back to the Stationery Office, then. There's no need at all for you to worry about the future.'

He clutched the cricket ball in tense fingers. 'You mustn't think, Mr Pye, that I was worrying about myself. It's the Prof I'm worrying about. What will *he* do?'

'I don't know. I realize it will be a blow to him.'

Quirk nodded slowly. 'This place means everything to him, Pye. It's his life, his passion.'

'Hasn't he a home to go to in Scotland?' I asked.

Quirk took a penknife out of his pocket, squatted down on his heels, and extracted a very small plantain from the cricket pitch. 'The Prof,' he said, 'was born in Glasgow, in the Gorbals. He told me that himself, in an expansive moment, years ago. When he was still a boy he went to live on his uncle's croft. His uncle is dead now. I don't think there's anywhere he could call his home.'

'I suppose he could go back to his University and take up some post there?'

Quirk sought vainly for more plantains.

'The Prof doesn't know I know this,' he said quietly. 'And I've never told anyone else: but he isn't really a professor at all.'

'What!'

'He was just a clerk in the Estates Bursar's office at Aberdeen University. One term, immediately after the outbreak of war, he lent a hand with correcting examination papers when one of the Lecturers in Statistics was called up. That's the sum total of the Prof's university career.'

'How do you know about this?'

Quirk rose to his feet. 'I only know because an old school friend of mine used to be on the staff at Aberdeen. I've told you about it because I think you ought to know; but I ask you, on your word of honour, never to breathe a word of it to anyone – least of all to the Prof himself.'

'Of course,' I said. 'I give you my word. But what will he do?'

'I just can't think,' said Quirk.

'Oh hell!' I said wretchedly.

'What are you two nattering about? Cricket, I suppose!' The Professor bore down upon us, walking with long strides across the green. 'There's a lot of preparation still to be done. Quirk, have ye looked out that bunting yet?'

'No, Prof,' said Quirk. 'I'll go and do it at once.' He shot an interrogative glance at me. 'We weren't nattering about cricket, sir. It was something more serious.'

'Mair serious than cricket, Quirk?' The Professor's dark, bushy eyebrows quivered into a smile. 'Surely there's nothing mair serious than cricket?'

'Well, yes, sir, actually there is,' said Quirk, haltingly. 'Mr Pye has just been telling me ... You might as well know now as later ... We've got our marching orders, got to shut up shop – innings declared closed.'

The Professor's smile faded: his lips tightened. He turned to me. 'What is this, Pye? Can you elucidate Quirk's sequence of mixed metaphors?'

I told him the facts, baldly, directly.

'When is this to take place?' he asked quietly, with scarcely a change in his expression.

' "Forthwith" was the term used,' I said. 'And I do hope you'll realize, Professor, that the decision was taken over my head, before I had even made my report.'

'I tak' your word for that, Pye,' he said. 'I'm relieved to hear it. However, one canna' pretend that the news is welcome.'

'I'm terribly sorry about it,' I said.

'You have told Quirk, obviously. What about Miss Mounsey?'

'I took the liberty of telling her, too,' I said. 'She happened to be in the room when I read the letter from Fairweather.'

'There seems to be little left for me to do,' he said, with a shrug of his shoulders. 'I assume you will also be notifying Lord Flamborough?'

'Just as you wish,' I said.

'Perhaps you would be so kind. His Lordship, as it happens, is expecting you to lunch with him in the train, before the Fête. I shall be busy up here, and' – he bit his lip, and I saw that the knuckles of his clenched hands were white – 'I find masel' a wee bit ... unnerved.'

'Of course,' I said. 'I will speak to Lord Flamborough at lunch.'

The Professor blinked; for a moment I thought I saw tears in his eyes; then his eyebrows rose in a gallant attempt at a smile. 'You have been most considerate, Pye. I hope you have enjoyed your stay here. Now Quirk, ma dear boy, there's a lot to be done if we're to have everything ready on time. Go and put up that bunting. Then look out the Flags of All Nations – they are in that croquet-box in the pavilion – and hang them up across the gates of the park. We must have the place looking gay and ... festive.'

I found there was a train to London which left Flaxfield Junction at 6.48 p.m. I packed my bag and parcelled up my easel and painting kit. Then I took them into

Flaxfield by taxi, and deposited them at the station. I decided I would slip quietly away from Arcady, without any fuss or commotion, as soon as the prize-giving was over.

Coming out of the station yard at Flaxfield I saw the Flamborough Flier standing just beyond the corrugated iron barrier, at the end of the Branch Line.

I hesitated. I had intended to go back to Arcady by bus; but if Lord Flamborough were expecting me to lunch I might as well join the train now, and break the news to him as soon as possible. I walked through the Goods Yard and across the waste land adjoining the Branch Line, and clambered up into the coach. 'May I come in?' I called.

Inside the saloon Lord Flamborough was sitting before his record cabinet, rearranging the contents. In another corner sat Lady Flamborough, looking through a pile of seedsmen's catalogues.

'Hullo, Jasper!' said Lord Flamborough. 'Didn't expect to pick you up here. I'm waiting for Ozzie Tipton.'

'I happened to be in Flaxfield,' I said, 'and saw the train, so I thought I'd join you now. I understand you have very kindly invited me to lunch.'

'That's it, my boy. We've got to fortify you for the Fiesta of Fallen Women. Don't forget you're presenting the prizes. I look forward to some trenchant observations on shameful bundles, the harlot with a heart of gold, and the call-girl menace in Flaxfield. Did you, by the way, see Ozzie Tipton hanging around the station?'

'I'm afraid I don't know Ozzie Tipton. Who is he?'

'Ozzie Tipton and his Stompers – quite a lively little jazz band that plays on the pier at Lowestoft. They promised to come over and put on a show for an hour or so at the Fête. They should be here by now. What's the time, Mabel?'

'Five past twelve,' said Lady Flamborough. 'I've been through all these shrub catalogues, Jasper, but I can't find either of those roses you mentioned last night, *fruticosa* or *Mancuniensis*. They must be extremely uncommon.'

I felt my embarrassments accumulating. 'Please don't bother, Lady Flamborough. I may perhaps have got the names wrong. I'll look them up when I get back to London.'

'When are you going back to London?' asked Lady Flamborough. 'I thought you were staying here for some time. There are a lot of things I wanted to ask you about the herbaceous border.'

'I'm going back this evening,' I said.

'This evening!' exclaimed Lord Flamborough. 'Whatever for? It's Whit Monday. There's only one train – leaves here at 6.48. You won't want to go at that hour.'

'I'm afraid I must,' I said, screwing up my courage.

'But you'll miss the dance,' said Lord Flamborough. 'I particularly wanted you to give a demonstration of the Charleston.'

'You aren't going to miss my fireworks, are you, darling?' said Belinda, who appeared at the door of the corridor leading to the kitchen. 'I'm putting on a wizard performance – Roman candles, Catherine wheels, tourbillions, Chinese fire-fountains – all specially in your honour!'

'I'm terribly sorry, but I have to go.' I steeled myself for the ordeal. 'And there's something rather important I have to speak to you about, Lord Flamborough. Perhaps we could have a few minutes' conversation privately, before this Mr Tipton turns up.'

'Privately?' Lord Flamborough turned and looked at me in surprise. 'Spit it out, dear boy. I've no secrets from my old woman – none that she doesn't know about, anyway.'

257

'I must go and get lunch,' said Lady Flamborough, getting up. 'Come and lend a hand, 'Linda.'

As soon as they had gone a smile crept over Lord Flamborough's Roman features. 'Wasn't that tactful! I suppose she guessed what you wanted to talk to me about. It's Belinda, I suppose? You want to marry her?'

I gaped.

'That's all right, my boy,' said Lord Flamborough genially. 'You don't have to plead your case. I know we Virleys have a tradition of not marrying out of the family. But it's a good thing to introduce new blood now and again. I think you'd make an excellent husband. Keep your eye on her though; she likes a lark. But I don't need to tell you that. She'll settle down if she's got plenty of children to look after.'

I stood speechless. Lord Flamborough turned his invalid chair and opened the drink cupboard. 'This calls for a celebration,' he said. 'What shall it be – champagne, if I can find a bottle?'

I was helpless with dismay. 'You are most kind, sir. But you are under a misapprehension. I'm not asking your consent to marry Lady Belinda. I . . . I don't want to marry her.'

'Eh?' Lord Flamborough looked puzzled. 'Don't want to marry her? Why not? Oh, I see: you're going to live in sin, Married already, perhaps? But why ask me about it? Seems odd.'

'I wasn't going to ask you anything at all about Lady Belinda,' I said. 'I'm afraid you jumped to the wrong conclusion.'

'It's not Tilly, surely? She's rather young.'

'No, sir,' I said desperately. 'It's nothing to do with any of your daughters. It's about the Hall.'

'But the Hall's nothing to do with me,' he said testily. 'That's the Professor's responsibility. You must speak to him if you want to know anything about the Hall.'

'The Professor himself asked me to speak to you,' I said. 'I have heard this morning from Whitehall that the Professor's unit is to be disbanded, and the Ministry will be discontinuing its tenancy of the Hall.'

'What! The Ministry's clearing out?'

'Yes,' I said. 'Proper notice will be given, of course, and due allowance made for any dilapidations.'

'But what will happen to the Prof? And Quirk?'

'I'm afraid they will be going,' I said.

Lord Flamborough, who had shown merely a slight irritability over the misunderstanding about Belinda, now gazed at me in consternation.

'But you can't do that,' he said. 'There must be some mistake. The Prof's been here – how long? Seventeen years, I think?'

'I know,' I said. 'But he and his unit are now considered redundant.'

'Redundant? What the devil does that mean?'

'Not wanted any more,' I said.

'But *I* want him,' roared Lord Flamborough. 'It suits me very well to have him here. He's an invaluable fellow. And, dammit! I've never charged the Ministry a penny of rent. I'm saving the country thousands.'

'I know, your Lordship,' I said soothingly. 'But the decision has been taken. It's a Treasury decision. It's nothing to do with me.'

Dismay had now given place to indignation. 'The Treasury, indeed! What does the Treasury know about it? Who runs the Treasury, anyway? The Chancellor of the Exchequer, I suppose. Who's that? Is he that fellow who was at Eton with me? Or is he some perishing Wykhamist?'

'I can't say off-hand where he was at school,' I said. 'But I've an idea it was Harrow.'

'Harrow! My God! That's the end!' Lord Flamborough slammed the door of the drink cupboard, and twirled

259

his chair towards the gramophone. 'I know what I'll do,' he said fiercely. 'I'll go up to the House o' Lords. Haven't been there since the last Coronation. But I'll go. I'll raise the matter in the House.'

'I'm extremely sorry,' I began.

'Cut out the apologies!' he snapped. 'Forget the whole thing! I'm not going to have my Whit Monday b——d up by a bloody Harrovian. Let's have a record. Pass me "Bye, Bye, Blues".'

I passed the record to him. In indignant silence he wound up the gramophone, inserted a needle, and set the machine going. A rasping chorus filled the saloon:

> 'Bye, bye, Blues,
> Bye, bye, Blues!
> Bells ring,
> Birds sing.
> Sun is shining,
> No more pining . . .'

The door of the saloon opened and a young man peered in. He was wearing a black polo-necked sweater and crimson jeans. His face was pale and pasty and he had a wispy blond beard. 'Hullo there!' he shouted, through the din of 'Bye, Bye, Blues'.

Lord Flamborough swung round in his chair. 'Ozzie Tipton?'

'That's me,' said the young man. 'Pleased to meet you, Earl.'

He advanced into the saloon, carrying a black trumpet case under his arm. Another young man followed him, carrying a guitar. He also was wearing a black polo-necked sweater and crimson jeans. He had a black beard.

'Jimmy,' said Ozzie Tipton, with a wave of the arm.

260

'Meet the Earl of Flamborough.'

'Hey!' said Jimmy, looking round the saloon. 'This is fabulous!'

A third young man appeared in the doorway, half-hidden behind a canvas-covered double bass. He, too, was wearing a black sweater and crimson jeans. His beard was red.

'And this is Jake,' said Ozzie Tipton.

'Hiya!' said Jake, lifting the double bass into the saloon.

'Jimmy and Jake are all I could pick out of the sand today,' said Ozzie Tipton. 'The rest of the boys are paddling.'

'Very decent of you to come at all,' said Lord Flamborough.

'Can you fix us with a drink, Earl?' said Ozzie Tipton. 'We're parched.'

Belinda came into the saloon. She looked from Ozzie Tipton to Jimmy, and from Jimmy to Jake. 'Crumbs!' she murmured. 'Crumbs!'

'I agree with Jake,' said Ozzie Tipton, swallowing his fourth glass of Angel's Tears. 'Since he broke away from Count Basie, Lester Young hasn't been the saxophonist he used to be.'

'What do you think of Charlie Parker?' said Lord Flamborough. 'Jasper, would you mind filling Ozzie's glass?'

'Charlie Parker's fabulous,' said Jimmy, plucking at his guitar.

'Charlie Parker?' said Jake, leaning back against the antimacassar and fingering his red beard. 'Charlie Parker was a modernist. He didn't restrict himself to elemental forms like the blues, or tunes that move in the conventional pattern of resolving sevenths.'

'Is that so!' said Lord Flamborough.

261

Jake continued: 'It must be conceded that Lester Young is the Grand Old Man of tenor saxophone playing. In his heyday he had a quicksilver technique. He's a master still, though musically he's living on his investments. There isn't the tension, the zip. As an executant he's been by-passed by the chromatic progressions of Charlie Parker and his contemporaries.'

'Has he, indeed!' said Lord Flamborough.

'Jake knows,' said Jimmy, putting his guitar aside and emptying his glass.

'Jasper,' said Lord Flamborough. 'Fill Jimmy's glass.'

'Nice little place you've got here, Earl,' said Ozzie Tipton. 'Quite a gimmick, eh?'

'I don't really know what a gimmick is,' said Lord Flamborough. He turned to Jake. 'What's your opinion of Duke Ellington?'

'The Duke's fabulous,' said Jimmy, putting down his glass and picking up his guitar again.

'Ellington,' said Jake, 'is musically a schizo. Working on the basic jazz structure he has created a synthesis of neo-negro technique and a tone-poetry that derives from Ravel or Delius rather than the folk music of the Mississippi.'

'You think that?' said Lord Flamborough.

'I for one,' proceeded Jake, 'am not proposing to take sides for or against Ellington on the issue of orchestration *versus* individual improvisation. But I see a psychic conflict running through the whole Ellington *oeuvre*. First he is toying with archaic jazz; then he is slipping into the idiom of swing; then he is trying to transcend what he regards as the limitations of his media and to create a *tempo*-free musical imagery expressed in pseudo-jazz phraseology. At all times we have to discount the element of show-biz.'

'Well, well!' said Lord Flamborough. 'Have another drink?'

I got up again and refilled Jake's glass. Lady Flamborough came in and announced that lunch was ready.

'Fabulous,' said Jimmy, strumming a brisk chord.

'All home comforts, eh?' said Ozzie Tipton. 'The boys on the beach don't know what they're missing. Whacko! I'm ready for some scoff.'

'Come along into the dining saloon,' said Lord Flamborough, propelling his chair towards the door. 'Jasper, I wonder if you'd mind lending Chloe a hand on the footplate?'

'Er – no. Certainly,' I said.

'Come in and eat, the rest of you,' said Lord Flamborough. 'I want you to tell me, Jake, exactly what you think of Lionel Hampton. I've got a record of " 's Wonderful", in which he plays the vibes with Benny Goodman's trio, but I'm told he has a band of his own now.'

As they passed down the corridor towards the dining saloon I heard Jake limbering up for a lecture on Lionel Hampton. I went the other way, jumped down to the ground, and walked forward to the engine. I was a little piqued at missing my lunch, but I was quite glad to avoid sitting through a series of disquisitions by Jake.

Chloe, wearing brown overalls, and with a red hand-kerchief tied round her hair, was leaning out of the engine cab.

'I've come to help,' I said. 'But I don't know what I have to do.'

'Never mind, darling,' she said, holding out a hand to help me up. 'You'll only have to do the firing. How nice to have you with me! But why aren't you at lunch?'

'I'm not in on the lunch party,' I said. 'It seems to have developed into a university extension lecture on jazz.'

'Ozzie What-not and his Stompers?'

'Two of his Stompers,' I said. 'But that's quite enough.'

'Never mind, darling,' said Chloe. 'You'll find it quite fun up here. And if you pull down that whistle cord you can make more noise than all Ozzie What-not's Stompers put together. Have a piece of bread and cheese to keep you going?'

I munched the bread and cheese, whilst Chloe, after a quick glance at the pressure gauge, put on an injector.

'Chloe,' I said. 'Have you heard the news?'

'What news?'

'About the Hall – and the Ministry.'

'No. What is it?'

I told her. She listened in silence.

'So that's why you escaped to the footplate,' she said at last. 'I suppose you found it all a bit embarrassing. Poor Jasper, how wretched for you!'

I was so touched by her consideration for me that I drew her to me and kissed her.

'That will do, my dear,' she said, gently pushing me away. 'The Footplate Regulations don't allow for kissing the engine-driver. Take this rag and rub up the hand-rail round the boiler. We must look spick and span for the Fête.'

I clambered out of the cab and edged my way alongside the boiler barrel. The locomotive was obviously an antique, but it appeared to be in beautiful order. The paint and varnish were lustrous. Although I soon found my hands were getting black with grease there was quite a satisfaction to be got out of polishing up the rail and the other brass fitments.

'Give the dome a rub over as well,' Chloe called.

I hoisted myself up on to the rail and did as I was told.

'That'll do,' she shouted. 'Now take this oil-can and

fill the oil cups on the coupling rods.' She handed me a large and greasy can and showed me where the oil had to go. 'Now you can make up the fire.'

As I climbed up into the cab I observed with dismay a long oil stain down the right leg of my trousers.

Chloe handed me an iron shovel. 'This is how you open the firehole door,' she said. She pulled a short length of chain and it swung open: a blast of heat hit me. 'Throw some coal towards the front,' she said.

The shovel seemed to me singularly awkward to handle, and it was by no means easy, in the confined space of the cab, to transfer the coal from the tender to the firehole without spilling it.

'That'll do,' said Chloe. 'Now, while we go along you must watch these gauge glasses to make sure the water-level's right in the boiler – tell me if it falls below the mark. And keep an eye on the pressure-gauge, too.'

In some bewilderment I tried to follow her directions and explanations.

'Now lean out and watch for the flag,' she said. There was a deafening roar of escaping steam as the safety-valve lifted.

Leaning out of the side window of the cab I saw regretfully that my shirt-cuffs were already black with coal-dust.

The bearded visage of Ozzie Tipton appeared from the window of the saloon. 'Hullo there! Let's go!' he yelled, and vigorously waved the green flag. I felt a childish and unaccountable twinge of envy that he had been accorded the privilege of flagging the train out.

Chloe released the screw-brake on the tender and pulled down the regulator. The locomotive shuddered and clanked into motion.

'Get cracking with the shovel now,' said Chloe. 'Don't let your fire get hollow at the front. You must chuck it well in.'

I got cracking. I found the task even less easy now that the train was in motion and the footplate was wobbling from side to side. It seemed impossible to avoid being flung with some violence against the sides of the cab.

'That'll do for now,' said Chloe. 'How's the pressure? Is the water-level all right? You should keep it about halfway up the glass.'

I answered her questions as best I could.

'I don't suppose you've ever done this sort of thing before,' said Chloe. 'It's quite a skilled job being a fireman. You've got to learn how to use your shovel. No need to move your feet at all. Keep your right hand up and swing with your body. Have another shot.'

I tried to do the job as she directed.

'It's all a question of stance,' she said. 'You're a cricketer. It ought to come easily to you.'

It didn't. After a few minutes the sweat was pouring down my cheeks. My collar felt insufferably tight. I had coal-dust in my eyes.

'You'd better take your jacket off,' said Chloe. 'Hang it on that hook. Take your tie off, too, if you like.'

I did as she suggested. I noticed that my grey tie was now disfigured with a huge stain of cylinder oil.

'It's fun, isn't it!' said Chloe. 'Aren't you enjoying it?'

'Yes,' I said untruthfully. 'It's great fun.'

'While you've nothing to do you might rub up those gauge-protector glasses,' she said. 'They've got a bit oily and steamed up.'

As I rubbed away at the thick glasses, close to the heat of the fire-box, I realized that my Harvie & Hudson shirt was not only streaked with coal-dust and oil, but was rapidly becoming saturated with sweat.

'Take a rest when you want one,' said Chloe. 'No need to overdo it.'

I staggered to the side window and leaned out. The rush of air against my face was blissfully refreshing.

The meadows, golden with buttercups, smiled in the sunshine. The passing hedges were bright with elder blossom and wild roses. Across the fields I saw the turrets of the gatehouse rising above the trees.

'Shan't be long now,' said Chloe.

She closed the regulator and put her hand on the vacuum brake handle. The locomotive began to slow down. I wiped my brow.

'You'll make a fireman yet,' said Chloe, as we pulled up at the Halt.

'Thank you for the compliment,' I said. 'Will you want me any more? If not, I'll go and try to clean myself up a little.'

'Oh dear!' said Chloe. 'I'd quite forgotten you were going to present the prizes. I suppose you want to look smart. But I shouldn't worry. Mummy usually does it, and she always dresses like a tramp.'

'I'd rather not look like a tramp, if it can be avoided,' I said stiffly, as I picked up my jacket and collar and tie and endeavoured to shake the coal-dust out of them.

'You've just about time to run up to the Hall and change,' said Chloe.

'Unfortunately all my clothes are in my case, at Flaxfield Junction,' I said.

'Why?'

'Because I'm leaving for London by the 6.48.'

'You're going?'

'Yes, I'm going – going for good.'

'Jasper darling, how *can* you?' she said, putting a very greasy hand on my arm.

'There's nothing to keep me here any longer,' I said.

'Oh dear!' she said. 'It's been such fun having you. Perhaps, after all, you might be allowed to kiss the engine-driver goodbye.'

'It's not allowed for in the Footplate Regulations,' I said, in dead-level tones.

I stepped down from the cab on to the platform. 'Hullo there!' I was hailed by Ozzie Tipton, who was standing at the exit with Jimmy and Jake. 'That was certainly a swell ride you gave us. Is it in order for me to tip the fireman?'

'It isn't allowed for in the Footplate Regulations,' I said coldly.

'Okay. That's saved me half a dollar,' he grinned. 'C'm'on, boys! Here's our barouche.' A farm hand was waiting for them with a tractor and trailer.

'Can we give you a lift to the fairground?' asked Ozzie Tipton, as they hoisted the double bass into the trailer.

'No, thank you,' I said. 'I'd rather walk.'

The church clock struck three as I reached the village green. I had washed the coal-dust off my hands and arms and face, but my shirt was filthy, my tie had a large greenish stain across it, and my suit was covered with patches of oil. I was almost ashamed to make my appearance.

The Fête was in full swing. Alongside the wall of the park was an array of tables and stalls stacked with flowers and vegetables. Chloe was dispensing home-made sweets to a sequence of small children who came running across the green with pennies and threepenny-bits clutched in sticky fingers.

'Hullo once more, Jasper,' she said cheerfully. 'Are you in need of fudge or marzipan bars, or would you rather have a lollipop?'

I bought half-a-dozen lollipops and distributed them to the surrounding children.

'Lady C's got a sticky assignment, Sir Jasper, eh?' said Jones, walking past with a cuckoo clock in his arms.

'Are you Sir Jasper?' said one of the children, advancing on me with an autograph book.

'Er – yes, I suppose so,' I said.

Jones turned and came hurrying back. 'Now, Frankie,' he said, taking the boy's autograph book and handing it to me, 'Sir Jasper will be pleased to sign your autograph book, but you'll have to give him a tanner for the funds.'

Frankie looked at me appraisingly. 'I ain't see yer on the Telly, as I know on,' he said. 'I'll have a lollipop instead.' And he took back the autograph book.

'Please bear in mind, Sir Jasper,' said Jones, 'that on no account must you sign yer autograph for less than ... well, perhaps threepence would be the right price.' And he dashed off again with his cuckoo clock.

I walked along the line of stalls. Behind a table stacked with bowls of delphiniums, iris, columbines, and roses, Lady Flamborough was sitting on a shooting stick, reading *The Transactions of the National Auricula Society*. I bought a dozen roses and gave them to a small girl who was gazing wide-eyed at the splendours of the stall.

'Coo! Thank you, mister!' she said. 'Coo! They're all stripey. What are they called, lady?'

'Rosa Mundi,' said Lady Flamborough. 'Or, more strictly, *Rosa gallica versicolor*. The name Rosa Mundi is supposed to derive from Fair Rosamund, the mistress of Henry the Second, but I don't believe a word of it myself.'

'Coo!' said the girl, clutching the bunch of roses.

At the end of the row of stalls was a long trestle-table laden with every kind of miscellaneous junk and surmounted with a white streamer on which was written: 'Arcady Antiques. Every Souvenir a Snip.'

'Roll up, roll up, ladies,' chanted Jones. 'This is the opportunity of a lifetime. Priceless antiques straight out of England's stately homes. How about these fire-tongs, madam? Good strong hinge, handy claws – you could pull the kiddies' teeth out with 'em. And antique – cor blimey, they're antique! This may 'ave been the very pair of tongs King Alfred was using when 'e burnt the cakes. Five and elevenpence, lady. That's right. Ta, lots!'

I picked up a charming little silhouette in a round black frame.

'Too pricey for you, Sir Jasper,' said Jones. 'That's a real collector's item. Who d'yer think the lady is?'

'I've no idea,' I said. 'Somebody's great-grandmama, I suppose.'

'That's where yer wrong, Sir Jasper. That is a portrait of Lady Hamilton, Horatio Nelson's one and only Emma. Don't blush, ladies: we know she wasn't the sort you'd find in the Mothers' Union, but Lord Nelson considered her a nice bit of stuff, and I think you'll all agree with him if you look at 'er profile in this ex-quisite silhouette.'

'Is it a right 'un?' said a burly farmer standing beside me.

'A right 'un!' exclaimed Jones, deeply offended. 'This 'ere silhouette is a properly authenticated pedigree portrait of Lady H. Look, the name's written on the back – in old writing, too. "Mrs Hamilton, 1843." '

'Why do they put "Mrs Hamilton"?' said the farmer suspiciously. 'You said it was Lady Hamilton.'

Jones winked. 'Don't be a proper charley, cock,' he said. ' "Mrs" means "Mistress", don't it? And even these respectable ladies here know what the word mistress means. Eh, ladies?'

There was a titter from the audience.

'How much?' asked the farmer, hesitantly.

'Sir Jasper 'ere 'as just offered me twelve-and-a-kick,' said Jones. 'It's yours for fifteen bob.'

'I'll give you fifteen shillings for it, Jones,' I said.

'Seventeen-and-six,' said the farmer.

'A pound,' I said.

'I'll make it a guinea,' said the farmer.

'Stop, gentlemen,' said Jones, holding up his hand. 'I

'aven't time for an auction. I've got plenty of other things to dispose of today. The first person who offers me two quid for this beautiful silhouette of Lady Hamilton gets it.'

'I'll take it,' said the farmer hastily, pulling a roll of notes out of his trousers pocket.

'You've got a bargain, sir,' said Jones. 'A real snip. Bad luck, Sir Jasper. This gentleman was just a little too smart for you.'

Jones gazed at me in wide-eyed innocence. I turned and walked across the green. I bought a few tickets for the Treasure Hunt and stuck my tallies into the ground. Then I stood for a while watching the youths of the village advancing blindfold towards a ham, which was suspended from a branch of an oak tree, and endeavouring to cut it down with Lord Flamborough's *scabiola*. As they were blindfolded at some ten paces' distance, and were made to turn round three times before launching their assault, their efforts were giving rise to hearty laughter amongst the bystanders. Two of the most persistent contestants were the ferret-faced Sticky Palmer and the ape-like Dod Hoxen, from Flaxfield. After each unsuccessful foray with the *scabiola* they glared at me resentfully, as though I were in some way to blame.

I walked to the far side of the green, where the traction engines were drawn up behind ropes, like horses in the paddock before a race. There were about ten of them, of different types and ages. Their owners or drivers stood around proudly, some in corduroy breeches, some in overalls, and some in white linen coats with the names of their engines embroidered on the pocket. A stream of spectators eddied in and out amongst the engines, examining and admiring them, discussing their points, assessing their prospects, and sniffing the mingled scents of trampled turf and hot cylinder oil.

The machine which was attracting most attention was a Showman's engine, with a brilliantly painted awning supported on six 'barley sugar' columns of twisted brass. Its huge driving wheels had the spokes intricately lined out in yellow, red, and green. The boiler was a rich dark green, and was bound by glittering brass lagging bands. There were brass stars on the cylinder covers, a brass ring to the fly-wheel, brass hub-caps, and a brass-segmented name-plate bearing the words 'Pride of Flaxfield'. A wisp of smoke rose from the chimney.

A red-faced man wearing an old-fashioned frock coat, a butterfly collar, and a brown billycock hat, clambered down from the driving platform and shook me by the hand. 'Good day, Sir Jasper,' he said. 'And 'ow do you like my little toy?'

I recognized him as Charley Aspall, who had umpired in the cricket match.

'I 'ope you'll be seeing more of me today,' he said heartily.

'I hope I shall,' I responded politely.

'I h'understand you'll be presenting the prizes.'

'Yes.'

He leered at me with his boozy eyes, then winked. Cocking his thumb at Pride of Flaxfield, he said: 'Not much doubt which is the most 'andsome engine on the field, eh? H'and in the best condition. Allow me to h'accompany you to the beer tent.'

He took me by the arm and led me towards the marquee. 'We don't need to drink beer,' he said. 'A drop o'Scotch would be more h'acceptable, eh?' He then gave me a detailed technical specification of Pride of Flaxfield, with diversions into her history, her past ownership, and her achievements on fairground and highway.

Inside the beer tent was Lionel, talking earnestly to a little wizened man who was wearing a round felt hat decorated with white braid.

272

'Jasper! Come in, dear boy!' cried Lionel. 'Meet Mr Crispin, our Starter. Hullo, you old rogue!' He dug a finger into Charley Aspall's ribs.

'Four treble Scotch, Perce,' said Mr Aspall to Percy Pott, who, in his shirt sleeves, was serving behind the trestle-table. 'And a small bottle of soda water.'

'No whisky for me,' said Lionel. 'Half a pint of bitter, that's all.'

Charley Aspall looked at him in astonishment.

'What, no Scotch!'

'No,' said Lionel solemnly. 'Not a drop of spirits passes my lips until Susie's been put through her paces.'

'Sufferin' snakes!' said Charley Aspall. 'Perce, bring Mr Lionel a pig's ear.'

I sipped at the outsize measure of whisky which Mr Aspall had forced upon me whilst the conversation ranged from Salter safety valves to feed pumps, from countershafts and blast pipes to injectors and clack-boxes. Through the fog of technicalities the only comprehensible fact which emerged was that Susie and Pride of Flaxfield were to be deadly rivals in the sporting events of the afternoon.

I felt a tap on my shoulder. 'Pye, thank heaven I've found ye at last!' I turned to see the Professor beside me, wearing a straw boater with faded club colours round it. 'I've been looking everywhere for ye. The Ankle Competition is due to start at any minute. Please drink up, ma boy, and come along with me.'

'I really don't want any more to drink,' I said, putting down my glass of whisky. 'I can't manage a treble Scotch in the middle of the afternoon.'

'Follow me!' said the Professor. Lionel and Mr Crispin were deep in conclave about steam glands. As I turned to push through the throng towards the exit I saw Charley Aspall pick up my glass of whisky and pour it into Lionel's glass.

The Professor hustled me out of the marquee and across the cricket pitch to the pavilion, before which one of the white canvas sight-screens had been erected, leaving about nine inches' space between the edge of the canvas and the ground.

'They're all lined up,' said the Professor, pointing to an array of ankles projecting under the bottom edge of the screen.

'No, my Rita isn't ready yet,' said a shrill voice at my elbow. A little woman with spectacles, wearing a blue beret, caught hold of my sleeve. 'Sir Jasper, I want you to meet my Rita. I expect you've seen her picture in the papers. She was Miss Felixstowe the year before last, and last year she was one of the finalists for Miss East Anglia. Say how-d'you-do to Sir Jasper, Rita.'

The former Miss Felixstowe struck a pose, advanced a wilting hand, and said, 'Ever so nice to meet you.'

'Rita's going in for the Ankle Competition, Sir Jasper,' said her mother. 'But only for a lark. It's all for a good cause, isn't it! She's got lovely ankles, hasn't she! Show Sir Jasper your ankles, dear. Aren't they winsome! And Rita always paints her toe-nails gold. Very stylish Rita is, aren't you, dear? Come along now: you must come behind the screen.'

'Ever so pleased to have met you,' said Rita, bestowing a dazzling smile upon me as she turned away.

'Now, ladies,' said the Professor, in lecture-hall tones. 'Are all the competitors lined up behind the screen? If so, will they all remove the shoe from their right foot. Now, ladies, will you please put your right foot forward under the screen, and the judging will begin. Come along, Pye. Will you start at this end?'

I walked along the line studying in bewilderment the objects extended for my inspection. It had never occurred to me before to examine the female foot aesthetically; and what I saw below the canvas was not rewarding. The assembly of hammer toes, dropped arches, swollen insteps, and bulging ankles was phenomenal.

I soon spotted Rita's gold-painted toe-nails, but it was evident that she was accustomed to walking about in extremely high heels, and the arch of her foot in consequence was almost deformed.

At last, after a sordid process of elimination, accompanied by gay shrieks and titters from the assembled spectators, I chose a foot which seemed less misshapen than the others.

'The winner,' announced the Professor, 'is Number Eight. Will Number Eight come forward and show herself?'

'You mean Number Twelve, don't you?' said a menacing female voice behind me. 'That's Rita's number.'

'Number Eight!' said the Professor loudly. There were movements behind the screen, and a girl appeared round the end of it. She was wearing steel-rimmed spectacles, and had a squint. Despite this – or perhaps because of it – she was greeted with cordial applause.

I felt a hand clawing at my sleeve. 'You must have made a mistake, Sir Jasper. It was Number Twelve you meant, wasn't it? That was my Rita's number.'

'No, this was the girl I chose,' I said.

'But my Rita's in the running for Miss England. She's got the daintiest ankles in East Anglia. You should have heard what Gilbert Harding said about them.'

'I wish I had,' I said feelingly.

'Professor!' said the little woman, her voice rising in anger. 'I object. Everyone *knows* my Rita's ankles are the best. I demand a recount.'

'Dear lady,' said the Professor, 'Rita is a singularly beautiful young woman. Nobody is disputing it. But the verdict has gone in favour of Number Eight, and I am sure ye won't grudge Number Eight her one crowded hour of glorious life. Rita's day will come. Pye, would ye follow me?'

With some difficulty, and to the accompaniment of grave imputations on my judgement, probity, and morality, I extricated myself from the clutches of Rita's mama and slipped away after the Professor.

'What a ghastly woman!' he exclaimed, as we hurried across the green. 'Why does one get involved in such vulgarity? However, the worst is over. Hello, Mouse, what is it?'

'What *have* you been doing to your suit, Mr Pye?' said the Mouse. 'And your tie, too? They're filthy.'

'I know,' I said unhappily. 'I had to fire the engine.'

'Give me your jacket and your tie at once,' she said firmly. 'And I'll go and clean them up. You won't catch cold without them, will you?'

'No, of course not,' I said, taking off my jacket and tie and giving them to her. 'How nice of you to bother.'

'I wish I could get you a clean shirt, too,' she said. 'I'll see what I can do.' And she hurried off towards the Hall.

'Yon's a guid lassie,' said the Professor.

A small boy came running up to him. 'Sir, the postman's come over queer and he's sent me to tell you he's gone home for a lie-down. Can you get someone to take his place in Tip-the-Topper?'

'Drat the postman!' said the Professor. 'He invariably does this; and Tip-the-Topper is one of the most lucrative side-shows. Pye, I've got an idea. Would ye be so guid as to take the postman's place?'

'What do I have to do?' I asked.

'Just walk up and doun behind a screen, with a top hat on your head. Couldn't be easier.'

'I don't mind doing that,' I said without enthusiasm.

'Splendid fellow!' said the Professor. 'I knew we could rely on you. Come this way.'

276

He took me to the far corner of the green, where another of the cricket sight-screens was rigged up, above a prominent notice, 'Tip-the-Topper. 3 shies for 6d.' Several men and youths, including Dod Hoxen and Sticky Palmer, were standing about, waiting to try their luck. The Professor took me behind the screen and handed me a battered grey top hat.

'Put this on your head,' he said, 'and walk up and down behind this screen in a crouching position. Stand upright every now and then, and let the contestants shy a tennis ball at you. If they knock your hat off they get another three shots free of charge.'

He hurried away. I put the top hat on my head. I had no sooner done so than a tennis ball struck it sharply and pitched it to the ground.

'Another three shies, please,' I heard Sticky Palmer saying.

I picked up the hat and replaced it on my head, taking care this time to remain in a crouching position.

'Let the dog see the rabbit!' called Dod Hoxen. I walked to and fro several times and then hesitantly straightened up. A volley of tennis balls crashed into the screen. Two hit me on the forehead. I ducked hastily. The hat was again on the ground.

'Three more, please,' said Dod Hoxen.

I picked up the hat and repeated the performance. After several attempts I discovered that it was possible, by moving swiftly from one point to another, and only showing one's head above the screen for a split second, to avoid being struck in the face too often. On a few fortunate occasions I was even able to retain the hat.

The effort of walking up and down with my back bent involved an increasing strain on the shoulder muscles, and I soon realized why the postman had 'come over queer'. I could see no such easy release for myself. My participation in the sport was clearly to the liking of Dod

Hoxen and Sticky Palmer, who seemed determined to spend most of the afternoon and a large sum of money in bombarding me. The Professor was quite correct in regarding Tip-the-Topper as a lucrative side-show.

I was beginning to feel a nagging ache in the lumbar region when a pale-faced young man with spectacles, carrying a notebook and pencil, appeared at the side of the screen.

'Are you Sir Jasper Pye?' he asked, regarding me sceptically.

'I suppose so,' I said, straightening up and immediately receiving a volley of tennis balls about the head.

The newcomer picked up the fallen top hat and handed it to me courteously. 'I didn't expect to find you here, sir,' he said. 'You're a sport, I must say.'

'Have you come to relieve me?' I asked hopefully.

'No fear,' he said hastily. 'I represent the *East Anglian Daily Courier*. I wonder if you'd be so kind as to grant me an interview.'

'I've nothing to say,' I said. 'But I'll try and answer any questions.'

The young man opened his notebook. 'I see, Sir Jasper, that you are billed as "the well-known TV Personality". Could you tell me what TV programmes you appear in?'

My heart sank. This was just what would happen. I was tempted to disillusion the reporter immediately; but on second thoughts it seemed a little unfair to Jones and the rest of them. I decided I had better bluff it out.

'I'm not really *famous* on Television,' I said modestly. 'I've only appeared occasionally.'

'In which programmes?' the young man asked.

'Let me think,' I said. 'I believe one of them was called "Animal, Vegetable, and Mineral". It was some time ago.'

'Let's 'ave a look at yer!' yelled Dod Hoxen irritably on the other side of the screen. I bobbed up for a moment and received a stinging blow on the ear. Fortunately the hat remained in situ.

The reporter gazed at me with respect. 'You're certainly a sport,' he said. 'So you appeared in "Animal, Vegetable, and Mineral". How interesting! May I ask on what special subject you are an authority?'

I cudgelled my wits for an answer. 'Palaeontology,' I said at last.

'How interesting!' The reporter wrote busily in his notebook. 'May I ask what palaeontology is?'

This defeated me. In my perplexity I allowed my head to rise above the screen. The top hat flew off and knocked the reporter's notebook out of his hand. When he had retrieved it and handed the hat back to me, he seemed, fortunately, to have forgotten what he had asked me.

'Have you been in any other TV programmes?' he continued.

'Oh yes, now and then,' I said airily, as I put the hat back on my head.

'Such as?'

'What was it?' I tried to remember the names of some of the programmes. 'Oh yes. I appeared once in something called "Six-Five Special".'

'You do surprise me!' said the reporter. 'May I ask what act you put on?'

'What act?' I echoed.

'Yes. What did you do in "Six-Five Special"? Did you sing, or play the steel guitar, or what?'

'I – I danced the Charleston,' I said.

'How interesting!' The reporter scribbled away in his notebook. 'Palaeontology and the Charleston!'

'Come on, come on,' shouted Sticky Palmer. 'Don't be bashful, Sir Jasper. We want to 'ave a look at you.'

I rose up wearily and took a sharp rap on the chin.

'Palaeontology and the Charleston and Tip-the-Topper!' said the reporter. 'We've got quite a story here, Sir Jasper. Oh, and by the way, are you one of the Pyes of Norfolk, or do you come from the Derbyshire family?'

'I come from Barons Court,' I said, making a desperate grab at the truth.

'I thought it as well to look you up in *Who's Who* before I came along. But I couldn't find your name there.'

'No,' I said hurriedly. 'I'm not in *Who's Who*. I don't care for publicity.'

'I couldn't find you in *Debrett* either,' said the reporter. 'Nor in *Burke's Peerage*.'

I rose to my feet and grinned fatuously over the top of the screen at Sticky Palmer and Dod Hoxen. 'Have a go!' I shouted. They were so astonished at the apparition that their shots flew wide of the target.

'Foxed them that time,' I said, as I dropped down beside the reporter.

'Are you a knight or a baronet, Sir Jasper?' the reporter asked.

'Just a common-or-garden knight,' I said desperately.

'I can't think why I couldn't find you in *Debrett*,' he said, 'or in *Burke's Peerage*.'

I had an inspiration. 'I've only just become a knight. In the last New Year's Honours. My name won't be in the reference books yet.'

'I looked through the New Year's Honours List, too,' said the reporter remorselessly. 'We print it in our paper. I always like to check my references.'

I rose to my full height and waved my arms at Sticky Palmer and Dod Hoxen. 'Come on, boys!' I shouted. 'You must do better than this.'

In his bewilderment the reporter also rose to his feet. A shot from Sticky Palmer knocked off his spectacles; then Dod Hoxen hit him squarely on the nose.

The reporter sank, moaning, to the ground. Blood began to trickle over his top lip. I picked up his spectacles and his notebook and shoved them into my pocket. Then I nipped round to the front of the screen.

'Pick up that man and carry him to the First Aid Tent,' I said sharply to Dod Hoxen and Sticky Palmer. 'You may have done him an irreparable injury.' And I walked swiftly across the green to where I saw the traction engines forming up for the parade.

The Parade of traction engines presented a strangely beautiful spectacle. The engines emerged, one by one, from their rope-enclosed paddock, and set off at a steady walking pace on a complete circuit of the green. They were led by a Steam Cart – built in the 'nineties by Messrs Soame of Marsham, so I was informed by Jones, who appeared to know the vintage and pedigree of every engine on the field. Under its gaily painted awning, suspended on brass columns, it looked more like a river launch than a road vehicle. It had wooden driving wheels, and was steered by a sort of tiller. The coal bunkers were placed under the seats, and the boiler was inconspicuously sited well behind the driving seat. The brass of the gauges glittered; the wheels sparkled in red, white, and blue paint.

Behind the Steam Cart lumbered a sequence of less-refined, but not less-impressive, iron horses of varied design and date, some belching clouds of black smoke, others emitting a quiet hiss of steam. Their tall chimneys moved proudly against the skyline, their fly-wheels twirled, their brasswork and name-plates caught and threw back the blaze of the sun.

As they passed me I was astonished at the quietness and smoothness of their motion – the muffled chuff-chuff of the engines, the smooth silence of the darting piston rods, and the occasional snap-crackle of steering chains. Only an occasional shrill whistle burst through the undertones.

The last in the line was Pride of Flaxfield, the only example of the traditional fairground engine. Under its wide projecting canopy, and behind its massive brass-bound, brass-starred boiler, Charley Aspall stood proudly at the wheel, his brown billycock perched on the side of his head, his check waistcoat studded with mother-of-pearl buttons, his countenance crimson with pomp.

It was not until Pride of Flaxfield had passed by – the grand final showpiece of the parade – that I realized I had seen no sign of Lionel or his Susie. I turned to Jones. 'What's become of Lionel?'

'Lionel?' exclaimed Jones. 'Strewth! Ain't 'e on parade?'

'Not as far as I can see.'

'Come quick!' said Jones. We slipped behind the line of cheering spectators and hurried round the green to the paddock. There, in the far corner, alone, unattended, was Susie, smoke faintly eddying round her chimney.

'To the beer tent!' said Jones. Together we ran back to the tent. At first glance it seemed to be empty. Even Percy Pott, in his apron and shirt sleeves, was standing outside, by the Ring, watching the engines go by.

Jones darted into the tent. I followed. There appeared to be nobody there. Then Jones went over to the serving-table and lifted up the edge of the table-cloth. Under the table, stretched out at full length on the grass, and snoring quietly, lay Lionel.

Jones bent down and shook him.

'Leave me 'lone,' murmured Lionel. 'Go 'way. Got to get a goo' night's rest. Ready for Susie t'morrow.'

Jones looked up at me. 'He's had it, cock. Flat out.

Pixilated. What do we do next? Where do we go from here?'

'Can you drive her?' I asked.

Jones shook his head. 'Haven't a clue.'

'Nor have I,' I said.

Outside on the green the Starter was making an announcement through a megaphone. 'We now come to the great event of the day, the Traction Engine Musical Chairs. The music is very kindly being provided by Ozzie Tipton and his Stompers. Will all drivers please halt their engines at the places marked with a flag. When the music commences the engines will start. When the music ceases the engines will stop and the drivers will jump down and sit on the chair that happens to be nearest to them. One chair will be removed, and one engine eliminated, after each break in the music. Please make your way to your stations now, gentlemen!'

Jones let the table-cloth fall over Lionel's recumbent body. Together we walked gloomily out of the marquee.

'Come along now, gentlemen!' The Starter was speaking again. 'Get to your marks. Just a moment; we seem to be one engine short. Mr Quirk, will you check the entries, please.'

'Poor ole Lion!' murmured Jones. ' 'E was mad keen to show what Susie could do. Why did 'e 'ave to get pixilated, today of all days?'

'I don't think it was entirely his own fault,' I said. 'I saw Charley Aspall pouring whisky into his beer. I don't suppose Lionel realized.'

'The devil take Charley Aspall!' said Jones bitterly. 'Look at 'im up there on 'is engine, grinnin' like a bloomin' Borgia!'

The Starter's voice rang out again through the megaphone. 'One engine is missing – Susie, entered by Mr Lionel Virley. I can only allow one more minute for Susie to get to her mark.'

283

Charley Aspall held his hand above his eyes and made a show of peering into the distance. 'Has anyone here seen Susie?' he asked, leering down at the spectators. Jones and I turned away in disgust.

'Come and help me clear up my stall,' said Jones sadly.

As we walked away we became aware of an outburst of cheering on the far side of the ground. The cheers increased in volume. Soon the spectators on the near side began to join in.

'What's this in aid of?' said Jones. We went back to the ringside and worked our way into the crowd until we could see what was happening.

Through a gap in the ropes on the far side of the ground came Susie, her funnel throwing a triumphant black plume into the summer sky, her fly-wheel whirling, her great wheels biting into the turf as she raced towards her mark. At the iron steering wheel, her golden hair shining in the sunshine, stood Chloe.

The spectators rose to her. In a pandemonium of clapping, whistling, and cheering, Susie drew up at her mark. The Starter lowered his flag; Ozzie Tipton and his colleagues struck up 'Twelfth Street Rag'; and the Musical Chairs began.

From the outset there was no doubt that the sympathies of the crowd were with the only woman competitor. It also became apparent, very soon, that Susie, being smaller and less clumsy than most of the other contestants, could respond more readily than they to the driver's hand. Chloe, moreover, proved to be more agile than the male drivers in jumping down from her driving platform and seizing a chair.

One by one the competitors were eliminated, until at last only Chloe and Charley Aspall were left. Although Charley Aspall was by no means lively in movement himself, he was very adroit in control of his engine. He was also crafty in his tactics, driving at snail's pace whilst he lingered near a chair, and then driving Pride of Flaxfield at top speed towards the next.

During the final round the excitement amongst the spectators mounted. A great roar of shouts, shrieks, and adjurations rose up when at last the music stopped and Chloe and Charley Aspall ran neck and neck for the sole remaining chair.

They were heading for a photo-finish or a head-on collision when Chloe tripped, fell full length, and rolled over on the turf. A groan arose from the Ring.

Charley Aspall checked his step for a moment to see what had happened, before running forward with leisurely strides and grasping the back of the chair. Then, to the amazement of everyone present – not least Jones and myself – he lifted up the chair and carried it over to Chloe. As he set it down before her he removed his billycock and executed a courtly bow.

'The winner is Mr Lionel Virley's Susie,' the Starter announced through the megaphone. 'Driven by the Lady Chloe Virley.'

The crowd roared. This was Charley Aspall's finest hour.

For the prize-giving a dais had been constructed alongside the marquee out of planks stretched across a pair of old farm waggons. It was also serving as a bandstand. When I climbed up, wearing the new shirt and cleaned clothes which the Mouse had brought for me, Lord Flamborough, in his railway guard's peaked cap, was sitting there behind his set of drums. Jake's double bass was propped against the upturned shafts.

'Come on up, my dear fellow!' said Lord Flamborough to me, with great geniality. 'You've met Miss Tidy, of course.' Miss Tidy, who was sitting between Lord Flamborough and the local parson, smiled a greeting.

'I'm going to ask the Prof to say a few words first,' said Lord Flamborough, 'as it's his farewell appearance.'

I saw the Professor, in his antique straw boater, wending his way through the crowd. His face looked strained and drawn. He climbed up the steps that had been placed against the side of the waggon, and shook hands formally and silently with the Earl. I found myself unexpectedly moved by this unspoken salutation and valediction.

The crowd gathered round. Immediately below me was Ozzie Tipton, holding his trumpet, and engaged in an earnest conversation, whose subject baffled conjecture, with the be-whiskered Chitty Buckthorn. Quirk and Chloe and the Mouse were standing in a group on the other side of the waggon. Towards the back of the crowd I saw some of the men of Flaxfield – Charley Aspall, in great good humour, talking to Dod Hoxen and Sticky Palmer. In the middle of the throng I picked out the billowing lines of Dimple Pott, standing between Jones and her husband. I could not see Lionel, who presumably was still lying in a drunken slumber. And I was a little surprised to see no sign of Matilda or Belinda. I had imagined Belinda would be well to the fore.

Lord Flamborough picked up a drumstick and gave a sharp tap on the cymbals. 'Ladies and gentlemen, my wife tells me this is the one-hundredth Fête to be held at Arcady in aid of the Fallen Women.' (*Applause.*) 'I understand that the charming creatures still continue to fall.' (*Laughter.*) 'So I suppose we shall have several hundred more Fêtes in Arcady before we've finished. But, alas, we shall not have with us to organize them and keep all you unruly people in order' (*laughter*) 'our very, very dear friend, Professor Pollux. Some dumb cluck in Whitehall has decided that the nation can dispense with the Prof. All of us in Arcady know what a ghastly mistake they're making; but there's nothing we can do about it – except to thank him from the bottom of our hearts for all he's done for us. I now call upon the Prof.'

The Professor removed his straw hat and rose, a little unsteadily, to his feet. His emphatic, bushy eyebrows were in stronger contrast than ever to his ashen face. I noticed that his clenched hands were trembling.

'Ma Lord, ladies and gentlemen,' he said. 'It is I who should be thanking you . . . for . . . for the happiest years o' ma life . . .' He turned and bowed to Lord Flamborough, then, after gazing into the air for a few moments as though in search of words, he shrugged his shoulders, sat down suddenly, and covered his face with his hands.

There was an unexpected and impressive silence. Then I saw Chitty Buckthorn nudge Ozzie Tipton, who put his trumpet to his lips and played the first notes of 'For he's a jolly good fellow'. The crowd did the rest.

When the tribute had ended in the usual outburst of cheers and clapping Lord Flamborough struck the cymbals once more.

'It is now my pleasure,' he said, 'to call for the prizes to be presented by our distinguished guest, Sir Jasper ∴ Sir Jasper . . .' He turned to the Professor. 'What's the fellow's surname?' he asked in a loud whisper. I looked fixedly into the distance to hide my discomfiture.

'Sir Jasper PYE,' Lord Flamborough resumed with emphasis, 'will now present the prizes. Sir Jasper PYE!'

I rose, to the accompaniment of mild clapping. I stumbled through my few prepared words of appreciation and congratulation. When I came to mention Lady Flamborough's particular interest in the Fête and in the welfare of fallen women I looked round anxiously for her, so that I could address my remarks to her personally, but she was not to be seen. 'She's digging in the garden,' muttered Lord Flamborough. Deprived of the full effect of my peroration I sat down as soon as I decently could.

Lord Flamborough tapped the cymbals and began to call out the prizewinners' names. One by one they came up to the waggon and I handed out the prizes. The desultory clapping which greeted each award only rose to any degree of animation when the squint-eyed girl, who had won the Ankle Competition, came up for her prize.

'I protest! It's a scandal,' yelled Rita's mother. 'I shall sue the promoters!'

'Who is this extraordinary woman?' said Lord Flamborough, turning to me. I briefly explained the Rita situation.

Lord Flamborough delivered a blast on the cymbals. 'Send your daughter down to my train when the proceedings are over, and I'll look at her ankles personally,' he said. There was a scream of delight from the audience.

There was further applause when Charley Aspall came up to receive the Red Riband for Pride of Flaxfield's showing in the *concours d'élégance*.

The last award to be made was the prize for the winner of the Musical Chairs. Lord Flamborough called out the name, 'Mr Lionel Virley'. There was a pause, and I saw Quirk indicating to Lady Chloe that she should come forward to collect the prize.

Then, through the throng of people gathered outside the marquee, Lionel appeared. He was in his shirt sleeves, his hair was dishevelled, and his tie was undone. He held in his hand a glass of beer. 'Good ol' Susie!' he cried, stumbling through the crowd. 'Good old Lion!' the crowd responded. Amidst cheers Lionel made his way to the dais.

I handed him the prize. 'Well done, Lionel darling,' said Chloe, clapping excitedly.

'Steady, the Buffs!' said Jones.

'*Hic manemus!*' said Lionel. 'Thish calls for a celebration.' And he emptied the glass of beer down his throat. Setting the empty glass down shakily on the dais he beat upon the drum. 'I'd like y'all to unnerstand,' he said in a thick voice, 'tha' 's all due to my wife. Goo' night, Susie.' And he kissed Chloe's hand.

There was a sympathetic cheer. Lionel passed a hand over his forehead and turned to me. 'This's a Fête worse than death,' he said, and subsided on his back underneath the waggon.

Lord Flamborough rattled the cymbals. There was silence. 'I am sure you will all join with me,' he said, 'in thanking our distinguished guest, Sir Jasper PYE, for presenting the prizes.' (*Applause*.) 'And now I have a little surprise for you. Sir Jasper is not only a distinguished Civil Servant; he is one of the few people öf his generation who really understands how to dance the Charleston. I'm going to ask him to be so good as to give a demonstration now, to music provided by Ozzie Tipton and his Stompers.' (*Applause*.)

I went white with embarrassment. But Ozzie Tipton and Jake had climbed on to the dais and had begun a lively rendering of 'Ain't She Sweet' on trumpet and double bass, accompanied enthusiastically by his Lordship on the drums. I looked round feverishly for Belinda or Chloe or the Mouse to come and relieve me in my predicament. None of them was to be seen; but through the crowd, with heavy and purposeful steps, came Dimple Pott. As she clambered up the steps the applause rose to a *crescendo*.

'Come on, dearie,' said Dimple, putting her arm round me and drawing me to her bosom. 'We'll show them.'

> Ain't she sweet?
> See her coming down the street!

Now I ask you very confidentially
Ain't she sweet?

There was nothing I could do about it. I was, literally,
in Dimple's hands. She took charge. 'Isn't this lovely,
dearie?' she murmured, laying her cheek against mine.
'Don't you wish we was at the Café de Paris?'

> Just cast an eye
> In her direction.
> Oh me, oh my!
> Ain't that perfection? . . .

By the time Ozzie Tipton had blown himself to a halt I
had reached rock bottom physically and emotionally.
Dimple put her arms round my neck, pulled me to her,
and gave me a smacking kiss. The crowd were ecstatic.

Lord Flamborough beat on the cymbals. 'Hotcha,
hotcha, hotcha,' he roared. 'What did I tell you? And
now I understand that Mr Jones wishes to make a little
presentation to Sir Jasper, as a memento of the occasion.'

Jones, who had joined the group on the dais, stepped
forward and handed me a large parcel. I opened it. It
contained the battered grey top hat which had seen such
gruelling service in 'Tip-the-Topper'. Inside the top hat
was something done up in tissue paper. I unfolded it. It
was Miss Tidy's completed needlework picture of Pan,
who was now manifestly depicted in the image of the
Earl of Flamborough.

I shook Jones feebly by the hand, and bowed to Miss
Tidy. I waved the top hat in salutation to the audience.

This proved to be an unfortunate gesture. There was
an eddying movement at the back of the assembly.
Through a gap in the crowd appeared the figures of Dod
Hoxen and Sticky Palmer, their eyes gleaming. The next
thing I knew was that the top hat was flying over Jake's

double bass and a quantity of tennis balls were bouncing off my person.

Clutching Miss Tidy's needlework, I jumped down from the dais and crept into safety underneath the waggon. Lionel was snoring placidly. Gladly, gladly, would I have changed places with him.

Above my head there was another clash on the cymbals. Lord Flamborough spoke. 'I am now going to call on our dear friend Miss Tidy, whom many of you will remember as the daughter of the late Canon Tidy, to say a few words. Miss Tidy!'

'A very few words only,' said Miss Tidy in a surprisingly clear and confident voice. 'You have heard this afternoon the sad news about the Professor's departure. You will all miss him greatly. But I thought you would like to know that Arcady Hall is, after all, still to be looked after by the powers that be. I happen to be in the service of the Ministry of Works, and I have been going about the country in search of a suitable site for an Atomic Research Station. I am glad to tell you that there is every chance that it will be set up here at Arcady. Don't be put off by the word Atomic. Nothing messy or dangerous will happen here. I dare say life will go on much as before – and I'm glad to tell you that Mr Quirk has kindly consented to stay on as caretaker – and groundsman. Thank you!'

I lay under the waggon listening in a stupor of disbelief. Miss Tidy! The Ministry of Works! Atomic Research Station! This was the ultimate peak of fantasy.

Lionel snored contentedly. What did he care? Why should he care? The crowd began to move away, and gradually quietness returned. I got up on my hands and knees and scrambled to the back of the dais. As I straightened up between the waggon and the marquee I heard low voices behind the canvas.

'Which do you like to kiss most?' Belinda was saying. 'Lips, cheek, ear, or eyes?'

There was a long pause. . .

'You're fabulous!' said Jimmy.

I crept out from between the waggon and the marquee and made my way as inconspicuously as I could through the dispersing crowds. As I pushed open the door in the wall of the park I looked at my watch: it was twenty minutes past five.

I turned aside into the shrubbery and stood for a few moments in the glade between the laurels and the yews. Then I sat down on the fallen tree-trunk and lit a cigarette.

I looked across the glade to the ancient oak tree by the wall. I longed – absurdly, unreasonably – for a low voice to call to me again from its massive crown of branches. I waited. I listened. But, apart from the distant shouting and laughter on the green, there was silence.

So I should have to leave Arcady without saying goodbye to Matilda. Why she had not come to the Fête I could not imagine. It was too late for me to go in search of her now. I stubbed out my cigarette on the fallen tree-trunk and stood up. Was this the end? Was this the moment of disenchantment? I walked over to the oak tree and looked up into the branches. 'Goodbye, Matilda,' I said quietly – absurdly, sentimentally. There was, of course, no answer.

I turned to go. There was a whirr, a thud; a splinter of bark fell on my shoulder. Incredulously I looked up.

The arrow was quivering in the bark of the tree about two feet above my head. I reached up and tried to pull it out, but it was too firmly embedded. Standing on tiptoe I untied the message that was wrapped round the shaft, and unfolded it.

Where nettles and the noxious nightshade dwell,
　　And spiders spin their webs o'er crumbling towers,
There Solitude withdraws within her cell,
　　And Contemplation seeks her solace in the flowers.

I read the message twice, then I looked at my watch. It was half past five. I folded up the message, put it in my pocket and set off.

There was nobody in the long, yew-lined walk. I broke into a run. As I hurried down the steps in the ha-ha, I saw a flicker of white among the trees across the park. When I reached the thicket beside the path I was breathless and very hot, but it was only twenty minutes to six. I took off my jacket and pushed my way through the branches and brambles towards the chapel ruins.

I found her sitting among the primulas, wearing her white frock, and twining the pink and yellow blossoms into a chaplet. Her bow and arrows lay beside her in the grass.

'I got the message,' I said. 'And here I am.'

'So I see.' She didn't look up at me.

'Your system of signals is uncannily efficient,' I said. 'How did you know that I'd be standing in the shrubbery just at that moment?'

'I have second sight. I told you I lead a life of the spirit. I know things other people don't know.'

I stood looking down at her. Her curiously old-fashioned white frock and her long dark hair made a vivid contrast to the Pre-Raphaelite prettiness of the nodding primula heads. There was a legendary, faerie air about her.

'I don't suppose you know what I'm going to say to you now,' I said.

'Yes, I think I do. You're going to tell me that tomorrow never comes.'

'I wasn't going to put it quite like that,' I said.

293

'Then you are going to tell me that you are going away, for ever.'

'How did you know?' I said.

She looked up at me swiftly, with panic in her eyes. 'Oh dear! Am I right?'

'Yes, you're quite right,' I said. 'Not only am I going, but so also are the Professor and the Mouse.'

'Why can't they go, and leave you here?' she asked.

'What should I do here? I don't belong here.'

'No,' she said, gazing reflectively at the chaplet of flowers in her hand. 'I suppose you don't. You're just a passer-by – one who goes whistling on his way.'

'I've nothing to whistle about,' I said. 'And I've certainly no wish to go on my way.'

'But you must, of course. It's fated.'

I set my jacket on the ground and knelt beside her. 'May I say goodbye to you now . . . here?'

She slowly turned her dark eyes towards me.

'Are you going to give me something to remember you by?' she asked.

'What would you like me to give you?'

'You know very, very well what I would like you to give me.'

I kissed her forehead. 'Goodbye, Matilda.'

She sat quite still, gazing at the chaplet of flowers. 'That wasn't much to remember you by,' she said. 'I'm forgetting it already.'

I put my arms round her and kissed her again, on the lips. She sat very still, and seemed hardly aware of what I was doing. I stood up and reached for my jacket.

'That won't last very long, either,' she said.

'I'm sorry, but what else can I give you?'

'You could give me something nobody has ever given me before,' she said. 'Something that I would never forget.'

'It's quite impossible, my dear.'

294

'You mean,' she said, looking up at me with searching and serious eyes, 'that I don't interest you – you don't care for me?'

I knelt down again and drew her to me. 'You interest me as no one else has ever done,' I said. 'You're out of this world.'

'I'm not out of this world at all,' she said. 'I'm here at your feet, at your mercy. Aren't you going to take me?'

'I care about you far, far too much for that,' I said.

'Are you being scrupulous, Sir Jasper? You don't seem to be running true to type at all.'

'Perhaps I am. As I told you before, I'm not really Sir Jasper – not in any sense.'

She didn't seem to be listening. 'You don't have to marry me, you know. It's a very, very old tradition that lovers can make love among these ruins without benefit of clergy.'

I kissed her again and rose slowly and finally to my feet. 'I'm not disputing the tradition, my dear, but there are other and more prosaic factors to be taken into account. One of them is that I'm catching the 6.48 from Flaxfield Junction, and it's now ten minutes to six.'

She turned her head away and covered her eyes with her hand. Her shoulders quivered.

'What's the matter?' I said.

'What's the matter!' she sobbed. 'The 6.48 is the matter. Oh damn, damn, damn!'

I was bewildered.

'Goodbye, Tilly,' I said. 'I'm sorry about the 6.48.'

'I'm not sorry . . . really,' she said, struggling against her tears. 'It's all for the best. But don't call me Tilly: my name's Matilda.'

I picked up my jacket again and put it on. 'I *have* to go, Matilda,' I said.

'Good,' she said, pulling a handkerchief out of her

sleeve and blowing her nose. 'You'd better take this.' She picked up the chaplet of flowers and handed it to me, burying her face in her handkerchief as she did so.

'Thank you, Matilda,' I said.

She stood up and dabbed at her eyes.

'Goodbye, Sir Jasper,' she said, in an uncertain voice. 'I apologize for this unfortunate outburst. The fact is that I made a silly mistake. I thought I was in love with you. But now' – her shoulders shook with sobs again – 'I realize I was wrong. Actually,' she added, in a curiously unreal, stilted voice, 'I find you rather a bore.'

She picked up her bow and walked slowly, mopping her eyes with her handkerchief, into the ruined nave of the chapel.

As the church clock struck six I walked for the last time between the lavender and the high brick wall. The air was heavy with the scent of roses. Except for the distant rumble of traction engines moving away from the green there was nothing more to be heard of the festivities of the day. The crowds had dispersed, presumably to refresh themselves for the ardours of nightfall, for the fireworks and the dance.

In the middle of the herbaceous border, almost hidden amongst the tall delphiniums, was Lady Flamborough, hoeing. She looked up as I passed. 'All over now?'

'Yes, it's all over,' I said.

'Sorry I couldn't stay to hear your speech. I'm sure it was splendid. But when I'd sold the flowers off my stall I just had to get back and finish this weeding. The weather may break at any moment.' She looked up at the gathering clouds.

'You didn't miss much,' I said. 'I suppose you'd already heard the news about the Hall?'

'Tidy said something to me about it, but I didn't pay

much attention. I don't mind which Ministry looks after the place so long as they don't interfere with the garden.' She resumed her hoeing.

'You'll miss the Professor,' I said.

'Oh no, I shan't. I've asked him to stay on – as gardener.'

As she spoke the Professor came through the gate at the far end of the walk. He was wearing a green apron and pushing a barrow.

'I have tipped them on the compost heap, your Ladyship,' he said. 'Guid evening, Mr Pye. Are ye on your way? I hope ye don't find the train too crowded.'

I said goodbye to them.

'Don't forget to let me know where I can get that rose you recommended,' said Lady Flamborough. '*Fruticosa*, you said it was – a hybrid of *Mancuniensis*.'

I walked on to the little castellated garden house at the end of the path. Belinda, I knew, would not be there, but perhaps the peacock would be.

He was standing very quietly behind a rose bush, his neck stretched forward his head cocked to one side. He ignored me completely. Suddenly he darted forward, described three circles round the rose bush, and hared away down the path, his head down, his great spurred claws flying out behind him.

I watched him run halfway along the path and then dart away into the bushes again, almost as though someone were in pursuit. As I turned to go through the wrought-iron gate towards the Hall, I saw that he had dropped at my feet a long white quill, fringed with gold, and ending in a green, blue, and golden eye. I picked it up.

There was a rustle under the yew hedge. A smaller, less spectacular, dove-grey bird appeared. She had no tail, and her coronet was green. She picked her way slowly but purposefully through the flowers and emerged on to the grass path. She was followed by four very small and very fluffy brown-and-yellow chicks.

The gate swung open. I felt a hand on my arm. 'I've brought these,' said the Mouse, giving me my hat, my briefcase and my umbrella. 'I don't think there's anything else of yours at the Hall. If we don't go soon we shall miss the bus.'

'Are you coming on the 6.48?' I asked.

'Yes,' she said. I saw she had a bag in her hand.

'Let me carry that,' I said.

'I'll take your briefcase, then.'

'Would you hold the peacock's feather, too?' I asked. 'Unless you consider it unlucky.'

'No, I don't consider it unlucky.'

'The bus will be leaving in a few minutes,' I said.

'If you come with me round the far side of the Hall,' she said, 'we can cut through the kitchen garden and pick it up at the end of the lane.'

I held the gate open for her. We walked through the intricate pattern of close-clipped box and coloured pebbles in the knot garden and across the broad lawns that skirted the moat. The gatehouse towered above us inscrutably, its sculptural grandeur thrown into high relief by the declining sun.

As we rounded the corner of the moat I saw the Flamborough Flier standing at the Halt. A little knot of people were climbing aboard. Chloe was on the footplate, with Lionel, surprisingly, wielding the shovel.

'So you are coming with me, are you?' I said to the Mouse.

'Yes,' she said.

'Any regrets?'

'Yes . . . and no. What about you?'

'Yes . . . and no,' I answered. 'Anyway, I'm not an Arcadian. I'm a Civil Servant.'

'I thought you were going to give it up?'

'I thought so, too. I intended to go to Paris. But I don't feel drawn to Paris any more.'

'Why not?'

'Somehow it seems rather tame . . . after Arcady.'

'What will you do, then?' she asked.

'Go back to the Ministry, I suppose.'

The sun went behind the clouds. I heard Lord Flamborough blow his whistle. A puff of smoke rose from the locomotive.

'I know my limitations,' I said. 'I'm only a Civil Servant.'

'So am I,' said the Mouse.

'I'm also a bore,' I said bitterly.

'A bore!' exclaimed the Mouse. She looked up at me in what seemed to be genuine surprise.

'Yes, a bore,' I repeated.

'I don't find you a bore,' she said. 'Far from it.'

As we came to the iron steps where the footpath crossed the railway line the train approached. Wistfully we watched it go by. Lionel waved gaily from the foot-plate: the Mouse flourished the peacock's feather in response. Chloe was too preoccupied with the regulator to notice us. Through the open windows of the saloon I saw Dimple with her arms around Jones, Belinda jiving with Jimmy, and Miss Tidy dancing rather stiffly with Quirk. Ozzie Tipton was blowing his trumpet and Jake playing his double bass. As Lord Flamborough bounced up and down in his invalid chair, belabouring his drums, he was singing:

> 'Happy days are here again!
> The skies above are clear again . . .
> Happy days are here again!'

The train puffed away into the distance. I felt heavy drops of rain on my face.

'You *really* don't find me a bore?' I said.

The Mouse shook her head, blinked, and began to weep, very quietly, on my shoulder. The peacock's feather tickled my chin. It was raining in earnest. Gingerly I opened my umbrella and held it over the two of us.

THE END